LAND OF HILLS AND VALLEYS

LAND

OF

HILLS

AND

VALLEYS

Elisabeth Grace Foley

ELISABETH GRACE FOLEY

With thanks to two Marys:
Mary Stewart and Mary O'Hara

For the land, whither ye go to
possess it, is a land of hills and valleys...

DEUTERONOMY 11:19

PART I: HILLS

CHAPTER I

I have been here before,
But when or how I cannot tell:
I know the grass beyond the door,
The sweet keen smell...

Dante Gabriel Rossetti: Sudden Light

I LEANED BACK against the faded seat-cushion of the passenger car, my face out of the sunlight that fell in flickering bars across my lap. The wide-open beauty of Wyoming on a clear, stunning June day was flying past the windows of the westbound train, and I had a guilty feeling that I was wasting a marvelous experience by not looking at it. But right now all I could think was that I was less than twenty minutes from my destination. My heart thumped in my ears despite my telling myself over and over that I was perfectly calm and there was nothing to be excited about. But even with this and half a dozen other very real sensations—the heat in the car, the smell of dusty fabric on the seats and smoke from the engine, the bright sunlight that almost hurt my eyes—I was still coming to terms with the reality of my situation.

I resisted the impulse to take the crinkled telegram out of my purse one more time. The single line it contained had already yielded everything it was going to tell me. *Wire received stop will meet two-thirty train Claxton station stop Robert Herrington.*

Mrs. Draper had been understanding and reasonable about the whole thing, even though she plainly thought my trip to Wyoming was a wild-goose chase. It would have been unreasonable of her to object, though: I had asked no favors and taken little vacation during the three years I had been Eunice Draper's private secretary. I had been happy enough with the Drapers, even if I sometimes found it a little dull. Eunice was a distant cousin of my father's, who had offered me the position more out of charity toward an eighteen-year-old orphan with practically no money and even less idea what to do with her life, than for any other reason. Dull or not, I knew it could have gone much harder with me if there had been no Eunice.

I hadn't for years even remembered I had a grandfather. When the letter came informing me of his death, my first and only emotion was surprise—and then a little guilt for feeling nothing else; but it was hardly possible to have felt anything, since I'd never known him and seldom thought of him. Had he ever thought of me—or even known I existed? Possibly not—I couldn't remember my mother ever writing to him during my childhood. All that Robert Herrington's letter said was that his property went to me as his next-of-kin. It consisted of a small ranch in Severn Valley, Wyoming, and evidently some money. Herrington, my grandfather's lawyer and executor, had advanced me money to make the trip west, and it was my own money. That was an odd feeling.

Severn Valley, Wyoming. I turned my head against the cushion to watch the sweep and roll of the grassy range, so endless around us that it almost felt like the train was making no headway in spite of its speed. Deep down I knew it was the name that had made me come, not the property. It was the little bundle of letters in my top bureau drawer, browned and faded by time, their envelopes slit jaggedly along the top; all dated nearly twenty-five years ago—letters written by my parents before their marriage, with the ones in my mother's handwriting bearing the return address of Severn Valley.

I had always wanted to know what it was like. I'd always had a sneaking fascination with the West, reading books about it now and then, lingering over pictures of Wyoming in magazines and advertisements. It must have been because of the animated look that came over my mother's face when she talked about Wyoming, a quickening of enthusiasm in her voice that I could still hear now, even though the occasions when she mentioned it had been rare. I had a dozen little fragmented pictures of the place in my mind from the way she described the hills, the clear air, the wildflowers, the horses.

And yet, after her marriage, she had never gone back.

The train began to slack speed. I drew a quick deep breath and gathered my gloves and purse from my lap, flicking an instinctive glance to my suitcase in the rack overhead. We were coming into Claxton now. The tracks crossed several wide streets lined with modest storefronts and parked automobiles; a network of cattle pens began to slide past. I stared with interest at what I could see of reddish polls and ears and the tips of short horns behind the wide slatted fences. It was a whole new world, an unfamiliar one; but I was not backward in either curiosity or willingness to explore it.

Only a handful of passengers got off at Claxton. They melted away in different directions even before I paused on the platform to get my bearings—alone within thirty seconds of my arrival. But I looked along the platform, with the sun-burnished double line of the tracks running away from Claxton shining alongside it, and saw two men standing near the ticket window watching the dispersing passengers as if waiting for somebody. One was a slight, gray-haired, middle-aged man in a three-piece suit, not much above my own height; the other wore blue jeans, a gray shirt and broad-brimmed Stetson hat. I took a half-hesitant step in their direction, and immediately the man in the suit whipped off his felt hat and advanced to meet me, holding out his hand.

He said, "You must be Lena Campbell? I'm Robert Herrington."

"Yes, I am. I'm glad to meet you."

Herrington shook my hand warmly, then turned to introduce his companion. "Miss Campbell, this is Ray Harper, your grandfather's foreman."

Ray Harper shook hands with me without speaking. He was taller than Herrington and considerably younger; under thirty, I thought. I was conscious of clear brown eyes studying me before I turned back toward Robert Herrington, who was speaking again. "I've got my car here; it's only about half an hour's drive to Severn Valley. Do you have any more luggage?"

"No, this is all. My employer—Mrs. Draper—she didn't think I ought to bring too much if I wasn't certain yet what I was going to do, and..."

And I hadn't been ready to tell her my real intentions just then. But Robert Herrington drew his own conclusions about my meaning and accepted it without a finished sentence. "Of course. Right this way, then; my car's just down here."

"Can I take that for you?" said Ray Harper, holding

out his hand for my suitcase, and I surrendered it with murmured thanks. I almost felt I'd have liked to have something
as familiar as a slightly sweaty suitcase-handle to hold on to,
but those are the kinds of things you can never explain at
short notice. I followed Herrington down the platform steps
to where his car, a brown Buick coupe that looked as middle-
aged and unpretentious as its owner, was parked on the other
side of the station building. Herrington opened the passenger
door for me to get in, then went around to the driver's side.
Ray Harper put in my suitcase and got in the back seat, and
slammed the door as Herrington started the engine.

No one said much until we had navigated a few dusty
Claxton streets and were out on the highway, speeding along
under the blue sky. "I've gathered," said Robert Herrington,
"that you don't know too much about your grandfather."

"No—practically nothing," I said, my eyes still fastened to the limitless view. "I never met him. In fact I wasn't
even sure whether he knew my mother had a child."

"It's possible he didn't," said Robert Herrington. "At
least we found nothing to suggest otherwise. He left no will,
you see. We had to locate his next-of-kin, and that, coupled
with the—circumstances of his death, accounts for the time
it took to notify you."

"The circumstances?" I glanced sideways at him. It
was the first unusual note in the conversation.

"About that," said Herrington, and stopped. I thought
the car's speed slacked off a little, as if he was thinking hard
and focusing less on his driving. "It has no bearing on your
inheritance, but you might as well know, your grandfather
was...killed."

The highway continued to flow toward us with
smooth regularity, as though we were driving into the blue
sky ahead. "Killed? You mean in an accident?"

"He died of a gunshot wound," said Robert Herrington.

There was silence in the car for a minute except for the grumble of the motor and the hum of the tires on the highway. Not knowing what to say, I looked out the window and my eyes caught the side-view mirror—it was angled so I could see Ray Harper in the back seat, and from the direction of his eyes I could tell he was watching me steadily from behind.

All sorts of thoughts flickered through my mind. Suicide?...an accident with a gun?...but Herrington's answer seemed to have ruled that out. I sat a minute searching for the words to ask, and finally said, "Did anyone...was someone arrested?"

"No," said Herrington. "He was found dead by the side of the road after having left the ranch alone one night— there was no evidence to point toward any particular person. The inquest brought in a verdict of murder by person or persons unknown."

"Oh," I said. I was silent again for a minute. Not just a new world, which had contained a grandfather I never knew, but one with layers and undercurrents I had no conception of—one in which someone had found reason to shoot my grandfather dead.

I thought Ray Harper was very silent too. I glanced again at the mirror, half expecting to find him still watching me, but this time he had turned his head and was looking out the window.

Herrington turned the steering wheel hand over hand as the road curved. "Would you prefer to go straight to my office, or see the ranch first? You can get a good room in town if you'd prefer to stay there."

"Oh, no, see the ranch first, please. I thought that's

where we were going," I said, feeling suddenly childish and shy at the sound of the mixed eagerness and disappointment in my own voice.

"Certainly, if that's what you want." I thought I saw Herrington flick a glance at the rear-view mirror, but couldn't be sure.

By mutual consent, it seemed, nothing else important was said for the rest of the drive. I sat and watched the landscape of broad pastures and rocky outcroppings with growing enthusiasm, turning to Herrington now and then with a question about places we passed. Ray Harper didn't enter the conversation except once or twice when Herrington referred a question to him, and then when he answered his voice sounded entirely natural. I decided I must have imagined there had been some constraint in his manner at first.

Severn Valley came on us quickly, small and surprising, about a mile after we left the two-lane highway for a narrow dirt road. First came a filling station, and here the dusty road widened, strung with a few houses and stores on each side. There was a general store, a feed and grain store, a bank and a few small offices, and a two-story clapboard building with a wooden sign bearing the imposing name Hotel Stevenson. Power lines dipped between poles; there were some widely spaced street lamps, and on one corner the unlit neon sign of a bar. A few thin, rangy men in faded jeans and impossibly big Stetsons lounged around the street lamp on this corner. A block later as we took a turn to the right, I glimpsed a white frame building in the other direction that I took for a church or a school until Robert Herrington nodded towards it. "County court house. Severn Valley's still the county seat, even though Claxton outgrew it thirty years ago."

The town dropped behind almost before I'd had time

to realize it was really there, and the increasingly narrow road dipped and wound, with barbed-wire fences lining the roadside ditches. My heart started to beat hard again, though I tried to stifle the nonsensical feeling. I was almost home.

Home? What home? A place I'd never seen, a place my mother had never returned to—a run-down little ranch off the beaten path of everything?

But foolish as it seemed, every hill and pasture and fence since Claxton seemed to have been reaching out to me, welcoming me, and my heart had already fallen hard for every one.

CHAPTER II

Though I have had no adventures, I feel capable of them.

Anna Katharine Green: That Affair Next Door

THE CAR TURNED into a narrow rutted lane, with weed-twined barbed-wire fences on both sides. I saw the house first. It was a faded and weathered white, with a gabled roof and a narrow front porch. Several big spreading cottonwood trees dappled the house and yard with their shade; off to the left were a gray-weathered barn with a corrugated tin roof and some outbuildings and high board corrals. Behind the house the trees thickened to a small grove, and in their shade at the foot of a slope was what must be the bunkhouse.

I opened the car door myself as soon as we stopped, and got out and stood looking up at the house. I stared at it almost as if I expected it to tell me something, to answer the hundred little questions wandering through my head. But it stood quietly, weathered white clapboards, worn-down porch steps, and sunlight falling on plain muslin curtains in the front windows.

I turned to look around the yard. There were some men over near the barn, and I sensed they were looking this way. Down in the barbed-wire pasture that the car had skirted coming up the rutted lane I could see horses grazing, bay and brown and black. And the ranch wasn't run-down. But I felt suddenly out of place standing there, in my blue cloche hat and the trim blue-and-white checked dress with red piping on the collar and sleeves that had seemed so neat and appropriate when I first boarded the train. To have a sentimental feeling for a place was not enough.

The rear door of the car slammed, and Ray Harper was beside me with my suitcase in his hand. "It may not look like much, but there's electric and indoor plumbing, and a telephone," he said. "Telephone was just put in last year."

I looked at Robert Herrington, who had come around the front of the car to join us, but it was his turn to be silent. He took my elbow and motioned me toward the porch. As I went up the steps, I felt the men by the barn were still watching me.

Ray Harper went ahead of us, and he pushed the door open and held it for me. "Mrs. Crawley—the Crawleys are the nearest neighbors—was over the other day to clean the place up a little," he said. "She thought you might want to stay overnight here, so she fixed one of the upstairs rooms for you. The house was a little cobwebby, being empty for a few months."

I stepped through the open door. In front of me was a steep staircase with a hallway running alongside it on the right to the kitchen. On my right was the living room; on the left another room where the door stood partly open, letting a crack of sunlight into the front entry. There was a closet under the stairs, and across the hall from it another door that was shut.

"If you plan on staying the night," said Ray Harper, "I'll take your bag upstairs for you."

I turned toward him, feeling inexplicably more myself. Maybe it was the sunlight, which streams in the same way through any window in the world, or maybe it was the honest simplicity of the little house. "Yes, I'll stay," I said. "Thank you."

I turned back to Robert Herrington. "Well, what do I need to know?"

I couldn't tell whether he looked annoyed or relieved. Relieved that he wouldn't have to shepherd me like the unworldly child I looked, maybe; or slightly annoyed that I was taking matters into my own hands so promptly? He pushed open the door to the left, which creaked. "Come in here and we'll talk," he said.

The room, with two windows looking out at the front and side, was furnished like an office: there was an old rolltop desk stuffed with papers and odds and ends against the back wall and a table with drawers in the middle of the room; there were a couple of cowhide-bottomed chairs and one faded green-upholstered chair on wooden rockers. Robert Herrington laid the briefcase he had brought from the car on the table, pulled one of the cowhide chairs up to it and motioned me to sit down across from him.

"To begin with," I said, taking a seat on the edge of the green rocker, "will you just tell me a little more about what I own? I know there's this ranch property and some money, but what exactly does the ranch include?"

Herrington opened his briefcase and drew out some documents. "Well," he said, "here is the description of the ranch and a list of the livestock, buildings, *et cetera* that I've compiled. You can look it over for yourself."

I scanned the sheets of paper he handed me, my eyes

widening progressively as I took in the totals of acres, cattle, horses, outbuildings...Herrington's initial letter had referred to a "small" ranch; I decided they must think in different proportions out here.

"In addition," Herrington was saying, "after paying off various small debts and bills, there is a very small sum in savings at the Severn Valley Savings and Loan Bank. The land and livestock itself is free from debt; your grandfather finished paying off a mortgage on it three years ago."

I sat and digested this for a moment, my elbow resting on my knee and the papers still in my hand. I looked round the office. Mrs. Crawley must have cleaned this room, too; except for the jumbled desk it was immaculate, looking as if its occupant had only gone out for the day. Outside somewhere there were men working; the ranch was going on as it always had, with only one place vacant: the place of the owner.

"Does the ranch pay? Enough to make a living, I mean."

Herrington hesitated a little over the answer, and tapped the end of his fountain-pen on the scarred table. "In theory—if it's properly run—and barring setbacks such as weather and diseased livestock—"

He broke off as Ray Harper came into the room. Ray did not interrupt, but moved over to the wall and leaned his elbow on the top of the rolltop desk. Herrington sat forward in his chair and spoke more crisply. "Essentially, you have three choices, Miss Campbell. You could stay here and try to run the ranch yourself. You could put the management into someone else's hands and return home—if you didn't want to break any ties back east, or give up your current position. However, you're not likely to see much extra income from the ranch, after operating expenses. Or—" he tapped the desk with his pen again "—you could simply sell the property outright. If you choose to do that, I believe I could successfully find a buyer for you at short notice."

Ray Harper shifted his position against the desk slightly. I glanced at him, then studied my right thumbnail for a few seconds to give myself time to build the courage for my next question. "If I did want to stay and run it—would I be able to? How much would I need to know?"

Robert Herrington looked over at Ray Harper. "Well...that's more Ray's department than mine. If you know nothing about ranching, you'll need a foreman to run it for you."

"You mean you don't work here any more?" I said, my eyes swinging to Ray in some surprise.

"As of right now I do. I agreed to stay on and run the ranch at least until the estate was settled. After that, it'll depend on whatever the new owner chooses to do, whoever that ends up being."

"Well," I said, trying to speak towards both of them, and to manage the little surge of excitement tickling my insides, "I'll tell you honestly. I don't know the first thing about ranching. But—I like the idea. I've always thought I would like it out here, from the way Mother talked about it; and from what I've seen so far, I do. I don't have any real ties to break and I wouldn't mind leaving my job. I'd like a change. I've been half certain this is what I wanted since before I left to come out here, and—well, it is. I want to stay here and give it a try."

Robert Herrington had leaned back in his chair at the beginning of my speech, rubbing his hand slowly across his chin. Now he straightened up. "Lena," he said, "it's a very big undertaking, for a girl with no experience. I hope you don't mind my speaking frankly—I wasn't just your grandfather's lawyer; he was also a friend. Of course the decision is yours, but I hope you'll take my advice into account. I would hesitate to take this course if I were you."

I sat back in my chair, feeling very put in my place. Did I really give such an impression of naïveté that he didn't credit me with even the ability to give something new a good shot? Or was it really too big for me to handle?

Robert Herrington repeated, "As I said, the decision is yours to make. But I wish you'd at least take the time to consider it."

I clasped my hands over my knee and tried obediently to consider. But my mind would offer me nothing but the conviction that had been beating at me ever since I entered the house: I wanted to stay.

On impulse I looked at Ray Harper. "What about you? Do *you* think I'm being foolish? Could I stay here if I wanted?"

Robert Herrington cleared his throat and shifted a little; I think he was a little put out at the bluntness of "foolish" being attributed to him. Ray was still leaning against the old desk, his elbow on the top and his knuckles against the side of his head. He looked at me for a second that felt longer, and then lifted his head away from his hand. "If you mean, could you live here and like it, that's for you to find out. As for the ranch, you can have someone manage it for you just the same staying here as if you went back east. If you're serious about learning the business yourself, you've got time to learn."

I flashed a vindicated glance at Robert Herrington, who tapped his pen on the table and looked lawyerishly noncommittal. I looked at Ray again. "Would you stay as foreman, if I decide to?"

I felt the pause more than heard it, it was so small.

"I'd stay. Yes."

I turned back to my grandfather's lawyer, arching my eyebrows as if to ask what more objections he could possibly make. Herrington only smiled rather dryly. "Is there anything I have to sign?" I said.

"Yes," he said, "there's the property deeds to transfer, and so forth—but I have one last request to make, Miss Campbell. As certain as you may feel right now, this is a big decision to make all in a moment. Why don't you take a few days here in Severn Valley, look about you, see if you like the ranch and the country as much as you thought you would. If after a few days you're still as enthusiastic as you are now, I won't say another word about it. Whenever you're ready, you can have Ray drive you into town and see me in my office at the courthouse—there'll be some papers to sign whichever way you decide. What do you say?"

"Well, that sounds reasonable enough," I admitted. "All right. I'll take a couple of days and then let you know."

Herrington gathered up the handful of papers and returned them to his briefcase, snapped it shut and rose. "Meanwhile, would you like to come back with me and have supper now? I expect you're pretty tired from your trip, and the Up & Down Café serves a meal that isn't bad at all."

I let out a breath. "It's nice of you, Mr. Herrington, but if you don't mind I'd rather just stay here. I'd like to just…take my time and look around, you know. I can make my own supper. If—that's not an inconvenience to anybody?" I looked at Ray.

Ray grinned openly for the first time. "No fear of that. Mrs. Crawley lugged in about a dozen covered dishes and baskets before she left. I think you'll find enough in the kitchen to live on for a week."

"She sounds like a nice kind of neighbor to have."

"She's that and more."

"Well," said Robert Herrington, "I'll be on my way, then. You're certain there's nothing more I can do for you tonight?"

"No, I don't think so. Thank you for being so"—I kept back the impulse to laugh from some irresistible little bubbling-up of my spirits—"understanding, Mr. Herrington."

Herrington, his briefcase under his arm, looked me over with that wry expression that made it hard for me to tell if he was pleased or displeased. "I remember your mother," he said unexpectedly. "She must have been around your age the last time I saw her. You take after her quite a lot. She was just as fair as you."

His eyes went past me and he nodded. "Ray. I'll be seeing you around."

"Be seeing you."

Herrington went out, and I walked after him to the front door and stood looking through the screen, watching him get into his car. When he had backed around and driven off down the lane I stood there a moment longer, watching the sun twinkling through the leaves of the big cottonwoods out front. Then I put up a hand and pulled off my hat, and combed my fingers through my short unruly fair hair to tidy it a little. I gave a little sigh and turned around. Ray Harper was standing in the office doorway, his hands resting on his hips. When my eyes met his he smiled a little—he had a nice smile, I thought.

"Do you want me to introduce you to the other boys?" he said.

"Later, I think," I said. A little shiver ran over me, not of apprehension, but because there were suddenly so many things to happen in that time called "later." "I'm sure

I should have a million questions to ask you, but I can't think of any of them now either. I guess I'd just like to look around the house, and...well...you know."

Somehow I thought he did know. Robert Herrington had been everything that was polite and considerate, but he did not.

Ray nodded. "Sure. I put your bag in the room to the left upstairs, if you want it. That's the room Mrs. Crawley fixed for you."

"Thank you. I wish I could thank Mrs. Crawley too."

"Oh, you'll be able to. No later than the day after tomorrow, is my guess."

I laughed—it was the first time I had let myself laugh all day, in spite of so many suppressed feelings of excitement and pleasure, and I felt it must sound rather giddy for such a simple moment. I ran my fingers through my hair again to hide my embarrassment. I was grateful to Ray for putting me at ease, for being so unhurrying, uncritical; but I also found myself looking forward to the moment when he would be gone, so I could be alone with myself and try to realize that this house, today's trip, today's sights, were not something I had imagined, but—if I had my way about it—my new reality.

Ray was already on his way out. He paused with his hand on the handle of the screen door to say, "If there's anything you need, there should be somebody around the barn or bunkhouse. Don't hesitate to ask."

"I will. Thanks."

The screen door creaked closed, and I heard his footsteps crossing the porch and fading down the steps, and I was alone in my grandfather's house.

CHAPTER III

…Not a whit
More tame for his gray hairs—

Keats: The Eve of St. Agnes

IT WAS THE light that woke me, filtering through the thin curtains on the windows. I lay still for a moment looking up at the slanted ceiling that sloped down to the head of the bed. I had a feeling it was very early, as the light looked different from what I was accustomed to seeing every morning.

I pushed back the quilt, slid out of bed and went to the window, and drew the curtains back to look down on the yard. The sky was bright and pale; under the trees was dim; the rising sun struck a faint gleam from the barn roof. I pushed the faded cotton curtains as far apart as they would go, and opened the window with a little difficulty; it stuck and some flakes of white paint from the sash came off on my hands. I knelt down by the window in my nightgown—the air that came in was cool, and I folded my arms on the sill and rubbed them a little, then rested my chin on my wrist, the ends of my sleep-tousled hair tickling my arm. It was so quiet—the whole morning seemed to be holding its breath. I realized it was the absence of the street noises I was used to hearing outside the Drapers' house every morning that made the difference.

I twisted on my knees and put my chin over my shoulder to look at the room. The walls were papered in a faded blue-and-white striped pattern, the bedstead was chipped white-painted iron. The floor was bare except for a braided rag rug next to the bed. There was a white-painted bureau with a mirror opposite the bed, a narrow, scratched oak wardrobe in the corner, and a clothes rack on the back of the door on which hung my dress and hat from yesterday, the only familiar objects except for my suitcase at the foot of the bed.

I wondered if this could have been the room my mother had slept in as a girl. It had been only Marjory McKay and her father in the house those last few years before she left to marry my father, Olsen Campbell. In my mind's eye I could see a fair-haired girl not unlike myself brushing her hair in front of the mirror, and going downstairs to join her father for breakfast in one of those rooms which, thanks to a neighbor's industry, looked as if they had been lived in only yesterday.

I had the strangest feeling that if I went downstairs now, I might meet my grandfather coming in from outdoors as big as life, as if he had never been away...

I scrambled up from the window and opened my suitcase, eager to get downstairs and see it all again as it really was. Yesterday was already a little filmy in my memory. And I still had a decision to make, though in my heart I knew I had made it already.

Ten minutes later I was down in the kitchen with a small fire started in the cookstove, breaking eggs into a skillet. Ray's prediction about the kitchen cupboards had been accurate, and I could only wonder what the Crawley family was living on this week. I had my breakfast at one end of the long bare table and washed my dishes afterward, and then set out to explore. I opened the back door, pushed through the screen door beyond it and went down the steps to the yard. The grass was wet with dew, the gaps in the trees streaming with sunshine, and smoke was rising from the stovepipe of the bunkhouse. I chose the path toward the barn and headed that way. I glanced back at the house as I walked, noting new details—there was a clothesline on poles near the back door, and sloping doors to a cellar beside the steps.

As I neared the barn the door creaked open and a man came out carrying two milk pails. He was short, with bowed legs and sloping shoulders and a battered hat pushed down on his head. He saw me before he had taken more than a few steps, and nodded to me. "Morning. Miss Campbell, ain't it?"

"Yes—good morning." I couldn't think of anything else to say.

"Looking for anything?"

"No, just—looking. You work here, don't you?"

"Sure." He grinned, his sunburned and rather aggressively lined face turning pleasant with a smile that disclosed crooked front teeth. "I'm Tim McGreevy. I been here around four years."

I glanced down at the milk pails. "I don't want to keep you from your work…There's milk cows too? I didn't know that."

"Just a couple. It ain't to sell; just milk and butter for the ranch. The cream separator's in the shed yonder. The old man"—he tried not to make the check in his sentence too obvious and got over it pretty well—"he didn't have much patience with machinery, but he preferred it to churning."

I pulled my sweater closer against the morning chill and smiled at the recollection of something said yesterday. "He must not have taken very kindly to the new telephone."

Tim's attention seemed to be on something else. "No."

The bunkhouse door slammed, and I looked that way to see Ray Harper coming down the path toward us.

"Morning," he said. "I was just coming down to the house to see if you needed anything done. Get along all right in the kitchen? That stove can be tricky to light."

"Beginner's luck, I guess. I haven't had to start a fire in a few years."

"I see you've met Tim—you want to come along and meet the others while they're around? There's just four of us all told."

I went with him to the tack room at the back of the barn, where the others were getting out their saddles. Ray made the introductions. "Lane Whitaker, and Tony Gleason. This is McKay's granddaughter, Lena Campbell."

I shook hands with each of them, feeling out of my depth again, but by no means unwelcome. Both were tall and lean—Lane was a red-headed boy of about nineteen with a winningly shy smile, and Tony, several years older, had brown hair and what appeared to be a constitutionally skeptical expression. "I'm glad to meet you," I said. "I've pretty much decided to stay here, so—Mr. Harper has agreed to stay on as foreman, and I don't see any reason to change anything else, if you'd all like to go on working here."

Tony Gleason gave a short laugh. "Like?" he said. "Catch me leaving on my own power. Jobs aren't so easy to come by these days."

I was still tingling all over from what I felt was an

awfully naïve and pretentious little speech, which I didn't know what had possessed me to make, when they had gone to saddle their horses and Ray and I had walked out of the barn. I said hesitantly to him, "Was it all right, my saying that?"

I thought he looked amused. "You're going to be my boss too, you know, if you stay on."

"I know, but—I don't want to start overruling you while I'm still too ignorant to know I'm doing it."

"If it makes you feel any better, I promise I'll let you know if you do. Deal?"

"Deal," I laughed.

We walked past the barn, alongside the corral, and stopped. I scanned the pastures, the dirt road running past, the rolling hills beyond, turning slowly to wind up with the house and barn again. I drew a deep breath. "Well, I want to see it all, but I don't know where to start."

"If you want to ride along with me this morning, I'll show you some of the ranch. Do you ride, by the way?"

"I *have* been on a horse, though only a couple of times. It was on a Western saddle, though."

"Well, that's one point in your favor," said Ray, that pleasant warm smile of his showing suddenly again. "Anytime you're ready. I'll go saddle a horse for you."

"You're sure it's not a bother? I mean, I don't want to take you away from anything more important…"

Ray shook his head. "Checking fences is routine work that needs doing anyway. You can call it your first lesson."

"All right. I'll go change and be back in five minutes!"

I flew up to the house, and rattled up the stairs to my bedroom, and turned my suitcase inside out. I had one pair of slacks with me, and a pair of lace-up boots which I'd once worn for some hiking and had packed for this trip with the idea that they might be useful. I put on these and a blouse, and having no hat, tied a blue scarf around my head like a headband to keep my hair back from my face. I was waiting on the front porch when Ray Harper rode down to the house, mounted on a big handsome bay gelding and leading another saddled horse, a dark-chestnut mare with a slim tapered head and delicate-looking feet.

"Ready?" he said, dismounting so easily that I envied him on the spot.

"Guess so," I said with a cheerful shrug. My heart was beating a little bit quickly again, but I still felt awfully happy.

Like I said, I'd been on a horse a few times, the last time about a year ago when the Drapers were at a weekend party in the country and I'd been invited to go along with some of the young people who were going riding. But those had been placid trail-riding hacks and I hadn't had much to do. Still this came easier than I'd expected. Ray didn't over-teach—he gave me a boost with his hand under my elbow as I mounted, showed me the right way to hold the reins and gave me a few pointers, and left the rest to come by experience as we went along. I was to find that to be his method of teaching me many things in the months to come.

Trix, my mount, stood perfectly still while Ray mounted Sarge, her daintily shaped ears alert and poised to catch sounds, the left one swiveled backward so I could see the furred inside. Sunlight caught the surprisingly long lashes fringing a large, soft dark eye. I gazed in fascination until Ray swung his horse alongside mine, then roused quickly and moved the reins as he had shown me to follow him.

We rode up the gentle slope behind the bunkhouse, through a gap between pine trees with the horses' feet thudding on a carpet of dry russet needles and crackling over the occasional twig. On the far side a longer slope of green pasture ran down, swelling up again perhaps half a mile away—or it might be twenty miles for all I knew—like a grassy sea. Beyond that steeper hills rose like ramparts against the sky, crowned with rock and seamed in places with the richer green of woods. Here and there across the landscape I could trace the lines of barbed-wire fences dividing the land into large pastures, and clusters of red-brown cattle dotted some of the lower fields. Over everything hung the vivid, shimmering light of morning.

I simply gazed, my eyes open as wide as they would go, too full of admiration and gladness to try and say anything. If I had it probably would have been inarticulate, fulsome exclamations over the beauty of the country, but I was riding with my ranch foreman and didn't want to make myself look even more of a neophyte than I already did by nature.

We rode for an hour or two, exploring the pastures, sometimes following a track marked out by truck tires and sometimes riding across open country or through sun-dappled woods that Ray of course knew well; and he gave me an idea how the land lay, where the pastures were, and showed me some livestock I had previously met on paper. We also met Tim, who fell in and joined us, and proved an entertaining companion, making me laugh with a droll story of hunting a wily saddle horse that had once gotten loose up in the hills. By then I'd long since forgotten to be nervous about my riding, and could even spare an occasional thought to be proud of myself.

We were riding along a north-facing slope of hill,

with a line of fence along the foot of the draw on our left, when I spotted a couple of other riders on the other side of the fence about fifty yards ahead. They must have seen us at about the same time, for they changed direction slightly and swung in closer to their side of the fence, coming toward us at a loose trot.

"Sutherland," said Tim. Something in his voice made me look at him, and I saw that his previously good-natured face had settled into a hard, almost ugly expression. "Figures."

Ray said, "Nobody said you had to talk to him."

"Thanks," said Tim, "I'll pass."

He wheeled his horse around and headed back in the direction we had come, angling up the slope. I stared after him for a second, then turned to face forward again. I had no idea what that had meant, and it probably hadn't been intended for me anyway, so I tried to look as if I hadn't noticed anything. I did steal a glance toward Ray to see if I could pick up some clue to how I ought to look or act, but his eyes were fastened on the approaching riders as we turned downhill on a course to meet them. The ground dropped off a bit steeply there and I caught at my saddle horn to steady myself with my right hand surreptitiously, as I remembered reading somewhere that "pulling leather" was considered a disgrace among Western riders.

There were two men—one of them must have been a ranch hand, but I never really noticed him because the one closer to the fence had grasped all my attention. He might have been seventy by his shock of white hair and seamed red face, but looked hale enough for an active man of fifty. His chin and brows both jutted a little so he seemed to be peering out from between them, and his small, rather unpleasantly alive eyes were fixed on me from the moment we drew rein on opposite sides of the barbed wire. "Hello, Ray," he said, but with only a brief glance at him; he was more interested in—and, I thought rather uncomfortably, amused by me.

"Miss Campbell, this is one of your neighbors. Bill Sutherland," said Ray.

The flatness of his voice surprised me. It gave me the impression he was introducing someone he didn't care for, but still in a way that nobody could find fault with.

"So you're Garth's granddaughter," said Sutherland in a harsh, creaking voice which, together with the heavy brow, reminded me of some aged bird of prey. He smiled, and the deep lines ran back from the corners of his mouth into his face. "Heard about you. Well, you're not much more than a kid. How old are you?"

"Twenty-one," I said, smiling half-heartedly and feeling younger.

"Just old enough, then." His eyes had a disconcerting gleam, like a burnished quartz rock I'd seen once. He looked like someone who had belonged to this country in an earlier time, before the trucks and the wire fences. "New to all this, aren't you? How do you like being in the cattle business?"

I might as well make the best of it. I smiled cheerfully and said, "I've only been here since yesterday, but I haven't met anything I dislike yet. Who knows, I might even get used to the cattle after a while."

Sutherland grinned again, sitting with one big fist resting on his hip, and I thought the gleam in his eye was almost like approval, though I didn't know why. "You might at that," he said. "At least you can be glad you've got a good man running the place for you. That goes for a lot."

I looked involuntarily at Ray, even more surprised. Evidently the dislike didn't run both ways. His tanned face was noncommittal, but there was something in his eyes that confirmed my first impression of his attitude toward the old man. Sutherland, though, was smiling. "Do you know, Miss Campbell, I tried to hire your foreman away from the Circle M once—and he turned me down flat? Offered him good money too. But he had his own ideas."

"I liked it where I was," said Ray.

One of Sutherland's white eyebrows twitched upward, thoughtfully. "Better than the chance of managing a ranch twice the size...and more money than McKay could afford to pay you. Well...your affair. But I gave you your chance."

"I'll take my own chances."

"You always will," said Sutherland, the creases in his face deepening again with his smile. I couldn't tell if it was scorn in his voice, or something like...admiration? I didn't know. I was tight as a fence wire with the confusion of trying to figure out things that were unsaid and maybe weren't there at all.

Bill Sutherland shifted in his saddle and the leather creaked, and all his attention was on me again. "Well," he said, "I hope you go on enjoying yourself. What's your first name?"

"Lena."

"Lena. Sounds kind of Swede. Pretty names they give girls nowadays, though. Time was, every girl I knew was called Martha, or Nell...Well...afternoon."

"He's...interesting," I ventured to Ray as we rode on along the fence line, with the two other horsemen disappearing round a curve of the draw behind us. "He seems like a real old-timer. I guess he was probably out here a long time before anybody else?"

"He's one of the last few," said Ray. "His spread is twice the size of most in Severn County, as he pointed out."

He glanced at me, and added, unexpectedly, "You did fine."

"Me? I hardly said a word!"

"That's all right. At least you answered him back—
you didn't let on you were afraid of him. Probably the best
thing you could have done to get in *his* good graces."

Was I afraid of Bill Sutherland? Of course: no
wonder I felt as wobbly now as you do after somebody has
jumped at you from behind a door. I was more impressed
with the fact that Ray had known it before I did. And if he
had, hadn't Bill Sutherland…? I remembered the gleam of
amusement in the old ranchman's eye and suddenly it all
made sense. "But I didn't—when I said that about the cattle
I wasn't trying to be smart! I just said the first thing that came
into my head—"

Ray was grinning, though I was sure I couldn't see
what *he* found so funny either. "It doesn't matter whether he
thought you were or not. He didn't get to bluff you. It's kind
of like with horses." He gestured toward the head of Trix,
pacing smoothly along with one foot in front of the other, the
sun gleaming off the chestnut curve of her neck in front of
me. "A horse can sense fear, or nervousness, and they'll act
just the way they know you expect them to. And men can be
the same way. If you can't trust a man, don't let him see
you're afraid of him."

We were coming over the shoulder of a low hill, the
green grass rippling to our horses' knees; the breeze stirred
in my hair and flicked the end of my scarf against my cheek.
Ray said, "I'll show you something better now. This way."

We turned into a stretch of woods, on ground rising
to the north—first a fairylike grove of wind-rustled young
aspens, and then higher up as the rocks broke more and more
from the moss-carpeted soil, dark, close-ranked, rich-
scented pines, their gnarled roots crawling over and winding

between the blocks of granite. I held unashamedly to the saddle horn as our horses climbed, and ducked the prickly evergreen branches that swept across the narrow trail we followed. And I wondered if Ray Harper had just told me not to trust Bill Sutherland.

CHAPTER IV

Prairie goes to the mountain,
   Mountain goes to the sky.
The sky sweeps across to the distant hills
And here, in the middle,
   Am I.

Kathryn & Byron Jackson: Open Range

WE BROKE FROM the woods onto a long, high, grassy ridge of land, running ahead against the sky as far as I could see. I followed Ray around outcroppings of rock in the tall grass, the ground still climbing all the time, until he drew rein and dismounted beside a big, roughly rectangular slab of granite, tilted so that it was perhaps four feet high at its higher end. I slid down into the knee-high grass, the ground feeling strange beneath my feet after a morning in the saddle. The fringe of grass and wildflowers along the crest of the hill was tall enough that from the little hollow behind the rock I could only see blue sky beyond it. Ray climbed up on the lower end of the granite slab, turned around and reached his hand down for me. I found a foothold on the rock and took hold of his hand, and with one strong swift pull he had me up beside him. I caught my breath as I saw what lay on the other side.

On the far side of the rock the ground fell steeply, not

in a cliff but a steep rocky slope clothed with scattered brush and lower down with tall pines; a hill that seemed to go down for miles. The view was like the one from the rise behind the Circle M ranch house, but ten times vaster in sweep and scope. Where before I had seen individual pastures, here I saw one huge valley breaking and folding in dozens of hills and draws and woods; rising on the right hand to rugged cliffs of gray rock, and fading gently away on the left into acres of rolling grassland, with the far sides of the valley like blue watercolors of hills in the distance. Beyond it all ran a garland of mountain peaks shining against the sky like silver and white meringues—so clear they looked barely half an hour away, though I later learned it was really miles and miles.

I didn't say anything. I just stood and looked and looked. I could have stayed on that rock and gazed for a lifetime.

It was minutes of silence before I even remembered that I wasn't alone. I turned to look at Ray Harper, and some of the glory must still have been reflected in my dazed eyes, for he just smiled. "I thought you'd like it," he said.

"If I hadn't already decided to stay," I said half to myself, gazing over the valley again, "this would've decided me. I don't think I could go back now even if I wanted to."

A wondering thought struck me, and I pivoted slowly to look up at him again. "Is any of that—*mine?*"

"Just a little. The Circle M's north boundary is about a hundred yards from the foot of this hill. Most of the eastern third of what you can see, and more of the upland above those cliffs, is Sutherland's." Ray put his hand on my shoulder and pointed off to the left, turning me a little to face that way. "Chambers' ranch is right down here in front of us, and the Crawleys are west of him. On the other side of both of them, bordering Sutherland most of the way up the valley, is Warren's. Over west and behind us a little is Severn Valley"—I looked over my shoulder, but could only see the long ridge running west and the indistinct green of woods beyond where it began to slope down—"and the highway is on the other side of that, then swings around to run east between here and the mountains—straight ahead, but you can't see it."

I drew a deep breath. The wind swayed the wildflowers below the rock, and whipped the loose sleeves of my blouse flat against my skin. "Someday," I said, "I'm going to pack a lunch up here, and a book or two, and just sit up here on this rock from morning till night." I glanced at Ray. "Have you ever seen the sun rise from up here?"

"A few times, yes. I'll bring you up here to see it sometime if you want."

"Oh, I didn't mean…I can come up myself sometime; I don't want to give you extra work chauffeuring me around."

"Well, I wouldn't let you come up here alone in the dark, Miss Campbell—boss or no boss" (this with a fleeting grin) "at least till you've learned how to shoot. There's mountain lions up in these hills."

"Oh, *I* see. Well, don't worry—I won't try to be stubbornly independent where mountain lions are involved. In fact I probably won't be asserting my independence noticeably anywhere for a while."

Ray said nothing, and I was assailed by a sudden qualm. I had a vision of all this vastness round me and all those acres and cattle without the anchor point of a reliable ranch foreman to make sense of it all for me; and I hoped I hadn't exaggerated my own helplessness to the point where Ray Harper might change his mind about staying on.

I said, with an uncomfortable attempt at a laugh, "I won't be such a millstone round your neck as all that. I'm a reasonably self-sufficient human, anyway, and—"

"Miss Campbell, I don't know what you're apologizing for. You're paying me to manage a ranch *for* you; you're not expected to have everything down pat in a week."

"Well, maybe not, but I do feel like your having to explain everything to a novice is going above and beyond what you're paid for."

Again, as he had done once or twice yesterday, he gave me a measured, almost searching look before replying, and I saw an expression in his brown eyes that I didn't quite understand. But he shook his head, and answered matter-of-factly. "I don't see it that way."

"Well," I said frankly, "I'm glad of that!"

Left alone at the ranch, later in the morning, I poked about and explored among the buildings at my leisure. I had a look at the chicken coop in its sagging wire-mesh enclosure, put my head in at the doors of the tool shed and the tack room, and wandered through the barn, with its box stalls and its high hayloft, mostly empty at this time of year. The doors at the far end stood open, framing a bright rectangle of sunlight and corral fences that was like an invitation, and I walked toward it. The doors led into one large empty corral, and there were a couple of smaller, interconnected ones beyond it, all adjoining the front pasture where the saddle horses grazed. Tony Gleason was in the next one, bent over cleaning a horse's feet with a hoof pick. I went over and climbed the fence just enough to rest my folded arms on the top, and leaned there watching for a minute.

"Picked up a stone?" I said casually, inwardly pleased I had at last found a place where I could demonstrate that I wasn't totally ignorant about horses. But Tony's answer rather deflated it. "Nope, just giving him the once-over."

He dropped one finished hoof, moved to another and hauled it up to brace it between his knees; and glanced at me with a look somewhere between friendly and sizing-up. "I heard Ray say you were coming from Chicago."

"Yep. I've lived somewhere near there pretty much all my life."

"First time outside the home corral, huh?"

I decide, first, that Tony might need some keeping in his place, and second, that he would be much easier to manage than Bill Sutherland. "Very first fore-hoof outside it. But it's not nearly so wild and woolly as I expected."

"Oh, yeah? How so?"

"Well, look at that train trip I took out here. Hundreds of miles across the prairie, and no hold-up men or Indian attacks at all—not even a little bit of dynamite on the tracks, can you believe it?"

Tony shook his head. "I've been telling people we've got to do something about that. Don't know what Wyoming's gonna come to if we keep on disappointing Easterners this way."

"Shameful," I agreed. "Seriously, though, going by most of the books I've read about the West, I think I know more about how to behave during a hold-up than I do about anything likely to serve me a practical turn nowadays. But I guess I'll just have to resign myself to the lack of excitement."

Tony nodded and shrugged. "Unless you count getting ten or a dozen of your cattle stolen every now and then as excitement. We've got that all right."

"Don't tell me! Real, live cattle rustlers? I thought Tom Mix had swept them all from the range in his last picture."

"He must have missed a few corners in Severn County," said Tony grimly, digging away with the hoof pick.

"You mean—there's really been cattle stolen? From the Circle M too?"

"Sure has. Darn good at it, too, whoever's been doing it—they've never left a trail that could be followed. They've been getting away with it for…gotta be six, seven years if I'm remembering right. It started before I was here."

I checked my first reply on the tip of my tongue. Having read *The Virginian* once, I had a nebulous suspicion that maybe my Eastern credulousness was being tested. But Tony's voice didn't seem to have the over-nonchalance or the solemnity of the trickster at work—and anyway, I was too curious to really care whether I was setting myself up to be laughed at. I said, "When was the last time it happened?"

Tony paused and squinted an eye upward in thought. "Last fall, round September. Crawleys lost a few head and so did we, and a couple others. The old man was—" He stopped, a little more obviously than Tim had earlier, and glanced at me before bending over the horse's hoof again and finishing, "—mad. It's a nuisance kind of rustling, just a few head here and a few there; but with the Depression on it's no joke to most people around here to lose the price of even two or three head of cattle that're already mortgaged to the tail."

The bitterness in his voice over the last words had nothing of joking about it. This was real, then. I wondered briefly why Robert Herrington hadn't used this to try and scare me off. It seemed like something logical to bolster his arguments that I would find ranching too daunting or troublesome.

Or maybe, I thought with a wry smile, Grandfather's lawyer really believed I was the kind of person who would be more delighted with the idea of a West that was wild.

That night after I had changed into pajamas, I got a pen and pad of writing paper from my suitcase and got into bed, sitting up at the head with the pad of paper resting on my knees and the light from the little lamp fixture on the wall falling over my shoulder onto it. I had a letter to write. But before I began, I put my head back against the rails of the bed and gazed off into the shadows of the room, thinking back over everything I had seen that day. I remembered the heavy, square-bodied Hereford cattle browsing the grassland; the alert chestnut ears of my horse, and the creak of saddle leather; the wind hushing through the pines on the slope below the great rock. It was all so new and yet somehow exactly as I had imagined it.

Complete with cattle rustlers, apparently.

I remembered Sutherland's flinty hawk-eyes beneath the brim of his big Stetson hat, and an ugly undertone in Tim McGreevy's voice that had prickled my nerves for a fleeting second. All my banter about train robbers and Indians aside, I knew there were things I did not know yet about these people and about this place that was so much bigger and more unpredictable than the city blocks that had bounded my growing-up years. A place where at least one person had taken the old path of settling a quarrel with a gun.

As they still did on street corners in Chicago, wearing

much more up-to-date hats, I reminded myself acidly. No doubt my grandfather could have made his share of enemies there too.

I opened my writing pad, and settled myself to compose the opening sentence of my letter. It wasn't easy. I hesitated several minutes with my pen hovering above the paper as I tried out different polite, convoluted phrases in my head, but none of them were quite right. At last I abandoned any attempt to be roundabout or apologetic, and settled for the only thing there was to say.

"Dear Mrs. Draper," I wrote, "I have decided to stay here in Wyoming and run my ranch."

CHAPTER V

Every man at the bottom of his heart believes that he is a born detective.

John Buchan: The Power House

I'D FORGOTTEN THAT you hurt all over the next day when you go horseback riding once in a blue moon. Next morning I could barely hobble around, and every time I had to stoop or reach for something my muscles wailed in protest. After I'd been up and about the house for a few hours my stiffened joints were loosened to the point where I no longer expected them to creak; but when I walked out the front door at nine o'clock it still required careful effort to move like a normal human being, which my pride required me to do.

Ray drove me into town in the ranch truck, an old green Ford with slatted wooden sides to the bed. Remembering how I'd felt the first day, I'd dressed simply: I wore a plain biscuit-colored cotton dress and my same blue hat and purse. As the truck, which didn't have any muffler to speak of, growled through the intersection toward the courthouse, I watched the people on the streets—women with deep shopping bags on their elbows looking over the bargain signs in front of stores, a few bare-legged, tow-headed children racing up and down the sidewalks, and the lank denim-clad men with their faces in the shade of their wide hats. I liked this place—I didn't want to stick out and look like a stranger here.

Robert Herrington's office was in one of the narrow corridors on the first floor of the courthouse, along with the county clerk, the district attorney, and various other public and private offices. He rose from his desk to welcome us as we entered, and once the first greetings were over, gave me a shrewd, somewhat resigned look. "Well," he said, "I see you have made up your mind."

It wasn't hard to see why; I know I felt and must have looked like a guilty child caught with a toy that didn't belong to it. But there was no sense in pretending. "I couldn't hold out any longer," I said, with a shrug and a smile. "I know what I want to do."

"Then we may as well get down to business," said Herrington, and having ushered me to a chair, turned to the filing cabinets lining the wall behind his desk.

Ray, standing just inside the office door with his hat in his hand, reached out and tapped my arm lightly with the brim of his hat and I looked around at him. "If you don't need me," he said, "I'm going to go pick up the mail and stop by the feed store, and then I'll come back and wait for you outside, if that's all right with you."

"Perfectly. Oh—if you're going to the post office would you mind mailing this letter for me? Thanks."

Last bridges burned, I reflected; and feeling somehow lighter now the letter was out of my hand, I settled back in my chair and waited comfortably as Herrington laid out various documents on the desk.

There probably weren't as many papers to sign as it *seemed*, but still the process of transferring the deeds to all Garth McKay's real property into my name took longer than I'd expected. Robert Herrington, a little more crisp and businesslike today than he had been the other day, was very precise in his explanations of everything, which I did find useful even though I suspect that wasn't the reason he did it.

"What would have happened if it wasn't for me?" I asked. It was hot in Herrington's office despite the electric fan, and the back of my neck was sweaty where my hat pressed down my hair. I was also beginning to get hungry. "I mean, if my mother didn't have any children. Who would it have gone to?"

"Since McKay died intestate, if we hadn't been able to locate any other relatives within a certain time, it would all have gone to the state." Herrington paused with pen in hand. "On that subject," he said, "it's a technicality I always recommend—now that you own a significant amount of property, it would be wise for you to draw up a will of your own, just so it would be disposed of in the way *you* would want in the chance-out-of-a-hundred it should be necessary."

"Do I *have* to?" I said, more because I was weary of signing papers and beginning to wonder when lunch was, than for any other reason. "I mean, I really don't see what good it would do. I can't think of anyone I would leave it to." The only relatives I knew of were the Drapers, who were quite well off, and at that moment I couldn't see that they needed my property any more than the State of Wyoming did.

Robert Herrington tapped his pen on the desk, and I added, hoping to avoid any more legal lectures, "At least not today? I'll try to think of some way to leave it, and you could draw it up for me sometime soon.

He inclined his head at a slight angle, in a way I was coming to recognize meant he accepted something without really liking it. "Very well, if that's what you'd prefer. Now, let's just go over this deed..." He slid another paper over to me.

It was past eleven-thirty when I signed my name for the last time and laid down the pen with a sigh of relief. Herrington shook my hand and congratulated me on my inheritance as I rose to go. I appreciated it, but I'm afraid the real property I was thinking about most was the six dollars and seventy-five cents in my purse, some of which I was meditating converting into lunch.

As Herrington was bidding me goodbye in the corridor outside his office, a door opened a few feet away and a man put his head out. His short-cropped hair was rough and iron-gray, his face hard-weathered and unsmiling, and there was a badge pinned on the pocket of his khaki shirt. Herrington saw him and nodded to him. "Oh, George. This is Lena Campbell, Garth's granddaughter. George Burwell, Severn County sheriff."

Burwell looked me over without expression, and I felt even more warm and wilted, more young, and more Eastern than I had a minute before. He didn't even seem critical; he just gave an impression of *being* critical by nature. "Staying long?" he said.

"I'm staying for good...at least I'm going to try it," I said. (For a minute I wondered if this was what it was like to have a grandfather.)

"H'm," said Burwell. "Hope things work out for you. The Circle M's not in bad shape, considering."

I glanced at Robert Herrington, wondering if I might get a clue as to what "considering" meant, but I didn't. George Burwell gave a not unfriendly but short nod that encompassed both of us, and disappeared back into the office. I felt, for the first time in Severn Valley, dismissed.

I felt better when I got outside the courthouse into the sunshine—it was a hot day but at least there was a breeze blowing. I looked about and spotted Ray Harper leaning against a car parked down in front of the corner of the building, talking to another man, but when he saw me coming down the courthouse steps he excused himself and came over to meet me by the truck.

"Everything all right?" he said.

"I guess so," I said. "I have to stop at the bank—and then go home for lunch; I'm starving already."

"We could get lunch here in town if you'd rather have it right away. Stevenson's and the Up & Down both serve a good lunch; whichever one you want."

"Stevenson's," I said promptly, for I'd been curious about the hotel ever since I saw the sign yesterday. "How about going there first? If the bank's going to take anywhere near as long as this did I'm not sure I can last it out without lunch."

It was a minute's drive of a couple dusty blocks to the hotel, with its high false front and raised boardwalk in front. Ray pulled the truck in alongside the boardwalk and shut off the engine, got out and came around to open the door for me, and we went up the steps to the boardwalk together.

A bell jangled over our heads as Ray pushed the door open and held it for me. I'm not sure what I expected the lobby to be like, but it was rather like the waiting-room of a country railroad depot. There were straight-backed, cushioned benches around the walls, some striped straw matting on the bare wood floor, and behind the desk in the corner with its rows of numbered pigeonholes on the wall there was a window that let in bright sunlight through a row of dashingly cheerful potted geraniums. There was a steep staircase to the second floor, and through an archway I saw a dining-room with half a dozen tables and a lunch counter across one side. On the walls of both rooms the usual advertisements for Coca-Cola and cigarettes were accompanied by some old framed posters for rodeos and livestock shows and pictures of horses and cows—cattle, I reminded myself. I took a closer look at one rodeo poster faded to pinkish-orange with age, and saw that the date was 1919.

There was a girl behind the front desk, leaning her elbows on it reading a magazine, who looked up when the bell over the door rang. She had on an everyday cotton dress in a cheerful yellow print and a checked wrap apron like my mother always wore, with the pattern blurred a little in front with many washings and hand-wipings, but her brown hair was waved in a good imitation of the latest style. She let the magazine drop and looked at me with undisguised interest— I think she'd been expecting the Eastern girl to be something more glamorous and unusual, but after the first look that told her I was a thoroughly ordinary person she seemed just as pleased with that. "You must be Lena Campbell," she said, sliding out from behind the desk and offering me her hand with disarming directness. "I'm Cathy Stevenson. I heard you were coming and I've been wanting to meet you."

I liked her right away—it would be hard not to with a greeting like that. She reeled off a rapid-fire string of questions with a kind of frank innocence that robbed them of any possible rudeness. "Did you just get here? Are you staying out at the ranch? We've got plenty of good rooms vacant if you want to be in town instead. Are you going to stay here for a while at least?"

"For good, I hope," I said, feeling much more con-fident about it than when I'd spoken to George Burwell.

"I've been over at the courthouse tying up all the legalities. I'm a rancher now for better or worse."

"Good for you!" said Cathy. "I was hoping you'd stay. So what can I do for you now? Lunch? How about you, Ray?" She turned and shouted through a door which must have led to the kitchen, "Hey, Mom! Two for lunch. I'll get their orders. Go on and sit down, I'll be right with you." This last to us, before she whisked round the corner into the dining-room and disappeared behind the lunch counter.

Ray and I sat down at a table in the dining-room—I careful not to show any sign of wincing as the effects of yesterday's ride gave me a twinge again. I put my purse on the table, picked up the menu card from where it leaned against the salt and pepper shakers and studied it attentively. Ray reached over and tapped the corner of the card with one finger. "Get the black bean soup with rye bread," he said, "and the lemon layer cake. You won't regret it."

"Never let a cheapskate order for you!" said Cathy Stevenson, reappearing to plunk down a pitcher of ice water on our table with a thud that made all the cutlery jump and ring. Then she grinned. "He's right, though. Mom's black bean soup can't be beat."

"I'm easily persuaded," I laughed, putting the menu card back. "I'll have that, please, and the lemon cake too."

"Same for me," said Ray.

Cathy whisked off into the kitchen again, and Ray tossed his hat on the seat of the empty chair next to him. Studying him across the table, I decided my first impression of him the other day had been wrong. I'd figured he was under thirty, but really he couldn't be more than twenty-five or twenty-six. What I had taken for extra years was merely the serious, level expression his face settled into when he wasn't speaking or smiling.

"How long have you worked at the Circle M?" I asked him, unfolding my napkin.

"About three years. Why?"

"Oh, no reason, I just wondered. You're from around here?"

"No, I'm from Colorado. I worked my way up here, going from one job to another."

I leaned back in my chair a little. "Mr. Herrington was very nice about everything," I said. I looked quizzically at Ray. "He didn't want me to keep the ranch, though. I could tell he didn't."

"I guess he just wanted you to take what looked like the safest route."

"You didn't agree with him—about that?"

Ray didn't answer for a second. Then he said, "Let's just say I wouldn't want to see the Circle M go to the buyer Herrington would have found for you."

I would have liked to ask more, but Cathy came back just then carrying a tray with our orders, and by the time we'd been served and begun eating the moment for that conversation seemed to have passed. There was one other thing I'd been thinking about, though, and once I'd made some headway with my soup (which was delicious), I determined to bring it up. "Mr. Harper—"

"Ray. Everybody calls me that."

"There's one thing I'd like to know," I said. "The other day, when Robert Herrington told me about my grandfather's death—was he telling the truth? When he said there was no clue to who did it?"

Ray looked at me for a few seconds with that steady, intent look of his, which, if it had lasted any longer, would have made me start to wonder if my hat was on crooked or if there was something else particularly unusual about the way I looked. Then he said, "Yes. It was true, to all intents and purposes. As far as what he meant—"

He transferred his gaze to the table in front of him, and slowly tore the crust from his slice of rye bread. "McKay wasn't the easiest man in the world to get along with. He had a temper, and not a lot of tact. You could find any number of people in Severn County who didn't *like* him, but that's not enough reason to charge anybody with murder. Any private hunches or suspicions the police had, there wasn't any evidence to back it up, is what Herrington meant. It amounts to the same thing."

I nodded, assimilating the idea. I moved forward a little in my chair and rested my chin on my hand. "You see, I had a kind of idea myself. What about the cattle rustling that was going on? Could the murder have had anything to do with that?"

Ray glanced up with a slight look of surprise. "The rustling? Who told you about that?"

"Tony. I mean, he never said anything about the murder—we were talking and he happened to mention the cattle being stolen, and afterwards I got to thinking about it. Couldn't it be possible that my grandfather found something out—found out who was doing the rustling—and that's why he was killed? To keep him quiet?"

Ray thought about it for a moment. "I suppose it's *possible*," he admitted slowly, "but the idea wasn't brought up, that I know of. I don't think anybody made that kind of connection, or at least never thought about it seriously, because there hadn't been any thefts lately around the time McKay was killed."

"But if it was something that'd been happening, off and on, for a few years—he could always have stumbled on somebody red-handed about to try it again, couldn't he? Or even, just came upon a clue or overheard something that told him who'd done it before. You can't say it isn't at least possible."

Ray stared thoughtfully at the menu card on our table as if thinking back, his lunch forgotten for a minute. He said, as if thinking aloud, "No...no, I see what you mean. It's not out of the question. It doesn't even mean he had to have proof...he could have privately suspected somebody all along, and then suppose he ran into the person that night... being half drunk and not thinking straight, he came out with an accusation that happened to be true."

"*Was* he drunk that night?" Herrington hadn't mentioned that either.

Ray looked at me for a second, and then said, "Yes. He was."

"I suppose it couldn't have really been an accident, or suicide..."

"He was shot in the back—and the bullet came from a rifle."

"Oh." I abandoned that theory, and returned to my original one with girl-detective persistence. "Do you think that's the explanation, then? I mean about the rustling."

"It could be, but even if it was there'd be no way to prove it."

"Why not?"

"Well, look at it this way—even if somebody was finally caught red-handed at the rustling, there'd be no evidence to link them with the murder, unless the police could match the gun (they'd be stupid to keep the gun around). And nobody's likely to confess to a murder on their own if all they're facing is some prison time for stealing cattle."

A single fly was buzzing against a window screen at the far end of the room, and I could hear a radio playing out

in the kitchen. I nodded slowly, in regretful acknowledgement of the logic. "Oh, well," I said, and picked up my fork
and cut into the lemon layer cake.

Ray gave me a look that seemed partly amused, and
partly something less agreeable, and seemed about to say
something but apparently changed his mind. I grinned a
little, embarrassed without knowing why. "Go on, say it."

He waited a second before speaking. "You sound
kind of disappointed."

I was almost certain that wasn't what he had
originally been about to say, but a flush stung my cheeks all
the same. I hadn't meant for my very real, niggling curiosity
about my grandfather's unsolved murder to look like playing
Nancy Drew for the novelty of it over his grave. Suggesting
theories over lunch and thinking I was the first, when the
police had probably been through it all before.

I forced a small smile. "Oh, no. I just wondered about
it, that's all."

The silence that followed lasted until Cathy Stevenson came back to see if our glasses needed refilling. I sat up
a little straighter and said, trying to sound as if I was continu-
ing an ongoing conversation, "There's a department store
here in town, isn't there? There's some shopping I'll want to
do, and I wondered whether I'd need to go to Claxton, or if
I can find what I need here."

"Oh, sure!" said Cathy, bouncing into the conversation before Ray could speak; "if you want anything fancy
you'll have to go to Claxton, but if it's just blue jeans and
everyday stuff you need, you go to Gundrum's. They'll have
all you need."

"Oh, good. Yes, that's what I had in mind—I didn't
bring much with me that's fit for riding and outdoors."

"I'll tell you what," said Cathy, "when you're finished eating, why don't I go with you and show you the stores myself. You'll find what you're looking for much quicker. And anyway I'm dying to get better acquainted with you. How about it?"

I laughed. "I'd love it. Only—I hadn't planned on doing it today; I don't know if you'll want to wait that long—" I turned questioningly towards Ray.

He was already getting up. "Don't worry about it. You said you had to go to the bank, right? Say I pick you up there in an hour."

"All right—"

"Swell!" said Cathy. "I'll just run and tell Mom so she can do the desk while I'm out. Ready when you are."

"I'm glad you decided to stay," Cathy told me as we walked along the sidewalk on Main Street—the only street, except for Severn Street by the courthouse, that had a sidewalk. "Ever since I heard you were coming I hoped we'd end up being friends. And listen, you've got to treat us like friends right away. Anything you need help with while you're getting settled, around the house or things like that, just call Mom and Dad and me. We run a hotel, so we're up at all hours."

"I will. Honestly, you're being so nice I don't even know what to say."

"Skip it," said Cathy cordially. "It's what we're here for. And you'll make more friends fast. Most people around here are pretty nice, take them for all in all. So long as you don't expect angels."

"I met the sheriff when I was at the courthouse," I said inconsequently. "He isn't very…talkative, is he."

"That's a very sweet way of putting it. He's a good enough sheriff, but nobody's ever accused him of having a good bedside manner."

"I'm glad it wasn't just me."

"Hmm...well...it wasn't anything against you personally, but he doesn't have much love lost toward anything to do with the Circle M. After the murder—that is—I suppose you know...?" Cathy trailed off a bit, the first check to her easy flow of speech, and gave me a questioning glance.

"Oh yes, I know all about that. All there is to know, anyway. In fact Ray and I were just talking about it, at lunch."

"You *were?* Oh, well, then..." Cathy looked and sounded relieved, though I didn't know why. "Well anyway, the sheriff's election a few years ago was a nasty one; one or two people who were against Burwell said some things about the way he did his job that rankled with him, so he's been touchy ever since about anything that could leave him open to criticism. Having the McKay murder left unsolved was just the kind of thing he thinks people would harp on if they wanted to talk him down."

"He thought it left him with a black eye."

"Yep. After a few months of dealing with all of it I think he wound up pretty thoroughly sick of anything and everything connected with the Circle M."

"Well if that's it, I feel better. I felt about ten years old and completely unfit to own property after he'd looked me over."

"There are some things about his face he can't help," said Cathy drily. "Here's Gundrum's."

An hour and a half later, having parted from Cathy on the street corner with mutual promises of telephoning later, and completed my business at the bank, I pushed an armful of parcels into the passenger seat of the green truck and clambered in after them, feeling like Mrs. Gamp departing for the countryside. My purse fell down by my feet and I philosophically left it to lie there till we got home. I was the owner of one Wyoming ranch, three pairs of blue jeans, a crisp white Stetson hat with a rawhide string, and shirts assorted, and I couldn't have been happier.

When the truck turned into the lane of the Circle M, I felt a funny little thrill at the fact that I recognized it already, after traveling the road three times coming and going. Then Ray Harper chuckled, and I looked at him curiously. He was looking ahead up the lane, and following the direction of his eyes, I saw a station wagon in the yard in front of the house and a man and a woman getting out.

"I did say the day after tomorrow, didn't I?" said Ray.

"Too bad you didn't get me to make a bet."

"It's bad manners to bet on a lady," said Ray, and I was still trying to choke back my laughter when the truck came to a stop by the house.

Mrs. Crawley was a small woman, just plump enough for you to notice it, with salt-and-pepper gray hair and a way of squinting carefully at you through the spectacles on her nose if you were close to her, and looking over them as if they weren't there when you were beyond arm's length. Her husband was a little taller, and almost stringily thin, with a prominent Adam's apple and a mild kindly smile.

I slithered out from beneath my parcels and out of the truck, leaving the things in the passenger seat, and shook hands with my neighbors. Mrs. Crawley held onto my hand with both of hers for a minute and looked at me closely through her spectacles. "You're Marjory's daughter right enough," she said. "Not the image of her, but the likeness is there. Maybe you're a little prettier."

I blushed, but there was a prickle at the back of my throat too. I kept forgetting that all these people had known my mother, maybe almost as well as I had. I said a bit hastily, "I wanted to thank you for all the—the food, and your cleaning the house."

"You're perfectly welcome, dear; I was glad to do it. We didn't want to disturb you your first night, or yesterday, but I told Rufus we ought to stop by here today and say hello and see if there was anything else we could do. We're just about three miles down the road, though we haven't got a telephone, so you feel free to run over any time you need something or want company." Mrs. Crawley gave my hand a final, brisk shake and released it, and then linked her arm through mine. "And now come inside and tell me all about yourself."

CHAPTER VI

Within lie snoods that bound her hair,
Slippers that have danced their last,
Faded flowers laid by with care…
Trifles that have borne their part
In girlish hopes and fears and shames…

Alcott: In the Garret

THAT AFTERNOON I had my first lesson in ranch management. In the office, Ray brought out all the books to the table and acquainted me with typical monthly expenses, the men's wages, cost of grain, haying, and so forth. I noticed that the only complete records seemed to be those of the last few months since my grandfather's death, in what was apparently Ray's own handwriting, different from the scratchy hand covering the mismatched sheets of paper of every kind that jammed the rolltop desk.

"My grandfather must not have been a very good bookkeeper?" I ventured with an amused glance toward the desk at one point.

"He had his own system," said Ray. "He was stubborn about money matters. He kept all the books himself, and he never let me handle anything financial for him, even down to making a deposit at the bank. I don't think he wrote everything down, either. When Herrington and I went through his papers, afterwards, there were so many gaps in his records that they weren't much use to us. From some things he'd said, I always thought McKay had another bank account or a safe-deposit box somewhere, but we never found a key or a record of one."

As he spoke I'd been going through the jumble on the desk, automatically smoothing and sorting the creased scraps of paper into stacks by their size. Ray said, "I wouldn't bother with any of that. It's all been gone through, and there's really nothing there that matters now."

"It's habit, I guess. I've been a secretary for a couple years and I'm used to organizing papers. I suppose I ought to clear all this up and put it away somewhere neatly, or burn it, if I'm going to use the desk."

"Whatever you like," said Ray. He got up and opened a table drawer. "I've been keeping the books in here, if you want to look at them any time. The key's kept in that top left compartment in the desk." He locked the drawer, and then put the key away in the place he'd indicated.

After Ray had gone I stood for a moment still absently turning over the litter of papers on the green desk blotter. If they were no use, I supposed I ought to burn them...but still...

I realized there were still parts of the house I hadn't explored yet. I spun around and left the office, and began with a good look at the living room. It had some nice old cherry-finished furniture and a big braided rag rug, rather faded; and an old sofa that looked pretty impossible but which I thought might be made over with slipcovers so long as it didn't actually have moths in it. I made a mental note to ask Cathy or Mrs. Crawley about where to borrow a sewing machine.

I investigated the closet under the stairs—old boots,

a couple of rain slickers, a coil of rope; a shelf of mis-
cellaneous items like wire-cutters, balls of twine, flashlight,
a tin of chewing tobacco and boxes of shotgun shells; and
the shotgun itself standing in a corner, from which I recoiled
a bit when I recognized its outline.

As I turned from shutting the closet my eyes fell on
the closed door across the hall. I stepped toward it and put
my hand on the doorknob, and then I paused. For a minute I
had the feeling that I was intruding somewhere where I had
no right to be. I pushed the thought away.

After all, it's my house now, I told myself, and
opened the door.

It was a bedroom. Nothing elaborate—a plain metal
bedstead against the left-hand wall, neatly made up with a
worn quilt and fresh untouched pillows; a night-table and
dresser and a closet. This had been Garth McKay's room. By
now I knew that he had been a plain man who bought no new
things and left behind few traces of individuality, unless they
had been cleared away by executor and neighbors.

But perhaps they hadn't. I found his clothes in the
dresser drawers—blue jeans many times washed and worn,
blue and gray shirts going threadbare in places, and plain
underclothing and socks. In the closet was a fairly good
quality winter overcoat that didn't look to have been worn as
often, and—

There was something long and made of thinner fabric
hanging against the wall in the dark corner of the closet. I
reached in—my fingers ran down its limp-hanging folds,
drew it out toward the light. It was a dress, an old party dress
made in the style of twenty-five years ago that had once been
moss-pink. I examined with delight the ruffled neck, the
bloused, embroidered bodice and loose elbow sleeves. I
wondered if I might try it on sometime, but the waist looked

smaller than mine. The eyelet lace on one of the sleeves was torn, and there was a place in the skirt where a long rip had been neatly mended, perhaps after a clumsy dance partner had stepped on the hem. An old party dress that had seen its best days and probably been replaced by another one—it was easy to see why my mother hadn't thought it worthwhile to pack when she left home to marry, especially if she had packed quickly, if there had been hard feelings to speed her on her way.

Had there been hard feelings? My mother had never said a word about it.

Garth McKay must have regretted it later, if he had kept a memento of his daughter like this—if he had cared enough to put an old dress away in his closet and preserve it. But why hadn't he written to her, or tried to find her? Was it just offended pride, or were there other things I didn't know about?

There was a shoebox on the floor almost out of sight under the hem of the dress, and in it was a little beaded purse with a broken clasp, a wide tortoiseshell comb such as girls used to put up their back hair in my mother's day, and a couple of ribbons. It was almost more than I could bear. Why hadn't he written? Why hadn't he set things right between them, or at least tried?

I ended up packing all the loose papers from the rolltop desk in a box and putting it away in the closet under the stairs. I don't know why I did it. Maybe it was because I had a feeling of something being still unfinished. Maybe I'd just inherited the instincts of a pack rat—but maybe I felt it wasn't quite right to burn even somebody's useless papers when their life had ended with a question mark.

CHAPTER VII

And this my neighbor too?

Shakespeare: The Winter's Tale

ON SATURDAYS, Severn Valley went to town. For most local ranch hands, Saturday afternoon and evening meant a game of pool in the back room of the bar or catching a moving picture and sampling some of the brighter lights of Claxton; housewives went visiting, and young people paired off for dates at the drugstore or movie house.

On my first Saturday in Severn Valley, I drove into town with the Circle M crew, who typically piled into the truck and went *en masse*. Once in town, Lane and Tony caught the bus to Claxton, Ray and Tim dispersed on errands or pleasure of their own, and I was left at liberty to find my own afternoon's amusement. At that stage Wyoming was still one great green and blue "talkie" to me, so I decided to skip the manufactured entertainments of Claxton and drop by the Hotel Stevenson to see Cathy.

The hotel dining-room was much busier today; there

were people at several of the tables and the lunch counter was crowded. I spotted Sheriff Burwell at the far end sitting over a cup of coffee and a sandwich. At the nearer end, Cathy Stevenson was leaning on the counter talking to a young man—a boy really—about my own age who was sitting on one of the stools. She caught sight of me and waved her hand. "Lena! I thought you might turn up today. Say, here's another one of your neighbors you should meet. This is Jimmy Warren."

Jimmy Warren swung around on his stool as Cathy spoke, and then slid off it and stood looking at me with a frankly pleased expression. He had dark hair and a bright youthful face, and was dressed like every other rancher on a Saturday, in clean blue jeans and a crisp shirt a degree nicer than the everyday. He was built differently than any of the Circle M hands; he was no taller than Tim McGreevy, but compact and quick-looking, more like the dapper cowboy heroes I'd been accustomed to see on a movie screen.

"That's right," he said, holding out his hand with a friendly smile, "everybody within fifty miles is considered a neighbor around here."

"Oh, I feel like a neighbor. I think I can see the tops of your trees from the highest point on my ranch," I said, shaking hands laughingly.

"Someday you'll have to come over and visit. It's just Dad and me, but we'd do our best to entertain you. Met any of your other neighbors yet?"

I slid onto the next stool and straightened my skirt. "I've met the Crawleys—they're awfully nice—and I met Mr. Sutherland my first day."

"Oh, *him.*"

I gave him a curious glance. "You too?"

"What can I get you, Lena? Coffee?" said Cathy,

giving a quick swipe with a dishcloth to the space of counter just vacated by a customer on my right.

"Oh, no thanks, I've had lunch. But—if *that* happens to be today's special—" I leaned forward to look after a plate with a slice of cake on it that had caught my eye as Mrs. Stevenson put it in front of a customer further down the counter.

"Double chocolate with almond frosting. It's a new experiment I'm trying out."

"I'm for that," said Jimmy, looking interested.

"Me too. I'll have a slice, Cathy."

As she went to get it, I folded my arms on the countertop and looked at Jimmy Warren. "You were saying?"

He grinned. "No, you were."

"Oh. Only that Mr. Sutherland doesn't seem to be anybody's favorite neighbor."

"Well, is he yours?"

I reflected. "Well, he has better *manners* than, say, Sheriff Burwell for instance, but for some reason I don't exactly feel comfortable with him. I never know what he's going to say next."

Jimmy nodded emphatically, as if I'd confirmed some opinion of his own. "I don't blame you. Burwell's just naturally grouchy, but Sutherland's got a streak of mountain lion in him—he takes every chance he gets to show off his claws."

I shot a rather guilty look over my shoulder at the sheriff and his sandwich, but concluded there was probably enough noise in the dining room that he wouldn't hear Jimmy's clear voice. Cathy slid a plate bearing a slice of the almond-frosted cake in front of me at that moment, and I picked up my fork and smiled at Jimmy. "Ray told me there were mountain lions up in the hills, but I had an idea he meant it literally."

"Oh, he did. He shot one up on the east boundary of the Circle M last year, you know. You'll have to get him to show you the hide sometime."

"How did we get onto mountain lions?" asked Cathy, putting her elbows on the counter again.

"We started with neighbors," said Jimmy.

"Yes. Cathy, this is absolutely *amazing*. You could open up a café in the city with just these layer cakes."

"Not enough excitement in the city for me. But go on about the neighbors and the lions; this sounds interesting."

I said (with my mouth full), "I think if I have to pick a favorite neighbor, I'll take Mrs. Crawley for starters. She seems like a very comfortable person to have for a friend."

"She is. She's been mother and aunt and grand-mother for years to all the kids around here who didn't have any of their own." He was deep into Cathy's cake, but I caught a look in Jimmy's eyes that told me he was one of those kids. I said, "Is that how she keeps up with what's going on, living away back there without a telephone? All that extended family must be useful."

"We-l-l-l, yes, in more ways than one. Her genuine niece Jenny Winship is the switchboard operator, so that helps too," said Cathy.

The bell over the front door had jangled every so often throughout our conversation, and as it rang now I glanced through the lobby and saw a couple more men who looked like ranchers coming in. I was scraping almond frosting from my plate when I realized one of them had come up behind us and Jimmy swung around on his stool to greet him. "Hey, Dad! How'd it go?"

His greeting was bright enough, but I thought there was a quick undertone of anxiety to it. I looked up.

"All right," said James Warren, in the slightly dismissive tone of somebody who doesn't want to talk about it right now. He looked from Jimmy to me, seeming to recognize that I was part of the group. I saw a slight resemblance to his son, mostly in coloring, but he was a much taller, long-limbed man, and his movements were slower. A face with a rather long jaw had likely once been handsome, but was now lined and a bit slack, and there was silver sprinkled through his dark hair. Jimmy introduced me with a pleased air that seemed partly for his discovery of me and partly pride at presenting his father.

"Yes, we've heard a lot about you," said James Warren, shaking hands with me. "Coffee, thanks, Cathy. So you're staying at the Circle M?"

We talked for a few minutes, going over the same ground of commonplaces I had with everybody else at introductions. Perhaps because I knew all my lines by now I was freer to observe the dynamics that existed between the Warrens. I couldn't help but notice how Jimmy hung on every word his father spoke, prompting him if he seemed to have forgotten something, echoing and corroborating his statements with an eager attentiveness that was almost pathetic. Warren had a laid-back, unconsciously grave manner that made him easy to talk to, but there was sometimes a preoccupied look in his eyes, rather like a man who has just come through a bad experience, and a line of perspiration on his forehead. I'd seen a similar look once on the face of a man who lived with chronic pain.

George Burwell had finished his lunch, and coming past on his way out as we were talking, stopped for a moment. "Hello, Jim," he said in his dispassionate way, "how's everything?"

"Oh...not too bad," said James Warren. "I think I've

finally got a buyer lined up for those Angus. Not for the price I hoped, though, not by a long shot."

"Times are hard. Other parts of the country it's a lot worse."

"I'm well up on the times," said Warren with a slight, strained laugh. "That's what I get from the bank when I visit them every month. Reminders of the times. I've just come from there."

"You put in for that loan?" said Burwell.

I noted how Jimmy Warren, sitting with one arm on the edge of the lunch counter, had his eyes fastened closely on his father's face, as if watching for any clue he could pick up from voice or expression—as if he wanted his father to look at him but knew he would not. "Not officially; not yet. Just feeling each other out...I know they won't give me a straight answer till after I've sold this year's stock in the fall."

"Like every year," said George Burwell.

Jimmy moved a little quickly on his stool, and dug in his jeans pocket for a coin that he pushed across the counter to Cathy. "Well, we'd better get going. You ready, Dad?"

"Coffee, son. Haven't finished it yet."

"Oh—right. I'll wait. The experiment was a success, by the way, Cathy."

"Experiment?" said James Warren quizzically, as he moved in between us at the counter.

"Double chocolate with almond frosting," I explained.

"Oh—oh, that."

As Warren lifted the half-finished cup of coffee, Jimmy moved around him to speak to me. "I'm awfully glad to have met you, Lena. I can call you Lena, can't I?"

"Of course."

"How'd you like to come riding some afternoon? You and Cathy, and she and I'll show you all the back roads and the best views."

"I'd love to," I said with enthusiasm (though in the back of my head I privately resolved to stave off that invitation until I was a little better horsewoman).

"Swell." He looked quite happy again; it seemed easy to put him in a good mood.

James Warren paid for his coffee, said goodbye to Cathy and to me, and the Warrens went out together. As they went through the dining room door into the lobby I saw Jimmy, half a step behind, put a hand on his father's back, and the gesture again conveyed an odd impression of protectiveness. I wondered why the need to take such anxious care of his father when he clearly looked up to him and was immensely proud of him? For I had distinctly received both of those impressions.

CHAPTER VIII

O, the land is fine, fine,
I could buy it a' for mine.

Scots Song: Strathairlie

T HE SUMMER WANED, and my education in ranch life progressed. I bought a pair of real riding boots. I learned to saddle a horse by myself. I began to memorize the layout of the pastures and to remember where the gates were. After it rained the first time I bought a slicker more my size at Gundrum's, as I'd completely disappeared inside the old ones from the hall closet. I was taught to look for bear and mountain lion sign around springs and creeks, and to always carry a pair of wire-cutters with me in case I found an entangled horse or cow. I got a pair of leather gloves for riding. I gradually became more knowledgeable about the care and feeding of livestock, and acquired a feel for what my income was and what I could afford to do with it.

I think I got off to a good start because the Circle M hands accepted me from the first—possibly because I didn't make any secret of either my ignorance or my eagerness to learn. They all seemed to take it as their business to watch out for me, but without being ostentatious about it. I was an amusing kid who needed looking after, but I was also a woman and their employer, and the combination of protect-tiveness and respect they gave me was just about one of the nicest things a girl can feel.

I think Lane had kind of a "crush" on me from the beginning, because when we were by ourselves he tended to stammer a bit and had a hard time looking me in the eye. He tried harder than any of the others to soften things for my Wyoming-ignorance, and wouldn't let on when I said or asked something particularly silly. I liked him: he was such a nice unassuming boy, and made me wish sometimes that I'd had a younger brother like him.

Tony was just about the opposite: he was the talker of the bunch, with a sarcastic bent, and rather fancied himself as a humorist; but he never crossed a certain line with me. Tim I thought the salt of the earth—he was the hardest-working, the most tireless, had the largest supply of good humor; but I also got the impression that he was pretty tough, and not someone you'd want to cross when he was in the wrong mood. I'd seen a flash of that once or twice and it was always a shock to me how quickly he could change.

There was just one subject none of them liked to discuss, and that was Garth McKay. Any time I mentioned him the response was the same: they answered respectfully, but in monosyllables, somehow became distracted by some-thing else, and drifted from the subject. It chilled me a little, and so eventually I stopped asking.

I wondered sometimes how Ray Harper had come to be hired as foreman. I never questioned his capability, but he was young for the position, even with the natural air of steadiness and authority that made him seem older. As far as

I could tell, the others had no problem taking orders from him, not even Tim, who was several years older but apparently had a thorough respect for Ray's judgment. And as for me—well, I figuratively hung on to Ray during those first months like a child hanging onto the coattails of the person in front of them in a dark hall at night. I followed him everywhere, listened to what he said and did as he instructed. Because he wasn't a terribly talkative person on his own, I learned to watch him for my cues. I came to know every shade of expression on his smooth tanned face, from the hard line above his brows when he was working out some problem to the almost invisible dimple in his right cheek when he smiled; and each inflection of his voice. And yet I didn't really *know* him yet, not in the deepest sense you can know a person, because they have to willingly give you something of themselves for that to be true; and Ray Harper wasn't the kind of person to give himself in that sense right away.

I can't say I thought all these things at the time. I was the sort who observed things and filed them as interesting and then went happily on my way without analyzing too deeply what they meant to me. It was only later, when I was going back over everything that had happened to me and trying to make sense of it all, that I could define it in such clear terms.

My riding was improving all the time too. Most of the time I rode Trix or Metis, a pretty little buckskin mare who eventually became my favorite mount. I'm afraid as soon as I gained a little confidence I became a terrible daredevil, and unnerved the boys by asking to ride all the most difficult horses on the ranch, which they very properly did not let me do. There was a handsome dark-brown gelding with splashy white stockings called Jericho, a favorite of

Tim's, that I longed to try—he had a little Paso Fino blood in him, and a stride so smooth it looked like swimming. But he could be hard to handle, and Ray and Tim both said no, wait till I was a little stronger and more experienced.

I did fall off a few times. The first time I inadvertently twitched the reins and made Metis think I wanted to go after a yearling steer that had just started lumbering away from us—she went and left me behind. Ray picked me up and asked me if I was okay—it always amazed me how he could get on and off his horse so fast—and I managed to nod yes, rubbing my hip and knowing there would be a bruise coming there later. It wasn't my last spill, but none of the others were quite so unexpected.

I was even learning how to drive the truck, probably the first area when I made myself genuinely useful, as I could free up a man for other work by taking the wheel when there was a load of fence posts or hay bales to haul. All the boys took a hand at teaching me, and even though the clutch and the gearshift both seemed to have minds of their own, I got the hang of it pretty quickly. I never did any worse damage than scraping some of the paint off the doors against fences, but one day under Tony's tutelage I got flustered and pulled the wrong lever and backed slap into a haystack. Tony never would school me again after that; I think he didn't want to be blamed for any havoc I caused.

Meanwhile, I was settling into the house. I unpacked the two small boxes of my belongings I'd had sent on from Chicago (blushing to remember that I'd packed them secretly before I took the train west), and spread them around the rooms. I learned that the radio in the living room worked when it felt like it—Tim claimed to be able to fix it, but I never found that the radio behaved any less arbitrarily after he'd gotten through with it than before he started. I'd covered the old sofa with slipcovers of flowered cretonne (Mrs. Crawley did ask me not to let Tim near her sewing machine when I borrowed it); and as I found there wasn't much reading material in the house except some old almanacs and livestock journals, I subscribed to *Collier's* and the *Saturday Evening Post* and a book-club-by-mail, and soon had a little library of my own between bookends on the table by the radio.

Eventually, though only after a little struggle with conscience or squeamishness, I did get rid of my grandfather's clothes, as it seemed pointless to have them lying there unused in the drawers. I bundled them up for the Salvation Army in Claxton, after first rather shyly asking the boys if there was anything they wanted to take for themselves. (There wasn't.) He had been a big man, I noted while folding the clothes to pack them; they were broader in the shoulders and hips than any of the other men on the Circle M.

His boots were too worn out to be of any use to anybody, so I threw them out. But I left my mother's dress hanging in the empty closet.

One quiet sunny afternoon, when I'd been out riding in the morning and come home and changed at lunchtime, I was reading on the front porch. Absorbed in my book, I paid little attention to my surroundings until footsteps near at hand made me look up, and Ray came around the corner of the house. I dropped the book into my lap and sat up straight, for the look on his face was one that I didn't know at all. Then I saw that he was holding his right arm awkwardly, bent a little in front of his body, and I realized that the slightly tense, flat expression was one of pain. I slid half out of my chair and my book plummeted the rest of the way to the porch floorboards. "What happened? Are you hurt?"

Ray shook his head a little as he reached the porch steps, but it seemed more to diffuse my concern than an answer to my question. "I don't know—not badly, I don't think. I was in the pen with the four-year-old bull, and he swung around all of a sudden and made a lunge at me. I almost made it out of the way, but he brushed me just enough to knock me down and I landed wrong on this wrist."

Ray was matter-of-fact, but I knew all about that bull by now, and a quick shudder ran through me at the thought of what could have happened beyond an injured wrist. I jumped up from my chair. "What should you do for it? Can I do anything?"

"If you would. I was just going to ask if you'd wrap it up as tight as you can for me, and maybe I can go on using it. I can't afford to knock off for the rest of the day. I rapped at the screen door in back but you must not have heard."

"Of course—but why don't you ice it first? Come in the kitchen and I'll get some for you, and find the first-aid kit."

Ray followed me inside and to the kitchen, and sat down at the table with his injured arm stretched out on it while I racketed around finding things I needed, a little noisier and clumsier than usual in my haste. I chipped off some ice from the big block in the icebox and wrapped it in a clean dishtowel for Ray to put on his wrist while I rummaged the cupboards for the first-aid kit I knew I'd seen somewhere.

"I should warn you I'm a complete amateur at this," I said, standing on tiptoe and straining to grope around on a top shelf; "so if you're sure you trust me...Where in the world—aha, I *knew* it was there somewhere! No, leave the ice on it for a minute while I cut this; it'll probably help." I brought the kit to the table and opened it and fiddled with a roll of bandage and the scissors for a minute—I felt like I'd been babbling, but I was still getting over the little scare I'd had. It was a little disconcerting to know I could be thrown off balance so easily.

"No worries," said Ray, pushing the ice pack aside in spite of my advice, and flexing the fingers of his right hand experimentally, with a wince that showed it hurt. "It doesn't need anything fancy. Besides, you're pretty good at trying out new things. Your first aid should be all right."

"*Really?*" I said, sitting down at the table opposite him and forgetting all about the bandages for a minute. "Do you really think I'm doing all right, or are you just saying that to be nice?"

"Just saying something to be nice can get a person killed in this country," said Ray a trifle dryly, and I blushed even before I knew what was coming next. "Don't ask Lane about Jericho again, please? He wants to be nice, as you put it, but he knows as well as I do that you shouldn't ride him yet."

"How did you know about that?" I asked, feeling rightfully abashed, but unable to help smiling half-heartedly as I started to unwind the roll of bandage.

"Lane asked me, the other day, if I didn't think you were maybe getting better able to handle a more spirited horse than Metis, and I could tell he was feeling me out over whether he'd get in trouble for letting you have your way." Ray stopped to grit his teeth for a second as I wound the bandage around his wrist, over between his thumb and forefinger and around again, as tightly as I could manage. "I told him yes, categorically."

"Yes, that I could handle another horse?"

"Yes, that he'd be in trouble. And so would you."

"From the horse, I take it."

"There's no need to go twisting my words when you're already twisting my arm," said Ray, half laughing through his clenched teeth, and I had to laugh too.

"All right," I said, reaching for the scissors, "I'll be good. And I'll *try* to remember that all this started with a compliment."

Ray just smiled a little, watching my hands as I clipped the bandage and knotted it. That quiet smile was easy to read: it meant that for the moment, all was right with the world.

Whether my first aid was all right or not, Ray's wrist continued to bother him for a few days. I suspect it was because he persisted in treating it as a minor thing, trying to go on using the hand as usual and neglecting my suggested ice packs; but in any case, on the third day he reluctantly decided to go into Severn Valley and have the doctor take a look at it. I offered to drive, since Ray couldn't and the others had plenty to keep them busy; and so the forenoon found us rumbling along the dirt road to town in the old truck, flying banners of dust behind.

Dr. Burns, the local M.D., lived above his office on the outskirts of Severn Valley, on a side street a few blocks up from the courthouse cul-de-sac. I pulled up outside the low picket fence, behind a black sedan filmed over with dust. "Good," said Ray, "he's home. Can't always count on it, with the way his calls take him all over the county."

"You want me to wait for you?"

"Well, I've got no idea how long I'll be. If it's more than a few minutes you don't have to wait; I'll catch up with you in town."

"All right. I'll probably fetch up at Stevenson's if you don't see me on Main Street."

As it happened, I had a little difficulty with the gearshift, and was still in front of the house when the front door opened, just before Ray reached the porch steps, and Dr. Burns himself came out to check his mailbox. My first glimpse of him rather surprised me. I'd expected a typical gray-haired country doctor in spectacles and shirtsleeves, but Dr. Burns was about as different from that as could be imagined. He had a high, massive forehead and a deep golden beard, a head that made me think of a lion; and a dignified bearing that seemed more like that of a professor or scholar. He was not someone you would expect to find behind a picket fence in a little town way out in Wyoming. I sat for a moment with my arms on the steering wheel and watched as he greeted Ray, and they stood and talked for a few seconds on the porch; from their manner and the way Dr. Burns put a hand on Ray's shoulder as they turned to go into the house, they seemed to be good friends. I watched them through the doorway until the doctor glanced back briefly, and then I remembered I hadn't meant to wait. I let in the clutch and pulled the truck out away from the fence.

As I drove through town, I tried to place an odd little feeling that had come over me. Something similar had plagued me more than once before when I'd been introduced to some other resident of Severn Valley. It was like a subdued curiosity, half apprehension. It was...now for the first time I identified it. It was something in the back of my mind saying, "This person knew my grandfather...I wonder what they thought of him."

I twisted the steering wheel over impatiently in a way that would have earned me a rebuke from more than one of my driving instructors as I pulled the truck to the curb a block above the Hotel Stevenson. That fruitless, pestering curiosity cropping up again. I wouldn't feel this way if Garth McKay had died in his bed. Yet even while I told myself that my own curiosity was ill-advised and perhaps inappropriate, I had a hard time understanding how the police, or anyone else around here, could *not* go on thinking about it, asking questions in their own minds. Perhaps having threshed it all out as far as they could, they were able to accept the lack of closure more easily because they had no personal reason to wonder.

But for me...well, you couldn't just step into some-one else's place and carry on without ever thinking about the way they had been so swiftly removed from it. It wasn't the same as if a stranger had bought the place; they couldn't be expected to care. Perhaps I'd always be fancying I was connected in some way with Garth McKay in other people's minds, even though there hadn't been the ghost of a connec-tion between us in life.

Maybe that was why the unsettling feeling. Maybe I was always thinking, in the back of my head, that any one of these new people I met might be the one looking at me and thinking about the man they'd killed.

I shook the thought away hastily. I got out and slammed the truck door and started to go around the front of it. I'd just reached the sidewalk when I heard my name called out from behind me. "Miss Campbell."

I turned, just a little too quickly, to see Bill Suther-land crossing the street, evidently with the intention of overtaking me. His hat was in his hand. The sun striking on his white hair made it look unusually bright above his reddened face, and like other men I'd seen since I came west, his way of moving seemed almost ungainly when he was on foot—he belonged on a horse.

"I've been wanting to talk to you," he said, as he came up and stopped. He eyed me for a second and then spoke with flat simplicity. "I'll come right to the point, Miss Campbell. I want to buy the Circle M. How much will you take for it?"

"It's not for sale," I said, too surprised to do anything but stare.

Sutherland spoke as if impatient to get something over with. "Anything's for sale, if the owner decides to sell it. Look. I'll make you any reasonable offer; you can get anyone you like to confirm it's a fair price. I'll even take on the wages of any of your men who want to go on working for me. I can make good use of that land, and selling it will save you a lot of time and trouble."

"No one seems to be able to take seriously my choosing to live here," I said a bit petulantly. "Even the very nicest people can't help letting on that they think it was all a whim. I didn't make my decision recklessly, Mr. Sutherland, even if I did make it quickly. And I don't want to sell the Circle M."

Sutherland's eyes hung on me with that same rough amusement I had seen on our first meeting. "You won't last, Lena. You'll get tired of playing cowgirl sooner or later. When the weather turns bad and the bills mount up you'll find it isn't all fun and games, and you'll be glad to get out for whatever price you can. You might as well get a better deal out of it and sell out to me now—because I warn you: turn me down now, and when you try to sell later, I won't do you any favors any more than the next buyer. I'll get it for the lowest price I can."

My face was hot. "I don't want to sell," I said. His words had roused a lash of anger in me, but his steel-chip eyes on me still made me feel shaky inside. "I'm not a little girl, Mr. Sutherland, and I'm capable of making my own decisions."

"I wonder," said Sutherland. He gave me a close, contemplative look that I felt meant something more than he was saying. "One day you may find you haven't been deciding as much as you thought."

He added, "But at least you know where I stand. My offer's open, any time you change your mind, but I can't guarantee it'll be as good an offer if you wait too long."

I said nothing, but pressed my lips in a straight line and fixed my eyes on the third button of his frayed denim coat. I'd said I wasn't a little girl, but I *felt* like an obstinate child whose only weapon is silence.

Sutherland's harsh laugh grated on my skin. "Have it your way, Lena. I'll be seeing you."

He turned away from me and tramped across the street, his stride a long swinging one for a man of his age in spite of the ungainliness. I leaned back against the warm metal bumper of the truck and watched him go, sorting out my mixed feelings of relief and anger. Sutherland's offer had taken me by surprise, but I felt I'd come out of the conversation all right, maybe because I'd been so sure of my answer that I hadn't had time to stammer over it.

Somehow I didn't feel like going on to the hotel, so I strolled slowly along Main Street, looking in at store windows, and spending rather more time in front of the hardware store than the window display warranted. I was still standing there frowning absently at it when Ray caught up with me.

"How'd you make out?" I asked.

He lifted his wrist, bandaged much more securely and professionally now. "Sprain, he said. All I can do is go easy on it till it heals, which is darned inconvenient."

"But darned advisable too," I said. "I warn you, if you don't follow doctor's orders, I'll snarl up the account books so badly it'll take you till your wrist is healed to help me straighten them out."

"Blackmail?" said Ray amusedly.

"No, just good management."

As we walked back to the truck I debated whether I ought to tell Ray what had passed with Sutherland. I wasn't obligated to tell my foreman I'd received an offer for the ranch and turned it down. But if I did tell him, his reaction might help me understand some of the things I'd been groping after. Once in the truck, I sat still with my hands on the steering wheel for a second, biting my lower lip and looking out at the dusty length of Main Street. Then I said, "Mr. Sutherland spoke to me while I was waiting for you."

I felt rather than saw Ray's sideways glance at me. Somehow the slight sharpness in his voice was not unexpected. "Was he bothering you?"

"No—at least not in any way you could—well, no, he wasn't. He just offered to buy the ranch."

There was an infinitesimal pause. "What'd you tell him?"

"I said no, of course. He told me the offer would stay open, but the price wouldn't be as good later on. He was really pretty rude about it…just about told me that I wouldn't make it here and would end up selling out in the end."

"It's the kind of thing he would say, considering how much he wants the place." Ray leaned back into the corner of the truck and rested his elbow on the inside edge of the window, with a restlessness in the motion that did not seem like him. "Let's get going, hmm?"

As I leaned forward to start the truck, something else occurred to me. Had Sutherland been the buyer Ray had mentioned once, the one he'd said he wouldn't want to see the Circle M in the hands of?

I was about to ask him—but on the heels of that thought came the conviction that if Ray didn't want to say, he would be able to make an answer that satisfied all the technical requirements of truthfulness without really telling me anything I wanted to know. It struck me for the first time that that was something he was very good at.

CHAPTER IX

'Tis a villain, sir, I do not love to look on.

Shakespeare: The Tempest

"Y OU SHOULD LEARN how to use a gun," Ray reminded me one morning. "Even if you never need it, it's a good thing to know."

"I used to be pretty decent with a slingshot when I was about ten. Will that be any help?"

Ray grinned. "It could mean you've got an eye—which helps. Come on out this morning and I'll give you a few lessons."

I'd promised to go riding with Jimmy Warren later that morning, so I was dressed for outdoors in jeans and a blue-flowered blouse that had come west with me. I added my new hat, slung down my back by its rawhide string, and left the screen door to creak closed behind me as I tripped down the back steps and went in search of Ray for my shooting lesson. I turned left behind the barn, where a rutted road skimmed under the pines that shaded the outbuildings and ran along behind the barn and horse pasture before curving right to skirt a small open meadow. I followed the road, my heart singing lightly at the sweet morning air, the tang of pine and the mellower smell of barn and pasture and the light sound of my boots on the hard-baked tire ruts. Tim was coming out of the back pasture gate as I passed, leading his horse, and I waved a hand to him.

Ray was over on the other side of the field waiting for me, in the shade of a belt of trees. He'd tacked up a paper target with a few holes already in it on the smooth trunk of a tree, and had just finished pacing off the distance from it when I joined him. He had brought one of the light .22s from the bunkhouse, and showed me how to load, cock, and uncock it, and how to make sure the safety was on or off.

"You can shoot small game with this if you want to," he said, "and it'll do if you need to take a shot at a pest like a coyote or bobcat."

"Good for shootin'-galleries too," put in Tim, who had followed me down, and was watching the proceedings with evident entertainment.

Ray threw him a look, half-exasperated, but with a repressed impulse to smile pulling at the side of his mouth. Tim merely grinned, and I wished I knew what the joke was. Ray handed me the rifle. "Try sighting it now."

I drew a bead on the center of the paper target, and Ray put a hand on the barrel of the .22 and corrected my posture slightly. "Don't bend your head down to it so much...Keep it high on your shoulder and your head a little straighter. That's good. All right, now try it."

I squeezed the trigger and the report echoed back from the trees and more faintly from the barn across the meadow. I'd thought the aim was pretty good, but the recoil from the gun must have thrown me off a little. "Not bad," said Ray. "Try it a few more times—try and correct your aim as you see where they're hitting."

I shook my hair back from my face, as the breeze was coming from behind me, took aim again, and fired carefully half a dozen times more, taking a little time between each shot to correct the aim. Behind me, Tim's horse shifted and pivoted a little on the ends of its reins, but stood his ground, probably being somewhat accustomed to the crack of a gun. I put all six shots successfully inside the three inner rings of the target, and took some satisfaction from the fact that two of them were in the center. I lowered the gun and glanced up at Ray for a verdict, trying not to look too elated but definitely hopeful.

"Yep, you've got a good eye," he said. "It just takes practice to get used to the feel of the gun and to judge the range of what you're shooting at. Once you can put half a dozen shots in the middle of the target from this distance, then you can try from further back."

"What about moving targets? Or do I just hope the coyote stays still?" I asked, carefully checking the cartridge chamber.

"Which coyote?" said Tim.

"A hypothetical one," I said.

"That kind stays still," said Tim; and we all laughed, as Ray took the box of .22 cartridges from his shirt pocket and handed it to me.

I hadn't heard the trampling of an approaching horse across the grass, but as I loaded the rifle again Tim's horse pricked its ears and swung its head around, and Jimmy Warren's voice said cheerfully, "What's going on over here? Target practice?"

"Oh, hello, Jimmy! I've just been getting my first lesson," I said, leaning to look past Tim. "Ray says I've got a good eye, so I guess that's a start."

"I'll say it's a start," said Jimmy, swinging a leg over his horse's back and dropping lightly to the ground. "I haven't got an eye at all. I have to get along without."

Tim chuckled. "You're gonna wish next time you meet a mountain lion, that you'd gone and cultivated an eye."

"You forgot 'alone,' didn't you? Next time I meet one alone. They're never going to let me forget that one, Lena."

"What, is that the same lion you mentioned before? I hadn't heard."

"You mean you haven't seen the hide yet? Well, I'll tell you, it'd be in my room right now if I hadn't shot an inch to the left."

"An *inch!*" said Tim, skeptically.

"Jimmy told me you'd shot a mountain lion, but he didn't mention he was there when it happened," I said to Ray. "Now I guess I know why. Jimmy—since nobody around here tells tales out of school, maybe you can tell me: what's the joke about shooting-galleries?"

"Oh, that," said Jimmy, laughing. "That was last year. Everybody was at the rodeo over in Claxton, and Tim talked our foreman Brooks into betting all the cash he had that Ray couldn't knock down every target in the rifle gallery at one clean sweep."

"And what happened?"

Jimmy grinned, and looked a little quizzically at Ray. "I'm too broke to bet—and I don't know any other way to get him to show off."

"Seeing a demonstration might do me some good," I suggested mischievously. I offered the .22 to Ray.

Ray's eyes met mine for half a second as he took it. He didn't look wholly enthusiastic, but there was that suggestion of a half-rueful smile as he glanced from the gun to the riddled target on the tree. He said, "Well…"

Then almost before I knew what he was doing the rifle was at his shoulder and he fired four times. I almost jumped out of my skin even though I'd been expecting the sound. Both horses shied, and Tim caught at their bridles and steadied them, as a little whiff of smoke blew away from us and I stood staring at the target. There were four neat holes in the top, bottom, and both sides of the outside ring, spaced as if they had been put there with a compass.

"Well—I guess I've got my answer!" I said, a little breathlessly.

"Essentially," said Jimmy, "yes. Brooks wasn't happy."

"I'd imagine not. It's too bad you didn't have anything to bet, Jimmy."

Ray offered me the .22. "It's still loaded. Want to take a few more shots?"

"After that? I'd miss the whole tree out of sheer inferiority complex. Anyway, I promised Jimmy I'd go riding with him. I'll practice some more tomorrow."

"Probably a good idea," said Jimmy. "Still, it's no shame being beaten by the best shot in Severn County. Hey, at least you've got him teaching you."

As I turned around with the stock of the rifle under my arm, my fingers occupied with the safety-catch, I caught a glimpse of Tim's face and saw his good-natured expression disappear in a flicker of distinct annoyance. It didn't seem to fit with anything that had been said or done. But I only saw it in passing and didn't think much about it.

"Come on over to the barn," I said to Jimmy. "I've just got to get my horse and I'll be ready to go."

We took the road that ran past the Circle M and on up the valley. I hadn't been any further out it yet than a couple of visits to the Crawleys. Once past the end of the long winding drive that led to their ranch, and through a little dip in the road lined with trees on both sides, we were out in open country for a while, between sun-warmed pastures stroked by long fingers of breeze that rippled their rich grasses.

Jimmy was good company. His friendly disposition and fresh open face, combined with an obvious desire to please, made him easy to get along with even on short acquaintance. He was an easy talker, ready and willing to fill me in on anything I asked about. He seemed to have definite and quickly-formed opinions about both people and things— and from the recurrence of "Dad says" and "Dad thinks" in his conversation, it was obvious that one of those opinions was near-worship of his father.

We passed the Chambers place, lying away across a creek with bridge and cattle guard and up a hillside on our right, and after that the road began to wind downhill. We rode under a cool archway of trees whose branches met over the road, which grew narrower and deeper-rutted as we went. A few miles on, Jimmy pointed out a low-lying pasture on the right, wire-fenced and bounded on the other side by the gray wall of a wooded bluff, which was the beginning of the Warren ranch. Shortly afterward we paused at the top of a steeper, twisting downturn in the road, and looked down on the house. It lay down in a hollow, long and low and buried in pines, so not much more could be seen from the road but part of the roof and a few spots of gold sunlight that pierced through the evergreen branches to touch the rustic-railed front porch. The whole place looked slightly tired and run-down, as if none of the energy put into running the ranch went toward keeping the buildings trim. All round the house was a little overgrown, and the roof of the barn was patched with rust and sagged at one corner.

"I'd ask you in," said Jimmy rather abruptly, after we'd sat our horses there for a moment looking down into the hollow, "but Dad's not home today, and the house isn't much to see anyway."

"It's a pretty spot for a house. That porch must be a nice place to sit in the evenings."

"It used to be," said Jimmy. "My mother and Dad used to like to sit out there after supper when I was a kid. Dad doesn't have much time for that sort of thing nowadays." He glanced over at me. "Oh, you don't have to try and fool me. The place hasn't looked its best for years now. Ever since Dad took out the second mortgage...But I don't know if it's that. Sometimes I think nothing's been right since Mom died, because I can never really put my finger on what the trouble is. Just every year, when you think things are finally straightening out, something happens to throw you back again."

"I suppose the Depression makes everything a little harder."

Jimmy shrugged his shoulders. "Maybe. I mean— there were always bills and things even when Mom was alive—every rancher's got bills—but the last ten years or so everything's just piled up. There's been the rustling, and the Depression, and all those little pieces of bad luck you can't do anything about. The thing is, I don't know half of what's going on. Dad's like that. He still believes I'm a kid who has to be kept from knowing just how bad off we are. Whenever

I try to talk to him about the mortgage, or how much we've lost on the missing cattle, or anything like that, he puts me off somehow. Tells me it's not my worry. But he doesn't understand: I don't want it to be all his. I'm here ready and willing to take as much of it off his shoulders as I can, but he won't let me."

"Could he sell the ranch if he wanted to?" I said.

"I don't think he'd do that. He's a rancher; I can't see him working in an office or selling tractors or insurance or something. And I don't think he could give it up."

His eyes ran over the rusty barn roof, the corrals half hidden by brush, and he gave a deep sigh. Then he turned to me and his voice sounded normal again, as if he'd shaken it all off and put it behind him for the time being. "Do you want to go back? It's getting past noon."

I nodded, and reined Metis around. As the clop of our horses' hooves merged into an irregular pattern of sound on the dry road, I said, "I had an offer for the Circle M, you know. Bill Sutherland wanted to buy it from me."

"Oh, did he?" said Jimmy, shooting me a glance with a gleam of interest in it. "I'm not surprised. He's wanted it for a while. He tried to buy it when McKay was alive, did you know that?"

"No, I didn't! When was that?"

"Oh, two-and-a-half, three years ago. The Circle M was in a bad way right around then—it was just after McKay hired Ray Harper as foreman—and came pretty close to going bankrupt. Sutherland made him an offer then, but McKay turned him down, and the Circle M did eventually pull through. Most people credit Ray with saving it."

All this was news to me. Not surprisingly, when I thought of it: I wouldn't have expected Ray to volunteer information to his own credit, and if Robert Herrington had wanted to persuade me to sell, he might not have thought it expedient to mention that my grandfather had refused an offer for the place. I said, "I guess that explains why Sutherland tried to hire Ray. You knew that, didn't you? I suppose after seeing the job he did with the Circle M, he wanted Ray working for him."

"Maybe. I've always had a different idea about that. *I* think he knew if he hired Ray away from the Circle M, the place would go downhill again without him and Sutherland would end up getting it cheap at auction after all."

My eyebrows lifted a little. That had a cold-blooded sound to it, and yet I could imagine Sutherland thinking that way. Yet Jimmy's theorizing was pretty glib for being just that. I looked at him curiously. "You've kind of got it in for Sutherland, haven't you?"

"I don't make any secret of that," said Jimmy. "There's been a kind of feud between him and us for a while now. He just never misses a chance to be as obnoxious as your next neighbor can be. First there was a bull of his that kept getting into one of our pastures—and Sutherland had the nerve to say it was our fences that were bad and he wouldn't do anything to keep the bull on his side if we couldn't. Then at the town council meeting a few months later, Dad put forward a proposition to build a dam on town property that would help with the flooding from the creek on our land that we always have trouble with every spring—and it might have passed, but Sutherland got up and said it was too much public money to spend on a project that only benefited one landowner, and we could irrigate our property differently if we had the sense and the money to make the improvements." Jimmy ran out of breath in his indignation. "But the worst was last fall—when a couple of our horses strayed off, Brooks went looking for them and traced them onto Sutherland's property. But when he got to the home ranch, one of Sutherland's hands came out to the gate with a shotgun and ordered him off. Brooks demanded to see Sutherland himself, and he came out and backed it up—told Brooks not to set foot on the place again. They sent our horses back when they found them a day later, but Brooks was boiling mad, and I don't blame him. Dad was upset too. So you can see there isn't much love lost between us and Sutherland."

"But for gosh sakes, Jimmy—if other people know all this, then they must feel the same way about him as you do—I wouldn't think he'd find it very pleasant living around here—"

"Well, you see how it is," said Jimmy, "Sutherland's one of the oldest residents, he's got a fair amount of clout in town and county affairs. A lot of men respect him for how he's carved out his piece of land and hung onto it for so long—that's what everybody wants, isn't it? He takes most of the prizes at the county livestock shows, and he's about the only rancher in Severn County who's been able to keep his head above water without going deep into debt. But public opinion and private opinion are two different things." Jimmy turned his head and looked at me. "I can tell you this, I'm not the only one around here who suspects Sutherland is responsible for the cattle-rustling trouble we've had."

My ears pricked. "You don't mean that!"

"Sure I do. He's claimed to have lost cattle himself, of course, but it sure hasn't hurt him as much as others. Anyway, whoever's responsible would have to fake some thefts from themselves as a cover."

"But how could—I mean, I admit that most of what I know about rustling comes from the movies, but—Tony told me it had been going on for about seven years. I don't see how, in this day and age, they could keep it up for so long without getting caught."

"It's this day and age that's the problem. They're not hiding them out in a brush corral and running the brands anymore. They load them into trucks and hustle them across the state line. There's lots of little back roads and tracks where somebody can sneak a truck in at night, load up a few head, and then they get right out on the highway where it cuts across the north end of the valley and they're miles away before you know it. We've even found the tracks at the turnings onto the highway. But they're smart, you see—they pick off a few here, a few there, never from the same ranch twice in a row, so that it takes a while for somebody to wise up to the fact that they're losing cattle at all and ask the State Police to patrol the highway at night. By that time the rustlers have already made a nice little haul and shipped it out, and they just shut down operations and wait for the fuss to die down and the State Police to give up patrolling—wait for months sometimes. They can afford to wait."

"And it must be someone local," I said slowly, "who knows exactly when the police have been alerted to patrol the highway.

Jimmy gave me a swift, appreciative look, as if discovering that I was a little keener than he'd realized. "That's true. Well, you can see it."

"And if any of this is true—that could account for Sutherland ordering your foreman off with a gun, couldn't it? Say they were caught with some sort of evidence in sight at his ranch that they couldn't allow Brooks to see?"

"That's what I thought. Of course, people drop by their neighbors' places regularly enough around here, and I've never heard of anyone else getting a reception like that at Sutherland's, but there's always the chance Brooks turned up at exactly the wrong moment and they had to draw a hard line."

Jimmy lifted one hand and let it fall on his thigh with a gesture of resignation. "But you see it's all absolutely conjecture, no evidence to back it up, no matter how much sense it makes. Burwell would never go after someone on a case like this without something solid enough for a warrant, especially one of the old guard."

"But people really do suspect Sutherland."

"Some people do. They don't say it out loud all the time, but they do. You ask Tim McGreevy, for instance. He'll tell you the same thing I do."

I remembered the ugly look on Tim's face that day along the fence line. I didn't have to ask.

For a second I itched to ask Jimmy what he thought of my theory that Garth McKay's death and the cattle rustling were connected. But I thought better of it in time. If the idea had never occurred to Jimmy before, and I suggested it to him now—there would be nothing stopping him telling it far and wide to any willing listener. And cowardly or not, I did not want it getting around to Bill Sutherland that Lena Campbell thought he was responsible for her grandfather's murder.

"I'll tell you just one thing, though," Jimmy was saying. "The next time one single head of our cattle goes missing, I'm not going to take it lying down. If Dad doesn't do anything, I will. I'm going to nail those rustlers if I have to track them every step and drive the highway at night myself, no matter what Burwell or the State Police do."

"Be careful," I said.

Jimmy brightened, as if he was rather pleased that I should worry about him. "I will," he said, "but I'll get them."

CHAPTER X

And as I lay in bed awake,
I thought I heard a noise.

W. S. Gilbert: The Pirates of Penzance

AUGUST CAME ON, and haying time. The Circle M hired extra hands. I didn't see much of the haying itself, as I'd somewhat rashly taken on the job of cooking for the whole crew. In past years the Circle M had hired a cook, but in my eagerness to be part of the ranch working force I'd said I was sure I could handle it. I'd cooked for a boarding-house when my mother and I kept one for a few years. But I didn't realize that three widow ladies and an elderly clerk or two didn't eat like eight or nine hungry men. I'm not sure how I'd have coped if Cathy Stevenson hadn't come out to help me for a few days toward the end. For weeks that didn't seem to have any beginning or end I spent my days in the kitchen, my face hot and flushed and my dress patched with perspiration under my arms and between my shoulder-blades, all the windows standing open, with the hum and rattle of distant mowing-machines drifting in; and the smell of mown hay wafting

from all directions—our fields, Chambers', Crawleys'—
even over the food smells.

The men ate breakfast and supper and sometimes
midday dinner in the kitchen, and some days Ray would send
Lane home at noon to help me load the midday meal into the
truck and bring it down to them in the fields. I felt shyer
around the temporary hands, and when they were all in the
kitchen I was glad to keep myself busy and inconspicuous,
as if I'd been a hired girl instead of their employer. And
when Cathy was there, her livelier personality and the rapid-
fire banter she kept up with the men while serving them
made it easy for me to stay in the background.

I didn't see much of Jimmy Warren those weeks. The
Warrens were haying too, like everybody else, and the few
times I saw him in town while laying in supplies we had only
time for a quick hello. I ran into Robert Herrington on Main
Street one day with my arms full of groceries, my hair tied
back with a bandana and scarcely enough breath for a greeting, and I thought there was a little shake of the head along
with his smile—though it didn't seem like a chiding shake
now so much as wonder that I was actually sticking it out,
and moreover seeming to like it.

I saw and heard nothing more of Bill Sutherland
before the hay crop was in.

Then it was September, and the air crisped and
chilled, and tints of bronze and golden crept over the hills.
Yellow splashes of goldenrod and scarlet Indian-paintbrush
filled the roadside ditches, and the sky was smoky with
autumn storm clouds. I wore sweaters and piled extra quilts
on my bed, for the cold seeped in through the walls of the
old house upstairs.

On fine weekends I often went riding with Jimmy
and Cathy—we explored all the back roads, as I'd been

promised, galloped across unfenced fields going brown as the weather turned, and followed a rocky trail among the pines on the Warren place to a pretty little waterfall back in the hills. One Saturday Jimmy drove us over to Claxton for a matinee at the Grande, and we sat silent and breathless through a romantic drama, then ate peanuts and critiqued the second-feature cowboy picture in whispered giggles beneath the onscreen gunshots. It was great fun—it felt like a bit of my girlhood I'd missed out on during the boarding-house years, when I'd often been too busy helping my mother to spend much time larking with high-school chums.

Once the Circle M had had time to catch its breath after the hay crop was in, it was time for fall roundup. All the cattle on the ranch had to be gathered in and tallied, the breeding stock separated from the ones ready for sale this fall, and the latter driven to Claxton and shipped out by train. The boys were going on a four-days' trip into the hills to round up every head that had strayed to the farthest reaches of the Circle M's back pastures. They set off early one morning at first light, with bedrolls and rain slickers and a pack horse carrying their camp outfit, and I was left at the ranch house alone.

Cathy and I had planned, during the week before the roundup, for me to drive into Severn Valley that first night the boys were gone and spend a night with her. But midway through the afternoon the telephone on the wall beside the front door rang, and when I answered it was Cathy.

"Lena? Listen, would you hate me very much if I asked you to put off coming over tonight? Mom's sister over in Wingate is sick and Dad's going to drive her over there tonight, and we've had a crazy day today—the plumbing in the kitchen's on the blink again, and I've got all sorts of things to clean up tonight, and I'll be so tired afterwards I'm more liable to bite than be good company. How about tomorrow night instead?"

"Of course, I don't mind. But are you sure you don't want me to come tonight and help you out?"

"No, I think I'd rather just tear into the mess myself, and leave tomorrow night free to have fun like we planned. You're an angel to offer it, though. Sure you don't mind putting it off?"

"No, it's all right. It's a bit quiet here but that's what I expected."

"Do they really make that much noise when they're at home? No, I'm kidding. The boys got off all right this morning?"

"Yes, early."

"Well, I'll see you tomorrow then. If I don't call you again just take it that everything's on schedule."

"Okay, I'll see you then...goodbye."

It was funny how quiet the ranch seemed that night with the bunkhouse dark and empty. Joking aside, a glowing window and an occasional murmur of voices were the only usual signs of the men's presence, but I think it was just the knowledge that they were gone that gave me the feeling of loneliness. It surprised me a little. I spent a quiet evening in the living room as I usually did, listened to the radio and read for a while, and went to bed maybe just a shade earlier than usual.

I don't know what time it was when I woke. I only remember lying in bed conscious of the fact that I *was* awake, and wondering why. I was deep under the layered quilts and comfortable there, and all I could see was the dim gleam of the mirror opposite the foot of my bed—it was an overcast night, and as dark in my room as it was outside.

I turned partly on my side, nestled into my pillow and

shouldered the quilts up to my ear, and my eyes drifted closed. I think I was on the point of going back to sleep when something dragged them open again. I lay still, wide awake this time, staring into the darkness without moving. I thought I had heard a soft sound, like a footstep, and it seemed to come from beneath the ear that was pressed into my pillow. Downstairs...in the house?

It must be my imagination. There was nobody else in the house, nobody else at the ranch. But—

I heard it distinctly this time. A soft, muted scraping sound, like a chair being moved a few inches. It was repeated several times, with slight pauses of different lengths in between.

It's very strange to think of now, but I'm not even sure I felt afraid. Burglars were something you didn't think of in connection with a place like Severn Valley, and there hadn't been any other alarming crimes locally since I'd moved there. But there was someone downstairs in my house, moving about stealthily in the dark—I realized that no strip of light showed beneath my closed bedroom door—and I lay there listening, almost holding my breath in an effort to hear, every one of my senses on the alert with wondering who it could be...and whether they knew I was here.

Surely nobody would break into a house where they knew someone was asleep...or would they?

And if they thought the house was empty, why would they be feeling about without a light?

It had been so quiet for a minute that I was beginning to wonder again if I'd imagined it. And whether anyone knew I was in the house or not, I was at a disadvantage lying huddled here in bed. I sat up as quietly as I could and pushed the quilts off, letting in a draft of chill air, swung my legs over the side of the bed and touched my toes to the cold floor.

I put weight on my feet very gingerly, hoping the boards wouldn't creak. Slowly I slid off the bed and straightened up, and when I was standing upright I drew a deep breath. I made my way noiselessly across the room to the door, my hands stretched out to feel my way until my fingertips touched woodwork. I'd missed the door in the dark, of course, and I felt my way across it till I found the crack and stood there listening.

My door had a lock that could be turned from inside, but it was stiff and creaky and I wasn't even sure I could make it turn all the way. Even if I could it would make more noise than anything in the house. I stood there in my nightgown with my ear close to the crack of the door, cold toes curled on the bare floor. And then I must have moved my head slightly, because I brushed against a hat hanging on one of the hooks on the back of the door and it fell to the floor.

The light sound seemed like a terrible thud. I didn't breathe. The house was still—it seemed to me that every room and every piece of furniture must be listening. Then I heard it—the faintest, most cautious rustle of sound downstairs, clearly a movement made by someone who now knew there was another person in the house and was trying not to be heard.

My heart was thumping against my ribs and the palms of my hands were sweaty. I had my fingers over the lock, determined to wrench it into place as a last resort if I heard someone coming up the stairs.

But it was still quiet. After what seemed like several minutes...hours...I heard one step—what sounded like a footstep down in the hall. And then, after a pause, a soft sound that could have been the front door being shut. And then silence again.

Were they gone?

I must have stood there ten or fifteen full minutes, listening. Then I turned my doorknob, which grated almost as harshly as I'd expected the lock to do, and opened the door a few inches. Five minutes more with my head tilted toward the opening, and I could be sure. No one could keep perfectly quiet that long. I stepped out into the hall onto the thin strip of carpeting, listened for a few seconds more, and started downstairs.

My eyes were used to the dark by this time. I felt somehow safer wrapped by darkness than if I'd clicked the switch and filled the hall with blinding electric light. I made a tiptoe circuit of the house—kitchen, bedroom, living room, office. All were empty. And then I made a discovery: the front door was locked.

I looked at the clock in the living room, peering at the hands through the thick grayness of a house at night. It was twelve-thirty.

I went upstairs to my room and sat on the edge of my tumbled bed, feeling a little short of breath, and tried to think. I was sure both the front and back doors had been locked before I went to bed. I'd been brought up in the city; I always locked my outer doors from habit. I didn't think the back door lock in particular would have given somebody that much trouble if they'd wanted to force it, but surely that would have woken me? If I was soundly asleep, though, a key turning in the front door might not.

Could Ray or one of the others have come back to the house for something they had forgotten? It was entirely possible that Ray had a spare key, though I would have thought he'd have mentioned it. But that didn't make sense—if it was one of them they'd have come in openly and turned on a light and not bothered about the noise, since they'd think I was at Cathy's—

A light began to come on slowly in my brain. I wasn't supposed to be here tonight. Someone had thought I was staying overnight with Cathy, and not knowing of the last-minute change in our plans, had taken the opportunity to enter what they thought was an empty house. They must have taken less trouble to be quiet at first, and the sounds they made had woken me. But—and this was the unsettling part—they hadn't switched the lights on, and that could only mean they didn't want to run the risk of anyone seeing lights in the windows of a house that was supposed to be unoccupied.

I tried to think: who besides the Circle M boys knew I was planning to spend the night with Cathy? She and I had talked about it in the lobby of the hotel last Saturday, with plenty of lunch-goers in the dining room within earshot; and I think I'd mentioned it to Jimmy Warren afterwards. Cathy's parents knew, and she or they or anyone else who'd overheard could have mentioned it casually to someone else. In other words, practically anybody in Severn Valley *could* have known I was supposed to be away from home that night. This afternoon's telephone call, however, was likely known only to the Stevensons and presumably Jenny Winship on the switchboard, and none of them were very likely to have told anyone else—Mr. and Mrs. Stevenson would have been well on their way to Wingate not long afterwards.

But who in Severn Valley had a key to my house?

There was always the possibility I'd forgotten to lock the front door. Or that the back door could be opened with a skeleton key.

I lay awake a long time, staring at the wall of my room and thinking, and still instinctively straining my ears after every real or imagined sound. But I must have fallen asleep at last—and when I opened my eyes to bright sunlight and a bit of a headache the next morning, everything in the room looked so thoroughly normal and natural that I was tempted to believe I'd imagined the whole thing. After breakfast I went over the whole house thoroughly by daylight, looking for signs of anything missing or out of place, but didn't find any. I thought the chairs in the office were possibly in different places than yesterday, but they always stood around at random angles and it was impossible to say without positively remembering their exact positions before.

The whole thing seemed so insubstantial and inexplicable that I almost decided not to tell anyone about it, but common sense told me that was foolish if there was the slightest chance of a real threat—so I told Cathy about it that evening, though half trying to laugh over it, to cover up any signs of having taken it seriously if she thought it was ridiculous too. She stared at me in puzzlement, though she didn't seem overly concerned.

"Well, that's odd," she said. "You don't keep a lot of money in the house, do you?"

"No, never more than a little expense money—and there's certainly nothing else in the house that's worth much. That's part of what baffles me. I can't think *why* anybody would want to get in."

"Do you think you'd better stay there alone now? You're welcome to come stay here for the rest of the week if you want."

"I don't think I need to do that. You see, I've been thinking—if whoever it was took so much trouble to get into the house when they thought I wasn't there, they can't have meant me any harm. And then when I made that sound and they knew I was there—alone—well, that was certainly their chance if they'd wanted it, but instead they got out as quickly and quietly as they could. After that, I don't see them coming back when they *know* I'm in the house."

"Hm. And if they knew you were staying with us all week, they'd know the house was empty for sure."

"That's right—I guess I had better stay then." I shook my head, trying to bring myself back to reality. "Cathy, we're talking like a detective novel."

"I know. And you just made a nice job of the speech the heroine usually makes before going back to the scene of the crime to get predictably kidnapped by the criminal."

"Oh, don't be silly. If it makes you feel any better, I'll get one of the .22s out of the bunkhouse and keep it upstairs in my room till the boys get home."

"What good would a rifle do you at close quarters like that?"

"Well, I don't have a handgun and wouldn't know how to use it if I did. Besides, if I get the lock on that door turned all the way I'd have time to load a flintlock before somebody could break it open. And who's talking like a novel now?" I stared at her. "You know, Cathy, I could have imagined the whole thing."

"You could," Cathy admitted. "All kinds of ordinary things that creak in a house could sound like a footstep, or a door closing, if your nerves are on edge."

She sounded almost regretful. I think she'd have liked to see the rest of the detective story enacted if it could have reasonably been done without actual harm to me.

"Well, since that's the case, don't say anything about it, will you? You can tell your father if you think somebody ought to know, but there's no sense in making a big deal about it to anybody else if it's really nothing."

And that's what it was, apparently. I put the .22 in

the corner of my room by the wardrobe, and lay awake for about half an hour longer than usual at night, but there were no more sounds and no signs of anything else unusual around the ranch. I called up the Hotel Stevenson on some pretext each morning just to let Cathy know everything was all right, but after a couple days even that was a formality. We both seemed to have accepted that the incident was a freak thing, a mistake of my own imagining. But nevertheless it stuck in the back of my head. Deep down I felt the footstep and the careful shutting of the door hadn't been imagined. It may not have had anything to do with me, but I felt certain that it had been for a reason.

CHAPTER XI

Yet sometimes he rests on the dreary vast;
And his thoughts, like the thoughts of other men
Go back to his childhood days again,
And to many a loved one in the past.

John Antrobus: The Cowboy

I SAT ON the corner of a freight platform, one leg bent under me and the other foot swinging over the edge, eating an apple I'd brought along in my coat pocket and watching the cattle milling in the railroad pens. We had just delivered forty head of Herefords to a cattle buyer at the Claxton yards, and the rest of the Circle M crew had gone off to celebrate with some leisure time in town while Ray was with the buyer finishing up the transaction. For once I didn't feel I had to be part of it; I wanted to savor the impressions of a day that was another glorious novelty to me. So I'd found my corner, and was sitting alone enjoying myself in my own way. I took another bite of the apple, a little warm from my pocket but still crisp and tart, and listened to the clatter and clang of the railroad yards and the hum of Claxton street traffic, and gazed up at the great bulwark of pine-clothed and snow-tipped mountainside that towered over the town on the north.

After the roundup, the Circle M had been in a turmoil of activity for a week as we sorted the cattle for shipping. I lived with pencil and tally-book in hand, clambering up and down corral fences or sitting aboard Trix, pelting Ray with incessant questions; and watching as men and horses cut out steer after steer and cow after cow and shunted them into different pens.

And then finally, one crisp, brilliant morning, we set out to drive the forty Herefords over the back roads to Claxton. I wouldn't have been left behind from this trip for worlds. We trailed at a leisurely pace past shorn hayfields, swaying goldenrod with mottled leaves shedding a mellow spicy scent in the sunshine, and occasional wind-whipped cottonwoods beginning to scatter their leaves. There was next to no traffic on the dirt roads—only once or twice did we meet an automobile churning through the dust, which honked and slowed as the boys parted the cattle, and then nosed its way slowly through the herd. I waved to the driver as they picked up speed again on the other side, and the plodding Herefords closed over the road again like a slow-moving Red Sea.

And then the steam and smoke of the railroad yards, the blare of lowing cattle occasionally pierced by honking horns, as cars crawled past the outside of the fences a few dozen yards away to bring passengers to and from the depot: a twentieth-century trail's end.

I heard footsteps on the boards of the platform, and looked up as Ray squatted down beside me. "Here's the check," he said, handing me a folded slip of paper which flicked open in the breeze like a butterfly trying to escape. "We did pretty good, considering."

"Enough to keep the wolf from the door?" I said lightly, studying the check—my name in the buyer's handwriting, and a sum that certainly seemed satisfactory to me.

"For now."

I slid the check deep in my coat pocket and threw him a smile. "I know. It won't look quite so pretty once we've bought grain for the winter, and salt, and repaired the fences and the barn roof, and had the truck fixed three times, and bought all sorts of tools and spare parts that I never knew existed."

"Well, I didn't want to spoil your afternoon."

"You couldn't," I said. I leaned back against a crate and waved my half-eaten apple toward the cattle pens. "I suppose it's all routine to you, but to me it's Dodge City at the end of the Chisolm Trail."

Ray grinned briefly. "It's something I've done before, but it doesn't mean I don't still get a lot of satisfaction out of it."

That was like him, I thought—satisfaction, where I'd have said exhilaration. Maybe if I'd worked hard at something, so I was tired but pleased and just glad to have the job done with, I'd have said "satisfaction" too—or maybe, deep down, they were different names for the same feeling. Maybe after I'd lived here for years I'd take it more the way Ray did…but I had a feeling I'd always stay incorrigibly the same.

"What's that for?"

I realized my mouth was twisted into a wry smile over the thoughts passing through my head. I didn't have to ask what Ray meant; he noticed things like that. "Oh, I was just thinking. You know, no matter how well I adapt, I'm always going to feel kind of an interloper. Did you ever hear the story about the ninety-year-old man who died after living in a town seventy years, and they put on his tombstone, 'Well beloved though a stranger among us'? Well, that's me."

"Well, then that's going to be my epitaph too if I stick around here long enough to need cemetery room. You're forgetting I haven't been in Severn Valley five years yet myself."

"Yes, but you belong out here. To the West, I mean. You were born and grew up in it, while I—I spent my childhood in places where the biggest piece of grass was about the size of that pen there, and got all the knowledge *I* had about the West before this summer out of books and by hearsay."

"What's wrong with that? The West used to be a place where you could ditch your past, if you wanted, and start fresh. I guess it's good to have a place to belong... whether you're born into it, or make it yourself...but if everyone stayed just where they were born and raised and stuck only to the things they were used to, there wouldn't be any settled West at all."

"I remember my mother saying something like that once," I said slowly. "I don't remember what she was talking about or who she said it to, but I remember she sounded almost a little bitter. Like she'd said it to someone else before. I always wondered. Because she did leave home to marry my father."

"He wasn't from Wyoming? What brought him out here?"

"Tuberculosis. Or at least a possibility of it. He had trouble with weak lungs, and he had to give up his job on a Chicago paper and come out here for his health. He was a writer, you know. He traveled around out West and made his living by writing pieces for magazines—little things about the country, or people he met or towns he stayed in, and funny or interesting things he saw. I've always wished I could read some of them—my mother didn't have copies of anything he wrote before he met her. And somewhere along the way he came to Severn Valley, and met her here. I guess he stayed a little while. Then when he moved on they wrote to each other for a while, and eventually decided to get married."

"They went back East to live?"

"After a bit. I know they were in California for a little while, and then by the time I was born they'd moved back to Illinois. Dad had a job on a magazine, writing and editing the same kind of human-interest stuff he was always good at. He liked it, though I think he always regretted a tiny bit that it kept him too busy to try writing some other things he wanted to. I know he always talked about writing a play. I guess his lungs must not have been as strong as they thought when they moved back...he died of pneumonia when I was thirteen." I looked fixedly for a moment at the hazy gold where the sun struck the snowy peak of the mountain. "We'd lived comfortably enough with the job he had, but he didn't leave very much money. But we had a decent house in the suburbs with enough bedrooms to take in boarders, so Mother and I made out all right that way all through my high school years. And then she died suddenly of influenza one winter. And after that...I guess you know the rest." I shrugged. "The Drapers had money, more than I'd ever known, so it was kind of an adventure living with them at first. But once the newness wore off I realized they just weren't very interesting people—but I didn't know yet what else to do. So I was ready for a change when I got Robert Herrington's letter."

I looked at Ray. He had listened without comment, but from his expression I didn't think I was boring him. "How about you? Do you have any relatives living?"

"My mother, and two sisters," he said. "I left home pretty early. My father and I didn't get along too well. I went to work on my own when I was sixteen, and that made it kind of easier—having some space between us, instead of living together and grating on each other. But he was killed in a farming accident not too long after that; and a year later my mother remarried. I've got a half-brother and sister almost eighteen and twenty years younger than me. So she's had a whole new family and new set of things to keep her occupied, and I think she was kind of thankful that I was already able to take care of myself. She writes a couple times a year, and I've been home for a visit a few times, but less often now than I used to. Both my sisters are married now—one lives near home and the other's in California. I hear from them now and again."

I felt a sudden flick of pity that oughtn't to have made any sense. I was the orphan, after all. But to have family that you were comfortable with seeing and hearing from "now and again," and could talk about in a not unfriendly but not exceptional way, like any other acquaintances—surely that couldn't fill the hungry place in every human heart that needed a few close souls to love and be loved by. I wondered if he'd ever found that elsewhere, or if, like many people, he was getting along without it.

I was studying his profile, thinking this, and also deciding irrelevantly that he had nice ears. At precisely this juncture Ray looked toward me and caught me off guard, and to cover my confusion I held up my browned apple core, which I'd been twirling absent-mindedly by the stem. "I don't suppose this'll hurt the cattle if I throw it into the pen?"

"Only if you hit one of 'em in the eye," said Ray, getting up with a grin.

I accordingly pitched the core over the nearest fence

and scrambled to my feet. "Are we all finished here?"

"As long as there's nothing else you want to do in town. We can head home any time you like; no need to wait for the others."

"By the way," I said, adjusting the string of my hat as we started along the platform, "there's something I've been meaning to ask you. That first night after you left on the roundup, did one of you come back to the house for something?"

Ray glanced down sideways at me as he spoke. "Nope, nobody did. Why?"

"Oh...nothing...only I woke up during the night and thought I heard somebody moving around downstairs. I thought maybe you'd forgotten something and one of you came back for it."

"I thought you were supposed to be staying with Cathy Stevenson that night."

"I was, but she called up that afternoon and said they'd had a hectic day and asked me to put it off one night. Anyway...I could have sworn there was somebody downstairs in the office, though I *suppose* I could have heard a board creak and imagined it."

Ray's steps slowed on the planking, and automatically I came to a stop and turned to face him as he stood still. He said, a bit oddly, "The office?"

"Yes—my room is over it, you know. Why?"

"Nothing. But—you checked around the house? Nothing was missing, or looked out of place?"

I shook my head. "Not a thing. That's what made me wonder if I was imagining things. But you know, I'm still *sure* there was somebody there, and they ducked out quietly when they heard me."

There was a pause—and then Ray shook his head. "I

doubt it's anything to worry about. I'd forget it if I were you."

He moved on and I followed, trailing a half step or so behind. I was thoughtful. Ray's manner was odd—half of me wanted to say he knew something more than he had said, but the other half thought he was just as puzzled as I was. I wondered if he'd made little of it just to keep me from worrying. But Ray wasn't like that—he'd always given me exactly the information I needed for my own welfare or safety, even if it was disconcerting.

As he'd told me once, withholding the truth could be dangerous.

CHAPTER XII

It is so hard for the novice to tell what is a clew and what is not.

P. G. Wodehouse: Something Fresh

MY FIRST WYOMING winter flew by. The twin tasks of keeping warm and keeping the livestock fed and sheltered were enough to fill the days; and there were amusements too. When the roads weren't bad I'd often go over and spend an afternoon in Mrs. Crawley's kitchen, always fragrant with baking bread, spicy cinnamon cookies, or blueberry or apple pie, chatting with her and practicing the knitting I was sporadically trying to learn. At home, I sometimes had company over in the evenings—the Stevensons, the Crawleys, Jimmy Warren and his father, or sometimes just Jimmy and Cathy—warm, pleasant evenings where the living room was filled with lamplight and talk and laughter, the radio fuzzily playing a jazz band's broadcast from a Cheyenne hotel or Christmas carols from the local station in the background. I'd sometimes invite the Circle M boys to come up to the house on nights when I had other company, and those nights were often the most fun. Sometimes there was a game of bridge or rummy, sometimes it was just talk and storytelling and debate; and I got equally as much pleasure from laughing till my sides hurt at one of Tim's stories, listening to Mrs. Crawley and Mrs. Stevenson piecing together three generations of somebody's second cousin's family tree, or discussing cattle bloodlines and the outlook for agriculture in the state with Ray and James Warren.

Christmas I spent with the Stevensons, and a week later I was in town again for the New Year's Eve dance at the town hall, at which I think all of Severn Valley not invalid or newly-born was present. I hadn't expected Christmas gifts from anyone but Cathy and Mrs. Crawley, but on Christmas morning I found that the Circle M hands had clubbed together and bought me a beautiful tooled-leather saddle, like the one of Tim's I had often admired and which he said had taken him a year's savings to buy. I was so touched by this I could hardly find anything to say—I hoped they were able to see it.

After the holidays winter set in colder and fiercer, as it often seems to do—the days were short, the late-afternoon sunsets bleak and vivid smears of red and gold behind the mountain ranges, and the wind blew ferociously sometimes from dawn to dusk. The pipes in the house creaked and rattled even after Tim had wrapped them in burlap to keep them from freezing, and in the pasture beyond the barn the horses stood huddled together, their breath making clouds of steam on the bitter air. On sunny days, when the cold and the glitter of sun on the snow-covered pastures was enough to hurt my eyes, I'd bundle up and pick my way across the yard, plowed into ruts by the truck when it was slush and frozen into ridges of iron, and Trix, Junior, Knockout and the others, looking both familiar and strange in their shaggy, duller-colored winter coats, would line up along the barbed-wire fence for the carrots I brought them.

So it went on, for so many weeks that time seemed to lull you into believing that there was no other season, and weary winter would go on forever. And then—first a drip, then a trickle; and finally a stream—the melting began, and one day the rush and mud and freshness of spring was there with a sweep of wind.

It was already green but the air was still raw the day Tony came home from the store, I remember that. He'd gone into town to pick up some wire and staples for spring fence repairs, and I'd handed him a scrap of paper at the last minute with a few items I needed from the grocery store scribbled on it. I'd started spring-cleaning, and I was shaking out some rugs on the front porch when the truck came roaring up the lane at a much more than reasonable speed and hit the mudhole at the edge of the yard so hard I thought it had broken the front axle, splashing the sides with mud right up to the door-handles. Tony pulled over by the barn and shut off the engine, and I heard the truck door slam. Ray was just coming out of the barn, and I leaned out over the porch railing and saw Tony stride over to meet him and begin to tell him something illustrated with plentiful gestures. I draped the rugs over the railing and ran down the porch steps and picked my way across the muddy yard toward them.

As I drew near I heard Ray say, "He's absolutely sure? If he jumps to conclusions and sets the whole county by the ears—"

"I'm telling you, I'm getting to it! He told Everidge, and on a hunch Everidge and his kids did a count of all the cattle in their upper pastures and found the same thing: six or seven head short. Hobbs and Everidge both."

"What's wrong?" I said.

Tony swung around and answered without missing a beat. "Hobbs and Everidge are missing cattle. It's the same old story—no broken fences, no carcasses, no sign of lion or bear or anything like that. And all that rain last week washed away any tracks in those back lanes. They're smart. They're damn smart."

"What are we going to do about it?" I said.

"We're going to stop borrowing trouble, for one thing," said Ray. I caught the look he shot at Tony, and the clarity of the message I intercepted almost startled me: *now see what you've done.* Aloud he added, "And count heads, of course. If there's none missing I don't think we've got anything to worry about. They always tended to work over one area at a time—it's people like Stewart and the Warrens who'll be worrying right now. There won't be any more tries now the word's out, but they may already have lost some."

"Yeah," said Tony sourly, "the damage's already done, and nothing anybody can do about it, and they're just proving they can get away with it again and again. And next time it'll be us." He yanked open the passenger door on the truck and pulled out the brown paper bag that lay toppled over on the seat. "What's Burwell even there for, I'd like to know."

"You think you could do any better? Come on, Tony, stop wasting your breath. Go get Lane and we'll figure out where to start checking."

I held out my hands for the bag of groceries, and Tony plopped it into them. I peered in among the contents. "Did you get the baking powder?"

"Bak—" Words failed him, and when words failed Tony it usually meant he was making a choking effort not to swear. "I was right there in the store, and Everidge came in and I got talking to him and I forgot it. I'll go back for it if—"

"No, never mind, I'll get it myself tomorrow. You go ahead, this is more important."

Tony went. I turned to head for the house, and found Ray looking at me with a faint, wry expression around his mouth that wasn't exactly a smile. He said, "It's not a national emergency yet, you know. You don't have to get so worried about it."

It might have been meant as reassurance, but somehow I felt rebuked. I tried to smile. "All right. But when it is time to worry, let me know. I'll be ready."

He did laugh at that, and so on that note we parted. I went back to the house, where half-shaken rugs and a disarrayed living room awaited me. But the first thing I did when I got there, after setting down the bag of groceries in the kitchen, was to go through into the front hall and make a telephone call to Jimmy Warren.

I was thorough with my spring cleaning. I took a room at a time and pulled the furniture out away from the walls, took up the rugs, swept and dusted in all the corners and then put everything back together. Though the house had been reasonably well-kept, I had an idea this was the first spring cleaning it had had in a while.

I'm pretty sure it was the day after Tony had been into town. I was working in the office—there wasn't nearly as much furniture to move in there; really nothing but putting the chairs outside in the hall, aside from the rolltop desk. When I got to that side of the room, I put my hands on my hips and looked at the desk, then decided I didn't need to go ask for help; I could drag it out myself one end at a time. I dropped my dust-rag on the floor, slipped my fingers into the crack between the back of the desk and the wall and pulled. The legs of the desk moved over the floorboards with a heavy stuttering scrape, and the other back corner ground against the wall. I pulled it by the other front leg, and got that side out a few inches. A couple more pulls on each side and I had it out far enough from the wall to dust behind.

A few dust-balls stirred by my movements floated away along the floor by the woodwork. I wondered amusedly if anyone had ever dusted behind it, but noticed some older scratches on the floorboards beside the ones I'd just made, as if somebody had dragged it out the same way before. As I knelt to reach behind the desk with my rag, a scrap of paper dislodged from somewhere up in the back of it and fell on the floor at my side. I picked it up and unfolded it.

It was about four inches square, folded once and torn on three sides as if it had been part of a bigger piece of paper that had been torn up. I supposed it had been pushed to the back of a drawer and caught behind it, one of those freak things you'd never find or even realize was missing, until my moving the desk had somehow freed it and let it fall. I recognized Garth McKay's scratchy, hurried-looking handwriting, but as I apparently had just the first few words of about three lines of writing, it took me a minute to get any sense out of them.

> *...without getting caug...*
> *Harper nothing becaus...*
> *make sure the tru...*

There was a step in the office doorway and I nearly jumped out of my skin. I was sitting on my heels and almost lost my balance and fell over, and I dropped the scrap of paper. I caught it up and instinctively shoved it deep in my apron pocket, and then I looked up. Ray was standing there with his hand on the doorknob, his mouth open a little as if he'd been about to say something but halted in the process.

I scrambled awkwardly to my feet, almost falling again. The consciousness of those strange words on the paper in my pocket heated my face with what I felt must be a faint but visible flush, and for the first time I could remember I had a hard time looking straight into Ray's face.

"What's the matter?" he said.

I wonder sometimes how differently things might have happened afterwards if I had simply shown Ray that scrap of paper right then and asked him, as frankly and innocently as I'd asked a thousand other questions, what it meant. It's too late to wonder now. But I've thought more than once, if I could have that moment back...

"Nothing," I said just a little too quickly. "I was just pulling the desk out so I could clean behind it. Did—you want something?"

"I just wanted to ask you," said Ray, his eyes traveling slowly to the desk over my shoulder and coming back again—and, I was sure, taking in my apron pocket along the way—"if you wanted the truck this afternoon. I've got to take a load of fence posts down to that east section that needs replacing, but I can put it off till tomorrow if you want the truck to go into town."

"No, go ahead. I decided I'd just go with Tim tomorrow—I'm too busy to bake till the weekend anyway."

"Do you have the key? It wasn't in the bunkhouse."

"Oh, yes—I think it's in the kitchen. Tony gave it to me yesterday..."

Ray stepped aside so I could leave the office, and I

maneuvered my way around the knot of chairs in the hall and headed for the kitchen, glad of something trivial to give me the appearance of inattention. I found the truck key hanging on the nail where I sometimes kept it when I had it in the house, and took it down.

He'd known I wasn't telling the whole truth; anyone would have. He must have seen the scrap of paper in my hand. Anyone might have been curious; perhaps assumed it was something embarrassing or silly. But from the way Ray had looked past me to the desk, I found myself wondering suddenly if he knew or suspected something I might find there. In that case he knew more than I did, for that torn bit of paper held only parts of a riddle...

I remembered how when I had explored the papers in the desk my first week there, Ray had brushed off their importance. *"I wouldn't bother with any of that...there's really nothing there that matters now..."* Had there been something among them he would rather I didn't find?

I brought the truck key back to the front hall and handed it to Ray. "Thanks," he said. He tossed it in his hand once so it jingled on the ring, then turned abruptly and went out the front door.

I watched him through the closing screen door with a queer disconsolate feeling. Ray had seemed different these last few weeks of spring. He didn't come around the house half as much, and didn't go out of his way to invite me along for the ride when there was stock to be moved or some other work to be done out in the back pastures. When he had to consult with me about anything he was brief and business-like, as if he was in a hurry to get the conversation over with and move on. The friendly, desultory conversations about anything and everything that we'd drifted into so often last fall seemed to have dried up and vanished.

Oh, well, maybe Ray had finally grown tired of my tagging after him and pestering him with questions. But I wasn't a pest. I was clear-headed enough to be aware of that. I was young and inexperienced, but I'd asked the right questions and I hadn't pushed myself underfoot while learning. No—if Ray didn't want me around, there must be some other reason. Even knowing it wasn't my fault, I found it strangely depressing.

I drifted slowly back into the office. The sight of the desk standing at a slight angle out away from the wall brought me back to my original train of thought, and my forehead puckered slightly. Ray had been very definite, very offhand, the time I'd told him about hearing someone in the office. *"I'd forget about it if I was you."* But now I was even more convinced that I *had* heard those noises downstairs. Soft scraping sounds...like desk drawers being opened and closed, perhaps?

What had been in this office that somebody wanted to find? Could it...could it possibly be the seemingly meaningless scrap of paper in my apron pocket?

I dug it out and studied it again. There weren't enough words there to properly deduce anything from them. Yet somehow, none of those disjointed half-phrases sounded to me like they came from jottings about finances or ranch maintenance.

Ray had said that all the papers from the desk that I'd boxed up and put away had been gone through. Did he know there was something missing—something he wanted to find and dispose of without anyone else seeing it?

I wondered...if I could casually question Tim or Lane about whether Ray had gone back to the ranch that first night of the roundup...

I came to myself with a start and gave my head a

sharp shake, like a horse brushing away a fly. The whole thing was crazy. If Ray had wanted to destroy some complaining note or record left by my grandfather that showed him in a poor light, he would have had plenty of better chances before I ever came to the ranch. I'd just made an idiot of myself, jumping and hiding an insignificant piece of paper as if it was something worthy of blackmail—no wonder Ray had stared at me. It was all in my own head—and to prove it, I crumpled the paper and threw it in the kitchen stove the next time I was out there.

But it wasn't the last time I would think of it.

CHAPTER XIII

Rustlers, cattle, foremen, sheriffs, and Heaven only knows what.

Zane Grey: Nevada

T HE NEXT AFTERNOON, according to plan, Tim
had to go into town to pick up some supplies and I
went with him. It was about one o'clock when,
having done my own errands, I emerged from the grocery
store to find the truck idling at the curb as Tim waited to pick
me up. At the same moment Robert Herrington came out of
the Up & Down Café next door, where he usually had his
lunch. "Hello, Lena," he said. He gave a bit of a chuckle.
"What price democracy, eh? What did *you* think of the
meeting?"

"Meeting? What meeting?"

"Oh, weren't you there? A number of the ranchers
have been holding an indignation meeting of sorts over at the
courthouse. They came to see George Burwell and demand
action of some kind over this rustling business, but he's
away serving some papers, so it turned into a sort of
committee on ways and means. They were outside when I

left for lunch—feelings seemed to be running rather high. I thought perhaps that's what you were in town for."

"I didn't know about it," I said, "but I definitely want to hear it now. Why didn't anyone tell me?"

"I gather it wasn't really organized to begin with. Hobbs and Everidge and one or two others went to see Burwell together, and some others who happened to be in town joined to hear what was going on."

"Well, that's exactly what I'm going to do," I said, pulling open the truck door and tossing my purse in ahead of me on the seat. I climbed in and stowed my paper bag of groceries on the floor by my feet. "Drive over to the courthouse, will you, Tim? I'm sorry to run off like this, Mr. Herrington, but thank you for telling me." The grumble of the muffler as Tim pulled away from the curb punctuated my sentence, and Robert Herrington lifted a hand in farewell with his customary dryly amused expression.

What a trial I must be to that man's carefully-ordered legal mind, I thought. Though he ought to be able to take some comfort from the fact that he couldn't be held responsible for any of my impulsive behavior.

We turned onto Severn Street and trundled along the block and a half before the cul-de-sac. As Tim slowed to look for a spot along the curb to pull in, I saw the group of ranchers gathered on the sidewalk in front of the courthouse near the fire hydrant. There were eight or nine men, and even at this distance you could tell this wasn't just the usual street-corner gathering to shoot the breeze. I took in their now-familiar appearance—the Stetsons, the frayed blue jeans and worn-down boots and the bulge of cigarette packages in shirt pockets—and my heart failed me a little. They were all so much older than me, more knowledgeable, and doubtless much louder...

"Tim, I don't know about this," I said, wilting a little as I sat. "Now I'm here I feel kind of silly. I may own the Circle M, but when I look at *them* I know I'm just an ignorant snip of a girl with no business at a meeting like this."

"Fudge. You're a lady," said Tim, jamming on the parking brake with fine disregard for its age and stiffness. "You can walk right up to them and right through 'em if you feel like it, and none of them have got any business to complain."

It was the loveliest speech I'd ever heard.

We got out on opposite sides of the truck, and, being a lady, I took a brief glance at my reflection in the side mirror to see that my hat was on straight and to brush an imaginary shine from my nose with the back of my hand. Then I put my purse under my arm and walked toward the indignation meeting, which sounded quite as heated as Robert Herrington had described.

Bill Sutherland was there, along with several men from the western side of the valley, Hobbs and Everidge and Stewart; and I recognized Brooks, the Warrens' foreman, a black-haired man in his late thirties with a perpetually defensive attitude. As I stepped up on the sidewalk Will Everidge touched the brim of his hat and made room for me to stand beside him. Several voices were loud in discord, but Sutherland's won out over them: "What do you all expect from Burwell? He can't keep calling in the State Police without losing whatever face he's got with them, and he can't patrol the whole length of the county every night with only two deputies."

"Even the least effort he could make—"

"What's the use of law enforcement at all if—"

"It's impossible. The only thing that'd help is having men watching our gates and back pastures day and night, and

Burwell can't give us that," said Hobbs. "I can't even do it myself. I've only got two men working for me, and my place would go to rack and ruin if I have them and me out riding fences round the clock."

"Why not try organizing something ourselves, then?" I said. Most of them looked at me, and I looked from one face to the next, feeling surprisingly sensible and not as small as I had thought I would. "Couldn't we arrange a way to lend help to each other, so all of us can check our fence lines more frequently than we'd be able to with just our own hands?"

There was a brief bit of silence, the kind where everybody knows what needs to be said but is waiting to see who will say it, and then Stewart spoke. "The truth is, not many of us could afford to lend help that way no matter how much we wanted to. Sutherland here is probably the only one who has enough men working for him to take some of them off regular work and still keep his ranch going."

I turned toward Sutherland, having to lift my head to meet his stone-chip eyes. My look was a question even before I spoke aloud, and he knew it. "Would you be willing to lend help for something like that?"

Before he could answer Brooks spoke roughly: "Not if it doesn't suit him he won't. And it doesn't. So long as you're all right, Sutherland, you don't care what happens to any of the smaller ranches around here. That's why you won't give us any help with Burwell: it just doesn't matter to you."

Sutherland had barely even diverted his eyes toward Brooks as he spoke; he was looking at me. "That answer your question?"

"I didn't hear you answer it," I said, though with a little less composure.

"Looks like I don't need to, the way everybody else knows me so well." This may have been directed at Brooks, but his glance shot around the whole circle, and none of the mostly expressionless faces changed much. "But I'll answer it for your benefit: no, I won't lend any of my boys. There's no way on God's green earth you can watch every mile of fence in this county close enough to discourage anybody who's really bent on stealing your cattle, and I'm not going to lend time and men to anything so useless." He stopped, and the lines in his face creased into a harsh smile. "Besides," he said, "why should I help you in any case? You all like nothing better than to talk me down behind my back, and then when you're in trouble you come begging to me for help. I'd like to see the day."

I heard footsteps on the sidewalk behind me—Robert Herrington had just come up, and stopped to listen, his thumbs hooked in his waistcoat pockets. Brooks said, "Don't play injured, Sutherland. You've proved time and again you're only too willing to take advantage of another man's hard luck. It's easy when all it takes is doing nothing, isn't it?"

Tim McGreevy cut in, and an apprehensive prickle ran up my spine at the charged hostility in his voice; I'd heard it once before and it made me uneasy. "Sure. You'd be glad to see some of the small ranchers go under with all this rustling, wouldn't you—it'd give you the chance to snap up their land for not much trouble or money."

I almost caught my breath at his bluntness, but Sutherland laughed—that harsh, crowing laugh of his. "You've never forgiven me for that, have you, Tim? Tell me, you really think—you think some sort of fool pity, or some idea of justice, should've kept me from offering to buy a place that was already on its way to a sheriff's auction—"

Tim gave a short hard laugh of his own. "Justice! No, I'd seen enough close to home to give up the idea of ever meeting anybody who used that word right. If there'd been any kind of *justice,* the Circle M would've gone to—"

Tim's eyes fell on me and he broke off with a jerk, as if he'd just suddenly remembered I was there. For a moment he was tongue-tied. He glanced around the group of men, as if he'd become aware that he was the center of attention and didn't like it.

Then he pulled himself together and spoke to Sutherland one more time. "You and I both know what it was almost put the Circle M out of business," he said, "and if it happens again I'll know why, too."

He turned around abruptly, looking ill at ease, and stepped off the sidewalk. "I—I'll be at the truck, Miss Campbell. I got nothing more to say here."

"I don't think any of us do," said Will Everidge grimly. "Nothing that's of any practical use, at least till Burwell gets back."

"If you do decide on anything practical that can be done, please let me know," I said. "I guess I'll be getting home." I glanced around the circle and gave a just slightly self-conscious nod goodbye, which was answered by the touching of half a dozen hat brims.

I turned to go and almost ran into Robert Herrington. He seemed not to hear my apology for a minute, and then blinked out of a trance of thoughtfulness and looked at me as if he hadn't heard at all. "I beg your pardon," he said. Then he recalled himself fully to the moment. "Leaving? Well, goodbye, Lena, I'll see you soon."

Tim didn't say anything for half the ride home, and neither did I. Stealing a sideways glance at him as we took the left turn on the road to the Circle M, I could see that his chin was still set in a way that didn't encourage conversation even at the best of times. But I'd been thinking—thinking back to the discussion Jimmy Warren and I had had about the rustling problem months before. Impulsively I spoke out of my thoughts into the silence. "There's one thing I want to know. If these rustlers belong to Severn Valley, and know pretty much every measure being taken against them, then what good would even constant patrolling do if they know when we start and when we stop?"

"No good at all," said Tim. "Sutherland knows that. He's honest enough, or bare-faced enough, to say patrolling's useless, I'll give him that."

I shied around that topic in rather cowardly fashion; I wasn't quite ready for it yet. "But if that's the case, why is everybody so set on getting the sheriff involved, and talking about guarding their fences if they know it's no good?"

"Because if they admit that," said Tim, "that's as good as saying right out that it *is* somebody who belongs to Severn Valley. Nobody wants to admit that."

"Or wants to be forced to accuse someone publicly," I suggested, with an inflection in my voice that made it a hint, rather than a statement.

Tim said nothing, but I thought from his face he agreed with me.

I leaned back in my seat and folded my arms. "I agree with Sutherland about one thing. Everybody around here is way too willing to do a lot of talking behind people's backs, but not to say what they think in front of anyone."

"I'm with you there," said Tim grimly.

But I'm really no better, I thought to myself, because I can't come out and ask you my real question: *do you think Sutherland shot my grandfather?* I tried a more roundabout way. "What did…my grandfather think about all this rustling business?"

Tim eyed me for a second, and then said, "He didn't like it."

That, I felt, was the understatement of the year. I made myself very busy with the clasp of my purse. "If he'd had any really strong suspicions about who was behind it…do you think he would have confronted them?"

Tim was quiet for so long this time that I began to wonder nervously if I had made a big mistake. But all he said, presently, was, "It wouldn't surprise me."

"Well, anyway, back to right now," I said, retreating quickly to safer ground. "This patrolling business. I had one idea. Everybody checks and maintains their fences pretty regularly in ordinary circumstances, so you figure someone keeping a covert eye on a few ranches can make a fair guess about when the coast is clear to slip in and steal some cattle. What if we started staggering the times we check our furthest pastures—mixing it up, so to speak? If everybody did that, we might make it unpredictable enough that the thieves wouldn't risk an attempt. It might not stop the losses, but there'd be at least a chance you might happen on them in the act of stealing, if they had no idea you meant to check the pasture that particular day."

Tim considered this as he slowed the truck to turn into the Circle M—long enough that for a minute I was afraid it was such a terribly naïve suggestion that he was trying to figure out how best to let me down easily. But in the end he gave a kind of combined shrug and nod. "It's not a bad idea," he said. "Might not change much. But like you said, there's that one-in-a-million chance—"

"It might be better than nothing, anyway."

"It might," said Tim. "Put it to Ray, anyway, and see what he thinks about it."

CHAPTER XIV

If I do not respect a man when he is living, I shall not pretend to when he is dead. One does not make a claim upon my honor by going out of life.

Melville Davisson Post: The Age of Miracles

THE SPRING BREEZE touched my face as I rode up the lane to the Crawleys', cool and soothing and yet somehow exciting in spite of its gentleness. The curve of the lane through young trees hid the house until you were halfway there, with the inevitable mud hole right at the bend. Fastidious Trix picked her way neatly around it, and then the house came in view—gray-weathered and lower-eaved than my house, with a screen door painted blue, and in front of it bare lilac bushes and perennial beds that later in the year would be a riot of color.

I caught a flutter of sheets from the clothesline around the side of the house, and a saddle horse that I recognized as Jimmy Warren's stood tied at that end of the front porch, so I guessed that was where Mrs. Crawley would be. I dismounted and tied Trix near Jimmy's horse and went round the corner of the house. Mrs. Crawley was there all right, a big wicker laundry basket at her feet and a line of sheets and towels snapping lightly in the breeze from the line where she was pinning them. And Jimmy was there, walking restlessly up and down on the short springy new grass nearby.

"I just don't understand him," he was saying as I rounded the corner. "I share in all the work, so why not this? I'd like to know just how long Dad thinks he can keep pretending I'm not old enough to understand just how badly off we are."

"Perhaps he's pretending for his own sake, Jimmy," said Mrs. Crawley, holding a sheet in place with one hand and taking a clothespin from the few clipped on her apron pocket. "Admitting hard facts to you might mean he's got to acknowledge them himself. If he doesn't say the worst of it right out to somebody else, maybe it's easier for him to keep on telling himself that—"

"That prosperity is just around the corner?" said Jimmy. "Maybe. But it's all the same thing in the end." He sat down on the side of the old well, abandoned and vine-grown now that the Crawleys had the water piped into the house.

Mrs. Crawley bent to take a damp towel from the basket and shook it out, and gave me a welcoming smile as I joined them. "Hello, Lena."

"Hello. Hi, Jimmy."

"Hello," said Jimmy in tones of the deepest gloom.

"Well, if it's as bad as all that, I'll go away again," I said with lifted eyebrows.

"Nonsense," said Mrs. Crawley. "If you've got anything vexing you, Lena, you'll just have to wait a spell for your turn. It's spring fever cropping out in everybody, I do believe."

I smiled faintly, and leaned against the clothesline

post. I hadn't meant to say anything to Mrs. Crawley about the shadow cast by Ray's apparent unfriendliness this spring, but I couldn't help thinking of it. Oh, well, maybe spring fever had got him too.

"I've told Dad over and over again that I want to take as much off his shoulders as I can," said Jimmy, who never seemed to mind soliloquizing on personal matters with someone else by to hear, "but it's always the same thing. 'You don't need to trouble yourself, son.' But it's knowing nothing that *does* drive me crazy! I've got eyes, haven't I? I can see what's happening. I don't know, maybe you're right…maybe he's just trying to avoid it all. When I told him about Hobbs and Everidge losing cattle all he did was listen. Every suggestion I made, every time I tried to tell him we can't afford to be robbed again, all he did was listen, and nod, and seem like he wasn't really hearing me. I don't understand him."

"Has anybody down your way lost more cattle?" I asked.

"No…not yet…and we're not going to if I can help it," said Jimmy darkly. "That's one thing I can do, anyway. I've been thinking"—he sat up straighter on the edge of the well, his voice warming with interest—"the way to solve this thing is to try and trace the trucks. I've been hanging around the filling station, asking Dusty about any trucks that come through with drivers he doesn't know. One of these days I'm going to drive out to some of those roadhouses along the highway and see if I can pick up anything there. Somebody's got to *do* something, if we're ever going to catch them."

"Well, I feel the same way," I said, folding my arms. "If I can't help anyone else, at least I can take care of the Circle M. And if there's any way I can lend a hand with your sleuthing just let me know."

"Call me if you see or hear anything, anything at all suspicious. Nobody's ever been able to get on their trail as soon as a theft happens, and I'll bet I could do it if I get the chance."

Jimmy got up restlessly. "I should get home. There's a dozen things that need doing. But Mrs. Crawley—if Dad should ever talk to you about any of this, you will try to make him see how I feel, won't you?"

"If your father doesn't like to discuss unpleasant things with you, Jimmy, I can't see why he'd bring 'em to me," said Mrs. Crawley.

"Can't you?" I said slyly.

"Make yourself useful," said Mrs. Crawley, and handed me a pair of clothespins.

I smiled, and moved around to the other side of the sheet she had draped on the clothesline. "I'll see you later, Jimmy."

Jimmy slowed at the corner of the house to look back over his shoulder, and his face brightened for a second as his eyes touched on me, like the sun breaking through the clouds and immediately hidden again. "I'll see you, Lena."

I moved on down the clothesline, and slipped another clothespin in place. Neither Mrs. Crawley or I spoke for a moment, but when the trampling of Jimmy's horse had faded away down the lane, I said, "He takes everything hard, doesn't he."

"He always has," said Mrs. Crawley. "But he's got some excuse for it lately. Jimmy didn't say anything about it, but I know the bank turned James Warren down for an extension on his loan earlier this month. I believe he's scared of what it'll do to his father if they lose that ranch—it's all they've ever had." She straightened the hanging sheet with a pensive expression. "I suppose I should be glad if this detective business takes his mind off it somewhat, but I hope he doesn't get himself into trouble."

"You sound as if you don't take the—detective business very seriously," I said.

"Well," said Mrs. Crawley, with an inflection in her voice which didn't tell me much one way or the other.

"Well, I do," I said. I wandered over and sat down in Jimmy's place on the edge of the old well. "I hope he does find something. In fact I wish I could be in on it even more than I am."

"You sound as if you had a particular reason."

Mrs. Crawley had her back to me, bending over the laundry basket. She was evidently waiting for my answer. I said, with a little difficulty, "I guess it's because of the murder."

Mrs. Crawley straightened up and turned around to look at me, a pillowcase in either hand. "You've got an idea the two things were connected."

I admitted it with a shrug.

"Hmm," said Mrs. Crawley, again noncommittal.

I looked down at the still leafless ivy clinging to the splintering gray wood, and my hand curved over the edge. What I was thinking would sound so foolish put into words, but all of a sudden I wanted to get it off my mind, no matter how silly it made me look. "Mrs. Crawley, when I first came here I thought it wouldn't make any difference to me that my grandfather had been murdered. It happened before I came and didn't have anything to do with me, and I wouldn't have to think about it. But I was wrong. I can't get away from it. I think about it all the time. I pass people on the street, and I wonder how many times I've walked past my grandfather's murderer. I'm in the house, and I look at the furniture, or his desk, or the rain slicker in the closet, and I remember that he lived in this house, and that somebody killed him and it's still a mystery who and why."

Mrs. Crawley had shifted the pillowcases to hang over her arm, and stood looking at me and listening to me. When I finished, she took the pillowcases and draped them carefully on the clothesline, and pinned them in place with deliberate movements. "I understand what you're saying," she said after a minute. "The questioning doesn't go away just because there's no answer. But Lena, don't forget—you never knew your grandfather."

"What does that have to do with it?"

"Some," said Mrs. Crawley. "You'd still wonder who killed him, no matter what; so would anybody. But if you'd known him, you might be breathing a sigh of relief that you didn't have to live in that house with him there alive."

I stared. Mrs. Crawley's voice was firmer than I'd ever heard it. "He was a hard man—a hard man, Lena, unkindest to the very people who served him best—always driving them away. Whatever it was happened that night, it wouldn't surprise me if he brought it on himself."

She must have seen I looked shocked, for she added more temperately, "Don't think I'm excusing murder, because I'm not, by any means. Nor saying that the truth ought to be buried. All I'm saying is, there's no need for you to waste your pity on him."

I sat and digested this, while Mrs. Crawley finished the basket of laundry. I had never heard her speak so uncompromisingly of anyone, frank assessor of human nature as she was. In fact, it was the closest anyone had ever come to telling me exactly what they thought of Garth McKay.

Mrs. Crawley was opposite me as she hung the last sheet, and I looked up and met her eyes over the white barrier. "Did he drive my mother away?"

"He kept her away, in the end, and it amounts to the same thing," said Mrs. Crawley. "Olsen Campbell—your father—worked here one summer as a hand for the Everidges—that was in Bob Everidge's time, Will's father. Most folks around here liked Olsen, Garth included. They knew he was here for his health, but they didn't take all that writing business seriously—nobody'd ever seen any of the magazines his writing was in, and they figured it was just a funny thing he did for a hobby. To Garth he was just a passing fair ranch hand who was new to the work, but did all right. And he saw how things were between him and Marjory. I think he assumed Olsen planned to stay in Severn Valley, and he figured on hiring him over to the Circle M after a while—and that he and Marjory would get married, and they'd be there for Garth to pass the place on to when he died. That was what he was always so set on—having some-body to pass it on to."

She came around to my side of the clothesline and put her hands in her apron pockets. "When he realized Marjory meant to leave with Olsen, it wrecked every plan he'd made. And he let her hear about it, I'm sure."

"Did he ever talk about her after she left?"

"He'd talk of her, but not of his own accord. Lands, it wasn't the let-me-never-hear-her-name-again kind of thing. When folks asked after her he'd say he didn't know where she was, and we believed him—and so after a while we stopped asking." She said, "If he hadn't been so hard-headed over it, maybe she'd have come back—for visits, as daughters do, or perhaps for good, if she'd ever needed a place to stay."

"Like when my father died."

"Yes, just that."

"So far as I know," I said, "Mother never wrote to Grandfather or heard from him at all. And she wasn't at all a quarrelsome kind of person, or one to hold a grudge. Either she must have thought it was just better that way, or the grudge was on his side." I folded my hands over my knee and cocked my head up toward Mrs. Crawley. "I've wondered sometimes, since I got the letter about my inheriting—do you think he ever knew about me at all?"

Mrs. Crawley shook her head. "I don't think so. The winter before he died he took a bad cough—and of course being along in years, one day he said to me, 'Anything in the house that was Marjory's I want you to have.' He'd never have said that if he knew he had a live grandchild, no matter how far away—not with how strong he was on having family to pass things on to."

"But if he really wanted you to have them—I did find a few things of hers—"

"Land sakes, Lena, of course not. Didn't I just tell you? Like as not he only told me to take them because he couldn't stomach the thought of strangers who didn't even know who the McKays were going through her things."

I smiled. "Do you suppose he had that much sentiment in him?"

"Pride will do it—and he had that in spades," said Mrs. Crawley grimly. She picked up the laundry basket and balanced it on her hip. "Feeling any better?"

"I guess so," I said, drawing a resigned breath. "It doesn't really change anything, though, Mrs. Crawley."

"Well, nothing in the past. But neither can anything he did bother you now."

It was the one time I would find Mrs. Crawley's judgment to be completely wrong.

CHAPTER XV

Imperiously he leaps, he neighs, he bounds,
And now his woven girths he breaks asunder...

Shakespeare: Courser and Jennet

IT WAS CALVING season. Our expectant cows out in the pastures were inclined to hide away as their time drew near in the brush that grew thicker and greener with every spring day, so I learned to join in another facet of ranch work: hunting them out, checking on their welfare, and tallying up the white-faced calves as they began to appear. Closer to home, lights burned late in the barn or pens on a few nights as Ray and Tim or Tony assisted with a difficult birth, and I awoke to the sound of the results bawling joyfully and hungrily in the morning.

I disgraced myself completely in the eyes of anyone who may believe a ranch woman ought not to be sentimental over cows with my delight over the adorableness of the first calf I saw. Tim and Tony grinned at my effusions, but didn't tease me more than moderately. Lane, who after a year was less bashful but still my loyal slave, was usually my partner in calf-hunting, and seemed to get almost as much fun out of it as I did—not, I think, because he shared my affection for the calves, but because he enjoyed my reactions.

And in spite of everything, I hadn't lost interest in Jimmy Warren's detective endeavors. Jimmy ate, breathed, and slept rustlers these days. Every moment he had free he spent prowling remote back roads for tracks or questioning people at filling stations and roadhouses along the highway. We talked by telephone nearly every day, speculating, theorizing, and comparing opinions on Jimmy's latest leads or hunches with true detective fervor. Something of Jimmy's intensity had evidently communicated itself to me, because I fully believed that sooner or later he would come across the vital clue, and I reported progress eagerly to Tim and whoever else of the Circle M crew was present after every telephone conversation. Tim at least shared my interest; I never bothered to question whether all the others did until one morning I have cause to remember.

The telephone rang early, just as I was picking up gloves and hat to go out looking for calves, and I jumped for it, since I hadn't heard from Jimmy the day before. We talked earnestly for ten minutes, and then I hung up the phone, seized my gloves and ran out to the barn, because I knew Lane was waiting for me. He had Metis saddled for me and was waiting with her and Junior outside the first of the smaller corrals beyond the barn, and as it happened Ray and Tim were inside it saddling their own horses.

"Sorry I kept you waiting!" I said, flinging a slightly breathless smile Lane's way. I scrambled up to perch on the fence and spoke to Tim. "I was just talking to Jimmy Warren. He thinks he's maybe finally got something! You know he's been talking to people at highway roadhouses? Well, he found out from the manager at one place that there have definitely been some truckers in the past, not local, who would stop to eat on their westbound trip with empty trucks, but never stopped on their way back—and he thinks they usually go back eastbound at night."

"Did he get license numbers, or a description of 'em?" said Tim.

"No—but he did get the manager to say he'd let him know right away when any of them came through again."

"Well, that was dumb," said Tim. "How's Jimmy know the guy can be trusted? He could be getting his palm greased by the truckers to keep quiet. He could do a real swell job of keeping Jimmy away from the scent."

"But gee, Tim, wouldn't that be taking way too many people into a thing like this?"

"I don't mean he's in it. But there's guys who'll put in for a little hush money if they get the idea there's something going on that people don't want talked about. Even if they don't know what it is."

"Maybe I should tell Jimmy that."

"What you should do is leave well enough alone," said Ray, turning around abruptly with sharp annoyance in his voice that was startlingly unlike him. "Jimmy Warren thinks he knows everything. He's got one idea in his head and he's going to do what he wants about it no matter what anyone tells him. I don't know why you encourage him the way you do."

For a few seconds I was too taken aback to speak. Then the color rushed into my face as if I'd been slapped. "Maybe because he's the only person in Severn Valley who's *doing* anything about it! You make it sound like he's a little boy playing cops and robbers."

"Well, you've got him thinking he's F.B.I. material, which he's not."

I was about to blurt an angry and no doubt equally

petty response, but choked it back with the sudden re-membrance that I had higher ground to take. "Thank you for informing me so promptly that I've stepped out of line. I'll try not to *transgress* again in future."

That shot told, anyhow, for Ray changed color a little and an expression flicked across his face that would have made me regret it if I hadn't been so mad. "All right," he said; "it's none of my business; you've got a perfect right to remind me of that. But you did tell me once that you wanted to hear my opinions on things; I'm sorry I couldn't phrase them in a way that'd be easier for you to swallow."

I bit my lip, and glanced about me. Tim had faded discreetly away, and Lane was waiting a few yards off with our horses, trying to look as if he hadn't heard anything that had passed. I made an effort at composure, though I felt as if all my insides were trembling, and I was at a loss to under-stand why my feelings should react so vehemently. "You know how I appreciate your advice. But I don't see why you have to come down on Jimmy like that."

"Do you have any better reason to stick up for him?"

"This time I happen to agree with him," I said, and I turned my back and slid down from the fence. I didn't look back. I mounted Metis, and rode off with Lane following me.

I was short-tempered and edgy for a week. I was exasperated with myself because I really had no good reason for it, or anybody to take it out on. I was left to myself most of the week because regular work had come to a temporary halt for some repairs on the barn roof; and for a couple of days wet weather kept me indoors. On top of everything, communications from Jimmy Warren suddenly ceased; I didn't hear a word from him all week long. I tried to tell myself that my edginess was worry about Jimmy, or maybe the new calves, but that was patently untrue: my imagination couldn't even invent a credible picture of Jimmy in danger, and the calves were almost disgracefully healthy. I was slowly running out of excuses and looking for an outlet, preferably a petty one. I was, in a word, spoiling for trouble.

Thursday morning I woke with a sense of suffocation, and with the light dappling my bedroom wall opposite the window telling me the day had dawned fair, I decided that I had to get out of the house for a good gallop. I had some housework to do first, and improved my frame of mind not a whit by breaking a dish washing up after breakfast. I finally escaped from the house a little after nine, and went across to the barn pasture and cast my eye over the horses grazing up at the nearest end. Metis and Junior were there, grazing close together, and a little beyond them was Jericho. My eyes passed over him, came back, and lingered on him a minute. A feeling of deliberate rebelliousness suddenly rose in me, and I turned and headed for the tack room.

I met Tim just outside it, and as he didn't appear occupied at the moment I accosted him. "Tim, would you please saddle Jericho for me? I'm going out riding."

"Alone?" said Tim, his eyebrows contracting a trifle as he looked at me.

"Yes, alone. I know the ranch well enough not to get lost."

"I didn't mean that, I just thought—hadn't you better take another horse, Miss Campbell? I know you been on Jericho a few times, but it was always with one of us along. I don't think Ray would—"

"If Ray has any objection he can take it up with me,"

I said, and my voice cut so hard it didn't sound like my own. "Please put my saddle on Jericho. I'll be down in a few minutes."

I turned on my heel and left him, not even waiting to see his reaction, and went back to the house. Inside, I ran upstairs and changed my dress for jeans and a shirt. I continued my run of luck by snagging a fingernail, and had to trim it. My eyes were hot and dry, and my throat ached. I couldn't wait to be out in the open, alone, with the cool air whipping against my face as I rode. I gave a hard, dry sniff, snatched my hat from the rack on the door and rattled downstairs. Jericho would be waiting. It was the first time I had ever "pulled rank" in giving an order, but I didn't think Tim would refuse to put the saddle on the horse—though it was entirely possible he would find it necessary to follow me at a distance, or pass the word to Ray to do the same. Well, if they did—Jericho could run.

I was thinking this so hard, as I marched toward the barn with my eyes on the ground, that I almost ran straight into Jimmy Warren, who was coming from there leading his horse.

"Oh—Jimmy," I said stupidly.

He didn't seem to notice anything amiss; he seemed preoccupied, almost as distracted as I was. "I was looking for you," he said.

At a second look, I was shocked by the change in him since I'd seen him last. His eyes were so exhausted and shadowed they looked like black hollows in his unusually pale face. There was a twitchy air of tension about him, like he might have jumped if you touched him unexpectedly; and I thought he looked thinner.

"Oh—were you?" I said vaguely, scraping for a better answer and failing. My concentration was divided—I didn't want to say anything about going riding, because ordinarily Jimmy would have jumped at the remark and offered to go with me, and I just didn't feel like making conversation with him today. "What's up—any news?"

"No...nothing new," said Jimmy. "I just came over to...I wanted to ask you how things were going. How those random fence checks were working out. I thought we might try it, if...it's any good."

"Oh," I said, a little surprised, though I couldn't put my finger on why, "all right, I guess. Of course we haven't had any trouble—haven't seen so much as a suspicious hoofprint, and not a fence wire out of place—"

I had a feeling Jimmy wasn't really hearing anything I said, and when I finished his nod and reply were like a sleepwalker's. "That's good."

"You look like you've been on twenty-four-hour highway patrol yourself," I observed. For the first time I felt a small twinge of remorse for having had a part, however small, in encouraging him to take this thing so seriously. Was it fair to have him do this to himself, just because of my own secret theories? I said seriously, "Is it really worth it, Jimmy, if your father doesn't even care?"

Jimmy flinched visibly. "I don't want to talk about it, Lena."

"I'm sorry. I know it's none of my business, but—I was just trying to be a friend."

Jimmy gave a tight, strained smile. "I know that."

He turned to his horse, and put a hand on the saddle. "I'm going into town, I guess," he said. He flicked a glance at the Circle M's silent house and barn, and I had a sudden queer feeling that he thought we might be watched. But there was no one around.

The hoofbeats of Jimmy's horse had died away down

the lane by the time I rounded the barn and found Jericho standing tied at the back pasture gate, with my saddle on him. Much to my own annoyance, I was a little nervous. He was a big horse, and Tim's grave looks, coupled with my guilt over defying the men's advice, engendered a little flutter in my breast that I couldn't entirely ignore. But I was determined. I unwound the reins from the fence rail and backed Jericho a few steps, then put my foot in the stirrup and pulled myself up—I needed the horn; it was a long way up from the ground.

I had been on Jericho before. But I was alone with him now, and my sense of the power in his strong curved neck and muscled legs—like the drivers of a locomotive engine—was stronger than it had been before. I remembered how Ray had told me never to let a horse sense my nervousness, and I was a little worried that Jericho already knew...I was angry at myself, too, because I hadn't been afraid at all before I snapped at Tim. I reined Jericho around and started at a trot along the truck road out past the meadow.

I thought I heard a voice call somewhere behind me. I looked over my shoulder and caught just a glimpse of two riders coming down between the trees by the bunkhouse—I didn't wait to see who they were. I struck my heels into Jericho's sides and he took off down the road, sweeping around the curve to the right in that smooth, strong canter I had always loved to watch. I didn't look back to see if anyone was following. After the curve the road swung left under some trees whose branches met overhead, and then cut straight across the middle of a downward-sloping pasture that was hayed in late summer. Jericho took the left turn neatly and sharply. And then suddenly my heart gave a startled lurch as I felt the saddle slide sideways on his back.

He didn't like it. Instinctively I tightened the reins,

but I felt the resistance and a break in his stride. With the saddle coming loose, all I could think was that I had to *get him stopped,* and I pulled back again. It didn't work. Jericho took one great head-shaking leap and then he bolted, straight down the road at a terrifying speed. The saddle was slipping further over and I was hanging on by a precarious handful of mane, the reins tangled in it and swinging loose to the bit so I had no control over him. Then he began to buck. Even if I had been able to hang on somehow, the saddle couldn't— there was a jerk and rip and the whole thing came completely loose in mid-flight.

The world turned upside-down and hit me hard, and I lay gasping for breath, flat on my back in the ditch with the cheery blue and white of sky and floating clouds high above me. I stared at the clouds and fought for breath, with a kind of incredulity. I heard the hard sound of hoofbeats fading away and surging up again. Then I realized it was because one horse really was fading into the distance and another was pounding up nearer to me. Mechanically I put out a hand and groped in the grass, trying to find some purchase on reality again.

I had managed to sit up, and was unsuccessfully trying to get to my knees when Ray reached me. He grasped me by both arms and almost shook me. "Are you out of your mind?" he practically shouted in my face. "I thought I told you never to take that horse out alone! What were you trying to do, break your neck? You ought to know better than to think you could hold him!"

He had me on my feet—I swayed back from him, more crushed and bruised by the tongue-lashing than I had been by the fall. Ray had never, *ever* shouted at me like that. Quite possibly he had no right to do it, but I was too shaken up and unnerved and hurt to think of that just then.

"Yes, I could too!" I cried incoherently. "I didn't fall off—the saddle slipped, I felt it. He'd never have run away if it hadn't been for that!"

Ray's face was still a thundercloud, but I thought I saw something change in it a little as the stumbling words about the saddle slipped off my tongue. His grip on my arms loosened a little.

"Are you hurt?" he demanded abruptly.

"N-no," I said, and was maddened that my voice shook. I wasn't sure yet if I'd bitten my tongue, and certain parts of me were still partly numb from being jarred so hard, but I was fairly certain that I wasn't actually hurt.

Ray gave me a comprehensive glance as if to assure himself I was telling the truth, then dropped his hands from my arms and turned to pick up his horse's reins. "Here," he said, bringing Sarge a step closer and holding the reins out to me. "You take Sarge and ride back to the barn. I'll be along in a minute."

With my returning equilibrium came a renewed sensation of stubbornness. "I don't need your horse," I said. "I'll walk back."

"Will you stop acting like a little fool?" Ray exploded. He thrust the reins at me. "Here. Don't be ridiculous. Take him and go home."

I drew in a sniff and drew up my shaky dignity. "If it's my own fault that I got thrown, then it's only fair I should be the one to walk home. I'm not hurt and I'm perfectly able to do it."

For a second Ray stared at me, then clenched his teeth on a broken-off sound as if he was keeping himself from saying something even angrier. "Suit yourself, then," he said, and dropped Sarge's reins on the ground, and turned and strode across the road to the heap of my saddle lying in the grass.

I drew the back of my hand quickly across the end of my nose and turned toward the ranch, which all at once looked very far away. It was at this point I realized I'd lost my hat. I looked about and spotted it some twenty yards further down the road, where it must have blown or been kicked. I set off after it.

By the time I'd retrieved it and turned homeward again, Tony Gleason, who'd apparently been on an unsuccessful chase of Jericho, had come back and joined Ray on the road, and both of them were on foot and seemed to be bending over my saddle. I had to pass them, and as I drew near I heard they were arguing.

Tony was insisting, "It couldn't have happened like that unless something was wrong with it beforehand. No buckle that's any good should break like that just because the cinch is loose."

"She said she felt the saddle slip. Before he ran away. She'd have noticed if there was something wrong with it when she saddled him."

"All I'm saying is, it *couldn't* have broken like that if it was cinched right. I've never seen one twisted like that before."

"Miss Campbell, come here a minute, please," said Ray, in what was almost his everyday voice. I came, partly because the fragments of argument had caught my attention; and he showed me the buckle end of the single cinch. The metal tongue of the buckle was broken off about halfway down, and what remained of it was wrenched and twisted out of shape. "Did you notice anything wrong about this buckle when you saddled Jericho?" he said.

"I didn't saddle him—Tim did it for me."

"But you didn't check the cinch before you mounted?"

A flush of shame rose to my cheeks. I'd been so self-absorbed when I led Jericho out that I'd forgotten to do what every rider should. "No."

Ray looked across at Tony. "That's out anyway. Tim would have noticed if something was wrong with it."

"It just doesn't make sense," said Tony irritably.

"My new saddle, too," I said, struggling with an inward impulse to tears.

"Never mind," said Ray abruptly. "It's not damaged aside from the buckle. You can send it to Cheyenne to be repaired. Whatever went wrong with it, you're just lucky you didn't get hurt."

I left them without another word. It was a long walk back up the hayfield, under the trees and around the meadow, and past the barn to the house, especially with knees still wobbly under me; and before I got there I'd had time to become aware that there were streaks of fresh dirt ground into my clothes all along my left leg and the side of my arm, and that the shoulder seam of my shirt was split. I kept my teeth clenched tightly, though, till I'd got inside and closed the kitchen screen door behind me—and then I went upstairs and flopped facedown across my bed and had a good stormy cry.

Ray sought me out next morning when I was gathering eggs at the henhouse and apologized for having shouted at me yesterday. He didn't offer any excuse; he just said that he had been wrong and he was sorry.

CHAPTER XVI

Out blazed the rifle-blast.

Whittier: Barbara Frietchie

THE SUNLIGHT CAME gaily through the fluttering little leaves of the young aspen trees that leaned out from the top of the rocky ledge on our left. Lane Whitaker and I were sweeping the far extremities of the ranch for new calves again, today down in the rocky northwest corner adjoining Crawley land. It was a maze of little draws and creek beds, hidden from each other by hills and ridges of granite grown over with fairylike young thickets of aspen and pine. Down in the draws were close-grown clumps of green brush that were ideal hiding-places for a cow with a new calf, and already that morning we had found three and hazed them back up to the nearest open meadow.

Lane reined Junior to a halt and pointed to a stand of young trees whose vivid green leaves were already thickened almost to summer denseness, their slender trunks hidden behind a rampart of bushes. "In there, I'll bet," he said. He circled the thicket, looking for an opening, and I reined Metis in and sat waiting. I still found it hard to believe that a heavy Hereford could conceal herself in a thicket I'd have gotten stuck in if I tried to walk through it—but sure enough, from inside it came a rustle of branches and the crack of a twig. Lane whistled through his teeth and pushed Junior in between the shoulder-high bushes—there was a louder rustling, a heavy, annoyed cow groan, and then suddenly the bushes shook as if they were alive and a red-and-white calf popped out in front of me. His mother followed slowly, giving the impression that she was going not because Lane was driving her, but because of an evident determination not to be separated from her offspring.

I laughed as Lane rejoined me, and the cow and calf headed up the draw ahead of us. "She reminds me exactly of one of those women you see who have a little boy that never keeps still, and the best they can hope for is not to let him out of their sight."

Lane grinned. "And he's waiting for the first chance to give her the slip. I've seen both my littlest brothers waiting on that chance, and getting it."

"I didn't know you had brothers," I said.

Lane was quiet for a second, and then he said, "I've got five brothers and sisters. Times were hard…there were too many mouths to feed at home."

We didn't speak for a few minutes after that, but rode with loose rein, the cow and calf trotting ahead of us. I reflected how little you really knew of most people if you never asked them. There were a few who volunteered everything by nature, but for the most part, being acquainted with a person took something on both sides.

After we'd left the cow and calf with the others, we headed down another rocky draw angling west. This one was narrower; as the ground sloped down, the rock ledges rose above our heads on both sides, crowned with an especially thick stand of aspen on the left, and some gnarled pines on the right. For a minute it narrowed further so we had to ride single file and Lane dropped behind, and then as the sloping draw widened out I heard Junior's trot quicken as he started to come up alongside me again.

Without warning, something ripped through my arm with a force like a blow and a flash of pain, and on the heels of it came the loud report of a rifle. Metis jumped at the sound and then I must have yanked on the reins, because I almost went over her head. I lost my left stirrup and slipped over to one side, clutching at her neck to hang on. I didn't faint, or really lose any of my senses, but nothing seemed to register for a moment—I just knew I was trying to stay on my nervously dancing horse, and seemed to have lost the feeling in my right arm, and from somewhere Lane Whitaker's horrified voice was saying, "Miss Campbell! Miss Campbell—"

Then he was on the ground at my stirrup, and I let go of the reins and Metis' neck and slid down, on the wrong side of the horse, into Lane's arms. He helped me a step or two and lowered me down to sit on the ground with my back to the rock wall. The pain in my arm was starting to come in sharp nauseating waves. There were little blotched trickles of blood soaking through the sleeve of my blouse, but I couldn't see exactly where I'd been hit, though I knew it was somewhere high on my upper arm.

Lane, on one knee beside me, yanked a bandana from his hip pocket, hastily twisted it around my arm just below the armpit, and tied it as tightly as he could. He groped with one hand on the ground for a stick, pulled it to him and cracked off a length under his foot, then inserted it in the makeshift tourniquet and twisted it tight. I gave a weak yelp of combined pain and terror, for the tightening hurt worse than anything that had happened yet, and I was frankly more scared of tourniquets than I was of gunshot wounds.

The rock at my back thrummed faintly with the pounding of a galloping horse, approaching from the way we'd come. I heard the sound grow louder, and the rattling and thrashing of hoofs on stones as the horse pulled up almost on its haunches in front of me and the rider dropped to the ground. I knew it was Ray even before he pushed Lane out of the way and knelt beside me. Relief flooded me, but at the same time with a sense of *déjà vu* I shut my eyes and braced for a scolding.

Ray's hand touched my uninjured shoulder. "Lena. Lena, can you hear me?"

I opened my eyes and focused on his face, where I saw nothing but intense concern. I breathed in shakily and nodded as best I could with my head tipped back against the rock.

Lane tried to explain jerkily: "Somebody shot—from the ledge up there behind. It sounded like a rifle. I don't know how bad it is, but she was bleeding a lot—I tried to stop it." His teeth were chattering, and I realized with dim surprise that in spite of his quick thinking and action he was terrified.

Ray spoke over his shoulder: "Did you see anybody? did you go back and look around at all?"

"No! I couldn't—it happened so quick—and I couldn't leave her alone. I thought—"

"You did fine." I heard the snick of Ray's pocket-knife opening, and he ripped the sleeve of my blouse from the wrist up to the tourniquet. I lay still against the icy-cool face of the granite and tried to stop the shivering which my body seemed to want to do of its own volition, and watched Ray's face as he looked at the wound; but I couldn't read it at all.

He spoke to Lane again without turning around this time. "Ride over to Crawleys' and tell them to bring their car and turn it around by the corner gate. I'll bring her and meet them there. Then you get to a telephone and let Burwell know what happened."

He added as Lane got up to obey, "Stay here a minute and help me first. I've got to get her on my horse. Lena— we're going to help you up; do you think you can stand for just a second?"

I nodded, drawing a deep breath. If I could just keep a firm enough hold on my nerves and my imagination—if I could manage not to think about the pain and the creeping numbness in my arm—I would be all right.

Between them they lifted me carefully to my feet, and Lane held me for a minute while Ray mounted Sarge and swung him around. The sunlight coming through the trees was a little blurry to my eyes, but Lane's arm behind me was firm enough, and I concentrated on that...*don't think about anything else...*

Ray crowded Sarge close and reached down his hand for me to take, and Lane boosted me up in front of him. The quick movement sparked a new wave of pain, pulsing steadily stronger like radio waves, and everything around me blurred to a thick mist. My hearing came back clearly I don't know how many seconds later, to catch the tail end of something Ray was saying to Lane about the Crawleys. Then the clatter of Junior tearing away up the draw at a gallop was lost in the nearer jolt of hoofbeats I could both hear and feel as Ray turned Sarge in the opposite direction.

It's only ten minutes from that rocky draw to the gate

at the corner of the northwest pasture that gives onto the road. I held onto the jolting rhythm of Sarge's trot, which meant progress even though it made me feel sicker, and the solidness of Ray's shoulder to lean my head against, and tried not to let myself shiver, because it wasn't cold. A lot of the time I felt like I was floating—slipping away and then surging gently back like the tide on a shore, all inside my own head. That sound like rushing water must be the tide. I kept as still as I could, breathing hard, keeping my eyes squinted against the bright shards of light that flashed into them through gaps in the trees, and hearing the rhythm of hoofbeats, and a confused noise of birds singing, and occasionally other things that didn't make as much sense.

"It's okay, sweetheart."

I came awake clearly and suddenly. I had been drifting again. Ray hadn't said anything; the only sounds were the clop of Sarge's hooves and the cheerful, oblivious singing of a distant bird—not birds.

I don't think I ever fully lost consciousness, but my memories of the next few hours are foggy at best. I remember being put into the Crawleys' station wagon; I remember a seemingly endless period of seeing the back of Mr. Crawley's head, and the short-cropped white hair and the faintly speckled back of his thin neck beneath the brim of his hat; and clenching my teeth so hard as the station wagon bounced over every rut in the road that I thought I'd never get them unclenched again. I remember the storefronts of Severn Valley sliding past, looking odd from the low angle of the station wagon's back seat...I was used to being perched up in a truck.

Then when we reached Dr. Burns' office, and Ray carried me into the examining-room, I must have let go the hold I had been keeping on my nerves, for I began to sob weakly—not so much from pain as from the shock and the delayed scare, which I hadn't had time to think about since the moment the gun went off. The first excess of emotion relieved, I pulled myself partly together while Dr. Burns began to loosen the tourniquet, and waited soggily for him to tell me that he was sorry but I was going to lose my arm.

But he didn't. A flesh wound, he said (I had never expected to hear those words outside a moving-picture palace), not serious, though it would be painful and take a little while to heal. He gave me a local anesthetic to dress it, and then with the help of Mrs. Crawley and the doctor's housekeeper I was gotten to bed in the spare room kept for occasional emergency patients. By the time my head was resting exhaustedly on the soft pillows, a dull, throbbing pain like a toothache was beginning to seep through the numbness in my arm, and I could hear voices downstairs in Dr. Burns' waiting-room. From the impatient inflection in one of them I thought it might be George Burwell. But I was past caring at this point, too tired even to think, and I was glad to close my eyes and slip off into deep, genuine sleep.

Next morning I awoke feeling much better than I'd expected. My arm hurt, and I was weak and wobbly as if getting over influenza, but it still wasn't as bad as I had thought I would feel. I was able to eat a little breakfast, brought in by the doctor's housekeeper; and in mid-morning Cathy Stevenson arrived to see me. She was exactly the sort of visitor invalids like: she brought over a few items of clothing to lend me that I was very glad to have, and filled me in on everything that had happened while I was in no shape to take an interest in it.

George Burwell, after questioning Ray Harper and Lane Whitaker thoroughly, had gone out with them to look over the scene of the shooting for clues to the perpetrator. He found signs that someone had been up on the ledge from which the shot had seemed to come, but the shooter had had the presence of mind to carry away the spent rifle shell that might have betrayed them—and with the rocky ground in the draw and the surrounding area, had managed to leave next to no tracks to indicate where they had come from or which way they had gone.

"Ray stayed at the hotel last night," said Cathy, "and he was over here first thing this morning to see how you were, but Dr. Burns told him you were still asleep. Oh, and Jimmy Warren came to see me last night, and was *he* in a state. He heard about it late in the day and rushed over here, but of course Dr. Burns wouldn't let him see you and couldn't tell him all the details. So he came over to get it all from me. He was just about frantic." Here Cathy paused, and eyed me with a bit of a smirk that I didn't understand at all, but when she saw that I didn't bite she went on. "Have you got any ideas at all about it, Lena? It just seems crazy to me."

I said slowly, "From what I remember Ray and Lane saying to each other when it happened, neither of them even considered its being an accident."

"Well, I don't see why they would," said Cathy bluntly. "Who would have been fooling around with a rifle down there, this time of year? And even if they were, they'd have come straight down probably shaken to pieces over having hit somebody by mistake."

I shook my head. "I can't see anybody making a

mistake like that…they would have seen us; they'd have heard our horses. There just isn't any way to make it fit—as an accident."

Cathy got up to go. "Well, don't think about it any more right now. If it's a mistake, or a lunatic, Sheriff Burwell will have it sorted out by the end of the day. And you shouldn't be doing anything but resting yet."

I smiled faintly. "No objections. And thanks for coming over."

George Burwell came in the afternoon to question me. He sat uncomfortably on the edge of a chair pulled over near my bed, his short iron-gray hair plastered down flat on his forehead from the Stetson hat he always wore, which at the moment dangled from his hand. He seemed out of his element in an atmosphere as tranquil as that neat white bed-room. I, meanwhile, was feeling a little more human by that time, sitting up with pillows at my back and my arm in a sling, my hair brushed and Cathy's fleecy blue bed jacket tied at my throat with a satin ribbon; and more in a frame of mind to take interest in his reason for seeing me.

I was really not much help to him, since I could tell him even less than Lane had. I felt that at best my answers only confirmed the evidence, or lack of evidence, that Burwell already had. When he had asked me about every detail he could think of, he put his elbow on his knee and scratched the side of his head for a minute, and in the pause, I summoned up the nerve to put hesitantly into words something I'd been thinking all morning.

"Sheriff Burwell," I said, "do you think this has any-thing to do with—with my grandfather's murder?"

Burwell lifted his head from his hand and looked at me. "Why do you say that?"

"No *reason,*" I said, looking down at the coverlet and

feeling foolish, "only—I don't have any enemies. I can't think of a reason why anyone would have anything against me personally, so I thought..."

I looked the unfinished sentence, half questioningly, and Burwell nodded in his wooden way. "I see," he said. "I've got no reason to think that. I wouldn't concern yourself with the idea, since there's no evidence to suggest it."

How he must detest the name of the Circle M now, I thought. Two separate cases dead-ended with no evidence.

Burwell got up, and shifted his hat to his other hand. "Well, I guess I won't need to bother you any more. All I can say right now is, when you're back on your feet, be careful where you go riding, and don't go out alone."

I nodded, trying not to show how dismaying that sentence sounded to me. It wasn't that I was particularly set on riding alone; it was the unspoken implication that I needed to watch my back and look behind every tree. Living that way is not pleasant.

Burwell went out, and I settled back against my mound of pillows and listened to the sound of his boots fading away down the staircase. Barely twenty-four hours had passed, with a whirl of enough events and emotions to fill a week, and here I was sitting and rearranging the scattered pieces of my life again. I could only hope that eventually they would fall back into the same pattern that I had come to love, and didn't want to lose.

Chapter XVII

But like the rest we up and went and saw, and what we saw, we took
To monument our glory-trail and leave a name to know us by.

H. H. Knibbs: Songs of Men

AFTER THE FIRST couple of days, I stayed with the
Stevensons for the weeks of my convalescence.
Even after I had mostly recovered my strength, and
had only the tenderness of my healing arm in its sling to
remind me of what had happened, Cathy and her mother
spoiled me, refusing to let me help out around the hotel,
making me resign myself to being waited on; and generally
made my stay so pleasant that I didn't feel as much of the
gnawing restlessness to get home as I'd thought I would.

Dr. Burns had made a couple of brief house calls to
check on the healing of my arm, but toward the end of my
stay I went back to his office for one final examination. I was
nearly back to my old self by now, so Mr. Stevenson drove
me across town in their sedan and dropped me at the doctor's
gate, and I went up the walk and rang the doorbell myself.

Dr. Burns had a patient in his examining-room, so his
housekeeper told me to just step across the hall and wait in

his library for a minute or two till he was finished. I thanked her, and as she disappeared down the hall to the kitchen I stepped across the threshold of the doctor's library—and halted, taken aback by an unexpected blaze of color. The mid-morning light from the window gleamed on gold-leaf and the rich leather bindings of books that lined the shelves across one whole wall: crimson, mahogany, russet, blue, and green. The bookcase itself was simple, as was the big practical desk and the few other pieces of furniture and wall hangings; the books themselves were the main furnishing of the room.

Dr. Burns' medical library? No...the medical books were there, ranged on a lower shelf, well-thumbed and much more indifferent as to binding; the handsomer volumes on a variety of subjects must reflect the doctor's own literary tastes. I browsed along the shelves, tracing the bindings with a fingertip of my free hand. There was a clutch of Greeks and Romans...Shakespeare's history plays...Machiavelli's *The Prince*...Gibbon...Burke. On the shelf above a very different strain surprised me. *My Life on the Range* by John Clay. *Reminiscences of a Ranchman* by Edgar Beecher Bronson. *The Journals of Lewis and Clark. Ranch Life and the Hunting Trail* by Theodore Roosevelt. *Forty Years on the Frontier* by Granville Stuart. And on the left-hand side of the bookcase I found novels and poetry, bound in more muted hues, some with a particularly old-fashioned appearance. Earlier nineteenth century, most of them. On a hunch I slid a volume by Thomas Hardy off the shelf and cradled it against my hip, letting it fall open to the frontispiece. It was a first edition.

I heard the examining-room door open and Dr. Burns bidding goodbye to someone in the hall. A moment later he appeared in the doorway of the library, and I glanced back over my shoulder with a smile, the Hardy still in my left hand. "I didn't know you were a collector, Dr. Burns."

"My one hobby," he said, his face lightening a little with a slight smile as he crossed the room to join me by the bookcase. He had a grave, laid-back manner which, after you had seen him professionally a couple of times, was not intimidating but rather gave you a restful sense that he knew exactly what he was doing. But his voice was almost animated, for him, as he gestured toward his books. "It's a fairly small collection for thirty years' work...but none the worse for being chosen carefully, I suppose. I'm far out in the country most of the time, but once or twice a year I manage to get to the city, and my tame form of amusement is visiting antiquarian bookshops." He restored the book I'd handed him to its place on the shelf, and skimmed a hand over the rest, touching one or two favorites. "This one is the gem of the collection by most people's standards...Keats. The Austens are in remarkably good condition. You often stumble upon something good in a very unlikely out-of-the-way place. Do you know something about books?"

"Not rare ones. I like to read, but I wouldn't know anything about what editions like these are worth. Were they printed in England?"

"American first editions, most of them, but there's one or two English among them."

"They're a long way from home."

"I can show you one that isn't," said Dr. Burns with another quiet, remote smile, turning to a cabinet that stood against the wall at right angles to the bookcase. "In fact I believe it's one of the most unusual first editions in my collection. It might particularly interest you." He brought out a slender book with a plain, worn black cover, and opened it to a similarly plain title page slightly brown-spotted with age around the edges: *The Banditti of the Plains: The Cattlemen's Invasion of Wyoming in 1892*, by A.S. Mercer.

"You'll see the preface is dated Cheyenne, but this was probably printed in Denver," said Dr. Burns. "You've heard of the Johnson County War, I'm sure?"

"I have heard of it. But I have to admit I've never fully understood it. Most accounts I've read seem rather scrambled and contradict each other."

"That's not surprising," said Dr. Burns. "It was a bitter controversy, and barely forty years ago. It may be one of those things where the truth doesn't sift itself out till a century or so later. Mercer—" he gestured with the shabby-looking little first edition "—wrote in the heat of indignation, and while perhaps not every one of his theories were correct, he certainly struck a nerve somewhere. There are all sorts of stories about efforts to destroy the first printing from 1894, and it's certain that copies of it are rare. I was amazed to find this one stuck carelessly in the corner of a shelf in a junk shop in Laramie."

"I think I'd like to read that one sometime," I said.

"You're welcome to stop in here any time," said Dr. Burns. "There are plenty on my shelves...which I think would also interest you...that I'd be happy to loan you, but I prefer to keep the *Banditti* here—since I consider it one of my most valuable pieces."

"Along with Keats?" I said. I cast a glance at the shelf of books on the West that had surprised me, and in truth *had* intrigued me most of what I saw there. "But that's a pattern on your shelves already, isn't it?"

Dr. Burns, having returned the *Banditti* to its place in the cabinet, was smiling again as he turned back to me. "Which part of my tastes surprises you, Miss Campbell: the books on the West or the classics?"

"Well, I wouldn't say either *surprises* me," I said, though the tips of my ears turned warm at the doctor's perceptiveness; "it's more the juxtaposition. You don't often see *Forty Years on the Frontier* sitting cheek by jowl with Sophocles and Shakespeare."

"True; you don't. But one ought to more. There's quite as much drama, poetry, and unquestionably comedy out here as there is anywhere else—even if only those of us who live here know it as yet. Why is a classic universal, after all?—because anyone can see themselves in it. Shakespeare would have been the last person to have turned up his nose at human nature because it wore a Stetson."

I nodded reflectively, my eyes still lingering on the shelf of frontier titles. I ought to know that if anyone did. Since arriving in Wyoming I'd been living something that could be catalogued among a particularly imaginative dramatist's Unfinished Works.

"Speaking of drama," said Dr. Burns matter-of-factly but disconcertingly, "how about that arm? It hasn't been giving you any unusual discomfort, has it?"

"No, it doesn't hurt any more than you said it should."

"Good. Let's have a look at it, then."

I followed him across the hall, reflecting that Dr. Burns could be altogether too keen sometimes. Pleasant when he could accurately guess the sort of book you'd like best to read, but unsettling when he could accurately put a name to the thoughts running through your mind. Especially when he managed to be so inscrutable himself that you couldn't return the favor.

CHAPTER XVIII

Love took up the glass of Time, and turn'd it in his glowing hands;
Every moment, lightly shaken, ran itself in golden sands.

Tennyson: Locksley Hall

IT WAS GOOD to be home again. Just breathing the air of the Circle M once more gave me a feeling of freedom and release. The realization of how nice it was to sleep in my own bedroom again, to fuss around in my own kitchen, the homely familiarity of every scuffed floorboard, every creaking hinge and doorknob and every slant of light through the kitchen curtains that greeted me, made me aware just how much this place had become home.

By the time my arm was out of the sling, the crop of calves was complete, the pastures were rippling with deep green grass, and all the leaves were fully out on the trees. Life at the Circle M seemed back to normal. On the surface, Ray and I seemed to have slid back into our old comfortable, friendly relations, and over and over I tried to tell myself that the distance of this spring had been a passing mood or misconception. But there was still something just a little forced, a little artificial about our interactions; and I knew it was only the excitement surrounding the shooting that had pushed other things onto a back burner and brought about this temporary sense of normality. And I tried to cling to it, not knowing how long it would last.

And then, one balmy late afternoon, Ray knocked it to pieces for good.

He found me out beyond the barn leaning against the board fence, resting my chin on my folded arms and watching the horses grazing in the pasture, as I often found it restful to do after a day of housework indoors. The grass was at its most vivid green, and the chestnuts' coats were beginning to shine red in the lowering sun; Metis glowed pale gold and Jericho and Knockout were like burnished dark chocolate.

Ray put his hand on the fence and stood there for a second, and I turned my head to look at him, for I sensed he was about to say something. But nothing could have prepared me for what it was.

He said, "Miss Campbell, I just wanted to let you know that I'm quitting at the end of the month."

For a second I was stunned, frozen in place, bewildered by the sudden rush of unhappiness that filled the hollow place my heart had just dropped out of. Somehow I forced out the question: "But—but *why?*"

"I just want to move on," said Ray. He spoke in an abrupt, flat voice, looking past me rather than at me, and *never* before had he been unable to look me in the eye. "Tim can manage the place all right until you hire someone else, or you may just want to leave him in charge. You've got a pretty good handle on the bookkeeping by now, and I'll do anything else I need to before I leave to make sure you're not inconvenienced."

I hung onto the rough top board of the fence with one

hand, as if that could help me sort out the welter of my thoughts. "Is it Sutherland? You've decided you want to work for him after all?"

"No. Nobody's offered me a job—I'll probably be leaving Severn Valley."

"But *why?*" I cried, no longer trying to keep the dismay I felt out of my voice. "I thought you were—that you liked it here. You've never given the least hint of being dissatisfied before."

"I'm not. I've got no fault to find with the job or the ranch. It's—it's just time for me to move on, that's all."

"But there must be a reason. I don't understand why you're hedging about it—if you've got a reason, just say so! If there's some sort of problem, you don't need to worry about offending me; I'd far prefer that to this."

"I don't think I'm required to give you a reason for quitting."

"Maybe not—but at the very least it's extremely inconsiderate of you! You've always been straightforward and aboveboard with me before." I caught myself up a little, because the raw hurt in my voice was something that almost alarmed me, allowed out into the open like that. "I'm not blind; I've seen you've been acting different lately. What *is* it? Have *I* done something? I'd rather be told at once and at least understand!"

Ray hesitated for a second—then shook his head. "No. It's nothing you've done."

"You're not telling me the truth," I said. "I can tell you're not. Ray, I don't understand. If there's something wrong, why act like this and shut off any chance of anything being done about it?"

I suppose I had finally just worn him down. He stared across the pasture as if trying to put off the moment, then dragged his eyes back to look directly into mine. "Because I'm in love with you, Lena, and there's nothing I can do about that anytime soon."

I stood perfectly still for a minute again, and I think my mouth was open a little. But it wasn't dismay; it was a sudden, lightening sense of release and comprehension, because that speech had told me as much about my own feelings as it had about his.

Of course I loved him. That was why I'd felt so un-settled and unhappy when he seemed distant this spring; why I'd been hurt to tears when he yelled at me after Jericho threw me—why it had felt like a blow in the pit of my stomach when he told me he was leaving. That was why, even unconsciously, it was Ray that I missed when I had those unreasonable little fits of loneliness and restlessness when by myself—why it was his opinion I was most in-terested in when I had an idea or a problem.

I tried to get hold on the feeling of thrill that was bubbling up inside me like a balloon about to float out of reach. I'm not sure what I looked like; probably as if I'd been thrown and dazed again. Common sense told me the wisest thing was probably *not* to simply blurt out, "And I'm in love with you, too!" but I couldn't think of anything else to do. I could only look up at Ray with wide-open eyes, as I scraped unsuccessfully for something more sensible to say.

He said, "Maybe I should have known better. Maybe I should have known enough to see sooner what was likely to happen, and been able to be more careful, for my own peace of mind. But I wasn't—not soon enough. I might have been able to think logically about it once…but from where I stand now I can't think of any reason not to love you."

I said, "And you were going to go away—without telling me any of this? What if—"

I stopped. I knew I couldn't finish that sentence without everything about me declaring to the world that it was true.

Ray moved a little closer, unconsciously it seemed, without taking his hand from the fence; there was something both diffident and earnest in his manner. "You've had a steady diet of me for a year, Lena. I've been telling you what to do, how to do it, practically how to think. You're used to having me around...used to listening to me. I didn't want to take advantage of that to...I didn't want you to mistake an obligation, or gratitude, for...what I wanted you to feel."

He paused. The sun had dropped behind the tips of the trees that divided its rays into a hundred gentle shadows; the shade in the pasture was like a deep emerald; and my heart was tingling with all the lights and colors filling my sight and with hints of other things I'd yet to know. "I thought I'd go away for a while, a few months at least, and then come back and—see how you welcomed me. I thought it would be better that way—that I'd know better if there was anything in it."

"I understand," I said softly, after a moment. "Maybe you were right...maybe it would have been the best way. But I'm still glad I found out now, before you could leave... because I already know I'd be lost without you."

Something flickered just a little in Ray's eyes, which brought an answering flutter somewhere around the hollow of my throat. But all he said was, "You and Tim would have managed all right between you."

"That's not what I meant," I said, even more softly.

Ray stared at me—I saw hesitance, wariness, but even more, a slowly increasing look of hope. He said, "Lena—do you mean that—?"

"I've been unhappy too, if you've noticed."

"Unhappy wasn't what I wanted to make you."

"But I'm not unhappy now," I said, my own daring making me so short of breath that my chest hurt, "or at least I won't be if you tell me you'll give up this idea of leaving."

Ray had moved a step closer to me. "Are you sure that's best?"

"I don't know if it's best," I said honestly; "all I know is that right now it's what I want."

I don't know how long we stood there looking at each other, trying to read each other's faces and expressions. It seemed that just then there was nothing better we could ask for, nothing more we wanted.

"That day I was shot," I said, "I thought I heard you say something—"

"*Did* you? I didn't mean for you to hear it. I thought you were groggy."

"I was. I thought I'd imagined it. Anyway—I already didn't know whether I was on my head or my heels, after you *didn't* give me a chewing-out for being so dumb as to get shot in the first place. You've no idea how shattered I was after the way you yelled at me when I fell off Jericho. I thought you were furious with me."

"I was, but only because you'd scared me half to death. What I really wanted to do was to kiss you senseless."

I tried to laugh, feeling my cheeks turn sweetly hot as if from sunburn. "And here I thought I was in more danger from Jericho."

"You were," said Ray with a momentary return of his old dryness.

"If it makes you feel any better, I knew exactly what I was doing that day. I was out of sorts and felt like doing something deliberately reckless—and Jericho was it. But I knew it. I'm less stupid than I am stubborn."

The grin, the warmth in his brown eyes that I hadn't seen in a long time, made my heart swell with happiness. "Stupid, I know you're not. Stubborn, I can live with."

I still remember those next few weeks as the happiest of my life.

On the surface, little about our days was different. The daily routine of the ranch spun on: the same hours of rising, of meeting, of barn chores and work on the range. Only now Ray and I spent every moment we could manage in each other's company—on horseback in the pastures, around the barn and corrals, anywhere. We talked and *talked*—not always about anything important; just of anything and everything. It wasn't just making up for the past few months of distance. It felt like we were simply making up for the twenty-some years we had been on earth without knowing each other.

I was blissfully, contentedly happy. It was remarkable how simple everything had been. What had happened between Ray and me hadn't turned my existence on its head, or upset all my ideas or my calculations, or dramatically changed the way I looked at life. It felt more like something that was always meant to be. It *fitted*. After that first flop my heart had given when Ray said those words—"I'm in love with you"—it all seemed beautifully natural.

I think the Circle M boys knew pretty well what was going on, though none of them let on by word or look. Nothing that happened in front of them was any different, except perhaps a tone of voice or a way of looking at each other which we probably didn't have a clue about ourselves; and yet I don't think a blind man could have been in ignorance long.

I have so many memories—sharp, clear little images framed in the living gold of sunshine, for the sun always seemed to be shining those days. I remember how it shone out at last light one evening after a short rain shower, as we walked across the dusky yard toward the house—the feeling of my jacket damp across my shoulders, the sunset glimmering through the rain-wet trees so it looked like they were dripping with gold; how we lingered at the back steps, putting off the moment of parting until it was dark in earnest.

I remember how brightly it shone on a day when I rode up the long grassy ridge to the great rock overlooking the valley, with a lunch for two that I had packed at the house, to meet Ray, who had been repairing fences with the others along the north boundary. We sat on the sun-warmed granite and shared the lunch, quiet for once, looking out at the view and perfectly in accord with each other's ability to find satisfaction just in looking. The sky was a vivid blue, with fluffy white clouds floating overhead, and the air was still, with only an occasional ruffle of breeze in the long grass around the rock and the far-off music of birdsong on the slopes below.

When the last sandwich was eaten we lingered, lazy and contented in the warmth of the sun. Ray lay down and put his head in my lap, and I leaned back a little with my palms spread flat on the rock and smiled down at him.

"To think," said Ray, "this time a year ago, I thought there was nothing much I didn't have that I really cared about having. And then—I met you."

"Don't try to tell me it happened the first moment you saw me."

"No. No, it didn't. But I can tell you, I was planning on quitting this job before you told Herrington you were staying."

I'd often thought that, but this was the first time he'd said as much. "Why?"

Ray made a little movement like a shrug. "No future in it," he said. "I just didn't feel like carrying on under a new owner." He began to chuckle. "Until you walked in and sat down in that office and said to us, 'Tell me what I need to do and I'll do it.' From that point the job looked a whole lot more interesting."

He added, "Then, too, maybe I felt it would be too bad to abandon you to Robert Herrington and let him talk you into selling the place after all."

"Oh, so *you* really thought that too, that I wouldn't stick it out?" I flicked his ear.

"Come on, quit that…No, after knowing you a week or two I never thought that. But if Herrington had kept hold of your ear and talked enough in that practical way of his before you'd had a chance to get a good taste of life out here, he might've persuaded you out of trying it. Guess I thought that'd be a shame."

Ray turned his head a little to look up at me, squinting one eye against the sun. "Then again, it could have just been that you were so gosh-darn cute."

"I'm absolutely certain it was that," I told him.

"Oh, you are, are you," said Ray, and I leaned forward a little and he reached up and tangled his fingers in the loose hair behind my ear, and drew my face down toward his.

"Hello, up there!"

In an instant Ray was at one end of the rock and I was at the other, and I believe I was trying to put my left glove on my right hand when the head and shoulders of a rider appeared over the long grass of the ridge. His barrel-chested, wheezing horse clawed its way up the last few yards of the steep slope to the high ground by the rock. It was Brock Chambers, one of my near neighbors; a short, broad man with a heavy black moustache and a gregarious disposition. "Afternoon!" he said cheerily, serenely unaware of having caused any consternation. "Saw your horses up here, and thought I'd come up and pass the time of day. How're y', Miss Campbell?"

"Very well—thank you!" I said, giving up on the glove.

"Fine day, ain't it? I been out since first thing this morning. Was planning to drive into town for a roll of wire at the hardware this morning, but my wife said to me, 'Brock,' she said, 'you know the right kind o' wire won't be there, because you told me yourself last time the delivery truck from Claxton is always late on Thursdays.' I told her I wouldn't be able to bring home the bolts to fix the kitchen pump till a day later either that way, but she said no matter, there's no sense in driving all the way to town and back twice, and I guess she's right."

"I expect so," I said, as this seemed to require an answer; not trusting myself to look at Ray.

"You're right. 'I'll have just as good a chance of seeing Burwell on a Saturday as a Friday anyway,' I said. So I took Joe with me and we've been up here in the back pasture all morning."

He stopped to push his Stetson back from his forehead with a thick-fingered hand. "Mending fences?" he said, looking down eastward along the foot of the ridge, where the Circle M crew could be glimpsed working about half a mile away. "Thought so. I come through the gate up where my pasture backs up to Warren's. And I tell you, I didn't see a single thing out of the ordinary, or a track that ought not to be there, even though I was looking hard." His black brows came down a little from their accustomed place. "I lost more cattle this week. Six head. Thought one bunch of two-year-olds looked short somehow, and counted, and sure enough—six. That's what I'm going to see Burwell about, though you and I know it won't get me anywhere. He'll check over my gates and fences, and scratch his head, and I've already done all that. I swear, Ray, sometimes I think these rustlers are ghosts, that's all."

"There couldn't have been a weak place in our fence where they got through?" said Ray.

Brock Chambers shook his head. "No, Ray, I—I've been all along your boundary, and there's no place a steer could have pushed his way through. Where you're mending today's up against Sutherland's, looks like."

Not to my surprise, they didn't pursue that topic any further. "That's tough," said Ray. "Half a dozen head—"

"Yeah. And with times the way they are, that's about all I can blamed well afford to lose!" said Brock frankly. He shoved his hat back into place. "Well, I better be gettin'. Keep my back turned too long and I'll be short two or three head more when I get home. Afternoon to you, Miss Campbell, and I hope you have better luck over this way."

I said something polite about saying hello to Mrs. Chambers for me, and was favored with hearty thanks, an account of what Mrs. Chambers would likely say when she received my message, what Mrs. Chambers *had* said last time they talked about me, and a digression into the affairs of another neighbor Mrs. Chambers had recently visited, before he circled around again to his original aim of taking leave. Having said goodbye to Ray and to me again, he hauled his big horse around and departed the way he had come, his bulky form lurching in the saddle as the horse picked its way down the hill.

Neither of us said anything for a minute after he was gone, and then I remarked, "Well, at least you don't have to worry about holding up your end of the conversation with him."

Ray laughed, and said no, you didn't. He reached for his hat and slid over to the edge of the rock, but I remained sitting where I was for a moment, gazing down over the sunny valley with the slightly lost, unhappy feeling that had come up inside me while Brock Chambers was talking.

Ray paused and looked back at me. "What's the matter?"

I turned round to face toward the Circle M, and piled my hat and gloves in my lap. "All these unsolved crimes make me feel—angry," I said. "I know you don't like my talking about the rustling, but—"

"Where did you get that idea?" Ray sounded genuinely surprised, maybe even startled.

I stared back at him. "You know you don't. Every time I brought it up, or tried to tell you something Jimmy was doing about it, you'd cut me off or change the subject, or say something that made it plain you thought I was wasting my time..."

"Wasn't half as rational as that. You couldn't expect me to be exactly thrilled over you being on the phone with Jimmy Warren for what seemed like hours a day—quoting him left and right—being interested in what he was up to every morning and evening—could you?"

"Ray! You were *jealous!*"

"Well, could you blame me?"

"Oh, I didn't say I blamed you. It's highly gratifying, in fact. I just think it's funny."

"Go ahead and laugh then, I don't mind. But it's not

so far-fetched as you think—how was I supposed to know you weren't interested in him?"

"In Jimmy Warren!" I said, laughing indulgently. "But I guess I see what you mean. How we both got the wrong end of the stick! I was certain you thought I was a little fool for harping on the cattle-rustling all the time." The laugh faded from my voice as my thoughts returned to their original channel. "You don't, do you? You understand, even a little, why it upsets me?"

Ray answered that with another question. "You're still stuck on the idea of its being connected to the murder?"

"I don't know. But...suppose there *was* a connection, wouldn't that make me responsible, in a way?"

"You're not the police. It was never your job to find out who killed him."

"Well, but look at it this way. If I was anyone else who'd lost cattle, and thought there might be a clue in the McKay murder, wouldn't I be justified in feeling upset that the only people who could ask more questions weren't doing it?"

Ray said slowly, "You mean—if you could, you'd get the case opened again?"

"I almost think I would," I said.

There was a short silence. Ray leaned against the rock, crumpling a feathery seed-head of grass he had pulled from its stalk in one hand, and after a moment tossed it to the ground. "Lena, I don't want you to take this the wrong way," he said. "Are you sure this isn't gnawing on you just because you can't quiet your own curiosity about who killed him?"

"No. No, it isn't. Just look at how these thefts hurt people like the Chambers, and the Warrens! It isn't just something that doesn't matter one way or the other. Can I help being concerned about what happens to my neighbors and my friends, and wishing I could do something?"

Ray straightened up from against the rock and came over to stand beside it where I sat, resting a hand on it behind me so his arm was partly around me. "Of course you can't," he said. "I'd never tell you not to care. But just don't brood over it like this. It doesn't do any good, and it'll just make you unhappy."

"I know. I don't think about it all the time, honestly. It's just—it's like a little gray cloud that comes over every so often, when I think about my grandfather." I looked down, and slid the rawhide string of my hat through my fingers. "I wonder sometimes if it'll be that way forever."

"No. Lena, don't think like that."

Ray leaned against me and gave me a slight squeeze with his encircling arm. "Hey," he said gently, with a slight teasing note in his voice that made me look up and muster a small smile. Yet beneath it was that caressing undertone that was one of the subtle, but wonderful new realities of these golden days. "Don't worry about it—all right?"

The angle of the sun was saying early afternoon, and the cicadas were striking up their scratchy song in the heat. I collected the wax paper from our sandwiches and the bag I'd brought the lunch in; Ray helped me down from the great rock and we walked slowly toward our horses, his arm around my shoulders.

"Have you thought any more about what we talked about the other night?" he said.

I glanced up at him and nodded, brightening. "Some."

"I was thinking," said Ray, "maybe around the end of July, before haying starts, when things are slowest around the ranch—we could go to California for a week or two for our honeymoon. Somewhere by the ocean, do you think you'd like that?"

"I'd love it...I've always wanted to visit there once. Not too much sight-seeing, you know, just be lazy for a few days and wander around a little by ourselves if we felt like it."

"That's what I was thinking. And maybe if we have time on the way home we could stop over for an afternoon and see my sister out there. I'd like her to meet you."

"I'd like that too."

The gray cloud was gone. But it remained just beyond my horizon.

CHAPTER XIX

Let's choose executors and talk of wills.

Shakespeare: Richard II

I T OCCURRED TO ME one day that I now had a way
to do something Robert Herrington had urged me to do
almost a year ago. I don't know whether some of the
more perilous adventures I'd had that spring influenced my
thinking, but perhaps in the back of my mind I appreciated
better the common sense in providing against that chance-
out-of-a-hundred, now. So one warm afternoon Robert
Herrington's car came bumping out the dusty lane to the
Circle M, and he got out of it with his briefcase in hand. I
welcomed him in and offered him some lemonade, which he
accepted readily, and I served it at the table in the office.
After we'd chatted over our drinks for a few minutes,
Herrington set his empty glass aside and opened his brie-
case, and drew out a few sheets of paper.

"This should be very straightforward," he said; "I've
drawn up the simplest form of a will, and all that's left to do
is specify a legatee and have it signed and witnessed. I

assumed, from what you said over the telephone, that you wish to treat the entire property as one bequest."

"Yes—the ranch and any money there might be. Just leave it all to Ray Harper."

I had my head tilted on one side looking at the document on the table, and I saw Herrington's hand with the fountain-pen in it stop halfway to the blank space in the text. I glanced up, and met a look that I didn't quite understand. He replaced it at once with the entirely noncommittal expression of the lawyer, but it made me realize I must have been a bit naïve or simply had my head in the clouds a good deal lately not to think the bequest must look odd to Robert Herrington.

"To Raymond Harper," he repeated, not quite able to keep the questioning note out of his voice altogether, as his pen made careful, scratching strokes on the paper. "Is Ray— aware of this arrangement?"

"No, I didn't mention it to him yet. I'll tell him about it sometime later."

Robert Herrington still looked puzzled. Clearly in a personal sense he would have liked to ask questions, but professionalism prevented it. For a moment, I saw him not as my lawyer but as the dry little man who had been my grandfather's friend, and I decided I'd rather confide than leave him to form his own conjectures. I set my lemonade glass back on the tray, and said, tripping shyly over some of the words, "You see, Mr. Herrington, we—that is, Ray and I are—if you know what I mean—"

It may have been imagination, but I almost thought Herrington looked more startled than he had the first time. Certainly the intelligence was unlooked-for. "I see," he said. "I—you'll pardon me, of course, Lena, but—naturally, I had no idea." He smiled, but I could see he was still getting over his surprise—in fact when the smile was gone he looked almost uncomfortable.

"As for the will, it's simple," I said; "when you wanted me to make one last year, I couldn't think of anyone to put in it, because I didn't have anyone close to me. Now I do."

"Naturally," said Robert Herrington, quite himself again. He straightened the paper before him on the table and laid the fountain-pen neatly beside it. "Now, all that's left is for you to sign this before witnesses. Can you get a couple of your men in here for that?"

"Sure, I'll run and get them. Be just a minute."

I carried the lemonade tray to the kitchen, put the glasses in the sink and returned the pitcher to the icebox before I opened the back door and ran down the steps to the yard. Over near the corral, Tony Gleason and the Warrens' foreman, Brooks, who had dropped by that afternoon, were involved in a heated debate about the competitions at the approaching Cheyenne Frontier Days, backing their predicttions with detailed statistics and recollections from past rodeos. Fortunately I didn't have to try and interrupt that, for Tim and Lane were at the front of the barn lowering some bales of hay from the loft with the block and tackle. From my spot in the sun I shaded my eyes with my hand and looked up to where Lane stood at the edge of the hayloft door, reaching for the rope with its heavy iron hook to attach it to another bale. "Can you two come into the house for a minute and do me a favor? It won't take long. I'll even bribe you with lemonade if you want," I added, as Tim began to pull off his heavy work gloves.

"Sure thing," said Lane with a grin. He slid down the rope to the ground, tossed his gloves on the nearest bale of hay beside Tim's, and I turned to walk back to the house, leaving them to follow me a few yards behind. The sun was hot on the dry dust of the yard, and the smell of it and the slightly musty scent of the hay and the baking resin of the spruces out back followed me as I walked.

When I re-entered the office, Robert Herrington got up from the chair he had been sitting in and motioned me to take his place. He had laid a blank sheet of paper over the will so the witnesses couldn't read what was in it, leaving just the space for our signatures at the bottom. Tim and Lane came into the room, their boots sounding noisy on the wood floor. "Sign right here," said Herrington.

I picked up the fountain pen, my hair falling forward from behind my ear as I bent over the paper, and signed my name where Herrington indicated. As I looked up, I caught a strange expression on Lane's face—the tail end of a look sent towards Tim that I couldn't see the answer to, as Tim was standing around the corner of the table from him almost at my right shoulder. I smiled at Lane, for I thought he looked apprehensive. "These punctilious legal minds!" I said. "It's just a formality. I'll probably come across it in a drawer somewhere when I'm ninety and have to blow the dust off it."

Robert Herrington gave a dry little cough (the outside limit for expressing humor in a professional situation, I suppose), and Lane did smile a little. Herrington slid the document along the table towards Tim and said, "If you'll just sign your names, please," and I handed the fountain pen up to Tim. He wrote his name in short, thick strokes, then handed the pen to Lane and moved out of his way. Lane's boyish face was still serious as he bent over the table, his lips parted a little as he wrote, a sweaty crease from his hat across the white of his forehead beneath his rumpled dark-red hair. He rested his left hand flat on the table with his thumb steadying the paper as he signed it; bits of chaff from the hay bales still clung to his shirt.

He straightened up and handed the pen back to Robert Herrington, who thanked them and said that would be all. "The lemonade's in the icebox; help yourself if you like," I added as they turned to leave the office.

Herrington had already slipped the papers into his briefcase, and was stowing the fountain pen in the inside pocket of his coat. "So that's done," he said. "I'll put it on file, and you don't need to worry about it again, unless you ever want to change it, of course."

"Not anytime soon," I assured him. I reflected that if all his clients were as *laissez-faire* about their legal affairs as I was, he would soon be out of business.

I went out on the front porch with him to say goodbye, and he turned back on the steps to shake my hand and thank me again for the lemonade. "All the best, until I see you again. And"—his lips twitched slightly, accompanying a knowing expression—"may I add—the best of happiness?"

"I'm pretty sure I'll have that," I said, smiling.

Herrington touched his hat and went down the steps to his car. The car door slammed and the engine started, and he backed it around by the corner of the house and drove out the lane, trailing dust. As the noise of the motor faded, I wrapped my arm around the post of the porch and leaned my head against it, gazing out across the front pasture, and settled myself to dream a few dreams.

CHAPTER XX

And all went merry as a marriage bell;
But hush! hark! a deep sound strikes like a rising knell!

Byron: Childe Harold

I T WAS A QUARTER to six, and most of the preparations were complete. The living-room was dusted, the furniture arranged just so, and a nice new table runner on the coffee table. I'd run upstairs half an hour before to change my dress and do my hair, then came down to arrange the refreshments. I brought them in from the kitchen and set them out on the coffee table: a plate of finger sandwiches, two layer cakes, a plate of raspberry thumbprint cookies and a glass dish of mixed nuts; and there would be coffee and lemonade to go with them.

As I folded napkins, sorted teaspoons, and set out the creamer and sugar bowl on a tray, my eyes kept returning to the ring that glinted on my left hand. It seemed I had never seen anything so lovely as the flash of the small diamond as it caught the light from the kitchen windows with each movement of my hands, and a smile hovered on my lips every time I looked at it. Only last night Ray had brought it home with him from Claxton. Sitting alone, I'd heard the truck coming up the lane and seen the headlights swing in through the gloom and flash across the living-room curtains, and the sight and sound brought a quick sensation of gladness and contentment at the knowledge he was home—and, as I jumped up to go out and meet him, the sweetness of thinking this was the first of many times I would feel that way. And there had been a precious half-hour together on the front porch in the dusk, when Ray had put the ring on my finger and we had talked over all our plans again, and shared lingering kisses before parting for the night.

This evening's party was, ostensibly and truthfully, to celebrate the one-year anniversary of my moving to Wyoming; but there was also the surprise to spring on the friends I'd invited. I'd decided to be a little mischievous about it: I'd simply wear my engagement ring and see who was the first to notice.

In the kitchen, I took off the apron that protected my dress—the prettiest one I owned, white chiffon sprinkled with daffodil-yellow flowers, with fluttery sleeves and hem—glanced at the clock and touched my hair and went out into the hall. I paused there a minute. I could see out through the screen door into the yard, and on either side of me into the tidy office and the homey living-room. I could see the little touches I'd added: the new lamps, the slip-covers, the prints on the walls above the staircase and the round rug in the middle of the entry. A year ago I'd stood here as a stranger in an empty house. Tonight, as I waited here to welcome my guests, it was home.

The Crawleys arrived first, right around six. Robert Herrington's Buick and the Stevensons' big sedan pulled in shortly afterwards, and the Circle M boys came up from the bunkhouse. Ray came in last, and answered everyone's hellos just the same as usual, our only greeting a meeting of eyes across the room unnoticed in the general hubbub. Only the Warrens were late, and after ten more minutes of waiting and conversation and another glance at the clock, I decided to go ahead and pass around the refreshments without waiting for them.

"They'll be here," said Mr. Stevenson. "Might be the tire has burst on that old truck of theirs again. I saw Jim in town last week getting the spare patched."

"Don't you believe it," said Cathy. "Jimmy is always late for anything where he has to slick back his hair, and when he has to bring his father along with him it's even worse."

"James Warren isn't looking at all well," observed Mrs. Crawley, as she cut into her slice of cake. "I know he's looked a little worn for years, but lately whenever I see him I'm shocked at how haggard he is; and his eyes are practically sunken in his face. I can't help wondering whether he's actually ill."

Robert Herrington said, "Well, he's not as young as he was. It's no secret the Warrens have never been prosperous, and hard work and discouragement begin to leave their mark on a man when he reaches that age."

"That age! He's ten years younger than you, Robert, so don't make yourself absurd talking about age."

"Eight," said Herrington firmly. "And I'm no spring chicken myself, Ellen, no matter how much scratching and clucking I do." He smiled up at me knowingly as I handed him a coffee cup. I was pretty sure he'd already seen the ring, but since he already knew something, was amusing himself by staying out of my little game. "I've been thinking lately I'd like to retire in a year or two...do some fishing, perhaps relocate to a balmier sort of place. California, perhaps. Even my kind of work begins to grow wearisome at that certain age."

"You need more windows in your office, that's all. Anyone would get tired of being shut up in an air-tight box with a lot of briefs and forms and documents for years," I said.

"Listen to her, Bob," said Rufus Crawley, "that's the girl you told me wouldn't last out six months of living here."

"All right, all right!" said Herrington, holding up his hand. "I was wrong and I admit it. I suppose none of you will ever let me forget it, especially now you've brought me here to admit it in front of witnesses."

"No, no, I promise I didn't invite anyone here to eat their words," I said; and waited till the laughter had died down a bit to add—"however much I may have wanted to!"

In the midst of our merriment, the Warrens finally arrived, and I ran to the door to greet them gaily. Jimmy, I was glad to see, was looking more himself than he had back in the spring, though still a little subdued; and spruced for the occasion. James Warren was freshly shaved and more neatly dressed than I usually saw him and seemed to be in quietly good spirits, but I could still see some of the haggard look Mrs. Crawley had described in his face even behind the pleasant smile with which he shook my hand.

"Sorry we're late," he said. "Evening, Rufus...Tim, how are you. Well...what's been going on?"

Mrs. Crawley spoke up. "Nothing much yet. We're all waiting for Lena to tell us about the ring she's wearing, and now you're here maybe she'll finally take pity on our over-stretched curiosity."

"That's an engagement ring, isn't it?" said James Warren, looking at my hand. "Well, Lena, I didn't know. I guess congratulations are in order?"

More or less everyone in the room had been sitting with wide grins since Mrs. Crawley started to speak. Now the moment had come, I found all I wanted to do was laugh for sheer happiness. I looked across the room at Ray, and said helplessly, "You tell them, Ray. I—I didn't write a speech!"

After that, no speeches were necessary. We were deluged with congratulations, and I was hugged or had my hand shaken heartily by nearly everyone in turn. Last of all, Robert Herrington set his coffee cup on the table and got up and came over to where Ray and I were standing together. "My congratulations, Lena. And I have to thank you for partially vindicating my judgment after all. Now I'll be able to say that there's no telling whether you would have remained so enthusiastic about the ranch, if there hadn't been—other attractions!"

The laughter over this was nearly deafening, but Ray, my loyal defender, wrapped his arms around me and told Herrington that he had it all wrong, that I was intrepid and a cattle queen and had enough determination to have conquered Wyoming all by myself, till I was blushing harder than the little lawyer's rallying had made me. Everyone was beginning to settle down again, and after receiving a concluding kiss on the cheek from Ray, I extricated myself and returned to my duties as hostess, offering a second round of refreshments amid the cheerful clamor of talk.

I was cutting the last few slices of yellow cake when I heard a car outside. I leaned over toward the window and drew aside the curtain a few inches to look out. The car had come to a stop beside the others in the yard, and its lights went out just as my fingers brushed the curtain. Its outline seemed vaguely familiar, and in the fading light I made out the badge on the side panel just before the door opened and a man got out.

"It's George Burwell," I said. "Wonder what he wants? I'll go and see."

I pushed open the screen door, which creaked a little, as the sheriff reached the bottom of the porch steps. He had his hat in one hand and a folded paper in the other, and paused with one foot on the bottom step as I came out on the porch to meet him. "Hello," I said.

"Evening," said Burwell.

He looked at me for ten seconds in his expressionless way, and I didn't know whether he was trying to make up his mind about something or just formulating an opinion of my appearance after his usual impenetrable fashion. But it seemed he wasn't going to say more without being prompted. So I said, "Is there something I can do for you?"

Burwell glanced at the open living-room windows, where lights and voices drifted out, and then at the paper in his hand, and tapped it against the crown of his hat. He said, "Miss Campbell, can I come inside for a minute?"

"Certainly," I said, only a little surprised. I added over my shoulder as I turned toward the door, "I'm having a little party tonight—just a few friends and something to eat. Would you like a cup of coffee and a slice of cake while you're here?"

Burwell didn't answer this, but followed me inside and through the hall to the living-room. Several voices greeted him as he stood there in the doorway, and he nodded in acknowledgement, but still said nothing. Then he looked across the room at Ray Harper.

He said, "Ray, can I see you outside for a second?"

It seemed for a second or two Ray didn't move; and then he put his coffee cup down on the end table and moved toward the doorway. "Sure," he said, and there was nothing out of the ordinary about his voice.

They went out through the hall, and I heard the screen door squeak and knew they were outside on the porch. I looked at some of the faces around the living-room... Cathy...Mrs. Crawley...Lane...and it struck me oddly that no one looked surprised, or curious, or concerned. It just seemed to have grown very still in the room all of a sudden.

The breeze moved the curtains gently, and I noticed it was almost dark outside. I could hear the low murmur of men's voices on the porch, and I had the sense that everyone indoors had become quiet in order to try and hear what they were saying. I tried to cast my memory back—the last few business transactions the Circle M had completed—had something gone wrong with one of them?

The screen door squeaked and their footsteps sounded in the hall, and Ray and Burwell came back into the room. And I saw on Ray's face an expression I was to see many times in the months to come—a set, deliberately resigned expression, as if he had shut off every emotion you might expect him to feel.

He said, "Lena, I have to go into town with the sheriff for a little while, all right?"

"Why?" I said, throwing a questioning glance at George Burwell. "What's wrong? Is everything all right?"

"He has a warrant for my arrest," said Ray, slowly.

"For *what?*" I said, my voice shrilly incredulous. I looked at George Burwell again. "Sheriff Burwell—what's it about?"

Burwell gave Ray a short sidelong glance, as if he was a little resentful at having to do the explaining himself. He said, "Murder in the first degree. For the murder of Garth McKay."

I think, for the first slow ten seconds, I felt absolutely

nothing. My mind was still just endeavoring to understand.

Robert Herrington got up and came over to stand beside me. "What's all this about, George?" he said, and he was speaking in his crisp, even lawyer's voice.

Burwell spoke as if he were reciting something he had already gone over, unwillingly at that, several times before. "An envelope with no return address, postmarked Cheyenne, was delivered to the D.A.'s office a few days ago. There was a paper in it with the number of a safe-deposit box at a Cheyenne bank, and a line of typewriting saying this might be of help in solving the McKay murder. I got a court order to open the box, and found a will in it written by Garth McKay six months before his death."

"And?" said Robert Herrington sharply.

"He left everything he owned to his foreman, Ray Harper," said Burwell.

I looked at Ray, and at Robert Herrington. In theory, I understood. It provided a motive for murder, since Ray stood to benefit by McKay's death. But—

"But surely that's not enough," I said, my voice sounding like I was asking questions of the empty air. "Just that fact by itself—to make out a case for murder! It isn't *enough*...is it?"

No one spoke right away. I looked around the room, looking for some sort of answer or indication, from anyone, but they were silent. All I saw was sober faces. And I realized, with a growing sense of dread, that all these people knew something that I did not, and for a moment I didn't want to know.

PART II: VALLEYS

PARTIE VI

CHAPTER XXI

He never stole, he never slew
He never murdered any
He never injured any of you
Spare me the life of my Geordie.

Traditional: Geordie

MAIN STREET WAS choked with traffic. Parked automobiles lined the sides of it, and at every intersection horns honked and clouds of dust half obscured the cars as they tried to edge ahead of each other into the cross streets. There were more people than usual on the sidewalks, dressed as if for Sunday, many of the outsiders marked by the newspapers they carried folded in one hand or tucked under an arm. Not only was most of Severn Valley in town today, but crowds from Claxton and other parts of Severn County had converged upon the county seat for the trial.

I stared at the commotion through the windshield of the Crawleys' station wagon as we inched our way down Main Street. The windows were all rolled up tight against the dust, so the sounds outside were muffled and it was stuffy in the car. None of us had spoken a word since we reached the outskirts of town—Mr. Crawley was busy navigating the traffic, and I was too quietly tense for small talk. I was glad neither of my companions attempted to make it.

The Severn Street intersection was the most congested—not only were most of the cars trying to turn in there, but crowds of people on foot flowed that way too, occasionally bringing the whole automobile procession to a halt by crossing the road whenever there was enough of a gap between cars. Most of the courthouse cul-de-sac was solidly parked already, but Tim had saved us a spot at the curb in front of the ranch truck. He was standing at the front fender of the truck, in suit and tie, his eyes squinted against the dust and his face already red from the heat under the brim of a crisp new white hat. As our car slowed alongside the spot, he nodded to us and then swung up on the sidewalk to join the crowds making for the open double doors of the courthouse.

Mr. Crawley pulled the station wagon in to the curb and shut off the engine. I sat still a moment, the muffled sounds of voices and horns and coughing motors beating distantly against my ears like raindrops on the outside of a window, as I watched the congestion of white Sunday-best Stetsons and brightly-flowered women's hats moving up the courthouse steps. It was difficult to realize that the hard fight to prove Ray's innocence was only just about to begin. I felt like I'd been fighting for weeks.

It had been a fight from the night George Burwell served the warrant. Ray didn't want me to come into Severn Valley; he didn't see any need for me to go to the county jail; but I was just as sure I needed to go and I couldn't be talked out of it. Once there, another conflict developed: when the question of bail arose Ray reacted obstinately against the idea of my putting it up. We argued over it, but this time it was Ray who wouldn't give way. I could feel the idea hanging unspoken that he wouldn't put into words: that it was indecent for Circle M money to be posted as bail for a charge of murdering the man who had owned it. But at that hour I cared nothing for decency, I only cared about Ray; I was edging close to hysteria, and I don't know what I would have done if the matter had not been settled abruptly by the judge's decision to deny bail—which brought a sense of horror all its own, but put an end to conflict for the moment.

The ensuing days felt like the kind of struggle you experience in the blandest, most insidious kind of nightmare, where you try and try to do something but feel you're going nowhere. And what frustrated me most was that all the opposition seemed to come from Ray himself. From the very first he seemed to have resigned himself to the idea of being tried, and showed no inclination to make an effort to prepare for it. I peppered him with anxious questions, but he didn't want to talk about preparing a line of defense, he was indifferent about finding a lawyer—he seemed to want to avoid talking about the whole thing altogether. The more my efforts fell unheeded off his indifference, I began to be uneasy and even frightened.

"Ray, I just don't understand," I said. "You've got to do *something*. You can't just sit still and wait for a murder trial to come on without doing something to defend yourself."

Ray's voice sounded both listless and impatient. "Lena, I've already told you. There's nothing I can do except repeat everything I said in front of the coroner's jury last year. Nothing's changed. I told them the truth about where I was and what I did, and that's all I know."

"Yes, but you have to be ready to fight point by point when the district attorney tries to make a case against you! And if you don't even *try* to defend yourself, it might make you look guilty!"

"Lena," said Ray in a different tone. "Lena, look at me."

I stared at him across what seemed an acre of bare table between us, bleakly lit by an unshaded bulb. His eyes were clear and steady, though there was a weariness at the back of them that hurt me to see. "Lena, do you think I shot him?"

"You know I don't," I said, the tears springing to my eyes. "I *know* you didn't. I never thought that for a moment."

"That's all I care about, then," said Ray quietly.

My self-control deserted me; I blindly stretched my hand as far as I could across the table, and when our fingers touched I caught and held Ray's hand tighter than I ever had before. At that moment all I was afraid of was losing him. I could see all the wheels of legal machinery rolling over us and gathering up a victim in their need to exact a life in exchange for my grandfather's life, even if it wasn't the right one. *And I was the one who had once wanted to set it in motion?*

"But if that's true," I choked, "don't you care about us, about our future…all the plans we made? It's all no good, if they—if they don't acquit you."

"I've got to take my chances, Lena. All I can do is tell the truth—I didn't do it. I don't think the case will stick without something more than what the D.A.'s got."

I couldn't speak; all I could do was quiver with noiseless sobs, my head bowed down over my outstretched arm. Ray didn't try to remonstrate, just sat still and held onto my hand for a long time while I cried. But deep down inside I resolved fiercely that even if he didn't think there was anything else to be done, *I* did, and I would fight and scratch and claw on his behalf so long as I had an ounce of strength left in me.

I had my second shock when I went to consult Robert Herrington, and he told me regretfully but plainly that he wouldn't be able to play any part in Ray's defense.

"For one thing," he said, "criminal defense isn't exactly my forté; you'll want someone better. And for another—well, I'm fairly certain I'll be subpoenaed as a witness for the prosecution." He paused. "The truth is, Lena—I knew about that will."

"You *knew?*" I said, thickly, dumbfounded. "You knew all the time—that it was in that bank in Cheyenne—?"

"No, no, not about that! I didn't know the will was still in existence; I only knew it had been made. Earlier this spring I overheard a chance remark of Tim McGreevy's, and it made me wonder...Well, I approached him privately afterwards and questioned him, and he admitted what I'd already guessed: that Garth McKay *had* made a will several months prior to his death, which Tim witnessed."

I remembered Tim breaking off in the middle of a sentence, with Robert Herrington standing on the sidewalk nearby. *"If there'd been any kind of justice the Circle M would've gone to—"*

"You knew what was in it?"

"No, but Tim did tell me that Garth explicitly rejected Ray Harper as a witness of his signature, which could only mean there was a bequest in his favor. Tim and Lane Whitaker witnessed it, in the office there at the ranch."

So that had been the meaning of the startled look I'd caught on Lane's face...It must have been an unsettling case of *déjà vu,* putting their signatures to my will at the very same table where they'd done it for my grandfather not two years before.

Robert Herrington leaned forward and put his hand over mine. "I sincerely regret now that I chose to keep all this to myself. But you should know, both Tim and I were firmly convinced that the will had been destroyed before Garth's death."

But he had known. I felt a kind of coldness come over me as I looked at him, a creeping feeling that made every line of his face, the gray eyes with the wrinkles at the corners, the sympathetic expression, seem like a lifeless mask for nothingness. For a second I was looking at a shattered illusion that there was anything behind the face of any friend that I could rely on. Robert Herrington had known—Tim McGreevy had known—Lane Whitaker had known. And none of them had said a word.

"Why?" I demanded of Cathy Stevenson, flinging my hat and purse to the head of her bed as I sat down on it, by way of relieving my feelings. "Why do I get the feeling that you *all* knew more than I did, but nobody ever told me?"

Cathy leaned back against the little walnut dresser opposite, with a look on her face that I didn't quite understand. "But *gosh*, Lena—we thought you did know. We all figured Mr. Herrington had told you everything about the murder when you first came out here. I remember hearing Mrs. Crawley tell Mom that Bob Herrington had told her you knew about all of it—I could even have sworn that *you* told me once that you knew—"

"'All of it'? All of what?"

Cathy stared at me. "That Ray Harper was Sheriff

Burwell's main suspect back when it first happened…that he probably would have been arrested, only there just wasn't enough evidence for a warrant."

"No," I said. My mouth felt dry. "I don't understand. Why him? Just because he was there? You have to have *some* kind of reason to accuse somebody of murder—"

Cathy gave a sharp, hard little laugh, very unlike her usual. "The way Garth McKay treated him was enough to provide a ready-made motive for anybody."

Again that sense of unreality, as if I had woken up, the morning after Burwell served the warrant, in a different world than the one I had gone to bed in. "What did he do?"

Cathy gave me another half-incredulous look, eyebrows raised, and then she reached for the bedroom's only chair and dragged it forward from the corner and dropped into it facing me. I don't think she'd fully taken it in till then just how much in the dark I was. "My gosh, it was common knowledge way before the murder," she said. "You know Garth McKay had a temper. He'd chased off every hand he had before the boys who're there now—drove them to quit, they just couldn't stand him. But with Ray it was something else again. For a while when Ray first worked there they got along just fine, and then all of a sudden everything changed. McKay used to take these moods, once every month or so, where he'd fly off the handle at the least little thing, and he took it all out on Ray. He'd find fault with him for everything—yell at him, swear at him, call him names—for practically nothing, it seemed like. He'd even do it in town with other people standing right by. Just ask Dad, or Dan Stewart or James Warren or anybody. James Warren said they wouldn't know which way to look."

So many things made sense now. Odd little looks, moments of uncomfortableness, the way the Circle M boys didn't like to talk about my grandfather—the way other people sometimes brushed quickly over references to him in conversation.

I swallowed. "So that—the way Grandfather treated him—was the reason the sheriff focused on Ray?"

"Well, that plus other little things, but all the rest was circumstantial. Ray's a terrific shot with a rifle, and the shot that killed McKay was from distance. And of course he couldn't give an alibi for the middle of the night. But all that didn't add up to enough. They couldn't match the gun, you know. The bullet that killed him didn't come from any of the guns Burwell found at the Circle M. So it never went any further than questioning, and eventually Burwell had to let the whole thing drop. I guess in the end you can't charge somebody with murder just because the murdered man treated him like dirt. Because that was the rottenest part, Lena;" and Cathy clenched her fist on her knee, carried off on the tangent; "not just that he treated Ray like that, but that he could do it after Ray had practically saved the Circle M from going bankrupt. I know that's why the boys that are there now stayed on—they didn't want to let Ray down. They thought he was getting a rotten deal, and the least they could do was not leave him without any men to run the ranch."

"How do *you* know so well what they thought?" I said, feeling again that unhappy prickling of resentment at the differences in how much we knew. Why her and not me? When I'd thought they all liked me and meant well towards me?

"Oh, things get around. In a place like this they always do. Tony Gleason's not the most discreet person alive, you know, even though he was always on Ray's side. I'm pretty sure Tim felt the same way, and Lane of course."

"Why of course?"

"Oh, gosh, Lane would do just about anything for Ray. Ray hired him over at the yards in Claxton after he'd been kicked off a freight car with nothing but a nickel in his pocket."

I only half heard. I sat back, feeling a little overwhelmed by the torrent of information that had just rolled over me, and ran my fingers through my hair. I felt confused, upset, still disbelieving. The bright cheerfulness of Cathy's room, which on any other day always raised my spirits—the yellow curtains sprinkled with cherries, the gleaming little bottles and mirrors on the dresser, the colorful prints on the walls of red-lipped girls in wide floppy hats and chiffon dresses—made me almost angry. It was like a bright hollow representation of a friendship I had depended on, and which I felt had let me down.

"I still don't understand why nobody told me any of this," I said, "not you, or Mrs. Crawley, or—" I somehow found that I couldn't say Ray's name, and I left the sentence unfinished. "None of you ever said a word. Why not?"

"Well, gee whiz, Lena…he was your grandfather," said Cathy, a little inarticulately for the first time, "even if you didn't know him—and he's dead now. None of it was your fault, so what'd be the sense in telling you things like this? I guess nobody wanted to hurt you. And as for the murder, well, just about everybody in Severn Valley who knew Ray believed he was innocent and was glad to see it all dropped. Even if they didn't think you knew, it would've been pretty thoughtless to drag the whole story up again just for the sake of talking about it."

"I know that. But I'd think that as a friend, you could have said *something*—just dropped a hint somewhere—to find out whether I did know about Ray!"

"Would that have made any difference?" said Cathy, eyeing me curiously.

That brought me up short for a minute. "With me and Ray? No...I don't think so." I stared at her. "I don't think it would have changed anything. Because I've never for a minute considered thinking that he did it. But—but if I'd known how things stood beforehand then it all wouldn't have *burst* on me like this!"

"I am sorry, then," said Cathy honestly. "But I really did think that you knew, and so did Mom and Dad—and I guess everybody. I guess we all just dropped the ball, because we all thought somebody else had it."

It seemed incredible, but it had happened. Robert Herrington *had* told me about the murder the first day, but Ray had been sitting right behind us in the car, and Herrington could hardly have mentioned his being chief suspect then. Herrington had hoped I wouldn't stay—and after I upset his calculations on that score, I suppose he wasn't the type to edge around and say, "By the way ..." His old-fashioned sense of propriety didn't quite extend to that. And I remembered now, I *had* said something to Cathy once about discussing the murder case with Ray. What other conclusion could she have drawn, but that I knew? The chain of misunderstanding and mistaken delicacy had been complete.

I sighed. "I don't suppose there's anything *else* you haven't told me?"

It was only half serious, meant more as a weak attempt at humor; but I could have sworn that for a split second Cathy's eyelids fluttered and fell. But it couldn't have been; she didn't miss a beat before answering, with her usual impudent good humor. "No, I think you've got the lot."

She reached for my hands with both of hers and squeezed them reassuringly. "Anyway, don't worry about it,

Lena. This charge won't hold up; you get a good lawyer and a jury with the bare minimum of common sense and they'll take care of that. It'll all be over in a month or two, and once Ray's acquitted the whole silly idea will be put to rest for good."

That was exactly the kind of thing I wanted to hear, and which, in my more level-headed moments, I had told myself. Cathy was common sense personified, so it made me feel better to know she saw the coming trial this way. Robert Herrington had patted my hand and told me in so many words not to distress myself overmuch; Cathy had practically squeezed the blood from my fingers and told me not to be an idiot; if I adopted a point of view somewhere in the middle I should be all right.

But even after this, certain bits of that conversation with Cathy kept re-echoing in my mind. As I drove home, my eyes sliding unseeingly over the dusty wind-scoured roads and the wildflowers bobbing alongside them in the hot sunlight, they rang in my consciousness again and again. It wouldn't have made any difference to me if I had known …would it? It wouldn't have kept me from being drawn to Ray, even if I'd known. I knew him now; I knew what he was like, and I knew he couldn't have killed my grandfather—not in the way they said it happened. Ray had a temper when provoked; I'd seen proof enough of that. But a flash of anger, over in minutes and apologized for afterwards, doesn't make a man take a rifle and lay wait to shoot someone in the back on a lonely road at night.

The next day I had an unexpected telephone call from Dr. Burns.

With far less self-consciousness than most people who had spoken to me about the trial so far, he said he expected Ray would be wanting a good lawyer, and he had a suggestion to make. He, Dr. Burns, had a nephew who had only fairly recently been admitted to the bar, but had already won a number of plaudits for cases he had defended, including a rather high-profile embezzlement case in Laramie recently.

Of course I was under no obligation to accept the offer, Dr. Burns said, but if I liked, he would telephone his nephew and personally ask him to come to Severn Valley and take the case.

Had it been anyone else, I would have dismissed this as an understandably partial recommendation of a young relative's talents—but coming from Dr. Burns, it carried more weight. The fact that he had made the offer to me rather than directly to Ray hinted at another uncomfortably shrewd assessment of how matters stood as well. I'd seen some Laramie papers lying about in the lobby at Stevenson's, so I went there the next day and looked through them until I found some accounts of the embezzlement trial he'd mentioned. It had been a complex and bitter case, but even without much legal knowledge I couldn't help but be impressed by the young defense lawyer, Carleton Kent, some of whose speeches were printed in full.

It sounded better, at any rate, than just hiring an average lawyer of unknown talents and commitment from Claxton, which seemed like our only other option; and I'd already had my private anxieties over that. So that night I rang up Dr. Burns—without having told Ray—and asked him to send for his nephew. After that, I felt better.

CHAPTER XXII

O, full of careful business are his looks!

Shakespeare: Richard II

B
UT MY FIRST meeting with Carleton Kent was not encouraging.

He had been in Severn Valley several days by that time. I knew he had arrived on a Monday morning and was staying at the Hotel Stevenson; that he had already reviewed the proceedings of the coroner's jury and all the documents relevant to the case; that he had met and talked with Ray and formally agreed to appear for the defense. But I hadn't seen him yet.

Ray had taken the news of Kent's coming more calmly than I expected. There had to be a lawyer and it might as well be this one: I suppose that's what he thought—he had no objections to Carleton Kent after meeting with him, anyway. But I was anxious to meet Kent myself and find out what he thought about the case, so I was glad to receive a polite telephone call from him saying that he would like to interview me as well.

The Stevensons had generously given him the use of the little back office at the hotel, so it was there, in the middle of a blinding-hot summer afternoon with glaring sunlight coming in through the window-blinds, that I faced Carleton Kent for the first time—with dismay. I knew he was young, but I hadn't expected him to look it—*this* much. He was tall and slim, quietly dressed in a well-cut suit, but his features were so boyishly, almost painfully clean-cut that it gave him an air of being freshly scrubbed behind the ears. His forehead had a slight anxious knit to it as if he was trying very hard to please or to concentrate on something. Everything about him, from his neatly-combed light brown hair with its straight parting to the very way his shirt-collar and tie fitted his neck, made him look like a college boy on his first day of classes. Had Dr. Burns relapsed into fond uncle after all? I suppose it could happen to anybody.

I hope I didn't show what I was thinking too much, but at the very least it knocked all the things I had planned to say clean out of my head, so it was left to Carleton Kent to begin the conversation. He cleared his throat once or twice, and twisted his slim fingers together.

"I wanted to see you, and talk to you, Miss Campbell, even though I understand you're not really a witness," he said, "because I wanted to have a full understanding of everything surrounding this case. There are—well, there's some things about it that are very unusual. It's not usual, for instance, for a murdered man's relatives to call in a lawyer for the defense."

This seemed so elementary to me that I brushed past it almost with impatience. "Yes, I suppose on the surface it's unusual, but I'm sure you've been told that I never even met my grandfather. At this point, my fiancé is closer to being family than my grandfather ever was."

"Ye-es," said Carleton Kent, "I understand that. I—"
He leaned his elbow on Mr. Stevenson's desk, and rubbed
behind his ear. "I wonder if you understand the impact your
relationship with Ray Harper has on the murder case...con-
sidering the way the property was left."

I moved forward in my chair with alacrity; the will
was a point I had plenty of eagerly-prepared speech about
and I may have even fancied I was more knowledgeable
about it than him. "Yes, well, I know the prosecutor will try
to say that Ray knew there was a will in his favor even
though he says he didn't. But why, when Robert Herrington—my grandfather's lawyer—was going through all
Grandfather's papers and settling his affairs, why didn't Ray
make any sign when no will turned up? If he thought there
was one, why didn't he say so, or press for a longer search?
If he really had committed the murder, you'd think he would
have been pretty sick to realize it was all for nothing if the
will never turned up. And he'd have been pretty resentful of
me getting the property, wouldn't he? But it was just the
opposite: he made everything smooth for me, and was the
biggest help imaginable my whole first year while I was
getting used to living here."

"Well, that" (he cleared his throat) "was one of my
questions for you. What role did Ray Harper play in your
choosing to stay here? Did he influence you, or actively encourage you to keep the property rather than selling it?"

I opened my mouth a little, and shut it again, trying
to think back. *Had* he? I remembered that day on the hilltop
where he'd admitted that he had wanted me to stay; but I
couldn't recall his ever saying anything about it outright
back then.

Nothing more than a hint. *"If you mean, could you
live here and like it, that's for you to find out...you can have*

someone manage it for you just the same staying here as if you went back..."

"I don't know. I don't think so, but I can't say absolutely. I only know I already wanted to stay, so it wouldn't have made much difference. What *does* it matter anyway?"

"If Ray Harper had convinced you, an inexperienced newcomer, not to sell," said Carleton Kent, "it would have left him essentially in control of the ranch, in a way he wouldn't have been had some local ranchman bought it. And then—there's the long view." He stopped and looked at me as if he thought, or hoped, I already understood what he meant by that.

I didn't. "The what?"

"He's engaged to you now." Carleton Kent seemed to be having an awkward time coming to the point.

"Yes?"

"If he marries you, he'll gain the McKay property along with you, almost the same as if he'd inherited."

Hot color flared in my face, and the sun beating in at the window suddenly seemed to make my neck sweaty inside the collar of my dress. "That's a singularly malicious thing to say."

"I'm sorry," said Carleton Kent, who did indeed seem uncomfortable, "but—it's my job to anticipate every angle the prosecution may take. I'm afraid your engagement offers them a good one. A sharp prosecutor could suggest to a jury that winning you over and marrying you was Ray Harper's Plan B from the beginning, as soon as he accepted that the will wasn't going to materialize. And it would sound plausible."

"To dirty minds, maybe," I said in a brittle voice.

"That's a criminal lawyer's job description," said Carleton Kent, with a small smile that went no deeper than his lips. "I can understand how you feel. But I can't pretend that you're not going to hear all this again, in court. And to argue against it, I need to have as clear a picture as possible myself of everything that actually happened." He gave me a few seconds, and then said, "Is there anything else—anything at all of a personal nature that might be relevant to the case—that I ought to know?"

I'm afraid I said it rather nastily, feeling that he deserved a jolt. "Only that I made a will leaving all my property to Ray Harper three weeks ago."

I didn't have the chance to see how he reacted to that. There was a knock at the door, and before either of us had a chance to answer Cathy Stevenson came in and shut it behind her. "Sorry to butt in, but I had to make sure of something while you're here. Lena, you're going to tell him about your intruder, aren't you?"

"My…oh, you mean last fall? I hadn't thought about it, but I guess I should. Apparently nothing's sacred and everything's essential."

"Intruder?" said Carleton Kent in a somewhat stifled voice.

I explained as shortly as I could.

If I had expected Kent to dismiss it as irrelevant, I was wrong. Before I finished, any trace of discomfort or embarrassment had drained away from him; he listened with alert, serious eyes upon my face. He asked a brief question or two, and made a couple of jottings on a legal pad he had by him on the desk. That done, he sat for a moment thinking, turning his fountain pen round and round in his fingers.

The question he came out with was unexpected. "Who else knows about this?"

Cathy and I looked at each other. "Well, I told Ray," I said; "and you probably mentioned it to your parents? I never made a big deal about it, since nothing came of it."

Cathy shrugged. "Same here. The three of us knew— if Mom ever mentioned it to anybody it was just as a queer little thing that happened that they've probably forgotten by now."

Kent continued to rotate the fountain pen for a moment, then paused. "I'm going to ask both of you not to mention this to anyone else before the trial."

"If it's to help the defense I won't," said Cathy a little ungraciously.

"No, I had in mind helping the prosecution," retorted Kent, pardonably sarcastic.

"I hope you don't," said Cathy with more than her usual bluntness. "If you're as good as Dr. Burns says you are I guess it'll be all right. Anyway, I just wanted to make sure you knew."

Having accomplished her purpose she disappeared, shutting the office door with a bang. Carleton Kent, looking rather as if a tornado had gone over him and blown out of the room again, blinked once or twice as if to restore his focus and returned to the matter in hand.

"One other thing," he said. "I'm told that you your-self were recently shot at, and the perpetrator was never found. I'd like to know everything about that, please, every detail you can remember."

"You think that *was* connected?" I said with a pricking of interest.

Kent studied me curiously for a second, and I wondered if he might have picked up on my instinctive emphasis. "I don't think anything yet," he said. "But I want to know all about anything remotely unusual over the past year or two connected with the Circle M. So if you can just start at the beginning—"

"Well," I said, mentally gathering up my scattered recollections of the event, "it was back in the spring...I was out on horseback with one of my ranch hands..."

Carleton Kent heard out my account, and then cross-questioned me thoroughly. My opinion of him went up a little more during this. He was Wyoming-bred even if he did look like a Yale freshman, and comprehended my statements about the landscape and the horses perfectly. He established as solidly as he could the exact positions and actions of Lane Whitaker, Ray Harper and myself before, during, and after the actual shooting. He had a map of Severn Valley township on the desk before him and he had me show him the location of the draw where the incident took place, and as the map didn't have enough topographical detail for his taste he had me try to make a sketch of the draw and its surroundings, though I didn't do a very good job of it. Ray or Lane could do better, I told him.

"And the date?"

"The end of April—or was it the beginning of May? If you want the exact date you could look at your uncle's records, since he treated me...and I suppose the sheriff has a file on it too."

Kent said nothing, and I suddenly wondered if he had seen those records already. And I wondered what exactly Dr. Burns had said to him when he first contacted his nephew about the case.

Chapter XXIII

Let us meet,
And question this most bloody piece of work,
To know it further.

Shakespeare: Macbeth

T HE COURTROOM WAS almost full, though it was still an elbow-to-elbow crush in the doorway and the hall outside when we made our way through. Most of the seats were filled, but groups of people still stood about talking, and standing-room at the back was already tight. The hum of dozens of voices talking at ordinary volume seemed loud as it reverberated back from the bare walls, and the scents of tobacco, chewing gum, eau-de-cologne and perfume, street dust, and the hint of hay and grass smell that always seemed to be somewhere in a country crowd mingled in the air.

I didn't look to right or left as we worked our way down the center aisle, but I sensed the eyes that followed me, the heads tilted to the side as people spoke in undertones to their neighbors. I'd been too wrapped up in focus on the trial itself these last weeks to think much about what was being said in Severn Valley about my involvement with Ray, but I was sure it was that, rather than my relationship to the murdered man, that was the cause of any attention I was getting now. I wasn't naïve enough to imagine there had never been a whisper or a quirked eyebrow about us even a long time ago, and Ray's arrest had likely stirred up gossips' interest where people wouldn't have given much of a thought before. Carleton Kent's apologetic hints had made it impossible to wear blinders in that respect.

Cathy and her mother had saved seats for us in the second row, on the left-hand side of the aisle. I edged past the knees of several seated people and took my place, and then took a better look at the scene of action. The railed-off front section of the courtroom in front of the judge's desk looked curiously bare, with only the court reporter at his station, the bailiff by the side door, and the two lawyers at their tables. Over against the right-hand wall was the jury box—the twelve in it were strangers to me, gathered from other parts of the county; ordinary-looking men with the same consciously cleaned-up, best-clothes-for-the-occasion look as most of the spectators.

Stafford, the district attorney, sat over on the right side closer to the jury, and a few feet in front of us was Carleton Kent. I could only see his slim shoulders in a dark suit, and the back of his neatly-combed head. From behind, his ears seemed to stick out a little. His ears are going to spoil everything, I thought wildly, and for one irrational second I passionately regretted giving in to Dr. Burns' advice.

The side door beyond the judge's desk opened and Ray came in accompanied by deputy sheriff Ed Kenyon. The room hushed a little, and I heard the subdued rustle of everyone leaning forward to look past their neighbor or stretching to see over the heads of people in front of them. I felt the suffocating sense of shame for him, felt the desire to sink into the floor as strongly as if all the eyes had been focused on me instead. Ray never looked out toward the courtroom, but walked ahead of Ed Kenyon to the defense's desk and took his seat beside Carleton Kent, to all appearances fully composed.

I heard a door open again and the bailiff's "All rise" was almost lost in the surge of sound as the courtroom came to its feet. Judge Hampden came in and mounted to his desk and sat down, and the spectators and participants subsided as one. The room was quiet now, except for the occasional creak of a chair or subdued clearing of a throat. In the pause before Stafford got up to present his case I stole a look over my shoulder at the dense rows of seated people. There was a disconcerting number of strangers' faces, but I saw familiar ones too. Bill Sutherland was sitting near the middle on the other side of the aisle, and Jimmy Warren and his father were at the back of the courtroom.

The charge was read. Judge Hampden, a small man with a lined face and hair turning from a sandy color to white, addressed the defendant to ask how he pleaded, and I heard Ray's voice once: "Not guilty."

George Burwell was the first witness. His testimony was mostly a re-hash of the coroner's inquest. On the morning of April 12th, 1934, he had received a telephone call around five-thirty A.M. from Tony Gleason, one of the hands at the Circle M ranch, telling him that Garth McKay had been shot. Burwell had placed a call to Dr. Burns, who served as police surgeon for the county, and then had driven out to the spot on the road near the ranch where Tony had told him to come. He found Tony with Ray Harper and Tim McGreevy by the body of the dead man. McKay was lying on his face half on the grass and half on the edge of the dirt road; he had been shot in the back. According to Ray

Harper's account McKay had left the Circle M alone and on horseback shortly after eight o'clock the evening before. That morning just before five o'clock, Ray had found his employer's horse browsing outside the corral, still wearing saddle and bridle. He had wakened Tony Gleason and they went in search of McKay. They had found the body by the roadside, and Ray sent Tony back to the ranch to telephone the sheriff. Burwell said both Ray and Tony swore the body had not been moved before the sheriff's arrival, except once briefly at first to check for signs of life.

"Where exactly was the body found?"

"About a mile and a half from the ranch on the road that goes north past there. Between the Circle M and the turn-off to the Chambers ranch, but closer to Chambers'."

"Did you examine the surrounding area for tracks or traces left by the murderer?"

"As soon as it was light I went over the ground for a hundred yards around in every direction. I didn't find any tracks that I could definitely connect to the murder. The weather had been dry for several days and the road was fairly hard, so if the killer kept to the road there was a good chance they wouldn't have left any clear tracks."

"What type of bullet was removed from the body at the post-mortem?"

"A .38-55 Winchester."

"You searched the bunkhouse at the Circle M for evidence related to the killing?"

"Yes, I did."

"Did you find any .38-55 cartridges there?"

"Yes."

"Will you please tell the court where you found them."

Burwell said, "I found two boxes. One with only a

couple of cartridges in it on a shelf near where the guns were kept, and a mostly full box in a locker with Ray Harper's personal belongings."

Murmur in the courtroom.

Stafford said "Your witness" and returned to his seat, and Carleton Kent rose to take his place. "Sheriff Burwell, assuming that MacKay was likely shot off his horse, was it possible to tell from the way the body was lying which way the horse was traveling at the time?"

"It's hard to say. If he pitched forward when he was shot, and fell off sideways and rolled to where he was found, then the horse was probably moving south."

"In other words, returning to the Circle M."

"Yes. But if the horse was spooked by the shot and wheeled around at all he could have slung him off in any direction."

"Did you analyze all the rifles on the premises of the McKay ranch to see if any of them matched the bullet taken from the body?"

"Yes, I tested all the guns I found in the house and bunkhouse that would fire a .38-55. None of the rounds matched."

Kent sat down, and Stafford got up quickly to deal with what I felt were the fairly obvious points he had made. "You say you searched for evidence within a hundred-yard radius. Going north from where the body was found, was there cover along the road within that distance where someone could have laid in wait until McKay had passed them?"

"Yes...some."

"In other words, the murderer need not have been following McKay, but could have approached from the other direction and waited off the road until he had passed before shooting him."

"It could have happened that way, yes."

"If the murder weapon came from the McKay ranch, wouldn't it be extremely unlikely for the murderer to return it to its proper place to be examined as evidence?"

"You would think so." I couldn't tell whether Burwell was being intentionally dry or not.

The district attorney indicated that he was finished with the witness, and Burwell left the stand.

Dr. Burns' medical evidence was brief. He had not examined the body until nearly seven o'clock A.M.; he had been out on a call when Sheriff Burwell telephoned his house and it had taken his housekeeper some time to track him down by phone. He estimated that death had occurred after eleven but not less than four hours before he saw the body; in other words not after three A.M. Based on his findings at the post-mortem, the bullet had been fired from less than a hundred yards but more than fifty; it had reached the heart and death had been instantaneous.

"Anthony Gleason!"

Tony was sworn in and took the stand. He looked strangely different in his blue suit, and without his usual half-sour, half-amused expression; today his face was straight and almost stern.

Stafford, a tall middle-aged man with a neatly-trimmed moustache and assured demeanor, took up his position just outside the witness-box and commenced his questioning in an unhurrying, workmanlike manner.

"When was the last time you saw Garth McKay alive?"

"The night before he was killed. Seven o'clock or quarter after, maybe. I saw him moving around in the house because the kitchen light was on."

"Did you see him leave the ranch?"

"No, I went to the bunkhouse before he left."

"What time did the other ranch hands come into the bunkhouse?"

"Lane Whitaker was already there when I came in but he wasn't in bed yet. We both went to bed after a while, and Tim came in a little later."

"How did you know it was him?"

"He turned a light on for a minute. I could see him from my bunk."

I had picked up on the omission in Tony's abrupt, staccato statement; and Stafford pursued it. "What time did Ray Harper come into the bunkhouse?"

"I don't know. He must have come in after I was asleep."

The district attorney put his hand on the railing of the witness-box and leaned forward a little. "Did you hear anyone come into the bunkhouse later in the night?"

Tony hesitated. "I half woke up once and heard a noise like somebody either coming in or going out, but it could have been either."

"Do you know what time this was?"

"No."

"Wasn't there anything about the light that gave you an idea what time of night it was?"

Tony said reluctantly, "The moon was up."

"What happened after that?"

"I went back to sleep, and slept through till Ray woke me."

"What did he say to you?"

"He said the old man had never come home last night, and he was going out to look for him. He wanted me to come with him. So I crawled out and got dressed, and we saddled our horses and went out looking."

"Which road did you take first?"

"The one we found him on. North."

"Why did you go that way?"

I saw Tony's brows twitch faintly. "I—I don't know. We just went that way."

"You were together when you found the body?"

"Yes."

"What did you do then?"

"We checked to see if McKay was alive, but we could see right away he was dead. Ray told me to go back to the ranch to phone the sheriff. I did that and then came back. The others were up when I got there and I told them what happened, and Tim McGreevy went back with me. He told Lane to stay at the house and answer the phone if it rang."

How well he remembered the details. But you didn't forget a morning like that.

"When you got back to the scene of the crime, had the body been moved at all from how it was when you left?"

"I don't think so. Not that I could see."

Stafford allowed a very slight, effective pause, and then said, "Mr. Gleason, how would you describe Garth McKay's relationship with the defendant?"

Tony looked at him for a second, then said, "I don't know what you mean."

I thought that somewhere far back in the courtroom there was a stealthy, smothered sound like a whisper of chuckles. Stafford, with a little glance at Judge Hampden to emphasize that he was dealing with a wooden-headed witness, re-phrased his question. "Isn't it true that Garth McKay treated his foreman badly?"

Tony shrugged. "McKay treated everybody rough sometime or other. He cussed me out more than once."

"As often as he did Ray Harper?"

The sour look was in evidence around Tony's mouth. "Maybe not. I didn't keep score."

Stafford's next question was like an arrow shot point-blank at a target, his voice ringing full-bodied and forceful through the courtroom. "Isn't it true that you witnessed Garth McKay direct abusive language and personal insults at the defendant on multiple occasions?"

"Yes—"

"And isn't it also true that on other occasions McKay's behavior was that of a normal, fair-minded employer, even friendly at times?" He ploughed on almost before Tony's assent was made. "The overall impression being that McKay's behavior toward Ray Harper was unreasonable, arbitrary, and unpredictable?"

"Objection," said Carleton Kent and I started; I'd almost forgotten he was there. "Leading the witness, Your Honor."

"Objection sustained," said Judge Hampden.

Stafford behaved as if the interruption hadn't happened. "Did you on one occasion refer to McKay's treatment of his foreman as 'a damn shame,' and 'a damned rotten way to treat a guy who'd saved your bacon'?"

"Yeah."

"Your witness," said Stafford, and walked back to his table.

I looked at Carleton Kent, but he was writing on a legal pad and only briefly looked up to shake his head. "No further questions."

Tony left the witness-box, and as he returned to his chair the bailiff's loud voice rebounded off the walls again: "Timothy McGreevy!"

Tim was sworn in with an expressionless face, and the air of a man resolved upon doing his duty. He settled into the witness-chair with a little clearing of the throat and twitch of his mouth and nose that after a year was as familiar to me as sunrise and sundown, and fixed his eyes on Stafford to wait for the first question. And I found a cause for the feeling of queasy unreality that had been dogging me ever since the witnesses began to come—I had never imagined myself sitting in court for a murder trial where all the witnesses were people I knew so well.

"Mr. McGreevy, when did you last see Garth McKay alive?"

"When he left the ranch the night before he was killed."

"You saw him leave?"

"Yes."

"Please describe how that took place."

"He was drunk," said Tim. "He'd been drinking in the house, and sometime around eight o'clock he came stumbling out to the barn and threw a saddle on his horse. Ray went to him as he was coming out with the horse and talked to him, tried to get him to stay home, but McKay wouldn't listen; he got on the horse and rode out."

"Was there an altercation between them?"

"I wouldn't call it that. McKay was the only one who made any noise."

"Were you close enough to hear what was said?"

"Not all the words."

"Will you tell the court everything you did hear?"

"Ray said, 'Mr. McKay, you shouldn't go out right now'—something like that—he said something about 'stay home and get some sleep.' McKay cussed him out for interfering—said he wasn't going to be told what to do by anybody anymore. He was just bull-headed; wouldn't listen to reason."

"Did he strike the defendant?"

"Yes."

Stafford spared a glance for the jury. "How hard?"

"Hit him in the jaw and knocked him down."

My eyes flew across the room to Ray, as if I half expected to see the mark of the dead man's fist on his jaw, to see still the disgust and frustration and hurt he must have felt at having his endeavors flung back in his face by the railing, drunken man he had tried to protect from himself. I felt every eye in the room must have turned as one, though there was no sound to betray it. I could only see a little of Ray's profile; he was sitting quietly with his arms resting on the table in front of him, watching Tim; his expression did not change noticeably at anything that was said.

"What happened then?"

"McKay got on his horse and rode out, fast, while Ray was getting up. I went over and asked Ray if any of us should go after him, but he said no, let him go. A little after that I went to the bunkhouse."

Stafford quizzed him on a few of the same details he had Tony. What time had Ray come into the bunkhouse? It developed that Tim, too, had been asleep before Ray came in. What time had Tim woken up next morning? He had woken while Tony was getting dressed to go out searching with Ray, and after they were gone had gotten up and made some coffee. It was around quarter after five then.

"Did you hear anyone leave or re-enter the bunk-house during the night?"

"No."

Stafford ran his hand along the railing of the witness-box. "You weren't woken by the noise Mr. Gleason testified to hearing. I guess you're a pretty sound sleeper?"

Tim looked puzzled, but shrugged. "Average, I

guess."

"If you slept through the sound of someone coming into the bunkhouse and moving about near you, then it's a fair guess you wouldn't have been woken by any sound outside—the sound of someone taking a horse out of the barn and leaving the ranch, for instance?"

Carleton Kent's head bobbed up in front of me. "Objection!"

Judge Hampden nodded and said, "Sustained."

"Let me put it this way," said Stafford; "it's possible, isn't it, that someone could have saddled a horse and left the ranch during the night without waking anyone in the bunkhouse?"

"It might be possible, but my saying it's possible don't mean it happened."

Either the answer or the belligerent note in Tim's voice got the first real laugh from the courtroom. The district attorney ignored it. "Ranching's a round-the-clock affair. There probably isn't a rancher in this courtroom who hasn't been in the saddle during the night owing to weather or sick livestock or some other emergency. In the four years you've slept in the Circle M bunkhouse, I'm sure there's been more than one occasion where someone had to get up in the middle of the night and took a horse out without waking the rest of you. Hasn't this ever happened, to your knowledge?"

Tim was equal to the occasion.

"If it happened, it wasn't to my knowledge. I wasn't awake."

The room rocked with laughter, and I was sure I could hear Bill Sutherland's harsh deep laugh over them all. Even Ray was grinning a little. I leaned back in my seat, feeling much better, and tucked a wisp of hair inside my hat. Stafford, allowing himself to smile, went back to his desk and waited for a few raps of Judge Hampden's gavel to quiet the court. When the laughter had died away he went back to the witness-box with a paper in his hand and showed it to Tim. "Is this your signature on this document?"

Tim looked, and nodded. "Yes."

"Your Honor, this is a will made by the late Garth McKay, dated in September of 1933. It bequeaths his entire property to his foreman, Raymond Harper, 'in appreciation of services rendered.' I would like to submit this document as Exhibit A for the prosecution."

The paper was handed up to Judge Hampden, and the district attorney turned again to Tim. "Mr. McGreevy, will you please describe in your own words what happened the day you witnessed this document?"

"I was coming along from the barn. There wasn't anybody else around. McKay came out the back door of the house and saw me, and he came over and said, 'I need you to come in the house and do me a favor. Bring one of the others and come into my office.' I said, 'Yes sir, I'll go get Ray'—because I knew where Ray was, I'd seen him a few minutes before—and the old man said, 'No! I don't want him. Get Lane or Tony.' So he went back in the house and I went and found Lane, and we went into the office. McKay said, 'I want you two to witness this,' and he wrote his name on something he had on the table, and then we signed our names after him. He said that was all, and we left."

"Could you see any of what was in the document?"

"No, he had an old blotter or something over most of it."

"Did McKay ever speak to you on the subject again?"

"Just once."

"When was that, and what did he say?"

"It was a few days later—a week, maybe, or maybe less. I was in the shed working the cream separator one morning after milking, and McKay came in. He kind of looked around like he didn't want anyone else to hear, and he said, 'About that thing you boys signed the other day— you just forget about that, all right?' I said sure. He said, 'There's no need to mention it again. You tell Lane, too. You just forget about it.' I said all right, and he went out. That was the last he ever mentioned it."

"What did you think was the reason McKay asked you to 'forget about' the will?"

"I thought he'd changed his mind about it, tore it up."

"You thought this at the time?" Stafford looked at him alertly.

Tim shifted in his chair for the first time. "Well, I mostly minded my own business at the time. I didn't think much about it at all. But after he was dead, and nobody found a will, then I was sure he must have changed his mind afterwards like I said."

"Why did you never mention the will to anyone even after McKay's murder?"

"Because it didn't matter then. Lane and me talked it over, and we agreed since it was pretty plain McKay had destroyed the thing a long time ago, there was no sense in bringing it up now."

Stafford leaned toward him a little as he spoke. "Isn't it possible there could have been an entirely different reason for McKay's asking you not to mention the will? Couldn't it have been that he didn't want Ray Harper to know of its existence?"

"Objection!" said Carleton Kent shortly. "That's speculation."

"Relevant speculation, I think, Your Honor."

Judge Hampden nodded. "Overruled."

There followed a repeat of the wrangle over the bunkhouse question. Considering that we now knew the will *hadn't* been destroyed, wasn't it likely—Kent objected to the word, and this time was sustained—very well, wasn't it possible that McKay had had this other motive? Possible, maybe, but—Please confine yourself to answering the question, Mr. McGreevy, not offering your opinion. Having extracted the grudging admission of possibility from Tim, Stafford moved on.

"Did the defendant, to your knowledge, have any means of access to Garth McKay's private papers?"

"I don't know."

"Come on now, Mr. McGreevy, you worked under Ray Harper for four years, you shared living quarters with him; you must have known his habits; you don't know whether he could have accessed his employer's papers if he wished?"

"Your Honor," said Carleton Kent, with a dignified annoyance that sounded almost funny coming from him, "I think my opponent is spending far too much time trying to build theories out of things the witness *doesn't know.*"

Judge Hampden agreed. I thought fleetingly that Stafford wasn't doing a very good job right now; but in the very next instant he went in for the kill.

"Mr. McGreevy, when you withheld your knowledge of McKay's will at the time of his death, didn't it occur to you that you were withholding something that could have been vital evidence of a motive for his murder?"

"I did not. I knew it would have caused a lot of trouble over something that didn't matter," said Tim bluntly. "They suspected Ray because of a few other flimsy things strung together, and if we'd dragged up the will business it would have made things look worse. I knew Ray didn't deserve to be suspected anyway because I knew he didn't kill McKay."

"You can't say you *knew* that, Mr. McGreevy, unless you were an eyewitness to the crime."

"I know Ray Harper, that's what I mean, and that's enough for me to know he didn't do it. If I'd suspected him myself it would've been different; but I was sure the will was torn up long ago and that he never even knew about it, so there was no sense in bringing it up."

"You were *sure* the will was destroyed, you were *sure* Ray Harper never knew about it, you were *sure* he was innocent of the murder; you were sure about a lot of things, weren't you? Which contrasts strangely with the number of things you *didn't know*." Tim said nothing.

"Isn't it true that you deliberately concealed the fact that Garth McKay had made a will which almost certainly benefited the defendant, because you *knew* it would be damaging evidence against your friend?"

"No."

Stafford allowed a single beat of silence as he looked steadily at Tim. Then, "Your witness," he said, and walked back to his desk.

My eyes swung anxiously to Carleton Kent, but this time I had even missed the brief shake of the head with which he disclaimed any interest in cross-examination. Judge Hampden nodded to Tim, who left the witness-box and went back to his chair, amid an intent, focused silence in the courtroom.

I jumped when Judge Hampden spoke. His normal tone of voice was so jarring coming through what seemed to me the palpable tension of the room that it was as if somebody had set off a firecracker at a funeral. "It's getting on towards five o'clock, Mr. Stafford, and I believe you still have several witnesses to go; so how about we adjourn until tomorrow. That satisfactory to you?"

"Perfectly, Your Honor."

The judge nodded, and struck one businesslike blow with his gavel. "This court stands adjourned until nine o'clock tomorrow morning."

Nine o'clock, with the blazing August sun pouring in through the courtroom windows, and the same audience so far as I could see, with little change except for slightly less fresh Sunday-best, settling in with a lower murmur than the prelude to yesterday's session, as if preparing for a siege rather than a performance. The cross-questioning had been combative yesterday; it would be unsparing today.

The bailiff's loud voice summoned the day's first witness: "Lane Whitaker!"

"How long have you worked at the Circle M?" was Stafford's first question.

"Three years, just about."

"Who hired you?"

"Ray Harper." Lane didn't look toward him; they all had a hard time letting their eyes meet his while they were being questioned about him.

"Where did you meet him?"

"At the stockyard in Claxton."

"How did you come to be there?"

"I'd been kicked off a freight train."

"So you were out of work and stranded? Did you have any money?"

"Not much."

I could hear the unwillingness in Lane's voice, and my heart sank. The district attorney was efficiently under-cutting for the jury the credibility of anything Lane might say that was favorable to Ray. Stafford had done his home-work well.

Again he went over the ground of the men's move-ments on the night of the murder, and got Lane to admit that Ray had not come into the bunkhouse before he fell asleep. Next Lane was shown McKay's will and confirmed that he had witnessed it, and corroborated Tim's account of the signing—also that Tim had told him a few days later that the old man had asked them to "forget about" it. Lane couldn't remember if Tim had expressed a definite opinion about why, but he thought Tim had said something about McKay "probably having second thoughts." I perked up a little, for this seemed a bright spot. But it didn't last long. Stafford pressed Lane for what his own opinion had been at the time, and Lane twisted and turned painfully in attempts to avoid a definitely committal answer, until Carleton Kent bobbed up and rescued him by objecting to Stafford's trying to build a case on personal opinions again.

Stafford wasn't done yet. He cross-questioned Lane mercilessly on every angle he could think of. Had Ray ever said anything in his presence that gave the impression he knew about the will? had he ever betrayed how much he knew about McKay's financial affairs? Had Lane witnessed McKay direct abusive and threatening language toward Ray? Multiple times, wasn't that right? Did the other Circle M hands ever talk about it in private? What was the drift of their remarks? Had Ray Harper ever let on how he felt about Garth McKay?

It was a battering, and Lane stood up to it as best he could, but the truth was plain to everyone in the courtroom:

he believed in Ray's innocence out of loyalty, but was uneasily aware of the plausibility of the charges against him. When the district attorney finally said "Your witness" and returned to his seat, I pressed my fingertips to a tensely aching forehead, half shielding my face from view with my hand. Stafford had managed to extract every possible ounce of defensiveness, bias, and reluctance from Lane's testimony that he could, and to me the case had never looked worse.

Again, Carleton Kent declined to cross-question.

"Hendrick Brooks!"

I started a little at the name. What did Brooks have to do with anything? Then I remembered: Brooks had been foreman of the Circle M before Ray.

Instinctively I glanced back toward where the Warrens were sitting. Jimmy's face, I noticed, wore the same tense, pale, unwell expression I'd seen on him that spring, and I had just enough time to wonder about it before the district attorney's voice pulled my attention back to the front of the courtroom.

Brooks had formerly been Garth McKay's foreman on the Circle M, correct? How long had he worked there? About five years, ending in 1930. Why did he leave?

"I quit, because I'd had it with McKay."

"He was difficult to work for?"

"Too difficult for me anyway. And I wasn't the only one. He fired one guy for no good reason, just 'cause the guy rubbed him the wrong way, and herd-rode two others till they up and quit. I finally had enough of it and quit myself."

Stafford then extracted from Brooks an eyewitness account of an abusive tirade poured out by McKay at Ray Harper in front of a small group of ranchmen at the Severn Valley filling station. Next he switched to Ray's ability with a rifle, and we heard Brooks' version of the shooting-gallery story Jimmy had told me so long ago. Brooks sounded a little grumpy, as impartial witnesses sometimes do when they're required to substantiate something particularly damaging, as if he just didn't want anybody to blame *him*. But he didn't demonstrate any reluctance or evasion, and I felt that he personally didn't care much what happened to Ray.

Robert Herrington was next on the stand.

"Mr. Herrington, did Garth McKay ever consult you or engage your services to draw up a will?"

"No, never."

"You never discussed the subject at all?"

"Not for more years than I can remember. I knew he had quarreled with his only daughter years ago, and like many vigorous men he didn't care to be reminded that he was getting older, so in recent years I seldom ventured on what I knew might be a sensitive subject."

"You settled McKay's estate after his death, correct?"

"Yes, I was appointed executor."

"You must have interacted frequently with Ray Harper during this process."

"Yes, we worked together going through McKay's papers, compiling a list of his assets, and so forth."

"Did Ray Harper ever say anything that indicated he knew Garth McKay had made a will—any will?"

"Not in the way I think you mean, Mr. Stafford. We both discussed the possibility that there might be a will somewhere, but eventually concluded there was not."

"Did he ever indicate that he knew McKay had a safe-deposit box?"

I thought that Herrington's eyes flickered out to the courtroom for a second, but I couldn't be sure. "We discussed that as well. Ray had some reason to believe there might be one somewhere."

"He introduced the subject, then." Stafford was on that quickly.

Robert Herrington hesitated slightly. "I believe so. He asked me if I knew anything about a safe-deposit box Garth might have had, but I knew nothing of it."

"When and how did you first learn of the definite existence of the will we have seen today?"

"Early this spring. I learned of it from Tim McGreevy."

"Mr. Herrington, why did you, too, never choose to make this information known to the sheriff or the district attorney's office?"

"I concurred with Tim's judgement: that since the will had in all probability been destroyed, and it was unlikely that Ray Harper ever knew about it, the revelation would only have caused unnecessary trouble."

"Are you a friend of Ray Harper's, Mr. Herrington?"

"Why, yes, I suppose so. Friendly acquaintance would be more accurate, perhaps." Herrington leaned forward a little and added, "May I point something out, Mr. Stafford? This knowledge of mine would not necessarily have been very strong legal evidence. At the time of the murder, and afterwards when I first learned of the will, there was no evidence that the document existed or ever *had* existed except for the bare word of Tim McGreevy and Lane Whitaker who said they had seen it."

"Yet since these two men were friends and partisans of the defendant, it's highly unlikely they would invent a story so damaging to him."

Robert Herrington said nothing, until Stafford gave him a look that seemed to rouse him. "Was that a question? I'm sorry, I didn't realize it needed my acknowledgement to be a valid point."

A smothered laugh ran through the courtroom. Stafford, trying not to smile, turned toward Judge Hampden's desk and said, "The state rests, Your Honor."

Carleton Kent sprang up and came over to the witness-box and went to work without preliminaries. "Mr. Herrington, did you draft a will this summer for the present owner of the Circle M, Lena Campbell?"

"Yes, I did."

"In which Miss Campbell left her entire property to the defendant, her fiancé?"

"That is correct."

"Mr. Herrington, on what date was this will signed and witnessed?"

"It was June the 4th of this year."

"Was Ray Harper aware of Miss Campbell's intentions?"

"I don't think so. I remember her saying that she would tell him afterwards, or words to that effect."

"Exact words if you can remember them, Mr. Herrington?"

Herrington reflected for a few seconds. "She said, 'I'll tell him sometime soon'—or 'sometime later,' I believe that was it."

"Thank you."

Herrington departed, and now it was Kent's turn. He asked that Lane Whitaker be recalled as the first witness for the defense.

I caught a glimpse of Lane's face as he went forward and felt sorry for him. His first appearance had been a nightmare and he plainly dreaded going through the same thing all over again. He sat with elbows rigid on the arms of the chair and waited tensely for the defense attorney.

Carleton Kent walked over to the witness-box and began matter-of-factly, "On April 28th of this year, you were with your current employer, Lena Campbell, when she was injured by a gunshot from an unknown assailant; is that correct?"

This was unexpected. You could almost sense a pricking of ears throughout the courtroom, a little more attention on the part of the jury.

Lane looked bewildered for half a second, and then nodded. "Yes."

"Where did this happen?"

"In a draw down in the northwest corner of the Circle M ranch."

"Will you describe exactly what took place?"

A little haltingly at first, but gradually gaining fluency as he went on, Lane complied. And for the first time I began to get a faint inkling that Carleton Kent was, in fact, a very good lawyer. His raw youthful appearance and very ordinary manner put you at ease so that you didn't notice for some time how intelligent his questions were. His brief interjected queries throughout Lane's testimony sounded as if they were things that had just occurred to him at the moment, but they drew out every detail of the narrative and gave it direction. Under his handling Lane relaxed, his voice sounding much more normal, and forgot that he was on the witness-stand. I had no idea yet how Carleton Kent meant to make any of this bear upon the murder, but I thought he managed to lay emphasis on the fact that Ray's horse was traveling at a full gallop when he entered the draw—the implication being that he had started from a greater distance off than the distance from which the shot had been fired.

I realized suddenly what had never occurred to me before: that an outsider might conjecture that Ray had fired the shot himself, and then joined us a minute later.

The jury had followed all this with interest; one man was leaning forward with his elbow on the rail of the jury-box and his chin in his hand, and there were lines of concentration on several foreheads as if they were waiting to see where all this fit in. Kent never even looked at the jury, but I suspected this was exactly the impression he wanted to make.

When he had dealt fully with the shooting, he said to Lane, "Thank you. Now just one more question. Did you witness Miss Campbell's signature to a will on June 4th of this summer?"

"Yes."

Carleton Kent thanked him again and walked back across to the defense desk, with a nod and "Your witness" to Stafford. The district attorney had no further questions, and Lane was allowed to step down.

Tim McGreevy was recalled very briefly to confirm that he had also witnessed my signature to a will on June 4th. Stafford, who plainly didn't know what any of this was about, let him go without cross-questioning, only too glad not to lock horns with Tim again, I imagined.

Tim returned to his seat beside the other witnesses, but Carleton Kent remained standing. There was a subtle, shifting wave of sound throughout the courtroom: the rustle made up of people moving to a more comfortable position on hard chairs after sitting in one place for so long, and small movements like a purse being opened and closed, a muffled cough, a paper being dropped or passed from hand to hand. I didn't understand what was happening until I realized that there was another witness coming.

"Raymond Harper."

CHAPTER XXIV

The truth is rarely pure and never simple.

Wilde: The Importance of Being Earnest

I T'S HARD TO DESCRIBE what it feels like to watch someone you love on the witness-stand at their own trial…and I suppose it's just as well that not many people have to know. There was no sense of threat in the atmosphere of the courtroom, but even though Ray was still quiet and calm, I felt as if I was watching him face a firing-squad.

Carleton Kent leaned on the railing of the witness-box, and in a quiet conversational tone to match Ray's own appearance, asked him to describe his own movements on the night of the murder. I felt that the whole courtroom was intent upon Ray's words, holding its breath to listen.

He hadn't felt like sleeping after McKay left the ranch, and so he had gone for a walk out the road through the north pastures. He had lingered out there for some time alone, doing nothing in particular, just leaning against a fence post and thinking. He didn't know exactly what time it was when he started back, but he thought it was after nine o'clock, probably nearer nine-thirty. He had gone straight to the bunkhouse and gone to bed, and had not left it again until he got up and went out shortly before five in the morning. And that was all.

"What about the box of .38-55 cartridges found in your locker? Can you explain that?"

"They'd been there for months. I'd bought them the last time I went hunting."

"Did you know while Garth McKay was alive that he had made a will?"

"No, I didn't."

"When you were told last month that he had left a will bequeathing you all his property, were you surprised?"

"I was stunned," said Ray. "I never expected that at all."

Carleton Kent gave him a brief nod, similar to that with which he thanked all the witnesses, but caught Ray's eyes for a second so that it was also a wordless encouragement for what was about to come. He turned and went back to his desk, and as he passed the district attorney he said, "Your witness."

I stared after him with a feeling of panic. What was Kent doing? Why had he put Ray on the stand just for this, and left him to cross-examination? I plucked at Mrs. Crawley's elbow and tried to whisper to her but she shushed me. Stafford was getting up and advancing on the witness-box and she wanted to listen. I sat back in my chair with my hands twisted tight in my lap and tried to quiet the pounding of my heart.

I wondered how much of the same ground we were going to go over again—times, movements, bunkhouse comings and goings. What more could Stafford possibly get out of Ray about that night that he hadn't already gotten from the others? But as it turned out, he didn't take that tack at all, and I dryly congratulated myself that I was getting a little smarter.

Stafford said, "Mr. Harper, let's go back for a moment to the weeks after Garth McKay's death. Were you surprised when no will was found among his personal effects?"

"A little, maybe. I mean, with the way the land meant so much to him, I wouldn't have expected he'd have left to chance what became of it. I thought he might have left it to his daughter."

"So you were aware a will might have existed."

Ray looked slightly puzzled. "I can't say I ever really consciously thought about it while he was alive; I guess I just assumed."

Stafford turned half away from the witness-box and shot a brief look at the jury; I was beginning to recognize this as one of his favored pieces of stage business. "Did McKay ever mention a granddaughter?"

"No—he never even mentioned a daughter to me; I only knew about that from other people."

"How much did you know about your employer's finances?"

"Can you be a little more specific about that, Mr. Stafford? I don't know exactly in what respect you mean."

(*"Good* boy," murmured Mrs. Crawley emphatically beside me, as if she'd been at a ballgame and witnessed a particularly good hit.)

"Well, for example, did you know at any given time how much money McKay had in the bank?"

"No, never—only an educated guess."

"You saw the need to educate yourself enough to make a guess?"

Carleton Kent leaned forward with his palms on the table looking like he was of two minds whether to make an objection, but his eye rested on Ray for a moment and he decided against it. Ray said, "It's not easy to help manage a ranch if you've got no idea what its assets or liabilities are. McKay was always tight-lipped about that from the beginning. I had to ask him a lot of questions about finances, just in order to be able to give my opinion about any decision he was making."

"And he would answer them?"

"Only partly, and it was like pulling teeth to get that much."

"But you persisted in asking."

"Like I told you, I tried to figure out what I was working with so I could do my job properly."

"So you *were* able to form a fairly accurate picture of the Circle M's finances."

"Not a complete one. I was always working partly in the dark."

"Given the difficulty you had in obtaining information from McKay, did you ever take an opportunity of examining any papers he kept in his home office while he was away?"

"Of course I didn't." There was an edge to Ray's voice for the first time.

"Did McKay keep personal papers locked up?"

"Only some."

"How do you know that?" the district attorney rapped back instantly.

"Because I'd been in the office with him and seen him lock and unlock a drawer or two. But most stuff he just tossed in his desk and I never saw him lock that."

"According to Robert Herrington," said Stafford,

pronouncing each word precisely and deliberately, "you asked him if he knew the whereabouts of a safe-deposit box belonging to Garth McKay. You knew about the box's existence?"

"I thought there might be one, from something McKay had said once, or twice—I don't remember now exactly what it was."

"You were the only person to voice the idea that McKay had a safe-deposit box—an idea that has since been confirmed to be true." Stafford was not looking at the jury, but the repetition was plainly meant for them.

Ray pursed his lips for a second and seemed to think, but there was no other accurate answer he could make. "Yes."

"You suspected the will might be there?"

I saw the trap, but Ray saw it too. "I didn't know there was a will."

"Of course," said Stafford, throwing an inflection into his voice and a confidential smile toward the jury calculated to make anyone on the side of the defense want to hit him. "I had forgotten."

He went on. "Did you consider the Circle M ranch a desirable piece of property?"

"Well, the land itself—it's as good as any. Whether it could be made a good going concern, that'd depend on the right management."

"Management such as your own?"

"Objection!" came Carleton Kent's voice.

"Sustained," said Judge Hampden, giving Stafford a very slight admonishing raise of an eyebrow.

"As Garth McKay's foreman," pursued Stafford as if nothing had happened, "you believed you had the management skills to make a going concern out of the Circle M?"

"I did my best, that's all I can say."

What was it? Something about the way Ray said it, the way he fixed his eyes on a point in space out in front of him instead of Stafford or anybody else, started an uneasy feeling stirring somewhere in the pit of my stomach. I didn't know why, but it was different than any of the anxiety I'd felt so far.

"Is it true that when you were first hired the Circle M was close to bankruptcy?"

"It was in a pretty bad way, yes."

"If you knew that why would you take a job there?"

"It was a job, and jobs aren't always easy to get these days. And I didn't know all about the Circle M then; I was new to Severn County at the time. I was a little surprised by McKay's offer, and I couldn't pass it up."

"Why surprised?"

"Well, I was only twenty-three, pretty young for a foreman's job, or at least I thought that's how most bosses would see it. And he hardly knew me."

"Would you say it was mainly your efforts that saved the Circle M from bankruptcy for Garth McKay?"

"I suppose so...partly. I told you, I just did the best I was able."

"Didn't you consider you'd been pretty shabbily repaid for those efforts?"

How many times, when I'd asked him a question Ray didn't care to answer fully, had I known there was much more behind the few brief words of his answer, as truthful as those words might be? I watched him now, knowing him as Stafford couldn't, and knew beyond a doubt that was what was happening now.

Ray said, "I wasn't hired for any special great effort. I was only paid to be a ranch foreman."

"Most of your friends seem to feel you were given a raw deal. Can you tell me you never felt that way yourself?"

A warning tenseness in my clenched hands and in the back of my neck alerted me: this was the danger point. Ray said nothing for a few seconds. Somehow I knew that the answer was no, and Ray knew that if he was to be truthful it was no, but that he also knew it was an impossible answer to make when you were in the dock for murder.

"I never asked for any special consideration," he said.

Stafford leaned closer. "But you do feel you went above and beyond."

"If I did, that was my affair."

Stafford held his position for a moment, one hand on the railing of the witness-box, looking straight at Ray. Then he turned away; and as if that was the signal to release a collective breath, another one of those subtle ripples ran through the courtroom.

The district attorney strolled a few steps away and came back. "What time did McKay's horse come back to the ranch the night he was killed?"

"I don't know—I didn't find it till morning, around five o'clock."

"We've heard testimony to the effect that Garth McKay sometimes drank heavily. Would you say, when that happened, he was incapacitated by liquor?"

"Not exactly. It affected his temper more than his thinking. It was more like—well, when he was drinking he'd kind of let things go, and not seem to care whether work got done or not."

"When he was in this mood, I suppose you could more easily influence him?"

"Objection!" said Carleton Kent with energy.

Again the district attorney re-phrased. "When McKay was drinking, did you have more leeway to make decisions, more control over the ranch's business affairs than the average foreman?"

"I don't know. I don't have other experience to compare it to."

"Mr. Harper," said Stafford, "by your own admission, you worked for a man who drank, who had an unpredictable temper, who made it difficult for you to do your job, and who left to you extra responsibilities that should have been his. According to others' testimony, he subjected you to torrents of verbal abuse and even struck you. What I'd like to know is—why didn't you quit?"

Again there was a pause before Ray spoke, and again a flicker of almost-panic fluttered in my chest. *Say something—say something, but don't say anything that'll hurt you in the eyes of the jury...*

"I guess I was stubborn," he said. "I felt I'd taken on the responsibility of not letting the ranch go down the drain. McKay never asked me to try and save the place from bankruptcy, but I guess I took it on myself—I didn't want it to happen on my watch. Once I'd started, I wasn't about to give up." He looked abruptly at Stafford. "If you can't understand that, I don't think I can explain it to you. But that's the way it was."

"Even so, most men wouldn't put up with that kind of treatment from their employer unless they knew they were getting something out of it—something besides just a pay check. Wasn't it really because you thought you might benefit in a larger way from McKay eventually?"

There were harder, older lines in Ray's face than I had ever seen there before. "I never expected anything but my pay."

"By the time McKay's granddaughter inherited it, the ranch was on a much more stable footing financially, wasn't it?"

"Yes."

"Well, that would mean the reason you gave for your tenacity in staying with the job no longer existed. Why did you stay then?"

"I told you, there's nothing wrong with the ranch. Miss Campbell needed a foreman to run it and I agreed to stay on."

"You were fine with the idea of staying on in Severn Valley, at the Circle M, even after being questioned in connection with your employer's murder?"

"I didn't need to run away, if that's what you mean. I had no reason to leave unless I wanted to."

"You're engaged to be married to Miss Campbell now, aren't you?"

"Yes."

"That's quite convenient for you, isn't it? Even if McKay's will hadn't turned up, you stood to essentially gain control of the property in another way. As your wife's property the Circle M would be practically or even literally your own, supposing your name was added to the deeds after your marriage."

"Our engagement was an entirely separate thing, a personal matter. I couldn't ever have foreseen it."

"Are you so sure about that? Are you sure that after you were balked of the inheritance you expected, you didn't foresee this very opportunity when you found the new owner was a young and attractive woman who was willing to keep you on the Circle M payroll?"

"I told you I never expected any inheritance. Our engagement had nothing to do with McKay or any other person except ourselves."

Stafford looked at the judge, and looked at the jury, looked at Ray again, and said, "No further questions."

Well, this was what Carleton Kent had tried to prepare me for. To have what had been something beautiful between Ray and me pulled inside-out before a courtroom full of wide eyes and ears, and made to sound cheap and cold-blooded. I'd known it was coming, but the pit of my stomach still felt hot and cold and sick by turns, and I kept my eyes fastened to the back of the chair in front of me.

From seemingly a long ways off, I heard Judge Hampden's voice announcing a recess.

I went to lunch with the Crawleys at the Up & Down Café on Main Street. We didn't even try to go to Stevenson's, as Mr. Crawley was sure their dining-room would be packed to overflowing. Packed at closer quarters with out-of-town people too, he may have thought but didn't say. The Up & Down was packed enough, and loud with the accumulated volume of many voices talking at once, but at least there we had a booth to ourselves against the wall. I ate, because my stomach was growling after those long draining hours in the courtroom, but I don't remember tasting any of it. I tried to let the noise in the café remain a background, without separating out any individual voices from the crowd. I didn't care to hear what anyone had to say about the trial right now.

I was so focused on keeping within myself that when I realized someone had approached our table and stood almost at my elbow, I jumped. It was Dr. Burns, who was exchanging greetings with the Crawleys.

"Well," he said, "what do you think?"

"He's a clever boy," said Mrs. Crawley, who doubtless interpreted the question as she would have asked it herself had it been her nephew for the defense. "I think he's doing well. He made the jury sit up and pay attention a few times, as they're supposed to do."

"Mmm," said Rufus Crawley more moderately. "He made a good job out of that point about Lena getting shot, I thought. I don't know if any of them have put it together yet, but they're thinking about it. I wonder what he'd have done to counter all that stuff about Ray trying to get hold of the ranch through Lena if it wasn't for that?"

"If it wasn't for that, would there have been a case at all?" said Dr. Burns.

I was looking up at him as he spoke, and as he met my eyes something changed—his expression became shuttered, more non-committal, as if he had said more than he had intended to say. His overall manner then as always was so calm that it was only an infinitesimal change, but I was sure I had seen it. "That is, I think the circumstantial arguments would have been pretty evenly balanced on both sides. I wouldn't envy either counsel the job of fighting that one out."

Mr. Crawley said something about the district attorney that I didn't quite hear, and Dr. Burns answered him. I wasn't listening. My mind was analyzing what Dr. Burns had said, trying to find something wrong in it, or at least something to allow for that minute change in expression, but I couldn't find it. Nevertheless, I watched the doctor's back as he left our table and made his way toward the door of the crowded café. Not for the first time I wondered if he had had some ulterior motive in bringing his nephew here—or at least some reason he had not seen fit to confide in anyone else.

I remembered suddenly from yesterday's testimony that Dr. Burns had been away from home on the night of the murder—out on a call somewhere on those long, dark country roads where he spent most of his life. Where he and his old black car were an accepted presence at all hours and in all odd places.

Someone like that could fit the role of masterminding the cattle thieving which Garth McKay could have found out about. Someone with brains, and an expensive hobby…like rare books…

Suppose Dr. Burns had a very good reason to know Ray was innocent—could procuring a lawyer to defend him be a salve to conscience, or a debt to a sense of justice that would not permit a friend to pay unjustly for his crime?

I shook my head. Foolish. Foolish to jump at shadows now…

Stafford made his closing speech. Means, motive, and opportunity, he reminded the jury, were the criteria on which a case must be judged; and Ray Harper had all three. Three witnesses had testified he had never entered the Circle M bunkhouse before they fell asleep; the jury had only his own word for it that he had not left the ranch, only his own word for the time he had finally entered the bunkhouse. Ray Harper had no way of proving he had not been on the scene of the murder when the fatal shot was fired; he possessed the competence—more than competence—with a rifle to have fired that shot accurately from the distance indicated by the medical evidence. Motive? Again, the jury had only the defendant's own word for it that he did not know he would benefit by Garth McKay's death, to the tune of everything McKay owned. No other witness could positively affirm he had *not* known.

"Garth McKay's relentless harsh treatment of the defendant, which has been testified to by multiple witnesses," said Stafford, "was enough to provide a motive for revenge in itself; for far more significant, gentlemen, was the defendant's response to it. Or I should say his lack of response. The logical thing for a man in his situation would have been to leave it—to quit his job with McKay. That he stayed indicates an inducement strong enough to make him put up with McKay's treatment. If he believed he could succeed in getting his employer to bequeath him property he himself has described as desirable, any hardship or indignity he had to undergo would be worth it. If Garth McKay was dead, and Ray Harper inherited the Circle M, he would retain his position of control and management—minus the annoyance of being abused by McKay."

And no one had asked, no one seemed to have wondered (Stafford went on), *why* Garth McKay would bequeath his property to his foreman if he disliked him to the extent of browbeating and persecuting him as described. Adroitly he suggested to the jury that we had been looking at the situation the wrong way around. Ray Harper had been in a position to exercise significant influence and control over his employer, especially to take advantage of him when he was under the influence of drink. At some point he had manipulated McKay into making that will leaving the ranch to him. Stafford suggested that from that point on McKay was afraid of him, that his fear and dislike were manifested in the hostility and anger so many people had witnessed— and that his real reason for wanting the existence of the will kept secret was that he wanted Ray Harper to believe he had changed his mind and destroyed it. Stafford had to get a bit creative here; he theorized that McKay had originally put the will in the Cheyenne safe-deposit box and was waiting an opportunity to retrieve and destroy it, but that Ray had watched him too closely to allow him the chance to slip away to Cheyenne alone. This was what had precipitated the murder: McKay had to be killed before he could carry through with destroying the will.

The defendant's subsequent behavior following the murder, Stafford said, supported the idea that possession of the Circle M had been his aim from the first. It was easy to cite personal feelings as an explanation, but the fact remained that he had stayed at the Circle M, had managed to secure the confidence of McKay's granddaughter—reasserting himself in the same position of influence he had held over McKay—and now stood to gain by marriage the property that would have been his by inheritance. Stafford reiterated his opinion that this was not a careless, impulsive act of opportunism; it had all the hallmarks of being the defendant's fall-back plan from the moment he saw that the new owner was a young woman who would be open to this line of attack.

Based upon this strong line of reasoning, Stafford said, it was the jury's responsibility to find the defendant guilty of murder in the first degree.

He sat down. I took a deep breath, feeling like I was coming out of a bad attack of seasickness.

Carleton Kent got up. He still looked so much like a college boy that I half expected him to shuffle papers self-consciously, to shove his hands in his pockets, to stammer with a mixture of earnestness and naiveté. But he did none of those things. His face looked pale and his eyes unusually bright, and I realized that this was the moment when he was in his element. For the first time I could believe he was the person who had given those speeches printed in the newspapers. When he spoke, you listened, and paid no attention to anything except what he was saying.

"My opponent has invoked the time-honored trio of means, motive, and opportunity," he said, "which is logical in itself. But it's my intention to show you that two of these cannot stand without the third, and the third as the prosecution has presented it is weak.

"Opportunity can be summed up as a lack of alibi, and the fact that the defendant was outdoors alone for several hours on the night of the murder. He *could have* left the ranch to commit the crime, but the prosecution has failed to present any positive evidence that he did so.

"Means? Access to guns kept in the ranch house and bunkhouse. I would point out that three other men working there had that as well. For that matter, just about every man in this county owns one or more rifles, and so any man in the neighborhood would have had the means if he had decided to kill Garth McKay.

"This doesn't make a case. At the time of the murder, Ray Harper's inability to provide an alibi and slight circumstantial evidence linking him to the murder weapon were enough to direct suspicion toward him, but not enough to charge him with murder. No one could say that he had a motive aside from inferred dislike of McKay; and in that he wasn't necessarily unique. Remember, we've heard multiple witnesses testify that Garth McKay was"—I had the feeling that Carleton Kent was purposely not looking at me as he reeled off the words—"bad-tempered, abusive, unreasonable, and a drunkard; the sort of man who could have made many enemies. Plain dislike is not enough to be considered a motive, especially when it's common to many people.

"Let me say it again: *there was no case* until the discovery of a will bequeathing Garth McKay's property to his foreman. My opponent knows this, and that's why almost the entire case for the prosecution has focused on motive. Outside of that, *there is nothing but negative or circumstantial evidence to connect my client with this crime.*

"So let's examine the matter of Garth McKay's will. I want you to notice one thing, gentlemen of the jury—*we have not heard one single shred of positive evidence that Ray Harper had the slightest idea he would benefit by McKay's death!* All the testimony we *have* had about the controversial will has only served to shroud the reason for it, and the circumstances of its creation, in even deeper puzzlement and obscurity—obscurity that can never be penetrated now, unless the dead should speak.

"I submit that the very vagueness and uncertainty of the witnesses on this subject is a point in my client's favor. If they had wanted to, they could have invented much more definite-sounding lies to help clear him."

Kent was not a perambulator like the district attorney. He took a firm stand in one place with his feet slightly apart to speak. But he did turn to fix a quick, intent look on the jury when he came to a particularly vital point.

"Much has been made of Garth McKay's temper, and how he seemed to single out Ray Harper for harsh treatment. But I want to remind you that other witnesses freely acknowledged being on the receiving end of McKay's temper as well. Rather than draw the conclusion that Ray Harper was singled out for persecution, isn't it more reasonable to say that Garth McKay had a foul temper whenever provoked—and that he was hardest on Ray Harper simply because Ray was the only one who didn't allow himself to be pushed away? Everyone else, employees and acquaintances, were content to keep their distance and avoid the storm as much as possible—but Ray Harper's conscientiousness in the performance of his job made him keep closer to McKay, to press him for the answers and the authority he needed to keep the Circle M ranch above water and operating. Was it his fault if Garth McKay routinely bit the hand that helped him? It would have been easier to quit—but Ray Harper didn't take the easy way. His only reward was the loyalty of the men who worked under him—and a charge of murder.

"The idea that he could have pressured Garth McKay into making a will in his favor, presumably by threats of some sort, is frankly ridiculous. How do you threaten a man into writing his own death sentence? My opponent has actually made a very good point here, probably without intending it: you don't make a will leaving everything to a man you fear and distrust."

Kent was fully facing the jury now, choosing and shooting off his words like a man lighting firecrackers. "Have you considered the unlikeliness of an intelligent man like Ray Harper committing murder in a way that left him so completely open to suspicion if that will had turned up at the outset? His own actions on the night of the murder left him not even the slightest possibility of providing an alibi; everyone in Severn Valley knew he was a good shot. If Ray Harper had committed this murder in this particular way, it would have been a stupid crime…which doesn't fit with the carefully crafted, far-thinking plot the prosecution has tried to attribute to him."

Carlton Kent paused for a second, and then went on more deliberately. "As for the assertion that the defendant's relationship with Lena Campbell bears out his motive for wanting Garth McKay dead—again, it rests entirely on conjecture, entirely unable to be proved or disproved. You can't base your decision regarding a man's life on conjecture, gentlemen. But I do want you to pause and consider this assertion carefully for a minute, because here is the biggest flaw in the case against Ray Harper.

"The prosecution has behaved from the beginning," he said slowly, "as if there were no other possible suspects to be considered in the death of Garth McKay. In fact, the only reason attention focused on Ray Harper during the initial investigation was because there was no other person against whom even *this* much of a case could be made. Therefore, everyone seems to have assumed that no other such person exists.

"But I want you to remember one significant, very suggestive fact: On April 28th of this year, an attempt was made on Lena Campbell's life. The most positive statement I can make about *anything* connected with this case is that it is impossible for Ray Harper to have made that attempt! Not only is circumstantial evidence against it, but there was not the slightest shred of profit in it for him. She had made no will. The Circle M would have reverted to her next-of-kin or to the state on her death. She was not yet romantically involved with Ray Harper; he had not even the faintest grounds to *imagine* that he might profit by her death. He had no motive whatsoever. And yet, gentlemen of the jury, that attempt was made.

"Think very carefully about it for a moment. Lena Campbell had no known enemies in Severn County, and yet someone tried to kill her. Doesn't that present a very logical argument for the existence of someone else with a grudge against the McKay family? Someone whose hatred of Garth McKay did not stop with killing him, but extended even to a granddaughter that person had never seen before she came to this country last summer?

"I firmly believe you cannot consider the murder of Garth McKay without considering this attempted murder of his granddaughter as a piece that fits in somewhere. I've demonstrated conclusively that Ray Harper could have had no part in it. If my opponent were to hastily theorize some personal vendetta against Lena Campbell to suggest that he could, that would entirely invalidate his own argument that all Ray Harper's actions were directed toward the goal of obtaining the Circle M. Even if he *had* hated Lena Campbell for some reason, he would not have killed her—and this was no impulsive crime of passion, but a deliberate ambush— without first being secure of his inheritance.

"I also ask you to give some thought to the anonymous letter that led to the finding of the will and the formal charge of murder against the defendant. Here we *have* to acknowledge the action of an unknown person. The letter might have been sent by someone who merely had a grudge against Ray Harper, but also invites speculation that it was done by someone who wanted to see him charged in order to divert any possible suspicion from others. I feel entitled," said Carleton Kent sedately, "to engage in a little speculation of my own at this point.

"The motive of Garth McKay's real murderer is unknown. But because it is unknown does not mean it is less real, less valid than the conjectural, often contradictory motives the prosecution has tried to attribute to the defendant.

"If you are reasoning based on the prosecution's theories about motive, then you must also weigh in the balance the character of the man who stands accused, as it has been painted by the opinions of the people who know him best. Conjecture and opinion carry equal weight. But if, as I sincerely hope, gentlemen, you are going to make your decision based on facts...*only* those facts that can be stated as unquestionable...then I believe you will reach the correct verdict, and acquit Ray Harper of this charge of murder."

The jury was out for two hours.

It was now dusk. Through a window I could see the sky above the buildings in the cul-de-sac was pale, and there was a burnt-orange glow along the horizon in the west. The street lamps had come on, shedding small circles of glare over the dusty hoods of automobiles parked bumper to bumper along the curb.

The courtroom was still more than three-quarters full; most people had never left, or had only stepped out for a few minutes. I sat feeling very remote and alone, even though Mrs. Crawley and Mrs. Stevenson on either side of me were leaning back over their chairs to talk to each other behind my head.

Then the crack of the bailiff's gavel startled me, and for the final time that day the courtroom surged to its feet. Judge Hampden was back in his place; Ed Kenyon went to the corner door and brought Ray in again. The jury was filing back into the box, looking a little the worse for the heat and the long afternoon.

Judge Hampden spoke: "Gentlemen of the jury, have you reached a verdict?"

"We have, Your Honor. We find the defendant—not guilty."

CHAPTER XXV

The hills are shadows, and they flow
From form to form, and nothing stands;
They melt like mist, the solid lands,
Like clouds they shape themselves and go.

Tennyson: In Memoriam

M Y MEMORIES OF THOSE first few moments
come in patches. I heard exultation in Mrs.
Crawley's voice, though I didn't hear what she
said; I saw Carleton Kent jump to his feet, looking happy
and more boyish than ever. The dam of silence had broken;
the room was awash in voices. The reporters were climbing
over each other to be the first ones to the door. I felt warm
and sweaty. I caught a glimpse of Ray, who looked relieved,
but a little blank—he looked about the way I felt.

The banging of Judge Hampden's gavel hurt my
head, which was already beginning to ache with that little
piercing pain at the temples that comes from tension and
weariness. I remember laughing weakly for not much reason
and holding onto my hat as if I was afraid it would get
knocked off as Mr. Crawley steered us through the jostling
elbows of the outward-flowing crowd. Then Carleton Kent
somehow got us into an empty corridor outside where I was

reunited with Ray—Dr. Burns was there, and Robert Herrington, and there were congratulations and hand-shaking. I only remember standing there with Ray's arm around my shoulders, even that feeling a little mechanical, and neither of us saying very much, letting the others do all the exclaiming and expressions of satisfaction for us. I was tired—so tired. And that had to be the reason for the queer feeling of emptiness—didn't it?

When I closed my bedroom door behind me that night, I stood there for a moment in the near-dark with my hand still on the knob behind my back. I stood silently with all my senses turned inwards, trying to analyze my sensations.

What I had been striving for, hoping for, praying for all these last few weeks was accomplished. And yet now that I was alone with that knowledge, I didn't feel the enormous sense of relief and relaxing of strain I had expected to feel. It made no sense that with the matter of Ray's innocence finally resolved, I still had a nebulous feeling of something wrong.

There was a dim bar of illumination on the floor between the window and my bed; it was still comparatively lighter outside even though the night was mostly cloudy. Without switching on the light I took off my shoes and put them away, undressed and slipped on a nightgown. I went out and went barefoot down the hall to wash my face and hands in the bathroom, then came back and sat down by the bureau to brush out my hair, doing it by touch in the dark.

I couldn't see my reflection in the mirror, only a swimming dark outline of my head and the motions of my hands, but I scowled at it, picturing the bitter expression in my mind as if I could see it. How could I dare be dissatisfied already? Not three hours since the verdict was given and already I was giving way to the old uneasiness—childish, harping, rebellious because I couldn't have the answer to a question that never would be answered: *Who really killed him?*

I'd brushed my hair to silky smoothness, but my head felt tight. I put the brush down and ploughed all ten fingers through my hair, resting my elbows on the edge of the bureau and my temples in my palms. If Ray hadn't done it, someone else had. And for a reason that was knocking at my brain, that I didn't fully understand yet, I had to know who did it.

If the motive was unknown, the possibilities were broad. As Carleton Kent had said, any man in Severn County had the means—any man in the bunkhouse could have left it that night for as good an opportunity. And Garth McKay had not exactly endeared himself to anyone.

Tim McGreevy had had no love for his employer. I remembered the ugly look that could come over his face when he was angered, often by an outrage to justice as he saw it. And he had been very definite in court when he said he *knew* Ray was innocent.

Was it because he knew, as no one else could, what had really happened?

I wasn't sure whether I found the idea unsettling or attractive—which was alarming in itself. But I reasoned it out impartially. No—I summed up with a brief shake of my head—even a combination of Tim's sense of justice, loyalty to Ray, and dislike of Garth McKay didn't add up to an adequate motive for murder. The same went for Lane, who didn't have half Tim's resentful temper.

Suppose one of them—Tony, for instance—had been

involved in the rustling, and my grandfather had found him out? He could have killed him to prevent exposure. Tony might have regretted afterwards that his emphatically voiced opinions about McKay's treatment of his foreman had turned suspicion toward Ray, but he couldn't have backtracked on the witness-stand, not with himself to protect.

But that was all pure conjecture—all grasping at entirely imaginary straws. It would do even less than the other theory.

And if I couldn't make out a case against anyone within the small circle of the Circle M, I couldn't begin to try against anyone beyond it. A strange sense of desperation rose up in me.

I got up and went to the window. I couldn't see anything outside but the indistinct blackness of the great trees stretching their arms over the house. Why did I need to know the truth? Because only the truth could keep my thoughts from circling back to a creeping, sinuous doubt that had wound its coils through my mind. I hated it; I felt it was unfaithful and unworthy, but some other part of me hinted darkly that it was dangerous to stuff it down and try not to listen to it.

So many times during those nightmare weeks I'd said to myself, and meant it too, that I wouldn't care whether the murder was ever solved or not so long as Ray was safely acquitted. I'd never considered that the jury's verdict might not be enough to satisfy *me.*

I'd gone into that courtroom fully prepared for anything the prosecutor might say about him. But somehow, even while thinking I had not, I'd let Stafford's artfully strewed seeds of doubt fall into some crevice of my mind and take root there. The jury of twelve must have been made of stouter stuff than I—less fanciful, less credulous.

Or perhaps, not knowing Ray as I did, they hadn't seen the one thing that I did.

I knew that whatever had happened between Ray and my grandfather, the whole truth had not been told in court.

I turned abruptly away from the window and began to put away the clothes I'd left lying across my bed. I did it mechanically, but with every shutting of a drawer or click of the wardrobe latch I was reviewing things I'd heard in court. I knew just how Carleton Kent had won, and how finely his case turned on one point: the link he had stressed between my grandfather's murder and the shot fired at me. There was only one way a case against Ray would hang together: by taking that attempt on me out of the equation and treating it as what it first appeared to be on the surface, a totally random and unconnected event.

A sudden thought darted through my brain. Could that shot fired at me have possibly been because I had suggested a new way of combating the rustling problem?

I sat down abruptly on the foot of my bed, and my hand found a curve of the metal railing beside me and wrapped round it. Could it be that obvious, and I'd over-looked it this long? I'd always taken for granted the in-significance of my suggestion about random fence checks in the whole scheme of things. But Brock Chambers' half-dozen head had been the only casualties since most of the neighbors had adopted our suggestion—my suggestion.

No—no. It was stupid. More imagination. If I'd told that story to Carleton Kent, he'd have—

He'd have been dead sure never to let a breath of that idea be heard in court, because it could have wrecked his case.

I got into bed and pulled the quilt up over my shoulders, even though it was a warm night. I lay with my eyes wide open, staring up at the ceiling, but seeing other things. Remembering. I couldn't make judgments on anything that had happened before I came to Wyoming. But if I did what Kent had been careful not to do and put that random rifle-shot on one side, I could interpret every word, every look, every moment of my relationship with Ray, from the moment we first met, based on the assumption that he was guilty. That it was the ranch he had been after all along.

He'd admitted that he changed his mind about staying after he saw me. Had it been true what Stafford had said—that I was his second chance?

Had he seen that it would be easy for him? Seen that I was willing to be led, influenced—ready to look up to him in wide-eyed admiration? Ready to fall for him, if he took the trouble to attract me?

Perhaps that was why he didn't want Bill Sutherland to buy the ranch. Once out of my hands, that was the end of his chances. It had been very easy for him to prejudice me against Sutherland from the beginning, to foster a dislike in me for the harsh-spoken older man.

He couldn't have had anything to do with the attempt to kill me. I remembered the reassuring safety of leaning back into the crook of his arm when I was dizzy and sick with pain, and closed my eyes because the recollection suddenly hurt. Even then, all his solicitude, all his concern for me could have been because his chance of getting the ranch was gone if anything happened to me.

The day he had told me he loved me…everything he had said, about going away and leaving me to discover my own feelings, had all sounded so sincere. But even his attempt at quitting could have been deliberate, meant to force the issue between us without the advances seeming to come from him.

That day in the office, the way his eyes had gone to the scrap of paper in my hand...that fragment with his name and accusing words on it...

Those stealthy steps downstairs at midnight...which he had said so very positively were nothing...

With a sudden chill I understood why Carleton Kent had instructed Cathy and I to say nothing about that night.

Could Ray have been searching for my grandfather's missing will?

Far better to marry me and acquire the property that way, than to have the will turn up and re-open all the suspicions against him again.

It was crazy. It was stupid. I didn't really *believe* any of the things I was thinking. But that suggestible half of my brain kept telling me they *could have been.* The sane, calm, everyday part of me believed that every word, every touch, every look of Ray's, every bit of the love I believed I had, was truth. But the chilling thing was, if you made just one assumption—that he had killed my grandfather—everything he had ever said or done for me could also be interpreted to support it.

And the other half of me shrank in terror.

I shut my eyes and pulled the sheets up to my chin, twisting to hide half my face in my pillow. *The jury said 'not guilty.' The jury said 'not guilty...'*

CHAPTER XXVI

And wilt thou leave me thus,
And have no more pitye
Of him that loveth thee?
Alas, thy cruelty!
And wilt thou leave me thus?
    Say nay! say nay!

Sir Thomas Wyatt: An Appeal

HAYING SEASON WAS upon us as soon as the trial was over. Between the rush of hiring the extra crew, laying in supplies, and putting the machinery in order, and the all-day grind of haying and cooking, Ray and I were both so busy that we didn't have more than a few minutes in a day to spend alone together; and so we didn't talk of much besides the work at hand. Perhaps we could have made more time if we wanted, but I think that I, at least, made a temporary coward's refuge out of the busyness.

All through those weeks I couldn't escape a continual sense of tension, even though nothing unusual was happening to justify it. I began to have nightmares—disjointed, fragmented things in which only a moment or two stood out clearly and could be remembered next morning. Always those moments centered around Ray—around his hands. Sometimes I saw them turning over my grandfather's body on the side of a road in the gray dawn, sometimes cocking a rifle; but more often doing ordinary things, like knotting a rope or jerking open the stiff-rusted latch of a gate, which in the dream seemed to be invested with a peculiar horror that had nothing to do with the actions themselves.

The weather was gray and lowering, with thunder frequently muttering over behind the hills, so the pressure was on to get the hay in before the rains came. Ray looked haggard, as even the strenuous haying season hadn't made him look last year—I thought that he wasn't sleeping well either. You didn't come through being tried for murder, after all, without its leaving some mark upon you. My heart ached for him...and yet whenever I was around him I caught myself watching his hands. Watching them make the most common gestures: pointing out something down the field to one of the men, or taking the cold thermos I handed to him, and wondering if they had ever...Or finding my eyes lingering on one of his hands as it rested on his hip or on the side of a hayrack, while I thought I was listening to the men talk; but hearing Stafford's voice in my head, or those demons of doubt that had swirled around me the night after the trial.

One afternoon when I was in Severn Valley for groceries, I saw Carleton Kent taking leave of his uncle at the bus stop where the outbound bus was about to leave town. Neither of them saw me. Dr. Burns had his back to me, but in the brief glimpse I had of Kent's face I thought he looked troubled. I hadn't known he was in town. So far as I knew he was back in Laramie, where he'd returned immediately after the trial; I had no idea what he might be doing back in Severn Valley, though I suppose it ought to be natural for him to come and see his uncle. Somehow it added to my uneasiness.

At home, in the fields, in the kitchen, I felt I was waiting for something to happen; waiting for some kind of storm to break as inevitably as the heavy thunderheads were bound to break over the meadows before long. I was holding it off by pretending to ignore it, but it was coming.

At last the hay was in. The extra hands filtered off, either down the road to the next haying job or driven into town in the truck by Tim to catch the bus for Claxton or Cheyenne, and the Circle M was abruptly quiet, stripped of the extra voices and the noise of machinery.

I was in the office; it was dusk. We had paid off the last of the hay crew that day, and I was sitting at the table looking over grocery and hardware receipts, entries in my bank book, and scribbled notes of expenses, trying to figure up what had been spent during the haying weeks.

Because of where the office was situated, quite often I didn't hear right away if somebody came into the kitchen by the back door. But still Ray's step in the hallway outside the office door made me jump. Hastily to try and cover it, I gathered up my notes and receipts into a pile, a pen held between my fingers, and glanced up at him as he came in. Ray walked over to the window behind me and leaned his shoulder against the frame, his whole body slouching in a tired, indifferent way.

"Thank God that's over," he said, but somehow he didn't sound as if he meant it.

I wanted to say, "You look tired." But I couldn't bring myself to do it, because I knew that on our old footing it would draw us closer together, produce some show of affection, and I shrank from that.

But the silence was unnatural, and as the long moment stretched out I had a growing conviction that Ray knew it. When he turned his head I dropped my eyes to the paper under my hand, missing meeting his gaze by the fraction of a second.

He said, "Lena, what's wrong?"

I'd been dreading this. I knew we couldn't go on this way.

"Nothing," I said, my voice unnaturally normal, searching senselessly for a place to write something on the uppermost scrap of paper.

"It's not 'nothing.' You haven't looked me straight in the eye since the trial."

It sounded like an accusation, and it touched on the raw because I knew I was guilty. "That isn't so."

"Yes, it is. I'm not an idiot, Lena. You haven't been acting like yourself for weeks. Did you really think I wouldn't notice?"

I got up, my feet tangling with the chair legs a little, and leaned against the table. "Ray, it's just...frazzled nerves, I guess. I've been run off my feet and I haven't been sleeping well."

Ray stood very still and looked at me for a minute. I looked into his eyes, with the lines and shadows of tiredness around them, and saw only searching, searching; and for a minute I thought he believed me.

Then he said very quietly, "You think I did it, don't you."

I wanted to say no. But the sum of all my doubts seemed to be swelling up inside my throat, choking me, telling me it would be hypocrisy if I did. I wanted to speak, but found I needed all my strength just to breathe.

Ray still spoke quietly. "You think I haven't been here before? I went through it all, a year and a half ago. Seeing it in people's eyes, hearing it in their voices...people who knew me and liked me. Knowing that all that wasn't enough to keep them from wondering." His hands clenched and he rested the right one on the windowsill...my eyes flickered to it and back to his face. "I thought I'd lived it down. I thought I had another chance."

He went on, still in that flat, almost detached voice. "I thought, for a little while—you were innocent enough—stubborn enough—to stick to your first ideas. I should've known better. I could tell as soon as I saw you in the hall after the trial, something was different. I knew just looking at you."

"It wasn't," I said desperately. "I wasn't. Ray, could you ask any human being to sit through that and not be a little shaken, even if they *knew* everything they were hearing was twisted to look wrong?"

Ray took a step toward me, and like a spooked horse I fell back a step, stumbling past the corner of the table. For the first time there was a tinge of anger in his voice. "That's your trouble, isn't it, Lena—you'll believe anything you're told. There was a time when you believed anything I said to you was golden truth."

"Maybe I've grown up a little," I blurted, unthinking.

"I don't think so. There's only one difference: now you'll believe anything you're told about me. Nothing's really changed, has it?"

I realized that the gray dusk had grown so thick in the unlighted room that I could no longer see his face distinctly, even though he had come close. The furniture blended into the corners of the room like the shading in a charcoal drawing, and I suddenly felt adrift, groping for reality in a strange shadowland. But I heard the throb of intensity in Ray's voice: anger, passion, or a mix of both.

"I've got nothing left, Lena. I've lost my good name, I've lost the trust of everybody I know. They'll pretend, but

I know it's gone. I can't lose you too. Don't do this to me, Lena!"

The office was suddenly very dark, and the consciousness sprang up in me like the black shadows in the corners that we were alone in the house. Oddly enough it was Ray's own words that came back to me, from somewhere long ago: *"If you can't trust a man, don't let him see you're afraid of him…"*

I couldn't move, and the next instant Ray had me pulled close in his arms, his voice fierce and broken. "Lena, I love you—I love you—don't do this to me—"

His touch and my feeling toward him were so much a habit that my face turned up to his and I let him kiss me. But in the midst of it, I felt his hand on the back of my neck, and a dozen fragmented flashes of my nightmares swirled through my brain…and I tore away with a sharp intake of breath. Ray's encircling arms kept me close against him and he tried to kiss me again, but I suddenly struggled like a snared bird, and let out one breathless, frightened sob.

Ray stopped, though he still held me, and for a few seconds stood still in the dark. I had managed to bring my arms up and brace them between us, holding myself off from him a little, and in spite of my best efforts I could hear myself trembling as I breathed. "Lena," he whispered, "Lena, I didn't mean to…I'm sorry…"

He bent his head so for an instant his cheek brushed mine, but again I strained away. "Let me go," I panted, and turning, I pulled away from Ray's now unresisting arms and fled from the office. I ran up the stairs, into my room and shut the door behind me.

The house was quiet enough that even over the hammering of my heart in my ears I could hear Ray's footsteps as he came out into the hall and paused there. I fumbled for the lock on my bedroom door, took hold of it with both hands and turned it. It stuck, scraped, and then gave in to my efforts and rasped into place.

He had to have heard it.

The action suddenly seemed horrible, irrevocable— as if by turning the lock, with Ray there to hear and understand, I had put something between us far more implacable than a door. How had we come to this point, that I had been frightened enough to do it?

After half a minute of perfect silence, I heard him turn and cross the hall, and the screen door squeaked gently. He was gone.

CHAPTER XXVII

Since there's no help, come let us kiss and part.
Nay, I have done, you get no more of me;
And I am glad, yea glad with all my heart,
That thus so cleanly I myself can free.
Shake hands for ever, cancel all our vows...

Michael Drayton: Idea 61

I LET THE SCREEN door creak slowly closed behind me and went down the back steps to the yard. The sky was a solid, uniform gray, and here under the trees everything stood still in that dim, moist-feeling hush you get on cloudy mornings with a promise of rain. Over by the chicken-coop a rooster crowed—not the first crow of the morning, for I had been lying in bed wide awake before dawn when that one came.

Over behind the barn, near the back gate to the horse pasture, I could see Ray putting his saddle on Sarge. I slowly drew in my breath, straightening my shoulders a little, and walked in that direction.

Partway across the yard I met Lane, coming from the other pasture gate leading Junior. When he saw me he changed direction a little as if he wanted to speak to me, so I slowed my steps and waited for him. We both said "good morning," but after a first look at me Lane's glance dropped self-consciously to his boots for a second—I thought he must be able to plainly see the marks of strain and sleeplessness in my face, but felt it would be presumption to even let on that he noticed.

"I wanted to ask," he said, "do you want me to start doing the rounds on the fences again? We haven't been all around them since before—since before haying started, so I thought it might be time for another check."

"Yes, you're right," I said. I felt like I'd put a hundred miles between me and the old worry of cattle rustling, but I didn't want Lane to think I was unappreciative. His serious, sympathetic eyes, like a concerned faithful dog's, touched the little piece of unwrung heart that I had left. "Thanks, Lane. You can start on it whenever you're free."

He touched the brim of his hat and moved on. I waited for Junior to cross in front of me and then resumed my walk to the barn, toward Ray. I had no plans for anything to say, or any idea what he might say, or how he might look at me. But avoidance wasn't going to fix anything. After those draining sleepless hours, none of the wild swirling emotions of last night were left; just a sober calm, like a flat lake after a storm. I was willing to believe things might be mended. Maybe we had both behaved idiotically last night, and the light of morning would show it in proper perspective.

Ray glanced up from tightening his cinch as I slowly approached. His hat was pushed back so I could see how his brown hair waved over his forehead, and as his eyes met mine I felt a swell of yearning feeling toward him. I couldn't think of anything to say, but I looked the question instead—the question of how he would react to the sight of me.

Ray looked away for just long enough to thread the end of the cinch through the ring and pull the stirrup down, and then he turned and stood there with his hand resting on

Sarge's flank.

"I'm sorry about last night," he said. "I was...but it's no excuse. I'd never hurt you, Lena. But I never should have put my hands on you like that, or raised my voice the way I did." He leaned forward a little, looking into my face. "Are you okay?"

I managed a shaky smile. "I was a little—overwrought too. I guess we both were."

"I'm sorry," he said. "Can you forgive me?"

I nodded.

Ray exhaled as if in relief. He came over to me as he had done a hundred times before and put his hands on my waist. Without even consciously thinking it, I stiffened.

Ray stood perfectly still for a minute. I couldn't make myself look up, so I didn't see his face.

He said, in that quiet voice, "What's the matter?"

"N—nothing."

"Nothing, hell! You can't keep saying 'nothing' and then act like you've got an electric shock every time I touch you. What's happened?"

I felt helpless, because the whispered words that I wrenched out were the absolute truth. "I don't...know."

Ray had let his hands drop, so now there was a little space between us. There was another pause before he spoke. "You can't be sure, can you?"

He knew the answer, though I couldn't give it. There was silence again. Beside us, Sarge lifted a hind hoof and stamped it once, twice on the ground, and lowered his head to snuff at a few stray wisps of hay lying in the dust.

When Ray spoke at last, his voice had that remote, shut-off sound it had had in the first weeks of our ordeal. "Maybe we made a mistake."

The words were a stab of pain, but at the same time I

felt the relief of a heavy weight lifted off me. I had to look up at him, because I couldn't shirk my share of a moment like this.

Ray said, "If you can't be sure of this, you'd never be able to trust me about anything."

I was glad he'd said it, so I didn't have to. I didn't want to hurt him any more. I slid the engagement ring off my finger, working it over the one knuckle where it was tight, and made as if to hold it out to him, but Ray shook his head. "I don't want it. Keep it and do what you like with it."

"But you paid—"

"Never mind that; I don't want it." His voice was sharp.

Slowly I put the ring into the pocket of my corduroy jacket, desperately despising myself for being so inarticulate —longing for some sort of justification, some consolation. "Ray, I don't...I wish..."

Ray smiled, a small, tight smile. "It wasn't meant to be, that's all," he said. "Don't think any more about it."

He took Sarge by the bridle and turned him about, then put his foot in the stirrup and swung into the saddle. I heard the whip and slash of reins against the horse's flank, and then the hard clatter of Sarge's hooves striking out in a round gallop along the road around the meadow. I stood there biting my lip hard until the sound faded in the distance. Then I went out beyond the horse pasture and found a hay-stack and threw myself down against the far side of it and cried until I didn't have any strength left to cry more. I knew it was because I still loved him, even though I would never know whether he had murdered a man.

Then I got up and wiped my nose and eyes, and brushed the hay from my clothes, and went to find Tony and ask him how the salt blocks in the lower pastures were holding out.

The rain started in the night, a slow drizzle. It was still coming down next morning. I didn't think I could stand to be alone in the house all morning, with every window weeping with streams of water running down the panes, looking out at the water-sopped trees and muddy yard, with nothing to listen to but the ceaseless sloshing and trickling of rain in the gutters. So I put on my raincoat and rubbers and my oldest gray cloche hat, and took the truck and drove into town.

By the time I got to the hotel the sky was a lighter gray and there had been a break in the rain, though I could still feel light flecks of it on my face when I got out of the truck. Stevenson's looked deserted inside and out. I slammed the truck door with a spatter of wet drops and mounted to the boardwalk, the steamy smells of summer rain and wet wood washing around me. The bell over the door jangled as I opened it and stepped into the dim lobby. There was no one at the front desk, and the sound of the bell didn't bring anyone out from the office, but in the dining-room Cathy was at the far end of the lunch counter watching rather drearily as her one customer, a dried-up little old man, painstakingly counted out the price of his lunch in nickels and pennies. I pulled off my hat and unfastened the belt of my raincoat and went through into the dining-room, and then I saw there was one other person sitting at the nearer end of the lunch counter. It was Carleton Kent.

He glanced at me as I slid onto a stool to his right, and then looked away again. He was sitting hunched over with his arms folded on the counter, an empty plate and a half-empty coffee cup in front of him, and the few streaks of dampness on the sleeves of his coat were faded enough to show he had been sitting indoors some time. In keeping with the afternoon and with my own mood, he did not look happy.

We both sat in silence while the old man shuffled out behind us and Cathy put the coins in the cash register and shut the drawer. Then she turned around to face us. She gave me a grim, appraising look.

"You're in the wrong place too," she said. "The bar has a neon sign."

I looked at Carleton Kent. "Too?"

He gave a thin smile with an edge of sarcasm to it, and with one hand pushed his empty plate across the counter toward Cathy. "I've never had lunch before in a place where I got service so obviously meant to tell me not to come back again."

"We're not the only place in town that serves lunch."

"You happen to be the first one I've tried. My uncle is out on a call, and I didn't want to put his housekeeper to the extra trouble of giving me lunch."

"You've been hanging around Severn Valley for more than just lunch a lot lately."

"I have an uncle here, if it's any of your business."

"You don't need Dr. Burns for a diagnosis, if that's what you want. I can give it to you free." Cathy folded her arms and gave him a pointed look over the salt and pepper shakers. "You've got a galloping case of who-really-did-it."

Carleton Kent looked down at the countertop between his arms for a second. Then he looked up at Cathy, his forehead knit in the tense, earnest way that prompted sympathy for how keenly he felt things, no matter what the circumstances. "I won a case," he said. "I got a verdict of not guilty. That's supposed to be my job. But for the first time since I've been in practice, I'm not pleased with it. For the first time, I don't know whether my client told me the truth or not. And I don't like that, because I feel I should know. I want to be able to trust my own instincts."

"Maybe you just haven't had enough clients," said Cathy brutally.

Carleton Kent bowed ironically, as well as a man can do while sitting on a stool at a counter. "May be. If I had, maybe I'd have known better than to take this one."

There was a crash as Cathy's indignant unfolding of arms upset the salt and pepper. "Why, you—"

"No, *you* listen. I'll tell you something you don't know. Ray *wanted* me to put him on the stand; he *wanted* to face cross-examination by the prosecutor. He told me he wanted to clear himself in the eyes of everybody in this town, not just in the eyes of the jury; and yet—and yet—" He thumped his fist on the edge of the counter in frustration. "I had the feeling he was holding something back the whole time, just as I did when I talked to him before the trial. I *know* it, and it doesn't make sense!"

"Oh, so just because you've got a feeling in your bones—that's a swell thing for a lawyer to go on, isn't it?— you've got to go around stirring up doubts and making trouble—"

"No...no, Cathy, it isn't his fault," I said wearily.

"What isn't his fault? He did his job, didn't he? If the jury and every other reasonable person are satisfied, why does he have to keep haunting this town looking like a whipped dog, trying to pick holes in his own arguments and make problems where there aren't any!"

"Oh, let him do what he wants!" I said. "It's certainly better than anything you people achieved by looking the other way and keeping your mouths shut because you were afraid of whose toes you might step on."

In the utter silence that followed—Cathy being flabbergasted, I imagine—I realized that Carleton Kent's eyes had fastened on my left hand. I wanted to move it, to drop it out of sight in my lap, but I couldn't bring myself to such an obvious action...even though I knew, once a few seconds had passed, that Cathy must have seen what he was looking at too.

"Thanks for the vote of confidence," said Kent quietly. He got up from his stool, reached in his coat pocket for a dollar and put it on the counter, and walked out of the dining-room.

The bell over the front door jingled at his departure, and the chime of the cash register sounded in counterpoint as Cathy deposited the dollar and shoved the drawer closed again. She glanced at me. "Coffee?" she said neutrally.

I shook my head.

Cathy removed Kent's unfinished coffee and empty plate from the counter, emptied out the coffee cup and stacked the dishes in the sink. Then she came back and leaned her elbows on the counter, her hands clasped in front of her.

"Where's your ring, Lena?" she said.

All I could think of to say, after a weary ten seconds of searching for words, was to repeat what Ray had said: "Maybe we made a mistake."

"Oh, Lena!" Cathy burst out deploringly, and I put my head down, shaking it in futile protest, though I knew I should have expected this. "Do you think anybody who knew the two of you would believe that? Lena, *don't* tell me it's because of this stupid murder. All you've been through and you're going to let it come between you like this now?"

"Where do you suggest we put it? Under the rug?"

"It's ridiculous that you can even think such a thing about Ray! He didn't kill McKay. He's not that kind of a person!"

I spoke through clenched teeth. "It's much, much easier for you to talk like that than any of this is for me! I don't need you to tell me anything about Ray. Do you think I haven't heard it all a hundred times—from myself? Honestly, Cathy, you've talked more than enough already! The way you bite people's heads off over this case you might as well be in love with Ray yourself."

It was the sort of thing you throw in out of spite, not even half serious. I'd have fully expected Cathy to lash back scathingly, but instead, she flushed scarlet and bit her lip. She said nothing for the time it took the color in her face to die down. And I stared across the counter at her with the feeling that perhaps, finally, I'd arrived at the last straw.

"All right," Cathy said at last. "All right, you might as well know. But it's not like you think. I was sixteen the first time Ray came in here for lunch. And I thought he was wonderful. Back then, if he'd ever looked at me twice, I'd have been ready to jump. But he never did. And—" She lifted her hands, palms outward, in a futile, inarticulate gesture. "I don't know. It's not something you can explain very well. But when you see somebody every week for month after month and nothing clicks, I guess you realize it isn't meant to be. I got over it long before you ever came around, and I doubt Ray ever had a clue. But I still think he's a swell human being, as much as I ever did, and I *do—not—believe* he shot that old man!"

And that, I thought, was my last straw of hope washing away down a river. I put my head in my hands and let out a long, ragged sigh. Cathy's staunch belief in Ray's innocence had upheld me many a time, when, even though I wouldn't admit it to myself, I couldn't trust my own. But did her belief rest on any firmer a foundation than mine had done? No—it didn't.

"I believe you," I said at last. "I understand—really I do. But...that means you're just one more person who can never be completely objective about him."

"It's nice to know you've got such a high opinion of my intelligence," said Cathy bitterly.

"You know it's not that. But *stop* trying to make my judgments for me. All right, so you're not in love with him. For that very *reason*, it's different for you than it is for me. You can afford not to be objective. At the end of the day, it doesn't cost you anything to stick up for a friend. But you can't *marry* a man if you've got the least, faintest shadow of a doubt about him!"

"No," said Cathy after a long minute. "You can't." She sounded weary and resigned.

She turned her back to the counter again. I sat and look at the napkin-holder in front of me while she moved to the sink, turned on the tap and picked a cup off the stacked dishes there. There was silence for a few minutes excepting the running water and muted clink of dishes within, and the whistle of wind that had picked up without, as Cathy washed her last two customers' plates and cups and put them in the drying rack. Then she wiped her hands on a towel, turned around and leaned on the counter opposite me. "I'm sorry," she said. "I'm no help. I just want things to turn out right for both of you, that's all."

"I know," I said. "But just...don't try and twist things around to make them be perfect. Because you can't." I looked across at her, feeling the expression in my eyes to be even bleaker than that in her own. "You just can't."

CHAPTER XXVIII

Storm at the top, and when we gained it, storm
Round us and death…

Alfred Tennyson: Idylls of the King

B Y THE TIME I left Stevenson's the wind had stiffened, so it almost blew me back through the door as I came out. I pushed forward into it and got down off the boardwalk, the skirts of my raincoat flying, scrambled into the truck and shut the door with a bang, the shelter inside the cab a relief. The whole landscape had changed. The sky was charcoal-colored again; as I drove through town stray newspapers and bits of litter scudded across the streets; power lines swooped and danced between their poles, and the sign of the filling station was swinging wildly as I passed it.

     Out on the open road halfway home, the wind was so strong that the grasses lay down flat and small branches torn from trees who knows how far away flew on the gusts like storm-driven birds. The force with which it buffeted the truck so I could feel the pull on the steering wheel scared me a little. I had driven these roads many times in many weathers, but never in weather where I feared the truck might flip over if I didn't keep a steady grip on the wheel.

But I made it home safely at last. The wind had dropped a little by the time I parked the truck under the trees and got out, as if the worst of the windstorm had spent itself, though big sparse drops of rain were falling again as I ran for the house.

I hung up my damp raincoat in the hall and put my hat away upstairs. Then I sat down at the kitchen table with my chin in my hand and my eyes resting on vacancy. I had nothing to do and nothing to think about except for things I didn't want to think about. I'm not quite sure how long I sat there. The house was quiet except for the sound of the rain, which had increased to a steady, driving patter. From time to time it slashed a little harder against the window, then settled down again to blend with the steady ticking of the kitchen clock.

Suddenly I heard the swift clump of boots on the back steps and the door swung wide to admit Tim, his hat and slicker streaming. He went straight across to the cupboards and began opening and closing them one after another, rummaging through the shelves looking for something.

"Where's that old flask of brandy that used to be in here? You didn't get rid of it, did you?" he said.

"No—I think it's on the top shelf; try the one on the end." I was on my feet. "What's the matter?"

Tim didn't answer till he'd banged the door of one cupboard and reached deep into the top shelf of another. "I came back for the truck," he said. "Lane's hurt."

He turned from the cupboard with the flask in his hand, his face almost impersonally set under the wet brim of his Stetson. "Can you get a couple of blankets, and some clean towels, and those spare slickers? And an old sheet or something if you've got one we can tear up."

I moved quickly. "Yes. There's some blankets in a bottom drawer in the hall bedroom if you want to get those, and the slickers are in the hall closet. I'll get the other stuff."

I raced upstairs to the linen closet, loaded my arms with towels of a few different sizes and with one hand tugged out a threadbare cotton sheet to sacrifice. On the way back I made a detour into my bedroom and threw the stuff on my bed, and quickly changed my dress for shirt, jeans and boots.

When I got back to the kitchen Tim had the blankets and slickers on the table along with the old brandy flask and the first-aid kit, and I put the towels down beside them. I pulled my corduroy jacket from its hook by the door and thrust my arms into the sleeves, and then began to put on my hat and slicker. Tim said, "You don't have to come."

"I'm coming."

I made all the supplies into a bundle with the slickers on the outside to keep the rest dry, and Tim held the back door open for me. The truck was standing in the yard running with its lights on, the rain slanting down in the headlight beams, and Tony was around back of it just shoving something into the bed. As we got near Tim called over to him, "Wide enough?"

"Think so."

Tony started to swing up into the bed of the truck himself but Tim waved him off. "Take Jericho and follow us. You're gonna have to lead Knockout back."

Tim and I got into the truck and I wedged my slicker-wrapped bundle half between us and half on my lap. Tim let in the clutch, there was a clashing of gears, and the truck started. As we turned I caught a glimpse of Tony on Jericho, hat pulled low over his face, his slicker and the horse's dark coat shining under the headlights. The lights swept across the wet face of the barn as the truck completed the full circle, and then we drove under the trees behind it and out the rutted road between the horse pasture and the meadow.

I didn't speak until we had passed under the dripping belt of trees that arched over the road and were driving down the open slope beyond. In my mind I'd already been over every accident or injury involving horses that I could think of, and I knew there could be other possibilities beyond my knowledge. "Is it bad?"

"His leg's broken," said Tim. He slid his hand to the top of the steering wheel, his eyes on the road ahead.

"Was he thrown? Or did...his horse fall on him?"

"He was riding Knockout," said Tim slowly. "Knockout must have rolled over on his leg, unless it was just the fall that broke it—but Knockout didn't fall on his own. He was shot at."

For a few seconds I couldn't take the words in. I stared at the puddled road over the lurching hood of the truck. "Shot?"

"Yeah. Knockout had a graze across his flank, easy to see a bullet made it...it happened up on the ridge ...Knockout must have jumped when he was hit. They went right over the edge."

I felt sick. I couldn't think of anything to say. My hands stuck with moisture to the surface of the yellow slicker atop the bundle in my lap, and the windshield wiper worked steadily.

Tim took the left-hand fork at the bottom of the long pasture, a seldom-used way twisting up into the trees where I wasn't even sure the truck could go. The road was bumpy and narrow, winding between high banks with small but deep-washed ditches on each side that a wheel might easily slide into, and Tim had to slow down as we rocked over gnarled tree roots that raised great lumps in the ground. Here under the canopy of trees it was almost dark, but we were sheltered from the rain, with only an occasional splat of water from a branch hitting the windshield. Tim guided the truck around a climbing hairpin bend, the noisy engine sounding like it was laboring at the elevation, and then pressed his foot on the accelerator up the length of a short straight slope. At the top of the incline he turned off from the last vestiges of the petering-out track, threading a gap between two tree trunks. The truck tires clawed at the long wet grass and we skidded a little, and I sat up straight on the edge of my seat as if that would help keep our balance.

I hadn't given much thought to where we were heading. But as we emerged from the shelter of the trees onto the beginning of an open ridge climbing gradually ahead of us toward the sky, I recognized it, and said almost involuntarily, "Not—here?"

"Up at the top—the steepest part."

We trundled along the ridge, upward into the rain; the woods receding on our right, the valley somewhere down to the left. Ahead, the long, open expanse of beaten-down grass, against the stormy sky. The ceaselessly waggling windshield wiper cleared my view of it for only a few seconds at a time before the rain blotted it again. A blur that I knew was the great rock, and something else near it, were just beginning to loom up in my vision when Tim slowed down. He said, "Sit still, I'm going to turn the truck here where there's room."

The tires jounced over rocks as he made the three-point turn, and I didn't dare look out my window to see how close we were to the brow of the hill. When we were facing in the opposite direction Tim backed the truck, one eye on the rear-view mirror, as far up the ridge as he could go, and then finally shifted gears, set the brake and shut off the engine. I opened my door, shoving it and holding it with my foot because my arms were full, and slid down into the wet, matted tall grass.

In the lee of the big rock three saddle horses stood in a knot with heads and tails lowered against the wet wind. A little nearer, five or six yards from the rock, Lane lay flat in the trampled grass at the edge of the steep slope, covered over with Ray's rain slicker. Ray was kneeling beside him, and another man stood by leaning over them with his hands on his knees—as I drew near I recognized Brock Chambers. Lane's left leg was stretched out awkwardly, and after one glance I didn't look that way again. Ray looked up at me as I got down on my knees across from him, but he didn't say anything, seeming to accept my being there without questioning.

Lane was conscious, but shivering uncontrollably, and there was little recognition in his eyes as I leaned over him. His face was colorless except for a purple bruise along one scraped cheekbone, and his parted lips were a horrible bluish color. I knew it was the shock and exposure, more than the broken leg itself, that was the danger.

Behind me, I heard Tony's voice say, low, "I'm going to kill somebody for this."

I pulled apart my bundle and passed the heaviest of the folded blankets across to Ray. Nobody told me what to do, but in the need of the moment I seemed to have been here and done all this before. I slipped a folded towel carefully under Lane's head, and with another dried his face and hands as best as I could. His hands were filthy, grimed with dirt and lacerated with small slicing cuts such as might have been made by the tough foot-long grass of the ridge...my mind registered the fact without its making much sense. Tony said, "How long was he out here, anyway?"

Tim's voice was clipped and brief. "An hour, maybe. Half an hour at least before Chambers found him, and more since."

"I found his horse," said Brock Chambers, in a way that sounded like he had already told all this before, but was in the strained, excited state where one needs to tell it all over again. "I was out looking to see what damage the storm done along my fences and I seen the horse standing over on the Circle M side at the foot of the hill with an empty saddle. He was limping from that there cut on his flank, so I led him around the long way up onto the ridge, and then I started looking. I found the marks where they went over the edge, and then I found him a little ways below. Looked like he'd crawled back up as far's he could go, but give out partway. I dragged him up the rest of the way, and then I seen his leg was busted."

The picture sank in slowly. Knockout rearing or leaping as the bullet scored his hindquarter, scrabbling on the edge for a second, and then the plunging crash. And then Lane, badly injured and alone halfway down that hill, conscious enough to know how long he might lie there in the chill rain before someone found him...the excruciating effort of trying to crawl back up dragging a broken leg behind him. I understood now the significance of his cut hands, and I didn't know whether the tight knot of hurt in my chest was agonizing pity or helpless rage.

Tony was still muttering under his breath, things I wouldn't repeat but had to agree with. Ray and I worked together, exchanging only a few words in low voices. For the moment urgency had stripped everything else away, and I saw only his coolness under pressure and his gentleness with

Lane. Between us we put the blankets over him, and the spare rain slickers. Brock Chambers had taken off his slicker too and stood holding it trying to keep some of the blowing rain off of Lane's face. Tim had gone back to the truck for some boards of various lengths that must be for splints and a stretcher; and after he brought them back he stood for a minute just behind me, staring down over my shoulder at Lane's white face. Lane shuddered a little and I laid my hand against his cheek, wishing its warmth could help somehow, though my own fingers were already chilly from the wet.

Tim turned toward Brock Chambers and said shortly, "You see any sign of anybody down there when you found his horse?"

"Nope, nobody, but I didn't waste any time looking. 'Sides, they'd had plenty of time to clear out by then."

Tim turned toward the horses. "I'm going down and have a look around."

Ray lifted his head, a mist of wet glistening on his face in spite of his shielding hat brim. "Don't waste your time, Tim. It's been an hour; they're long gone."

"May be—and it may be in this weather they left some tracks. I ain't forgetting what Lane was up here for. And I'm sure as hell not sitting back and doing nothing this time."

He turned on his heel and strode over to the horses, mounted Jericho, and disappeared over the edge of the hill on the other side of the rock. I watched him out of sight and then turned back to meet Ray's eyes with a slightly apprehensive questioning, but he gave a brief shake of the head that told me not to worry.

"Tony, come help me with this splint, will you?" he said. "That one'll do...just keep them straight but try not to touch his leg. Tear off a strip of that...all right...Brock, I might need you for a minute, can you come give us a hand?"

Chambers handed me his slicker and went to help. I put the slicker over my arm and shoulder and made as much of a tent out of it as I could, and did not watch the process of splinting the broken leg. Careful as Ray was being, every touch on it had to hurt, and in the conditions we were working under, the occasional fumble or slip of a hand was hardly avoidable. Lane's breathing was short, and every now and then he gave a faint whimpering moan that cut me to the heart. Sitting with my knee touching his shoulder, once I felt his whole body jerk, and Ray said instantly, "Easy...almost done."

"All right," he said a minute later. "Now let's get him in the truck. Tony, you want to bring that board?... Okay...over here." Ray started to get up, but still on one knee, he leaned over and tucked the blankets up closer to Lane's chin. "Hang in there, kid. We'll have you out of here in a few minutes."

Ray stood up, looking toward the truck. "I want to take that canvas in the back and lash it over the top—not till we've got him in, though; it'll get in our way. If we—"

A gunshot ripped through the wet air of the valley below, echoing back from the ridge and the great rock and seemingly from every hill in sight. For a second every one of us froze where we were, our heads turned toward the sound like stiffened and alert deer. Then my eyes sought Ray's again, my mouth open in dismay and incredulity.

Brock Chambers took a couple of steps toward the edge of the hill, peering down into the pines at its base, and cast a questioning look back at Ray. "Want me to go down and see?"

"No," said Ray after a beat of consideration. "We need your help here. If he's not back by the time we're ready to leave someone can go, but—"

Chambers, about to turn away from the edge, suddenly stopped and pointed. "There he comes now! No, wait, it's—" He finished on a note of tight-reined excitement, "He's got somebody with him!"

"Where?" demanded Tony.

Chambers pointed again for reply, but I could already hear the trampling of horses coming up the hill beyond the rock. The head and shoulders of first one rider and then another came into view, as they rounded the corner of it. Ray strode forward to meet them. The first rider wore no slicker, and his clothes were soaked and dark. Tim's face was set like a flint as he drove the other ahead of him—had he had a gun with him all that time, since we left the house? The other man's shoulders were slumped; he was leaning over sideways in the saddle with what might have been drunkenness or exhaustion, or abject terror.

"Get down," said Ray in a hard voice I had seldom heard before, and he laid his hand on the man's shoulder and almost dragged him out of the saddle. The man staggered as his feet touched the ground, as if Ray's hold on his collar was the only thing keeping him up. Ray pulled him along toward us, and as the prisoner's head lifted, I saw beneath the brim of his sodden hat the white face and haunted eyes of Jimmy Warren.

CHAPTER XXIX

There's blackmail in it, or I am much mistaken.

Arthur Conan Doyle: The Yellow Face

THROUGH THE NARROW passageway of the jail I could see George Burwell, his hands on his hips, nodding his head once in a while as he listened to what Ray was saying to him. His face and jaw were set like those of a man who has just had all his ideas upset like a house of cards, and doesn't want to believe it yet. From time to time he glanced toward the cells at the other end of the passage. I couldn't hear what they were saying, and it made me nervous. It was the first emotion of any kind I had felt in some time. All the long ride into town, sitting beside Lane in the back of the truck under the wet canvas, I'd been in the absolute flat calm you get when you're so deep in the middle of disaster that it doesn't seem possible for things to get any worse.

I twisted my cold hands together and tried to warm them by sliding them between my knees. My jeans were soaked through and muddy from the knees down, and the old coal-oil stove in the jail couldn't seem to alleviate the chill hanging round me. The seat of the wooden chair I sat on was hard. Ed Kenyon was in the room, but he was standing over near the passageway trying to listen to Ray and Burwell's conversation too; we hadn't said much to each other during the time it had been just the two of us in the room.

The door to the street opened and Tim came in, and somehow not to my surprise, he was followed by Carleton Kent. At the sound of their entrance Ray turned and came out of the passage, followed by Burwell. Kent's glance went to me first, and I felt grateful to him for wanting to make sure I was all right. There was some of that disbelief that I think we all were feeling in his expression, but also an air of alertness, a kind of suppressed excitement I hadn't seen in anyone else yet.

"How's Lane?" said George Burwell.

Tim answered for them: "Doc Burns wanted to get him to the hospital in Claxton, but a lot of the phone lines are down with the storm, and Jenny thinks there's a bridge out somewhere between here and the highway. Doc didn't want to risk trying to get through in an ambulance and getting stuck. So he's keeping him under sedatives till morning, when he can get the ambulance here." Tim looked at Ray, and at me, and added, "Doc thinks he'll pull through all right."

Carleton Kent glanced toward the back of the jail. "Is it true, that Jimmy Warren shot at him? Have you found out anything?"

"It doesn't make sense to me," said George Burwell. "But something happened out there. And the gun he had with him was fired." He pointed to the rifle that lay across the sheriff's desk.

"He wouldn't tell us anything," I said. "He didn't

deny it, or object to our bringing him here, or anything. He just seemed to have gone to pieces."

"Let me talk to him," said Ray quietly. "Just five minutes back there, George, through the cell. I want to know what happened, and I'll ask him straight out."

Burwell's mouth twisted with reluctant disapproval. "That's pretty irregular. He ought to have a lawyer."

"He didn't ask for one. You were clear enough about his right not to speak when you took him back there; I heard you. You come with me, and if he chooses to talk in front of both of us that's his business."

George Burwell stood chewing on his thin lower lip for a minute, and then, after a glance round at the rest of us, he nodded to Ray and beckoned him toward the doorway with a jerk of his head.

Carleton Kent moved after them, and I got up and followed him. In the narrow confines of the passageway I heard the men's boots slap on the cement floor and then stop, some little distance ahead of us. The electric bulb overhead in the passage was dim compared with the glaring one that hung in the cellblock, so that where Kent and I halted a few feet behind Burwell, close to the wall, we could see and hear without being seen. I could see the back of Ray's shoulder, and in the cell in front of him, Jimmy Warren's white, strained face as he came up to grip the bars and look through them at Ray with a kind of terror in his eyes, as if he was about to hear a sentence read over him.

"I heard you," he began in a quavering voice, and then had to swallow before he could go any further; "I heard you saying something about Lane. Is he—is he all right?"

"Why should you care?" said Ray sharply.

"You don't understand," said Jimmy in a husky, high-pitched voice. "I didn't *want* to kill him. I didn't want to. When I saw his horse go over—his horse rolled over him, and then went on to the bottom—and then when he didn't move—" He broke off with a shudder. "I went away...but I had to go back...I had to go back and see. I couldn't stand not knowing..." His voice was trailing away into half-sobs, and even in my shadow I couldn't help cringing, my eyes shifting to the cement floor out of shame on his behalf. Ray's voice cut through the whimpering muddle like a bracing slap, bringing him back to the point. "Jimmy! *Did you shoot at him?*"

Jimmy leaned his forearm on the bars and hid his eyes against it, and took a breath through his clenched teeth. "I never wanted any of it. And I swear to you, Ray, I *never* meant for Lena to get hurt. I swear I didn't, you've got to believe me. He told me at first...then at the trial, I saw what he was really after...and how I'd played into his hands. But I couldn't—"

This time his voice seemed to run into something and then stick. I saw his hands were trembling. Beside me, I heard Carleton Kent suck in a quick, intent breath, as if something he'd just heard had made sense to him.

Ray moved a little closer to the cell. "What *who* was after?"

Jimmy looked at him for a second with his hands white-knuckled around the bars, his eyes wide and staring. He started to shake his head. "I can't. I can't—"

He jerked away out of my line of vision, and a creak of springs indicated that he had flung himself down on the cot in the cell. Ray stepped up close to the bars and grasped them and said sharply, "Jimmy! Jimmy, listen to me—"

He repeated Jimmy's name several times with no answer, until Burwell plucked at his sleeve and motioned him to come away. Carleton Kent put a hand on my arm and we retreated ahead of them; Tim, who had been listening from behind me as well, falling back to make way. We filed back out into the office, and this time George Burwell closed the door to the cellblock. We all looked at one another.

Ray said, "It sounds to me like somebody's got some kind of hold over him. He knows something and he's scared to tell."

Kent nodded. "Blackmail could make somebody act that desperate."

I said incredulously, "Blackmail? You don't mean that *Lane...?*"

"No," said Carleton Kent. "There were a lot of different pronouns in that speech. He gave away quite a lot, if we could just identify them."

The street door opened again and James Warren stepped in. At the sight of his heavy face, I forgot for a few seconds the reality of everything that had happened, and only wanted wildly to apologize to him and make up to him for what I knew this must be doing to the man. He took off his hat, showing the deeply-scored lines in his forehead, and said, "George, what is all this?"

Burwell told him, sparing nothing, all that we knew about what had happened that afternoon. Warren listened, the knuckles of one big hand resting on the corner of the sheriff's desk, a faint, distant look of unbelief on his face.

"It doesn't make sense," he said.

"I know it doesn't," returned Burwell. "But everything he said can be confirmed, up to a point. He was hanging around there about an hour afterwards, and he was soaking wet. Tim was looking the area over for tracks and surprised him in the brush down there. Jimmy pulled his horse around to run for it but Tim fired a shot in the air to stop him."

"He didn't actually admit to firing the shot at Lane," said James Warren.

"No, but he admitted to being on the spot and seeing it happen. And the gun he had with him had been fired," said Ray. "And he said, 'I didn't want to kill him.' That seems to me to imply pretty strongly that he was involved in almost doing it."

James Warren looked at Ray, started to open his mouth, and then closed it again.

"Look, Jim, I know how you feel," said Ray. "But a kid's been badly hurt, and if that shot had been a little more accurate he could be dead right now. What would you have said then?"

"Ray," said Burwell.

Carleton Kent, who had been keeping silent a little behind me, now moved forward. "Mr. Warren," he said, "do you have any idea, any idea at all, who might have some kind of hold over your son? Something they might have held over him as blackmail to get him to do something dangerous or illegal for them."

I thought that James Warren's eyes shifted away from Kent for just a fraction of a second before he spoke, and I wondered if Kent had seen it too. But Warren shook his head. "I've no idea. None."

"Did you know where Jimmy was this afternoon?" said Burwell.

"No. He left the house earlier when I was indoors…I don't know exactly what time it was and never asked him where he was going."

Carleton Kent said, "What was Lane Whitaker doing up on the ridge?"

"He was making the rounds of the fence lines," said Tim McGreevy. "We were overdue for one and Lane said that Miss Campbell had given him the O.K. to go ahead with it. There was a break in the rain a little before noon, so we had dinner early and started out to cover what ground we could while it was clear."

"Alone?"

"Yeah. Ray and I had just met up when Chambers found us and told us."

It was Ray who put into words what I knew Carleton Kent was getting at. "Maybe Lane saw something he wasn't supposed to from up on that ridge."

"If you're getting at what I think you are," said George Burwell, "that's crazy. Jimmy was worked up worse about the cattle rustlers than anybody else in the county. He spent half the spring and summer insisting he was going to catch them himself single-handed."

"A good cover if he wanted it that way," said Ray. "Of all the things going on in Severn County that somebody could have used as a handle on him, it's certainly the most obvious."

I sat down on the hard wooden chair again, my muddy boots stuck out in front of me. "I don't know," I said. "Somehow I wouldn't say Jimmy was a good enough actor for that."

"I don't see it either," said James Warren, shaking his head. He had taken this charge a lot more calmly than the first. Perhaps because he *knew* it wasn't worth considering? But a father's judgement wasn't necessarily the best in this case—especially since I had always suspected that James Warren knew much less of his son's mind than most people would assume.

Another chilling thought struck me. I knew the Warrens were in bad financial straits—again perhaps worse than people suspected. Suppose Jimmy had taken the knowledge he had gained from tracking the cattle rustlers, and turned to imitating them on his own account to try and save his father from bankruptcy? And if someone else had found him out—

"All right, all right," Tim was saying, "but if that's out, then *why Lane?*"

There was a brief silence as we considered. And then Carleton Kent said:

"There was one thing Jimmy said that I thought was interesting. He said that he never meant for Lena to *'get hurt.'* What did he mean by that?"

"I think you know what he meant," I said, looking at the floor.

"I'm not so sure," said Kent. "He wasn't talking about the trial yet. This came first. And anyway, if he'd been talking about figurative pain, wouldn't it have been more natural for him to have said something like 'I never meant for it to hurt Lena,' or 'I never meant for Lena to be hurt by it'?"

"What are you getting at?" said Burwell.

"I think it's worth thinking about," said Carleton Kent slowly, "that back in the spring when Lena was injured by a gunshot, she was *riding with Lane Whitaker.* Lena, you remember how you described it to me. You were riding in single file, and as the trail widened Lane was just coming up beside you again. If someone was up on that left-hand ridge behind them at a diagonal angle, and they were just coming into line with each other at the moment the trigger was pulled—"

"That would be stupid to shoot then," said George Burwell.

"But someone did shoot then. Everybody assumed it was meant for Lena, but really, wouldn't it be even more stupid to shoot at the person *beyond* at the moment another rider was coming into your line of fire?"

I opened my lips, which felt dry, and said, "Jimmy always used to joke about being a poor shot."

"And there's another thing," said Kent, "which just now begins to make sense. You might as well know, I got hold of Tony recently and talked to him about some things. Isn't it true that sometime in the spring, Lena was thrown from a horse because the saddle cinch had been tampered with?"

Ray said, "We couldn't say definitely it was tampered with. The buckle on the cinch broke, and there didn't seem to be a good reason for it, but—"

"But it was a horse she wasn't meant to be riding, wasn't it?"

"The horse was Tim's. Meaning he rode him most of the time. I didn't think Lena was ready to handle him yet, so she'd never taken him out alone."

"And what about the saddle? Was that hers?"

"Yes—it was her new saddle, the one that—" Ray suddenly seemed to see the point. He finished, "It was made like Tim's...the one she'd admired."

I said in a shaky voice, "And Tim saddled Jericho for me. Ray, Jimmy was at the ranch that day...he'd been at the barn looking for me; I met him coming back. He might have even seen Tim putting the saddle on Jericho."

"Just wait a moment," said James Warren. "What are you trying to suggest? That—"

"Leave out for a minute the question of who did it," Carleton Kent interposed swiftly, "but it looks very much like *somebody* made underhanded attempts to put Lane Whitaker and Tim McGreevy out of the way. If there was no obvious reason, I'd assume it was because they knew something without knowing the significance of it."

Tim said, "If it was anything I'd said too loud about who was to blame for the rustling—"

"No—it couldn't have been just opinion. It had to have been something that was materially damaging to someone. Something the two of you could have sworn to..." Kent's voice checked, faltered, changed; he finished in an entirely different tone: "...in court."

A hot sickness swirled around at the base of my throat. I knew. I heard James Warren saying, "What? What is it?"

Carleton Kent said, "Tim McGreevy and Lane Whitaker were the only ones who knew Garth McKay had made a will."

"The *will*," said George Burwell in an almost awestruck tone. "They witnessed it. So—" He looked at Kent. "What you're saying is that somebody else did know about it. Somebody tried to put them out of the way so they couldn't let slip there was a will. Meaning someone didn't want it known what had been in it..."

My cold hands gripped the hard edges of my chair. The room seemed to have grown colder and darker, with only the coal-oil stove a taunting, sinister glow straight in front of me. I wasn't looking at George Burwell, but I could almost see the sheriff's head turn. The intent, almost breathless attention of everyone in the room was focused on the two men who stood looking at each other and the cold, silent challenge between them. Burwell was looking at Ray Harper.

CHAPTER XXX

Let them have it as they will!
Thou art tired; best be still.

Matthew Arnold: The Last Word

RAY SAID, "All right, Burwell, why don't you just say it."

"You're crazy!" Tim cut in swiftly. "You expect me to believe that? Burwell, if you believe it you're out of your mind."

"No, go on, say it," said Ray. "I knew Jimmy Warren was stealing cattle, and I threatened to turn him in unless he killed two men who worked for me. That's pretty rich. There's nothing you won't try, is there, Burwell?"

"It doesn't have to be that complicated," said George Burwell. "I'm still not convinced any of this stuff about Jimmy makes sense. But somebody who was at the ranch would have had a lot better opportunity to tamper with that saddle than Jimmy did. You were nearby when she was shot; you could easily have backtracked and then caught up with them again once you saw you'd made a mistake. And there's no way to prove you didn't bushwhack Lane today, either."

Tim pushed in between them. "Are you forgetting Jimmy practically admitted to that?"

"The boy was half off his head. He'd had rustlers on the brain so long, it was getting to him. He might have spotted Lane along the fence and didn't recognize him, thought he was up to no good, and set out to stalk him—then when he heard the shot and saw what happened he thought *he'd* done it."

That was quite a flight of imagination for George Burwell, but just then nobody thought it was funny.

"You're the one who's off his nut," said Tim. "You've taken this case personally ever since you had to let it drop the first time, and you're just out to paper over the cracks so you won't look bad, no matter whose hide you have to do it with. Ray, don't listen to him. He's nuts."

"Shut up, McGreevy!" said Burwell, nettled. "I'm not running for re-election now, I'm trying to get some things straightened out. You've got something personal against me, we can take it up later outside this office."

Tim swung around to face Ray, his back to the sheriff, and the two men's eyes met, locked, and battled in a way I didn't fully understand. "You gonna just stand there?" said Tim. "Say something. You don't have to put up with this."

Ray shook his head, and as his eyes half-closed for a second I suddenly realized how utterly weary he was. "I'm not going to defend myself any more," he said. "I don't have to say anything. I don't have to give you one single word. I stood my trial in open court, Burwell, and you threw everything you had at me and it didn't stick. I don't have to be put through this all over again. I'm not having any part of it." He walked straight between James Warren and Ed Kenyon to the door, put on his hat and pulled his coat off the rack. "I'm done. I'm going over to Doc Burns'."

He opened the door and stepped out into the rain—
and as the door closed behind him a sudden wave of
conviction crashed over me, seeming to loosen the invisible
fetters that had bound my tongue and bound me to my seat,
and I half started up from my chair in horror. Why hadn't I
spoken? Why hadn't I added my indignant voice in his
defense, even if it was only for him, even if the sheriff
brushed me aside like a fly? For a moment I had forgotten
all my doubts—there was only that horrible dead, weary look
in Ray's eyes, the look of a man who simply does not care
any more and has lost all hope, and it was all my fault. Tim
was shouting after him: "Ray! Ray, come back here, you
damn stubborn—"

I sat down abruptly and a little unsteadily on my hard
chair. James Warren and Ed Kenyon had both begun to talk
protestingly at once, though I couldn't tell what they were
objecting to, but Burwell shut them up. "All right, Jim, all
right! You wanted to know about your boy, and now we're
just beginning to get somewhere. What I think—"

"Talk sense, will you?"

We had all forgotten Carleton Kent. While everyone
else was arguing he had been sitting on the corner of the
sheriff's desk, biting his thumbnail, apparently wrapped in
his own thoughts. But now he was among us, standing bolt
upright with his feet braced apart, his hands shoved in his
coat pockets and his eyes bright with suppressed triumph.
"You've thrown together a nice little case against Ray
Harper pretty quickly, but you're all missing something
important."

I lifted my head with the faint glimmering of an idea.
"Ray wouldn't have made that mistake with the saddles."

"That's true—but that's not what I'm thinking of,"

said Carleton Kent. "I meant this: everyone in Wyoming who reads a newspaper has known since the beginning of August what was in Garth McKay's will. In that case, *what-on-earth kind of motive did Ray Harper have for shooting Lane Whitaker today?*"

Nobody answered.

"But," I said into the silence, "even if Ray didn't do it, it must have had *something* to do with the will back in the spring. It wasn't until after Tim gave away that there'd *been* a will that I had that accident with the saddle, and I was shot at not long after that. You remember, Tim, Robert Herrington said he'd guessed about it from something he heard you say one day—and there were plenty of other men standing around then too. Bill Sutherland was there, and your Brooks, Mr. Warren; and Brock Chambers and a lot of others. That proves right there Ray wasn't the only one who could have known, or guessed."

"But there was a lot more time before the thing finally turned up," said Tim. "Neither Lane or me had any more narrow escapes that *I* know of. You think if somebody was trying to bump us off they'd have quit after one try?"

"He's right," said Burwell.

Carleton Kent stood with his head bent a little, staring in front of him. "It ought to fit," he said. "It ought to. But you're right—you don't have an urgent enough reason to try and kill someone, and then just give it up with a shrug when it doesn't pan out the first time. Not unless something's significantly changed in the meantime. After the attempt on Lena—I mean on Lane—"

He stopped. I saw his eyes widen. Then suddenly he wheeled around, pushed past Ed Kenyon into the front of the office where the floor was clear, and strode across the space and back, clutching at his head with both hands as if it hurt.

"No! I've got it! *I've got it!*"

"What? *What?*"

"I know what changed," said Kent. He strode back and sat down on the corner of the desk again, his boyish face lit and transformed with his intensity, and leaned toward me. "Lena—Lena, you made a will on June 4th, didn't you? And Tim and Lane witnessed it?"

"Ye-es—"

"Don't you see? *A genuine document with the same two signatures that were on Garth McKay's will.* And then just a few weeks later, the missing will suddenly turns up, providing a cut-and-dried motive for murder for Ray Harper —*and the signatures of the same witnesses.*"

"But—" I think I saw it all then, but it took a moment for my brain to translate it into words that could come off my tongue. "That would mean that—that—"

Carleton Kent nodded. His glowing eyes held not only triumph, but grim understanding. "Only one man had the opportunity to obtain those signatures. Robert Herrington."

CHAPTER XXXI

Every murderer is probably somebody's old friend.

Agatha Christie: The Mysterious Affair at Styles

I REPEATED incredulously, "Robert Herrington?"

A dozen pictures flashed through my mind: Robert Herrington, always brisk, always the same in his three-piece suit; his dry little cough, his good-humoredly skeptical raised eyebrow, his habit of tapping his pen on the table. Shaking my hand on the station platform, guiding me through the signing of papers; trying to reason me into being conventional with a tolerant smile. Grandfather's old friend, always a point of normalcy and reliability for me in my new world even when we didn't agree.

But it all fit.

"Now I can see where Jimmy fits in," said Carleton Kent. "Herrington must be the one with a hold over him, and he tried to use him to get rid of Tim and Lane. But both attempts went wrong—and before Herrington could settle on a new plan of attack, Lena asked him to draw up her will, and presented him with a perfect opportunity."

George Burwell hadn't said a word yet. From the look on his face, I thought that as incredible as the theory was, it had struck him hard enough that he was forced to see the logic in it. He said, "Why would Bob Herrington want Tim and Lane out of the way?"

I stared back at Carleton Kent with wide-open, comprehending eyes. "Because he wanted to produce a forged will in court! A will that would incriminate Ray for my grandfather's murder—and he couldn't do that so long as Tim and Lane were alive to maybe notice something wrong with their signatures."

"Right," said Kent. "For some reason, Herrington wanted the McKay murder safely wrapped up and tied with a bow and someone in prison for it. I think we can assume he knew who really did it and was helping to cover up. Or, for that matter, he may have simply killed McKay himself, though I don't know why yet—"

I caught my breath. "What if it was about the rustling after all? Grandfather found something out and was murdered for it. Suppose Robert Herrington was in on it with—with another client—and they wanted Ray safely convicted and out of the way so nobody would dig any further into it."

Burwell held up one hand. "Hold on a minute. You're moving pretty fast here. Before we even get to the murder, you're saying now that Herrington was behind the rustling racket too?"

Carleton Kent said, with a cough and a little deprecating air that would probably go farther with Burwell than anything else, "It's just a theory, Sheriff, but I think a man who could put over a forged will in court would be pretty adept in negotiating the sale of stolen livestock."

"Maybe Jimmy found out who was behind it after all," said Tim. "I don't know what in hell Herrington could have said to him to turn him around in his tracks like that—but I'll bet I know what story he spun him about why he wanted me and Lane out of the way."

"That the two of you were getting too close to stumbling on the rustlers yourselves. Of course," said Carleton Kent. "That would explain what Jimmy said tonight. He didn't know anything about the McKay murder at first. Then at the trial, listening to the testimony about the will, he must have realized that all the business with Tim and Lane had been meant to cover it up."

"It all fits," I said breathlessly.

Burwell said, "I've got to have more than that, though. I can't take a step against anyone, outside of Jimmy Warren—and that only for what he did today—unless some of this is substantiated."

"Jimmy could tell us, if he would," I said. I turned to James Warren. "Mr. Warren, can't you try and convince him to talk? He can't get out of what he did to Lane, but if he turned state's evidence over whoever put him up to it, it'd probably go a lot easier for him with whatever other trouble he's in. Wouldn't it, Sheriff?"

George Burwell considered his answer for a second, looking at Warren, and then he nodded. "Jim," he said, "there's been a lot of wild ideas and accusations thrown around here tonight, but we're never going to prove or disprove any of them without a ton of headaches unless your boy makes a statement of some kind. Will you try talking to him?"

James Warren, who seemed to be looking into space somewhere between Burwell and me, half opened his mouth and then shut it, and breathed hard once through his nose. For a second I thought I saw through his mind. Our importunings had brought him to a place where he had to face the fact that Jimmy had actually done some of the things he had been accused of. But he couldn't refuse us, couldn't continue to turn away from the facts, without denying Jimmy the only practical help he could get in his predicament.

"I'll talk to him," he said.

He unfolded his arms and followed George Burwell, who opened the heavy door to the cellblock and led the way down the passage. The rest of us followed, intending by common impulse to listen grouped around the outer door. The forms of the two tall men partly blocked the glare of electric light from the other end of the passage for a minute, and then suddenly I heard George Burwell stop and utter an exclamation. Then he was moving again, quickly, his boots scraping on the cement floor. "Ed, give me those keys!"

I heard the keys jingle, then hit the floor, and somebody swore. Burwell stooped and picked them up, shoved the key into the lock and the cell door opened with a scrape and a clang. Burwell and Warren were both inside, both kneeling. Through the frame of the passage doorway I saw that Jimmy was on the floor of the cell, face down. All I could see was the back of his head and one hand and arm lying alongside his body, and the hand was motionless. And there was a small spot or pool of something dark on the cement floor close by, something that was beginning to be soaked up by the blue sleeve...

George Burwell and his father were bent down, half lifting him and turning him over. "Shot," said Burwell tersely. "Ed, get on the phone and—"

There was a pause. I couldn't see the sheriff; I was watching Ed Kenyon, and I saw his hand slowly slip down from the bar of the cell door he had been holding and hang at his side.

Burwell said, "Never mind."

I don't remember feeling any particular sensation, but I must have looked queer, because Tim grasped me by the shoulders and brought me away from the door. In a moment George Burwell came out, looking five years older than when he went into the cellblock, and Carleton Kent followed him, white-faced.

I could only say, "But how? *How?*"

"Easy," said George Burwell. His voice was an abrupt monotone. "Small caliber gun, likely a silencer. The door was shut and it's pretty thick; we were all in here talking at the tops of our voices. We wouldn't have heard it."

He added, "There's streaks of mud on the cot, like he stepped up on it to talk to somebody at the window. If it was somebody he trusted, all they had to do was beckon to him to step up there, and then pull the trigger."

"I guess that pretty much proves that he was being blackmailed," said Carleton Kent quietly, "and that somebody felt he was about to break."

"They must have found out awfully quickly that he was in jail." Even as I spoke, something indefinable flickered through my mind that I felt was important, but it was gone before I could have a look at it.

"In this town?" said Tim with weary disgust. "Jenny Winship might have mentioned over the line to anybody that she put a call through to Warren's from the sheriff. Anybody with the goods on Jimmy could have put two and two together."

"It doesn't have to be as involved as that," said Burwell. "I'm not ruling out anything, absolutely anything yet. All that stuff we were talking about Herrington is still pure theory. And I'm not overlooking the fact that Ray Harper walked out of this office almost ten minutes before I opened the door to the cellblock."

Kent and Tim exploded simultaneously. I pressed my fingers to my forehead, hardly hearing what they were saying. Here we went again…Tim was almost shouting, "All right then, pick up the phone and call Doc Burns and see if he's there. I'm willing to bet on it."

"That wouldn't prove anything. He could have gone around to the back window and shot Jimmy and then headed for Doc's without it making more than a minute's difference in the time it took him to get there."

I couldn't stand it any more. I was sick of the whole thing. I turned and drifted numbly toward the door, fumbled my hat off the coat rack onto my head and dragged on my still-damp yellow slicker. I opened the door, and shut it behind me on the sounds of the men's arguing voices. I don't think they noticed I was gone.

The Circle M truck stood at the curb, and I climbed in at the passenger door, slid across to the driver's seat and turned the key. The headlight beams switched on into thick rain, a shower of shining needles against the deepening murk of dusk. I pulled out into the muddy street and took a left turn that would take me out of town. I was no more use here. All I wanted was to get home.

I didn't believe that Ray had shot Jimmy Warren. I didn't even take it seriously enough to fear for Ray's safety. But from Burwell's point of view, he would be the most logical person to question first because he had been on the scene—and if Kent's theory about the will couldn't be proved he was still a candidate for the role of Jimmy's blackmailer. The same thing all over again—the same technicalities, cross-questionings, and denials; the same soul-draining pressure and suspicion. And I was angry, in a tired, hopeless way, because it was all so unnecessary.

The rain blurred my side windows so a stretch of

muddy, rutted dirt road ahead, bounded on both sides by strands of wet barbed wire that seemed to flash and spark when my headlights glanced along them, was all I could see. If one was going to accept the theory of Robert Herrington's helping to cover up the murder, one had to believe there was someone else in it. Herrington may very well have been the one whose fingers played upon the financial strings, but he had to have had a more efficient partner than poor, wretched Jimmy—someone who had managed the practical side of spiriting stolen livestock out of Severn County for years.

And I thought I knew who fit that role.

He had been there all along—always obvious; almost flauntingly so. Bill Sutherland, the untouchable man of Severn County—the man whose barns and pastures no one was allowed to trespass in—the man whom everyone disliked, but no one dared accuse. The eternal elephant in the room. He'd probably had George Burwell in his pocket all this time. Burwell had turned a blind eye to the rustling because of Sutherland's political power, and now with someone else getting uncomfortably close to the truth, it would be in character for him to drag his feet about investigating Robert Herrington. He'd waste precious time cross-questioning Ray again, while Herrington—and Sutherland —would have ample opportunity to cover their tracks and destroy evidence. They would never be brought to account for this afternoon's work.

Once more I was looking down that dizzy, rough slope below the great rock; once again I saw Lane's blue lips and lacerated hands. And suddenly I was furious.

I was coming to the three-cornered fork in the road: the left-hand turn curving down towards the Circle M, and another road straight ahead that I seldom took. Abruptly I set my teeth and put my foot down on the gas pedal and the Ford roared ahead into the other fork, its tires slewing round a little in the mud before it straightened itself out.

CHAPTER XXXII

And here is truth; but an it please thee not,
Take thou the truth as thou hast told it me.

Tennyson: Idylls of the King

I T WAS STILL raining when I turned under Sutherland's ranch sign. I'd never been to his ranch before; I only knew that the buildings were well out of sight from the road. I also knew that I was several miles from another house, that there was a good possibility of the telephone wires being down, and that I had no idea who I would find at Sutherland's ranch or how they would receive me; but my nearly blinding anger carried me on without a tremor.

The ranch road twisted several times around outcroppings of rock, fringed with scrubby pines. Then I rounded another bend and there the ranch was—the long low house in the foreground, a few big solid barns, corrals, and a two-story bunkhouse at a little distance beyond.

I pulled the truck to a stop in front of the house, shut the engine off and tumbled out the driver's door. I splashed around the front of the truck and rapped on the door, not realizing how I was assaulting it until the hurt in my knuckles got through to me. I dropped my stinging hand and waited. It was only half a minute or less before the door opened, and Bill Sutherland stood there looking at me—the same big, slightly stooped but formidable frame, the same craggy face and heavy white eyebrows, like ice on a mountain ledge. I tried to speak, but nothing I had meant to do or say would form itself into words, and my teeth were chattering from the chilly dampness that clung about my knees and had worked its way inside the collar of my coat.

Sutherland gave me and my drowned-rat condition one look, and the eyebrows went up in flat amazement. "Good Lord, girl! What in the world are you doing out here in this weather? What's the matter with you?—you look sick. Here—get in here."

Without the slightest attempt at courtesy or ceremony he grasped me by the arm and pulled me in out of the rain, and shut the door. He gestured peremptorily for me to unfasten my wet rain slicker, which I did, and he took it from me and threw it on a hook in the hall. I pushed my hat off backwards and let it fall down my back on its string. Sutherland took my arm again and steered me into the living room, a large square room lighted by both a big gas lamp and an open fireplace, with a slight clinging atmosphere of cigarette smoke. There was an elk's head, some other hunting trophies and a rack of shotguns on the log walls, along with a few framed paintings of outdoor scenes that even in my preoccupied state I recognized were probably good ones. A few Navajo blankets were tossed over the backs of the heavy leather-covered furniture, which was rubbed and worn with age but still as solidly reliable-looking as if it had been put there yesterday.

"Sit over here and get warm," said Sutherland,

crossing to the fireplace.

I stood still in the middle of the room, shivering a little with my hands tucked under my folded arms, without taking my eyes from him as he took the poker and thrust it into the coals to stir up the fire. The red glare outlined his big frame and unkempt white hair, and threw a distorted version of his shadow on the ceiling. He put the poker back on its rack with a clang, and then turned around, realizing I hadn't moved or spoken.

I took a step closer, my eyes fixed on his face. "I want you to stop," I said. I swallowed convulsively. "It's what I came to tell you. I just want you to stop. I don't care what you've done before now, I don't care if you never pay for any of it; I just don't want anyone more to get hurt. I can't stand any more. I've had it. I'm telling you to stop." I pushed my fist into the palm of my other hand and squeezed it until my fingernails bit into the flesh.

Sutherland was standing looking at me, his mottled red forehead creased above the white eyebrows, with an expression that seemed half uncomprehending, half ironic. "And just what do you mean by that?"

"Jimmy Warren's dead," I said. The full realization of the fact seemed to go through me for the first time like a cold slice of wind, and my lips felt numb for a second. "Or did you know that already? Did somebody report to you?"

An eyebrow went up at that, but still his reaction wasn't one of either fear or violence. He came a little closer and peered straight into my eyes for a minute as if to be sure I wasn't suffering from shock or fever or something else unbalancing. He said, "Dead? Warren's boy? I haven't heard a thing about it. What are you talking about?"

"Jimmy shot at Lane Whitaker over on the north boundary of the Circle M today," I said, "and when he was in jail, someone shot him through the cell window to keep him from talking. And Lane's leg is broken, and they can't get him to the hospital in Claxton till the storm is over." I sat down on the nearest corner of the leather sofa and put my hand over my eyes. I wanted to cry, but couldn't get any nearer to it than a quivering ache in my throat. "I'm not going to pretend I don't know what it's about. I know Jimmy was mixed up with the rustling, even if I don't know how." I flung my head back, lifting my streaked face and set chin determinedly toward Sutherland. "Haven't you got enough? You've had everything the way you wanted it around here for years and years; won't you ever have enough? How much more can you want? Why do you have to do it?"

There was an ominous gleam in Sutherland's deep-set eyes now—I finally seemed to have aroused his interest or his anger, or both. He laughed—half under his breath, but still with that signature harsh sound. The strange part was that he seemed genuinely amused.

"Just so I'm sure," he said. "You're saying I'm the one responsible for this county's rustling problem these last few years?"

I couldn't keep my head up, faced with those piercing eyes, but I glowered up at him defiantly from under my lowered brows. "I've always thought so."

"I'm interested. That makes me interested. What made you think so?"

"You ought to know why," I retorted. "You're always after more than you've got, and you don't care who you trample down to get it. The sheriff won't touch you because you've got too much influence around here. Nobody dares say anything, but do you think they don't have any idea? I'm not the only one. Tim McGreevy says so—I know Ray thinks so—James Warren has to know it—and my grandfather—"

I stopped, catching my breath.

Bill Sutherland looked down at me keenly. Something like a smile flitted across his craggy face as he stood there, his feet in their battered boots a little apart, the thumbs of his big hands hooked on the pockets of his jeans.

"So you've got that far," he said. "You think I killed Garth—eh?"

I couldn't speak this time, but my shivering silence admitted it.

Sutherland said dryly, "If you're convinced I'm a killer, I've got to say you picked an odd way of dealing with it."

"What can I do to you?" I said bitterly, wearily. "For that matter, what more can you do to me? I don't care what happens to me any more." The tears came to my eyes then, but perversely I fought them back. I wouldn't cry in front of Bill Sutherland. "You've ruined everything. Ray—he hates me now, because he knows I couldn't trust him—I went back on him even worse than anyone else, but I couldn't help it! I couldn't help it! I was just *scared.*"

Sutherland gave a sort of sarcastic grunt. "And you're still breaking your little heart over him, even though you think he did it."

"I can't help how I feel, can I?" I cried. "You can't just stop caring about someone in an instant, even if you *know* they've done something terrible. And I *don't* know. I don't know anything."

"That's the first sensible thing you've said yet," said Sutherland. He turned away and took the poker and stirred up the fire again, and then, after a minute, looked back. "You don't really believe it's me. You just don't want it to be him. You're hoping it's me, so you can shove all this off onto somebody you don't like and keep the rest of your life all safe and tidy and comfortable. Well, I'm sorry to disappoint you, girl. But I didn't kill Garth."

I dried my eyes and looked at him as steadily as I could. I thought there was one thing that might possible shake him. "Then it wasn't you who sent that anonymous letter to the D.A. about the safe-deposit box?"

"No, it wasn't," said Sutherland emphatically. "I always thought there was something funny about that. Still do. The will was all wrong, the box was wrong, the whole story about it. All wrong."

I swallowed a little thrill of nerves. I wasn't going to mention Robert Herrington if I could help it, but there might be something here if I could get at it carefully. "Why was it wrong?"

"Because I knew Garth. We weren't exactly what you'd call friends; had too much of our share of fallings-out for that—but we had each other's measure. I knew the way he saw things and he could fair enough have told you how I did." Sutherland took a step to the side and sat down on the arm of the big chair opposite me, and as he did he put one hand to the small of his back as if it was a little stiff. It was the first time I had ever seen him acknowledge the possibility of age or infirmity in word or deed.

He slid the hand to rest on his knee, leaning forward a little, and went on. "See, Garth's whole life was his land. Maybe you don't know what it took him to get it. He and I were cowboys out here in the eighties, and back then it wasn't so easy for a cowboy to get land and start up a ranch of his own—big ranchers didn't want to let us have a share, and they'd make it hard for a man, fight him fair or foul. When I say big ranchers I don't mean men like me, I mean men with more land and more money and power than anybody who's left around here nowadays. Well, Garth McKay and me got ours, and we kept it. I guess you could say I've been luckier than he was, or smarter, or something. But he had his land, and he was hell-bent to keep it to the death and pass it on to his children. That's why nothing about that will made sense to me. Garth would never have left what became of the Circle M to chance—it didn't make sense that they couldn't find a will, and it didn't make sense that when there *was* one it was stowed away in a city bank where nobody might ever have found it. He'd have wanted to make dead sure the land went where *he* wanted."

I was listening closely, with my hands folded between my knees again. "And what about the will itself? You said—"

Sutherland rubbed the side of his head, behind his ear. "I don't know—might just be me. But I didn't think he'd have left the place to Ray Harper. Not even if Ray was like a son to him, if Garth knew he had kin living. Some men set more store by blood kin than anything else. He was like that."

"Even though he'd quarreled with my mother?"

"Even so. 'Sides, if he'd known your mother was dead, he'd have known about you."

He shifted on the arm of the chair and it creaked. "Everything I've heard said about this murder in the papers or in court has got all kinds of lumps and holes that nobody's bothered to look at. Garth McKay didn't have those drinking spells and pitch into Ray for nothing. He was an ornery old son of a...gun, but ordinarily he didn't act like he was wrong in the head. There was something behind it if you ask me. And if I knew McKay at all, he wasn't the kind to take something quietly if it was pricking him. Sooner or later, he'd have to yell his fill about it or bust."

"Maybe," I said in a low voice, "somebody knew that sooner or later he was bound to yell, and they silenced him before he could do it."

"Maybe. But he was a crafty old bird too. If he knew somebody was after him, he might have found a way to put a spoke in their wheel, even after he was dead. I recall a time back in the eighties, when he was running crossways to somebody who wanted him off that land, he said to me one day—he said, 'Bill, if you ever hear I've fallen off my horse and busted my neck, or my gun went off while I was cleaning it, it'd be a good idea to find out what'—a man we both knew—'was doing that day.'"

"If it was something like that, why didn't he tell you this time? Would he have?"

"I dunno. We hadn't been so friendly as that of late years. It was different back when we had the same enemies."

We sat in silence for a minute. Then I lifted my eyes to Sutherland's face again, and found the steely eyes watching me, not without amusement.

The lines of his face deepened with his somewhat mocking smile. "Cleared me yet?"

I gave a weary little sigh. "Mr. Sutherland," I said, "there's one more thing I want to ask you. Why did you warn James Warren's foreman off at gunpoint when he came here looking for their horses?"

Sutherland's jaw jutted a little and color came into his face. "I've got the right," he said, "when a man marches on my property and demands the sight of a horse as if he thought I'd stolen it—"

He checked himself and lowered his voice to a more normal level. "My differences with the Warrens are between them and me, Lena. Leave what doesn't concern you be."

I said again, "And now Jimmy Warren's dead."

Sutherland shook his head. "You know as much about that as I do."

I got up, and stood uncertainly for a minute looking at him. Sutherland laughed out. "Wondering if I'm going to let you walk out of here alive? Go on, I've got nothing to hide—and like you said, even if I did, there's nothing you could do about it."

"I should go home," I said, feeling a certain uncoiling of tension in spite of my prior conviction that I hadn't been afraid. "Tim might try to call me from Dr. Burns'…and I walked out of the sheriff's office without saying where I was going…I don't want to get anyone worried about me."

"No, you shouldn't do that," said Sutherland, and I wasn't sure if he was being ironic or not.

And he saw me to the door, watched me put on my slicker and hat, and I went out into the dusk and the wet and he shut the door behind me.

CHAPTER XXXIII

We find what we have been told to search for.

Anna Katharine Green: The Forsaken Inn

THE RAIN HAD tapered off to a mist but it was nearly pitch dark. I kept my hands firmly on the steering wheel and my eyes searching ahead as I drove, scanning the swatch of puddled road picked out by my headlights, but my mind was working busily.

I hadn't said a word to Bill Sutherland regarding our deductions about Robert Herrington and the forged will, but he had unwittingly confirmed them. And he had given me something further to think about.

There *had* been a real will. Tim had believed it was destroyed—assiduously encouraged in this idea by Robert Herrington, incidentally—but now I was convinced that it hadn't, and Herrington knew it. And there was something so vital about it that he had tried to have two men murdered to keep anyone else from knowing of its existence.

Robert Herrington, as executor, would have been the first person to examine Garth McKay's office after his murder. If he had found the will among McKay's papers he could have easily destroyed it without anyone else ever knowing about it, but his actions since then indicated that he hadn't found one.

And months later, someone had still been searching for something in my grandfather's office by night.

Sutherland had given me the clue. Robert Herrington knew my grandfather too, knew him well enough to suspect he might have left behind something incriminating to the lawyer—perhaps in the form of a confessional will. And he must have reason to believe that it was still hidden somewhere in the house at the Circle M.

Gradually the thing was coming clear to me. The incriminating material, whatever it was, had been put into the will; but Grandfather had known that if the document came into the hands of his executor first, Herrington would destroy it—and so he had hidden it. In fact, he may have been a little too clever for himself, since it hadn't come into the hands of anyone at all.

I swung the wheel over and turned the truck into the lane leading to the Circle M. In the dark I couldn't see across the horse pasture to the barn. And when I reached the yard there were no lights in the house and none that I could see in the bunkhouse. Tony must have gone to bed. I pulled the truck around the side of the house under the trees and shut off the engine, and got out and slammed the door. I knew the place so well by now that even in the dark I didn't miss a step as I went around to the front porch and up the steps.

I opened the front door…I'd lived long enough in the country that it wasn't locked…and pulled it to behind me as I scuffed my muddy boots on the hall doormat. I felt the wall with my left hand and flicked the electric light switch, and nothing happened.

The wires must be down somewhere from the storm. I went into the office, where there was an oil lamp I'd used on occasions like this once or twice before. I had a bit of a hard time finding the matches in the rolltop desk, so I went out and groped in the hall closet for the flashlight off the shelf and brought it back with me. With that I found the matches easily, about an inch from where my hand had been pawing in the desk drawer, and lit the lamp and set it on the table in the middle of the room.

Where could you hide something in an ordinary little house like this? I looked at the desk, with a vague idea about secret compartments or a false back to a drawer...but Robert Herrington had no doubt already turned it inside out. I remembered those scratches I'd noticed on the floor when I pulled the desk out to dust—somebody had definitely dragged it out from the wall before. I stood and looked around the room, as if hoping my eyes would light randomly on something that would give me the clue. A loose floorboard? The back corner of a cupboard? I'd lived here more than a year and been in and out of the cupboards and closets every day—and what was more, I had a feeling whoever had searched the house had already tried all the obvious places.

Sticking something under a random floorboard would be foolish, unless you left some sort of clue for the person you did want to find it.

I took the flashlight out into the hall and shined it around, at the stairs, down toward the kitchen, trying to think of a hiding-place that was somehow logical and yet would never have occurred to the man who was searching. Assuming he had managed to visit this house and search it several times—what *wouldn't* he have touched? Was there anything in the house that hadn't been disturbed since my grandfather died?

His clothes had been there when I moved in...but somebody could easily have gone through those drawers. Probably the first place they would look after the desk. The closet in his room was bare except for—

My flashlight beam halted midway across a blank wall. I was hearing Mrs. Crawley's voice saying, *"He said to me, 'Anything in the house that was Marjory's I want you to have.'"*

My mother's old dress hanging in the closet, and the shoebox of trinkets that had been hers...had *they* been touched by anyone since his death?

Surely, Robert Herrington wouldn't have neglected to...?

But there was always that chance...

My footsteps on the floorboards sounded curiously detached and far away as I entered the empty bedroom, my flashlight beam probing in front of me. I opened the closet and shone it on the faded pink dress, then dropped to my knees and opened the dusty shoebox.

There was nothing there. I turned the little purse inside-out and felt the lining; I shone the flashlight all over the box and lid, but it was plain flat cardboard that concealed nothing. I set the box aside and rested the flashlight against it at an angle so it shone upward onto the dress, and turned my attention to that. I went over every inch of the ruffled hem; I felt all along the side seams and gores, the waistband, the full sleeves. I got to my feet and unhooked the back of the bodice, and shone the flashlight all inside on the lining to see if there were any signs of its having been mended. There was nothing, and my hopes were sinking with every inch of lining examined. But when I came to the top of the bodice near the neckline, for a split second my fingers touched a spot that felt stiff and crackled.

I sank to the floor again, sitting back on my heels with the dress in my arms, the soft worn silk spilling over my knees and onto the closet floor. With shaking hands I propped the flashlight up again and fumbled at the neckline of the party dress. I turned up the wide ruffled collar, and there beneath it was an inch-long gap in the stitching that joined it to the dress. I slid two fingers into it, and felt paper between them. It took me a few tries to get it out. It was long and narrow, something folded lengthwise so it lay along the seam under the collar. But at last I had it in my hand and could just make it out by the flashlight. It seemed to be two or three thin pieces of paper folded together, and along the outside was written, "To be opened after my death." I knew the handwriting from the jumbled papers in the desk.

I scrambled to my feet, and as I did so my foot hit the flashlight and it went out, and I heard it rolling away across the floor into some far corner of the room. I was in too much of a hurry to look for it. I felt my way out of the room and across the hall to the office, where the oil lamp was still burning. I moved the lamp to the nearer side of the table and sat down with it close by my elbow, and unfolded the paper. My chest hurt, and not just because I was a little short of breath.

"I Garth McKay am of a sound mind while writing this, my last will and testament and confession."

On a hunch I shuffled the pages and looked at the bottom of the last one. It was dated in September 1933 and was witnessed by Tim McGreevy and Lane Whitaker.

"I leave all property of which I die possessed to my daughter Marjory McKay now Campbell or to any children of hers should she not survive me. The land I own was gotten honestly and the thing I have thought about my whole life was keeping it and passing it on to my offspring. It was

honestly gotten, but in late years when times got hard I was willing to do anything to keep it. I am writing down here the truth about everything I did because Robert Herrington a man I trusted has trapped me and is cheating me of everything I made honestly or dishonestly. He knows there is nothing I can do to him without going to jail, but if I ever die and he lives after me I want him to pay for his part in it, because he has sucked my blood and ruined me by knowing how far I was willing to go to keep my land.

"For three years beginning in 1927 I was part of a scheme to steal cattle from the other ranches in Severn County. Robert Herrington was the one who planned it and arranged for shipping and selling the cattle. He suggested it to me as a way to make the money I needed to pay my mortgage that was pressing on me, and he would get a share himself. I and one other man took part in stealing and moving the cattle and so did some men who worked for us. I will not say anything about anyone else outside the Circle M, they can speak or choose not to speak for themselves. Only my part is my business.

"After that three years my ranch was better off from the extra money I had to put into it, and I decided not to take part in the scheme any more because I thought it was risky. I told Herrington I was finished and at the time he didn't make too much fuss though he did try to persuade me to keep on a little. I paid off all the men who worked for me and told them to leave the county so nothing would ever come out through them, and we had it given out that I had fired some of them and others had quit because they did not like working for me. Except one of them did not leave the county but went to Robert Herrington for more money and stayed on in his pay.

"After the cattle money stopped coming in I fell on

hard times again. I have never been very lucky. But after I hired Ray Harper as foreman things got better, and I don't know if the worst thing that ever happened to me was being prosperous, because it was then Robert Herrington started to bleed me. He knew I had some money in the bank, and he blackmailed me for a share of it by threatening to inform to the law about my part in the cattle stealing. His hold over me was the man called Hendrick Brooks who had stayed in Severn County and in his pay. Brooks had been one of the ones to give it out that he quit the Circle M, and Herrington's threat was that Brooks would claim he left because he suspected about the rustling, but both he and Herrington would deny having any part in it. Herrington claimed he had covered his tracks too well with the shipping and selling to ever be caught, but Brooks' word could put me in jail. He may be right. I couldn't see anything to do, so I have paid. The money is put in safe deposit box 438 in the Stockmen's Associated Bank in Cheyenne, which is where Herrington used to leave me my share of the rustling profits, once every month and Herrington collects it—he has the other key to the box. As long as he knows I have a red cent in the world he will go on turning the screws until he has everything and the Circle M is run into the ground.

"Herrington has got me. I think he is clever enough to turn me in without getting caught himself, and so I pay. I have told Ray Harper nothing because I know he is honest to the core and would either make sure the truth is told or leave the Circle M straight away. He thinks I am an addle-headed old fool who can't even keep straight how much money I have, but the truth is I know too well how much of it Herrington has had and how much he will go on having. Because Robert Herrington knows I will never go to jail and leave this place that I have spent all my life for. I know it too,

so all I can do is write this, and because I am likely to die before he does I hope that one day he will get his deserts.

"Maybe it is my punishment that my daughter left me and so now the land may never be lived on by her and her children the way I wanted it."

Garth McKay

He had hidden it there in the dress, and left his clue in the only way he could think of, telling Mrs. Crawley he wanted her to have my mother's things—had gambled on the hope that Robert Herrington would not find it, and that Mrs. Crawley would. And ironically it was my coming there to the house that had almost kept it from ever being found.

I realized, too, that I held in my hands the document that I had once found a disquieting piece of—a torn fragment of an early draft, no doubt, which had somehow escaped destruction and jammed in the back of the desk drawer. How wrongly I had interpreted it...but how could I, how could any of us have guessed?

I don't remember if I had just come to the end of the document for the first time, or if I was reading over some of the passages again—but I know my eyes were still on the closely-written paper when there was the faint creak of a floorboard, and I realized there was someone in the doorway of the office. I leaped to my feet with a startled surge of my heart, clutching the papers and almost overturning my chair. And then with recognition of the face the panic ebbed away and left me feeling shaken and rather foolish, for it was only James Warren.

"Oh!" I said, letting out a breath of relief, and I think my voice must have sounded rather unnatural. "You startled me. I didn't hear the front door—I must have been—"

James Warren came forward slowly, into the light

from the lamp. His dark overcoat and clothes and his sodden hat blended with the shadows of the room, so his pallid, age-carved face seemed luminous, hovering there at a fixed height. His eyes went very slowly from my face, to the paper clutched in my hand, and back again, and I recognized that the sight gave him some sort of knowledge. The look in his eyes was almost lifeless, but it frightened me. And then the last piece of the puzzle clicked into place.

Jimmy. The rifle shots. Hendrick Brooks. Turning the screws. Robert Herrington.

"So you found it," said James Warren. "I wish you hadn't."

CHAPTER XXXIV

Which is the villain? Let me see his eyes,
That, when I note another man like him,
I may avoid him.

Shakespeare: Much Ado About Nothing

I MUST HAVE lived a hundred lives in the ten seconds before he spoke again.

"I wish you hadn't," he repeated, his voice dull, almost gentle. "It would have been easier for everybody. It would have been closed...finished."

And I hadn't even meant to do it. He had seen my jump, my startled face as I clutched the papers to me, as if I had been trying to hide them, and had reached a conclusion that in the same instant was both true and false.

James Warren thought his name was in my grandfather's confession. And it wasn't. But it no longer mattered, for he had given himself away.

I said, at last, "Did Jimmy know?"

"No," said James Warren. "I didn't want him to know. It was one of my conditions for going into it."

"And you didn't know that—that he was the one who tried to kill Tim and Lane?"

Warren shook his head. "He never told me anything," he said. He seemed to try and smile faintly. "I suppose he thought I would turn myself in. At least, he knew I'd never let him kill someone to protect me." He paused, and then added, as if speaking to himself, "He should have told me. I could have handled it myself."

That was the moment I began to shake, at least inwardly. It came home to me that I was in the same room with a murderer—standing opposite me in the person of this big, grave man whom I had never been afraid of.

I looked down at the pages of my grandfather's confession, beginning to crinkle where my sweaty fingers dampened the paper. "But how—why—what made you come here?"

"Oh," said Warren. "I had a flat tire just past your lane, and the spare was bad too, so I walked up here. I thought the house was dark. Then I saw a light move in this room, and I thought—I thought it was—" Again he paused for a second, with a convulsive movement of his throat muscles—"I thought you had an intruder."

My voice came creaking through a dry throat. "Did you know that...that my grandfather wrote something before he died?"

"Herrington never told me," he said, "till afterwards."

Somehow, imperceptibly, he had moved a little closer to me, and I had drawn backwards. But I had nowhere else to go.

"None of this has ever done you any good," I said in a whisper. "Why bother now? What—what good will one more murder do? Will it ever be—enough?"

James Warren shook his head. His fixed eyes seemed to stare right through me, unseeing in his haggard face. "It was never enough. Always more, and more—he had to have more of the cattle, and more; and I always believed the money from next time would do it for us—And then McKay—"

His eyes focused in directly on me, as if he had become aware of me, of my actual presence, for the first time. "If you'd never come here," he said, "if you hadn't stayed, my son would still be alive. If it wasn't for you none of it would have been stirred up again."

He was beyond reason now. And I had nothing left to do except make a desperate dash around behind the table and try to make it to the door, though I knew he could likely beat me to the other end of the table in one stride. Still that's most likely what I would have done, and been finished then and there, if it had not been for a sound from outside the house at that moment that arrested both of us.

It was a horse. The thud of trotting hooves in mud, coming in from the road…unhurried…passing near the corner of the house, and coming to a halt somewhere under the cottonwood trees, near where I had parked the truck.

Both of us had turned our heads toward the window to listen. But I caught a flicker of movement out of the corner of my eye, and when I looked back at James Warren he had a gun in his hand.

And a sudden realization zinged along my nerves. Whether it was Ray or Tim outside—if he had intended to go on to the bunkhouse as usual he would have ridden straight to the barn, not stopped there under the trees. He was coming to the house.

The front door opened, and the squeak of hinges and the sound of footsteps in the hall, unwary, with no attempt at concealment or idea of danger, tore all the breath from my lungs. James Warren moved closer to me and pushed the muzzle of the gun against my ribs. I suppose I ought to have yelled out or dived to the floor or done *something* to give warning, but my mind was too scrambled to think of anything until it was too late.

With a feeling of unreality I listened to the footsteps. A pause, a change of direction toward the office, and Ray's voice said, "Lena?"

He stepped into the doorway, and saw us and stopped. He opened his mouth as if to say something, and then he took a second look and saw more. The gun in Warren's hand, the papers clutched in mine. The look on my face as I stared desperately at him.

"Come on in," said James Warren. "It's all right. It doesn't change anything."

Ray moved a slow step or two closer, looking at me, at Warren; and I could tell his mind was working, trying to put things together, dismissing all but the essential fact; looking for a way out. James Warren put his other hand on the back of my neck, guiding me a step to the side as if arranging a tableau.

Ray spoke in a very carefully conversational tone, as if he were dealing with a spooked horse—I think he too had had a look at Warren's eyes. "You'd better not try it, Jim. There's no way on earth you'll get away with it. There won't be any good explanation for another shooting."

"Maybe," said Warren, "but with you being here, it's all right. If I shoot you, it'll be because I caught you having just murdered a woman. After all that's gone down, people will believe me. They know a lovers' quarrel can go bad."

I felt his fingers tighten on the back of my neck, and I went hot and cold and half faint, knowing instinctively what he meant to do. But at the same time my heart was singing with the exultance of a bird released from a cage, because I knew once for all that that was not Ray. It never had been. I had him back, he belonged to me again, even if it was only for the few short seconds I had left; and it was almost worth the shortness of the time to be able to look into his eyes one more time knowing he really was the man I had known and loved.

"Don't, Jim," said Ray. "It won't work. It isn't worth it."

He was looking at me, but I could tell he was aware of the gun in Warren's hand, which was pointing at him now. "You'll regret it afterwards, Jim—"

Sometimes a person can think too quickly. I just know it flashed through my head that for Warren to arrange the scene of the "crime" to suit him, he couldn't possibly shoot me. And I gambled on it. I jerked away from his hand and rushed at Ray, throwing myself in front of him to shield him. If I'd had more time to think I ought to have known Ray would instinctively do just what he did do: he shoved me aside out of the line of fire. I fell against the table, jolting it so two of its legs rocked up off the floor, and the oil lamp tipped. In the midst of losing my balance I made a wild grasp at it, but it was out of my reach. It went end over end and then somehow—I don't know how—went out an instant before it smashed on the floor and plunged the room into darkness. One, two, three gunshots crashed through the blackness as I hit the floor—I heard thuds, the clatter and screech of a chair being knocked into, and a man's strained voice gasped a curse.

Then suddenly it was over, and I was cowering on the floor in the pitch black, my thigh throbbing where I had banged it hard against the edge of the table, the sulphurous taste and smell of gunsmoke filling the air around me. I heard footsteps running down the hall to the kitchen and the back door wrenched open, and at the same time became aware of another faint sound in the opposite direction—another horse pounding down the lane from the road.

For a second I couldn't move, almost couldn't breathe. There wasn't a sound, not a flicker of movement to indicate I wasn't alone in the office. But I had a horrible dread that I was not. I crawled to my hands and knees, and felt blindly in front of me. My fingers met shards of glass on the floor, and a wetness that must have been spilled oil...and then touched a sleeve. With a shaking hand I felt my way up across a shoulder, a chest, and touched his motionless face. I began to cry, the hot tears spilling down my cheeks. "No...Ray, *no*..."

The front door banged open; there was a confused noise in the hall and somebody tried the useless light switch. "Lena!" shouted Tim's voice. "Lena, where are you?"

"Here—in here," I cried.

Tim strode toward the office and halted for a second in the doorway—I heard him try to strike a match, and swear as it failed to catch. "Don't light a match!" I cried. "The lamp broke—there's oil on the floor."

"Where's there another one?"

"In the kitchen. Oh, Tim, hurry!"

I heard him turn and grope his way out into the hall, but before he had gone more than a few steps the hall lights suddenly came back on with an unearthly flicker. I choked back a scream. Ray was lying with his head turned to one side, his eyes closed, an ugly gash across the side of his head and blood trickling down over his ear and neck. Tim came swiftly back and knelt down across from me, put his fingers on Ray's wrist, and bent down to lay an ear against his chest. He straightened up, pulled a bandana from his pocket and started to wipe some of the blood away from the cut on Ray's head.

"I don't think it's that bad," he said; "the cut's kinda deep, but he's breathing okay...Who was it?"

"James Warren. He went out the back—I don't know where—"

"Don't worry. He won't come back now. Here—it's bleeding a little still—you hold this against it for a minute while I go phone the doctor."

He lifted Ray's head and helped me ease it onto my lap, and I sat there holding him, keeping the folded bandana pressed against the cut, while Tim sprang up and went out in the hall, took down the receiver and cranked the telephone.

The front door burst open again and Tim whirled around to face it, almost jerking the receiver off its cord. It was Tony, wearing a rain slicker over pajamas stuffed into the tops of his boots, with a gun in his hand. Tim swore on an exhaling note of mixed exasperation and relief. "What's going on?" demanded Tony.

"Tell you later," said Tim. "Get outside and—what? —hello—hang on, Jenny, just a second—Make sure nobody comes near this house till the sheriff gets here. And if you see James Warren watch out; he's got a gun. Go on, get out there."

"Will somebody please tell me why the Warrens keep shooting at us?" said Tony, and vanished.

Tim turned back to the telephone. "Jenny? Get me Doc Burns, quick. Yeah." He waited a few seconds, and then, "What? Yeah, probably—okay, call the sheriff then, and if you can't get through to him call somebody else and have them go over there. I want the sheriff out here, and Doc Burns too. No, he doesn't have to call back, just tell him to get out here. Okay."

CHAPTER XXXV

This is true love to anyone, to do the best for him we can.

John Tillotson: Sermon LIII

THE SHERIFF'S CAR arrived first, its headlights cutting and sweeping through the dark as it lurched through the mud hole at the end of the lane; and Dr. Burns' big black station wagon pulled in not a minute behind it. Tony came from the shadows to meet them at the porch steps, and then for a few minutes the house was all bright lights and muddy boots and men's voices. They had carried Ray to the bedroom off the hall—empty since the last time one of James Warren's victims had lain there—and while Dr. Burns was with him I sat in the living room and tried to give Sheriff Burwell a coherent account of what had happened. Tim stood by in the corner of the room and listened silently, clearly ready to interfere if it looked like I needed defending. But this time there was no conflict. A permanent expression of incredulity seemed to be stamped upon Burwell's features by now. I answered all his questions as best I could, but my mind wasn't more than half there in the room. I kept looking toward the doorway, waiting.

It would be some time before the sequence of that night's events was officially pieced together, but one fact was easily established: Jenny Winship had put through a call to Robert Herrington from the Warren ranch just after James Warren had left for town and the county jail in answer to the sheriff's telephone summons. Regrettably from a police point of view, Jenny hadn't listened in—there were many other things happening on the switchboard that night with all the damage from the storm. But it was pretty clear the call had been Hendrick Brooks warning Herrington that Jimmy had been arrested. Robert Herrington had then evidently taken matters into his own hands, for the first and last time. And then, he had either decided the game was already up, or realized he had overstepped himself this time, for James Warren would surely put two and two together—for he had disappeared. James Warren, we later learned, had gone straight to Herrington's house and then to his office after leaving the jail, and I think it's pretty safe to assume what would have happened if he found him. But Herrington had already gone.

What George Burwell's sentiments were that night at my house, upon learning that all three men implicated in the McKay murder were at large with a head start, no one will ever be privileged to know. But he was convinced of the truth by now. I had given him the crumpled document I had found in the lining of my mother's dress, and he read it, standing by the living-room lamp with the pages angled toward the light. I sat on the sofa opposite, with my feet very close together and my hands balled up in the pockets of my corduroy jacket, for I was still a little chilled from my damp clothes drying on me, and watched.

I shifted my position a little, hunching my shoulders

against the chill feeling, and my right hand touched something small and hard deep in my jacket pocket. I uncurled my fingers and felt for the shape of it. It was my engagement ring. I drew a deep breath, and waited until I felt steady, for an intimidating tide of emotion shook me from inside. Then I took my hands unobtrusively from my coat pockets, and in a moment when no one was looking at me, I put the ring back on the third finger of my left hand.

Dr. Burns appeared in the doorway. I jumped to my feet, my attention leaving George Burwell as if he had never been there, and faced the doctor without speaking, a living question mark from head to foot. Dr. Burns smiled a bit dryly.

"He wants to see you," he said, nodding toward the hall. "He won't stop asking me whether you're all right. I'm growing rather tired of having my truthfulness impugned, so you had better go."

I went. But I caught myself in the doorway and turned back to George Burwell. "Can I have that for a few minutes? I'll bring it right back."

He folded the confession and handed it to me, and I slipped it into my coat pocket as I hurried down the hall to the bedroom.

The door was ajar, and I pushed it open. Ray was sitting half propped up against the pillows on the bed, with a heavy bandage around his head. His face was pale under its tan and marked by weariness, but looking straight into his eyes, I could see that he was himself and that he was all right. Then my eyes blurred up so I couldn't see him at all—I stumbled forward and somehow found the edge of the bed and sat down on it, and leaned over and buried my face against his shoulder. I felt Ray's arms around me, and his hand on my hair. It was an incredible relief to feel him warm and alive and still strong, and after everything I'd been through that night, it was a relief simply to cry.

Ray murmured, "It's okay. I'm okay."

It was a few minutes before I could pull myself together, but I didn't grudge any of them. Then I sat up and pushed my tangled hair back from my tear-streaked face. Ray's hand slid to rest on my shoulder. "You sure you're all right? You know you could have gotten yourself killed."

I laughed shakily. "If you start in on that I'm going straight back to the sheriff. Anyway, you don't have to tell me; I know. I thought I'd gotten *you* killed this time." I wiped away another tear that slid down my face of its own accord, and then I took the folded paper out of my pocket. "Ray, I want you to hear something."

I read him Garth McKay's confession, and somehow kept my voice steady, except for an occasional tremor of pure tiredness. Ray lay still and listened, staring past me into the room with somber, absent eyes. He didn't move or say anything until I had finished and looked toward him to see how he took it.

"So that was it," he said, at last. "I never guessed. Never even suspected."

He started to shake his head slowly and then stopped, as if it gave him a twinge of pain. "I never understood at all; that was the trouble."

"I only wish I did," I said.

Ray's eyes swung to meet mine; he had caught the accent of bitterness that I didn't even trouble to restrain now.

"When I first came here we hit it off so well," he began, after a moment. "He seemed pleased with everything I did...he treated me almost like a son. And that was—" He paused. "I guess I felt that. I hadn't always had it. And then, for no reason—everything changed."

Clipped and halting as the sentences were, I sensed a vulnerability that had never been there whenever I had tried to talk to him about my grandfather before—almost an entreaty, as if he truly wanted me to understand. "I didn't understand. I didn't know what he was blaming me for, or if he was blaming me. But I thought he was in some kind of trouble, and I thought I could help him if I only knew what it was. What I said in court about being stubborn was true. It was plain hard-headed not wanting to fail, almost... almost...as much as wanting to help the old man straighten out whatever was wrong. But every time I tried all I got was a kick in the teeth. And after a while it made me angry." Ray shut his eyes, and an expression like pain drifted across his face. "That's what made it so hard, Lena...every time Burwell, or Stafford or somebody was hammering me with questions, all I could say was that I didn't do it; but down inside I was remembering all the times I'd been so angry I downright hated him. Lena—that last night, I knew he shouldn't go out drunk, and I tried to keep him there, for his own good, and he turned and swore at me and knocked me down. And for a minute when I was on the ground I really felt like I hated him enough to kill him. When Tim asked me if we should go after him, I said—what I really said was, 'Let him go to hell.'"

His voice thickened, ground to a halt. My throat hurt from clenching my teeth so hard.

"It was my fault. I let him go to his death—I knew all along I was halfway to blame—"

I interrupted him heatedly. "*No,* Ray, you weren't! James Warren killed him. You didn't. And Grandfather brought it on himself. It's all right here in his own words. All that time you were trying to help him, you were trying to save him from himself. He *could* have let you help him if he'd wanted to, but he didn't—and so he died." I paused, letting my eyes drift to the floor. "And you could have let me help you."

I lifted my eyes again and they were full of tears. "I tried so hard, Ray, before the trial—but you never would tell me what was wrong. You never told me the whole truth. Even back at the very beginning, one word would have explained—I'd never have spent so much time agonizing over why you didn't want me to know you'd been questioned about the murder. Why *didn't* you?"

Ray didn't say anything for a few seconds. Then he drew a breath, and gave something like a faint, rueful smile. "Being pretty much the only suspect in a murder does something to you," he said. "It—it beats you down a little. I'd convinced myself it was all behind me, that it didn't matter. That I didn't care who knew what about me or what they thought. And then you came along. I wasn't even in love with you then, but you were so sweet and honest and innocent, I knew if you found out I'd been suspected you would pull away from me, and rightly so. I was just coward enough not to say the one word I should have. Later on—by the time we got engaged—I was in too deep to say anything without you questioning why I hadn't said it at the first. And I didn't..."

His voice died away. He was holding my hand, and he had seen the ring.

Ray's eyes lifted to meet mine. He said very seriously, "Lena, are you sure?"

"I'm sure."

"But—you shouldn't be. After everything I've told you—"

"Ray, the *only* reason I ever broke it off was the murder. Because I couldn't be sure. There was never anything else wrong between us."

"I knew that," he said. "I knew from the first minute you found out I was suspected that you couldn't marry me and be comfortable about it, unless you knew for *sure* I didn't do it. That's part of the reason I was so low before the trial. I knew I could never prove definitely to another human being that I was innocent, even if a jury said 'not guilty.' I saw it coming all along that I'd end up losing you."

"If you'd only told me then what you have tonight," I said; "if you'd been completely honest, and just spilled out everything you were afraid of and angry about...I think I would have believed you."

"And I was too stupid to see it." There was a sound of finality to his words.

"You can see it now."

"It's not as simple as that," said Ray impatiently. "I behaved like a fool—I gave you every reason to doubt me and distrust me, and then I was angry with you for doing it—"

"I know. I'm not trying to pretend it never happened. But I love you—and I understand you better, now—and I *don't* believe that we don't have another chance."

Ray put his head back against the pillow with a sigh. He turned it slightly to look at me again. I could see both the doubt and wistfulness in his eyes—the deep desire to give in to me struggling with the stubborn conviction that it wasn't right. He said, "Lena, don't you understand? I'm only saying it for your own good."

I began to laugh; I couldn't help it. "You're proving my point," I said. Impulsively I reached out and put my hands on either side of his face. "It sticks out all over you, especially when you're trying to run yourself down. Even if you *haven't* always been the smartest about knowing what was best for me, I know now that's what you've cared about all along."

CHAPTER XXXVI

Let the dead Past bury its dead.

Longfellow: A Psalm of Life

MRS. CRAWLEY, her spectacles sitting halfway down her nose, folded up the wrinkled pages of Garth McKay's last will and testament and looked up from it with a little sigh and shake of the head.

"Well, that was Garth all over," she said. "A stubborn, stubborn man. He never could learn to back down when he'd made a mistake, and I guess it got him in the end."

We were sitting in the living room with the rays of an early sunset falling through the windows—the Crawleys, Carleton Kent, Ray and I. It was nearly two weeks after the events that had caused a sensation such as Severn Valley had scarcely ever known before; and the first chance we had had to sit down together and compare notes, for the whole story to be fully told.

James Warren had been apprehended that same night of the storm, offering no resistance, and the state police had picked up Robert Herrington two days later—making tracks for California with all the liquid assets he had been able to lay his hands on at short notice. Only Hendrick Brooks, who had also disappeared that night, had been able to make good his escape so far, but with a warrant out for his arrest he would probably be found eventually.

In addition, sheriff's deputies with a warrant had searched the Warren ranch the day after the storm, and had found a concealed wire corral in one of the remote back pastures that held about a dozen Circle M and Chambers cattle. Jimmy, still terrified lest anyone should stumble on the truth of his father's guilt, must have found out about this latest theft, and when he spotted Lane Whitaker reconnoitering along the Circle M boundary where traces of cattle being moved might have remained, had lost his head and shot at him—something which certainly hadn't been in Robert Herrington's plans.

The authorities didn't expect they would be able to trace all of Herrington's transactions in stolen cattle or recover much of the profits he had made, but between a confession made by James Warren and a few things they had gotten out of Herrington they had been able to put together a fairly complete picture of the McKay murder."

"Robert Herrington was the one who came up with the rustling racket," I told the Crawleys. "It sounds like he'd grown tired of being a lawyer in a little country town and was planning a luxurious retirement in some other state. He proposed it to my grandfather and James Warren because he knew they were both hard up and in debt and could use the money. Grandfather got out when he thought he'd made enough, but nothing James Warren did ever turned out right, and he depended on the money from the rustling just to keep his head above water."

Mrs. Crawley said tartly, "Garth didn't do so well out

of it as he thought, either. He was back in debt up to his neck before a year was out."

"They faked some thefts from themselves as a cover too, just like we always knew somebody must be doing. And after Brooks moved to Warren's, he managed to concoct a 'feud' between the Warrens and Bill Sutherland, by doing things to cross Sutherland wherever he could, and then telling the stories a little twisted to make it sound like it was Sutherland doing the provocation instead of Brooks himself. They wanted to divert people's suspicions about the rustling toward Sutherland, and it wasn't hard to do, since he wasn't very well liked."

"Not that Bill Sutherland ever did anything to counteract that feeling," observed Mrs. Crawley.

I smiled. "In his own way I think he's just as stiff-necked as Grandfather was. He thought he was above having to excuse and explain his quarrels with the Warrens."

"Brooks probably learned a thing or two about stiff-necked old men working for McKay," said Ray dryly. "He knew all the right strings to pull. Burwell told me some of what Warren told him. Brooks connived at Sutherland's bull getting into Warren's pastures and then raised Cain about it—he made a big deal of going up there and demanding to search for missing horses in as insulting a way as he could—and Warren played up too, by making a proposition at a town council meeting that Sutherland would be sure to shoot down hard, and make Warren look like the victim."

"There *was* one thing that might have been a give-away, you know," said Carleton Kent. "I didn't even know this until I was working on Tony for clues, after the trial: none of the new hands McKay hired after he got rid of his old crew were local boys. If anyone had been paying attention, it might have been a hint that McKay had something to hide."

"I don't think it ever went as well for Herrington and Warren after McKay quit," said Ray. "I remember that was a quiet spell for rustling, when I was first here. And it's really only been in fits and starts ever since, even though there's been enough to upset people. I'll bet Herrington held a grudge against McKay for getting out, and that went into the blackmail too."

"Did Jim Warren get any of the blackmail money?" said Rufus Crawley.

"He didn't even know about it," I said. "Robert Herrington told him Garth McKay was threatening to spill the whole thing to the law because he'd had a personal quarrel with Herrington and wanted to spite him."

Crawley nodded slowly. "And what with Garth's drinking and spells of temper, it looked like he might lose hold on himself and spill at any time...with Jim depending on the rustling money, and desperate to keep his boy from finding out what he'd been doing...it was a good handle for Bob Herrington to convince him that McKay needed to be shut up for good."

"It was an evil thing," said Mrs. Crawley firmly. "It's all very well to talk about Herrington forcing him into it, but James Warren was just as guilty—more. He could have faced up to the lesser evil, gone to jail for rustling and kept at least some of his self-respect—but he chose murder."

There was silence for a moment. It was Carleton Kent who eventually broke it: "Herrington must have got his hands on McKay's key to the safe-deposit box and pocketed it the first time he set foot in the house after the murder. I'm guessing he kept quiet about the box because it could have pointed toward the blackmail if anybody in Cheyenne had seen him visiting it. Later on when he saw how it could be useful in 'discovering' the forged will, he decided to take the risk."

Rufus Crawley rubbed his chin thoughtfully. "Do you think he was planning to forge a will from the time he tried to have Tim and Lane killed?"

"I don't think so," said Carleton Kent. "It would have been too much of a risk. If Tim and Lane weren't alive to swear to their signatures, the whole thing would have been subjected to much more scrutiny. Even though it was just a basic typed will form with a few insertions in a pretty good imitation of McKay's writing, it probably wouldn't have passed with a handwriting expert. But the forgery with the real signatures was brilliant. If the signatures were genuine, and Tim and Lane could honestly testify to having witnessed it in McKay's presence, who was going to look too closely at the rest of it?"

"I think the whole trouble was that Robert Herrington had an uneasy conscience," I said. "It sounds like Grandfather *had* made some kind of a threat about a written confession, but Herrington didn't know if he'd actually carried it out. But when no ordinary will turned up, he was almost *sure* there was a will with a confession somewhere. We think he searched here a few times when the house was still empty, maybe Saturdays when all the boys were away. Then when I moved in, that was a problem. But he still tried to search the house at least once more, one night when he thought I wasn't home."

"It wasn't the first time, for sure," said Ray. "I thought I heard somebody at the house one night soon after the murder. I went to look, checked all around, but didn't find anything out of order. When Lena told me later on what had happened to her, it startled me a little. But I had absolutely no clue about any of this, about the rustling or the will, so I didn't know what to think."

"Ray actually told me all this before the trial," explained Kent, "but I didn't want to bring any of it up in court. It would have been easy for the prosecutor to suggest Ray had invented the story to cover for himself, if *he* had been the one searching the house and thought somebody had overheard him."

He went on, "Herrington got even more uneasy when Tim almost let slip about the will. Now he was sure it existed. But I guess he decided to bank on the fact that if *he* couldn't find it, nobody else would; and to eliminate Tim and Lane just in case. That was where Jimmy Warren came in."

"You mean he blackmailed him with Jim's being the murderer?"

"Nobody's sure whether he ever found out it was actually his father who murdered Grandfather," I said. "But what Herrington did use was enough. Jimmy was dead set on catching the rustlers himself—and then Robert Herrington approached him and revealed that it was his own father. It must have been the worst shock he could have had."

Carleton Kent added, "Herrington probably used the same blackmail tactics he had with McKay—threatening to turn James Warren over to the law for cattle rustling—but for Jimmy the price of silence was to be bumping off Tim and Lane. Luckily for them, Jimmy turned out to be a pretty inept assassin."

"You know, I don't think it was inept," I said slowly, "so much as unwilling. I've thought about it a lot...and I don't think he could have bungled both attempts so badly if it wasn't that deep down he hated what he was doing, it terrified him and made him sick even though he felt he *had* to do it because it was the only way out. Who knows, maybe he hoped Herrington would let him off the hook if he claimed he'd tried and failed. The tampering with Tim's saddle was half-hearted—and even if he was a poor shot, he picked absolutely the worst moment he could have when he shot at Lane and hit me. It's almost as if he was secretly hoping he would miss."

"A much simpler way of putting it," said Mrs. Crawley with some acerbity, "is that a guilty conscience spoils one's aim."

I nodded. It still hurt to think of Jimmy, perhaps because in spite of everything I could still find it in me to pity him. Poor wretched, misguided Jimmy, who had idolized his father, had in the end been weak in the same way as him—unable to face up to the penalty for one wrongdoing, had committed worse. Had made shipwreck because he had had no other moral compass besides "Dad says."

I pulled myself back to the present, where Mrs. Crawley was saying, "But why drag Jimmy into it? Why not have used James Warren again, or that man Brooks? It seems like too much trouble to go to."

"We were talking about that," said Carleton Kent, "Sheriff Burwell and my uncle and I, and I think there may have been a couple of reasons. One, he'd have had an extra hold over Jimmy—it seems he always liked having something to hold over people—if Jimmy had tried to disentangle the Warrens from the rustling racket later. Jimmy could even have been getting too close to the truth about that himself. And I think what he may have had in mind was to let Jimmy take the fall if anybody got too curious about what happened to the Circle M boys. It could be said that Tim or Lane found out about the rustling and Jimmy tried to shut them up. Any story of Jimmy's about being blackmailed by Herrington would sound crazy, since Herrington didn't have any motive to kill Tim or Lane—that anyone knew of. No one else knew about the will, not even Ray or Tony."

I shook my head. "I don't even want to imagine what he might have done next—after Jimmy failed him. But then …I suppose fortunately…I played right into his hands, when I asked him to draw up my will."

"He had some nerve," said Kent, studying the signatures on my grandfather's confession. "It was a long chance that he'd be able to wangle Tim and Lane being the witnesses again. Because at that point he had no idea that Ray was disqualified by being a beneficiary, didn't you say that, Lena?"

Ray cut in: "But he might have known that I wasn't around. I was in town that day; it's just possible Herrington might have known somehow that I was going to be. And you know, Lena told me—she remembered that Brooks was here that day, that when she went out looking for the boys he was over by the corral and had Tony's ear about something. I wouldn't be surprised if he was here on purpose to keep Tony out of the way."

"What nerve," said Carleton Kent with a kind of professional relish.

"Even with all that, I still can't believe he had the face to bring it into court," I said.

"I don't think going to trial was as risky as it looks now," said Ray, "when you put together that Tim and Lane honestly believed that was the will they'd signed, and that I hadn't been very satisfactory in front of the coroner's jury. I guess Herrington probably figured if he could get me solidly framed and convicted and the case closed, everyone would just forget about McKay and his will."

"But had no idea he'd already made his big mistake," said Mrs. Crawley, "by giving a very clever young lawyer that other shooting to show as contradictory evidence."

"It was all due to my uncle, really," said Carleton Kent modestly. "He thought there was something rotten in Denmark ever since Lena was shot at, and he pointed me in that direction. He's quite a remarkable person."

I looked a trifle sheepish. "I've noticed. So remarkable that I once even considered him for the role of First Murderer."

Carleton Kent grinned boyishly. "You should tell him that sometime; he'd be amused."

"Well, I certainly owe him a vote of thanks," said Ray. "Of course it would have been comforting to know it at the time"—there was still something a little strained about his smile—"but really Herrington's whole plan was doomed from the minute Jimmy took that first shot at Lane."

"Because I was in the way," I finished, with a rueful smile. I added, "I certainly never tried, but I seem to have been getting in everyone's way ever since I came to Wyoming."

"Based upon results," said Mrs. Crawley, "I'd advise you to keep right on doing it."

EPILOGUE

How much can come
And much can go,
And yet abide the world!

Emily Dickinson: There Came a Wind Like a Bugle

I ROUSED FROM sleep, stirring a little on my pillow. The room was dark, except for a dim glow from a candle over on the bureau, and Ray was leaning over me shaking me gently by the shoulder. He was already dressed, though the empty side of the bed beside me was still warm. "Better get up now," he said. "It's almost five. I'll go downstairs and make some coffee."

I crawled out of bed and dressed in jeans and flannel shirt and sweater, waking up by degrees as I did so. I blew out the candle, took my boots in my hand and padded downstairs in my socks. The only light downstairs was in the kitchen. Ray had started a small fire in the stove and put on the coffeepot to brew, and while he got out cups for the two of us I pulled on my boots, sitting by the kitchen table. It felt like the middle of the night still, with only indistinct squares of blackness beyond the windows. When the coffee was ready we had a cup, hot, and then Ray turned down the damper on the stove and we put on our coats and hats. On my way out the back door I switched off the light; the kitchen went dark and the sky outside the windows showed pale gray—a switch from night to morning.

The crisp, chill air of early dawn filled my lungs, and I tipped my head back and inhaled deeply. Comfortably warm inside my coat and sweater, I relished the nip of the air on my cheeks and nose and its bracing freshness that seemed to clear out my mind and quicken my blood. It was utterly still; the only sound our boots on the dry hard-packed ground as we crossed the yard to the barn.

By the light of a single hanging electric bulb in the barn, we saddled Sarge and Metis, and led them out through the far door, out under the trees, to the back pasture road. We mounted there and started down the half-seen road through the grayness. The horses knew this way better even than we did, and their feet kept surely to the track, even when the shadow of the trees arching over it on the other side of the meadow made everything black as night again. Now and then amid the clop of their hooves I thought I heard the rustle of a frost-dried leaf drifting to the ground. The sleeping woods were gold and bronze and ochre, blanketed by night, waiting for the sunrise to set them on fire.

We had been married for a month. The cloudless summer we had promised ourselves had long since slipped away; but by the time life had settled back down to some semblance of normal, we decided that we didn't want to wait any longer, and so we were married very quietly at the end of September. Only a few people were present: the Crawleys, the Stevensons, Dr. Burns, and the Circle M boys. Lane was on crutches by that time; he was recovering well, and Ray and I had promised him his job would still be waiting for him when he was fit to work again. Brock Chambers and his hired man had helped us to keep things together in the meantime, especially during those first chaotic weeks when Lane was in the hospital, Ray still recovering from concussion and the stitches Dr. Burns had put in his head, and all of us grappling with a welter of interviews with police and lawyers and the occasional forays of reporters.

At the far end of the valley road an auction sign now hung on the closed gate of the silent Warren ranch. James Warren had pleaded guilty to murder and his sentence had been commuted to life in prison; and considering the reflections he had to live with I wasn't sure any punishment could be worse. Robert Herrington was still awaiting trial, admitting nothing on any count; the authorities were hoping to recover at least some of what local ranchers had lost through stolen livestock, but it promised to be a tedious and complicated prosecution before conviction for that or the murder was accomplished.

And autumn came on, and I thought I had never seen one so beautiful, even though I had lived it in Wyoming once before. Every slant of light, every touch of color, every leaf on the breeze was doubly precious to me, seen through eyes taught to appreciate that I was still here to see it and that I had safe all I most loved. For a long time I felt like I was walking in a waking dream, that a nudge might awaken me. It took many days of blessedly ordinary living and working—many times of seeing Ray across the table from me, at my side on horseback during the day, or in the living room in the evening, and finding him close to me when I woke in the morning—to realize that the long nightmare was over, and this was the dawning of our future together.

The light was pale, colorless, but stronger now, as it filtered down through the aspen trees, whose twinkling leaves hung still for once. The horses' hooves thudded on the moss, with an occasional steel-shod ring on granite. Ahead of me Sarge's hooves rattled for a second on the stony crest of the ridge, and I saw Ray's head and shoulders silhouetted between the trees against a sky that now held a faint touch of lemon. Then Metis made it up over the top, and we could ride side by side again as we left the aspen wood behind for the long open ridge. On both sides the shadow-filled valleys were like a great dark sea, the mountain peaks to the north like the rocks of a distant shore; we seemed to be riding along a single strip of land that led straight up into the limitless sky.

We dismounted by the great rock. It was getting so I could see the texture of the knee-high grass, whispery and tough after autumn frosts, and the corners and contours of the rock instead of just a dark shape. Ray climbed up ahead of me, and gave me both his hands to help me up. We stood side by side there on the flat top, high above the silent valley, waiting for the coming of the light.

It was hard to tell just when it began. I noticed presently that the eastern slopes of the far-off mountains were shining, lit by the full blaze of a sun that we could not yet see. Fine shafts of light sprayed upward from behind the hills of the eastern skyline; the soft blue overhead gradually grew brighter and brighter, and suddenly the rippled white clouds dappling the sky were suffused with a shade of apricot.

I looked sideways at Ray. I had often felt that, despite the upheaval I had been through, of the two of us I was the less changed by our experiences. The half-healed scar above his ear, soon to be hidden when his hair grew to cover it, was the only external mark left upon him; but the other scars left by shame, bitterness, and self-blame were only half-healed as well. We had talked about all of it far into the night, many times, and every time it seemed afterwards that he could stand straighter, breathe freer, and smile more.

All around the whole horizon glowed a vivid soft yellow, and the clouds had turned white again. At last I spoke: "I haven't been up here since—that day."

"I know," said Ray. He glanced down at me. "There's a lot of places around here with bad memories attached to them. I figured it's time we started making some new ones."

He moved over behind me and wrapped his arms around me, and I folded my gloved hands over his and leaned back against him. I stared off at the glowing mountain range. "Have you ever been sorry you didn't move on when you had the chance? You could have started fresh, instead of having to rebuild everything."

"No...never for very long, anyway. I don't regret it now. If I had left, I'd never have known the truth."

He added, "It's not all bad memories, anyway. Remember the first day I brought you up here?"

"I'll never forget it."

"Me neither. I'll always remember the look on your face...it was like seeing the world all over again for the first time, through your eyes."

I leaned my head against his arm, and he rested his chin on top of my head. I said slowly, my eyes fixed on the pines coming into focus down in the valley, "There's one thing I've wondered sometimes...I've wondered if you ever look at me, and think—about him. If it ever makes you feel unhappy or resentful, because I'm his granddaughter— because I came from him, and after all he did to you—"

"No. No, Lena, don't ever think like that. If I ever did look at you and think of him, it was to be amazed that you were so completely different, and to be glad about it for your sake and mine."

My hand tightened over his, and Ray leaned down and kissed my ear. A single bright diamond-point of light appeared in a cleft of the eastern skyline, and shot a sunburst of thin golden rays in all directions. I drew a deep breath.

"It seems like after I read that confession, I ought to have had some qualms about taking what he left," I said. "But you know, I don't. Grandfather paid for everything he'd done—paid dearly at the end. But now I feel like the slate's been wiped clean, and you and I have the chance to make this place what he always wanted it to be. What he couldn't make it, because of his own failings. A place for a family. It wasn't meant to be in Mother's time, but when it came to me I was ready."

The sunlight spilled over the eastern hills and poured down across the range, illuminating each fold and ridge and slope. The air was crisp, but the stands of trees warmed to color, rich russet and yellow-gold. The brilliance of the sun increased minute by minute until I fancied I could feel its warmth on my face; and somewhere down in the valley a bird began to sing fearlessly.

Acknowledgements

I OWE MY family many thanks for putting up with me
through years of my trying to vent about my struggles
with this book without sharing plot spoilers. Special
thanks to my mother (one of the world's sharpest whodunit
readers) and my sister Anna for being the first readers of the
manuscript, and to my brother Davey for letting me use his
laptop for final editing and formatting when my own
computer crashed a month and a half from release.

Thank you to Jenni Schrock for reading and giving feedback
on the Wyoming setting, to Hanna-col Pokone and Tony
Dekker for being some of my biggest fans and giving me the
encouragement to keep on working even through seasons of
doubt and discouragement, and to Jennifer Zemanek for the

beautiful cover that "put a face" to the story I've lived with in my head for so long.

And thanks above all to my Heavenly Father for giving me the desire to write, the gift of being able to write, for keeping me going and being exceedingly patient with me through the years it took to write this book.

ABOUT *the* AUTHOR

ELISABETH GRACE FOLEY has been an insatiable reader and eager history buff ever since she learned to read, has been scribbling stories ever since she learned to write, and now combines those loves in writing historical fiction. She has been twice nominated for the Western Fictioneers' Peace-maker Award, and *Land of Hills and Valleys* was voted into the top ten of Readfree.ly's 50 Best Indie Books of 2021. When not reading or writing, she enjoys spending time outdoors, music, crocheting, and watching sports and old movies. She lives in upstate New York with her family and the world's best German Shepherd. Visit her online at www.elisabethgracefoley.com.

LISA JEWELL... RACHEL JOLLEY has [been] an author... books... has been... since... has written... She also ...for the ...

...We con... ...the ...and American life and Europe... on the ... ...as well as ...

See her ... ... (2011) ... ...as writing, she ... enjoys ...other ... ...music, ... and ...in her own ...idols though ... She lives in Upstate New York ... ...now with ... German Shepherd... ...online at www.either... .com

Made in the USA
Middletown, DE
12 July 2023